OUT OF THE STRONG

James Daniel was born in Portsmouth, and educated at Gosport County Grammar School, Welbeck College and the Royal Military Academy Sandhurst. After a service career spanning 33 years during which he served in a variety of theatres world-wide, he left to take up employment in local government. Married for 30 years, he has one son and lives in the south-west of England.

G000061285

Also by James Daniel

They Told Me You Were Dead

JAMES DANIEL

OUT OF THE STRONG

PAN BOOKS

First published 1995 by Pan Books

an imprint of Macmillan General Books
Cavaye Place London SW10 9PG
and Basingstoke

Associated companies throughout the world

ISBN 0 330 33125 6

3 5 7 9 8 6 4 2

A CIP catalogue record for this book is available from
the British Library

Phototypeset by Intype, London
Printed and bound in Great Britain by BPC Paperbacks Ltd

And they said unto him, Put forth thy riddle,
that we may hear it.
And he said unto them,
Out of the eater came forth meat,
and out of the strong came forth sweetness

Judges 14: 13–14

PROLOGUE

Late May 1982

A thunderstorm threatened.

The air was heavy, oppressive, charged with electricity. A sudden wind, a harbinger of the coming storm, gathered the capital's litter, bowling it along the pavements. The late-evening sun filtered through the trees, throwing a kaleidoscope of dappled colour on to the surface of Horse Guards where the Blues and Royals trooper, motionless astride his horse, waited for the approaching rain. To the gawping tourists, the animal seemed embalmed; a twitching nerve, the flick of an ear, the only indication the animal was alive.

A pigeon paraded importantly between the polished hoofs.

The trooper gave no thought to the impending storm. His thoughts instead were with his comrades, three thousand miles to the south. Perhaps, even now, their armoured cars were clanking ashore from the landing craft beached in San Carlos Water.

The occupants of the room were unaware of the sun, and the pretty effect on the road above. None spared a thought for the trooper astride his mount, their minds busy with more pressing business. In the underground chamber, insulated from the effects of the first rolls of thunder, they could not see the darkening sky as the first heavy drops started to fall, thickening until they became too heavy, dropping painfully from the black clouds that hung like a dark blanket overhead.

Above, the trooper sat impervious to the rain that suddenly, without warning, cascaded from the sky on to the

1

horse's flanks, resting there momentarily before running off the polished surface like globules of mercury. With consummate skill, the trooper jiggled the reins. The animal, at one with its rider, took four majestic paces backwards, into the shelter of the sentry box beside the archway leading into Horse Guards Parade.

They had been inside the building all day, summoned by the Special Despatcher to attend a meeting in the Cabinet Office Briefing Room, nicknamed COBRA. Those with paging facilities had scampered to telephones. Others, more senior in rank, with the benefit of mobile communication systems, had hurried from their places of work in order to arrive here punctually.

Nobody was ever late for the Prime Minister.

The group sitting around the polished oak table in the underground chamber consisted of the War Cabinet and the Joint Chiefs of Staff. The mood in the room was sombre, for the briefing had been depressing, the strain clearly registered, the tiredness showing. Not many had slept decently since the conflict had begun. As a result of this gathering, few, if any, would sleep soundly again.

The war was not going well.

The days of euphoria were over. The jingoists had been silenced. The tabloid press was beginning to sound subdued, publishing half-truths to disguise the real anxiety felt by the correspondents who penned the editorials. With the imposition of such strict censorship by the Ministry of Defence, there was no alternative. At best, Hobson's choice. Any news from the South Atlantic, exiguous at best, was first processed and filtered before despatch, courtesy of the Royal Navy with its SCOT satellite terminals.

Censorship.

And the press hated it.

The muted conversation died quite suddenly, absorbed

by the mellow oak panelling, the curtains that covered the operations maps on the soundproofed walls and the individual booths along the wall behind. The Prime Minister had entered the room through the wide doors at the east end, and walked quickly with short steps to that hallowed position at the centre of the table, her footfall muffled by the pile of the carpet. She placed the briefing papers carefully on to the polished surface in front of her, then arranged them neatly into piles before squaring them off with irritating, punctilious fussiness. Finally, satisfied with this simple housekeeping, she looked up and glanced around the room.

'What the hell is going on?'

The Prime Minister had never been known to mince her words.

A few papers rustled. No one dared even cough, lest it draw attention, bringing those piercing, angry – some thought worried – eyes in their direction. Aware of her imperious personality, some tried to shrink down into their chairs, hoping to avoid the verbal onslaught that would surely follow. The Prime Minister was in that sort of mood. Finally, when the silence had stretched embarrassingly, the Chief of the Naval Staff cleared his throat, raising a gently clenched fist to his mouth and coughing silently into it.

He stood.

'Prime Minister.' He coughed again. 'The Navy is experiencing a few difficulties at present. You will be aware—'

'Difficulties? *Difficulties?* One of Her Majesty's ships already at the bottom of the South Atlantic. *Sheffield.*' Her tone was sharp, accusing. 'God knows how many more with unexploded bombs in them and out of action as a result. *Antrim, Ardent, Argonaut, Brilliant* and *Broadsword.*' The Prime Minister recited the list alphabetically. He supposed it was easier to remember that way. 'You certainly are experiencing difficulties!'

'Prime Minister.' The Chief of the Naval Staff kept his voice even. 'The Argentine pilots are performing better than even they could have anticipated. This, coupled with the devastating effect of the Super Etendard and the Exocet missile—'

'The Intelligence assessment of the Argentine Air Force led me to believe that they were not a serious threat, that the A4 Sky Hawk, Dagger and Mirage were no match for Sea Harrier. An assumption both erroneous and premature, I suspect.' She interrupted, somewhat ungraciously. 'Furthermore, according to the INTREPS, the Super E and the Exocet were not yet battle-ready. I repeat. What the hell is going on?'

The Rear Admiral held the Prime Minister's gaze unflinchingly, feeling her eyes boring into him. He was as worried as anyone over the damage to the fleet. They were, after all, *his* ships. He, more than anyone in the room, felt the pain of the sinking. But there were further casualties, as yet undisclosed, known only to him and a select number of his staff. He had received the SITREP not five minutes before coming to this briefing. A disaster. He wondered what the Prime Minister's reaction would be.

He could guess.

The Navy is getting clobbered. The first time we've been shot at since Amethyst *on the Yangtze, and look what's happening to us.*

The Rear Admiral, an imperturbable and courageous man, did not shirk from his responsibility. He steeled himself, then told the Prime Minister of the additional casualties that had been brought to his attention. The agitated 'two-ringer' had dashed along the corridor at Northwood, catching him as he had been about to leave for his staff car. With the flimsy signal clutched in his hand, he had looked dejected, sick with worry.

Now, he told the Prime Minister of the sinking of HMS *Coventry*.

She looked away with a sharp intake of breath. There

4

was a pause as she digested the news, aware of the implications. Turning slowly to face him, she asked: 'Sir James, can you still protect the troop-carriers? Do I still have a Task Force capable of retaking the Falkland Islands? Can we expand the beachhead? And if we do,' – she looked at him directly, challenging – 'can we win?'

'Prime Minister.' He weighed his words carefully, wondering which of her questions to answer first. 'You were aware of the risks in the very beginning, when *Intrepid* and *Fearless* set sail from Portsmouth. We are suffering a few setbacks, but nothing we cannot overcome.' He paused, waiting for the right moment before proceeding. 'The landing at San Carlos must continue as planned. We are committed. Everything is in place. The weather will break, very soon now, denying us another chance before winter.' He glanced around the table. Everyone looked at him. 'The advantage is with the Argentine. You have seen the aerial photographs, the SAS and SBS reports. If we do not go now, he will have yet more time to improve his defensive positions and hone up his so-far-crude air tactics.'

He wondered if the Prime Minister had considered the state of the fleet had their enemy possessed an even half-decent low-level attack aircraft, a command-and-control system to support it. As if reading his thoughts, the Prime Minister replied: 'I suspect that if the Argentine Air Force owned a few MiG 27 Foxbats and the requisite training, our position would be even more tenuous.'

Ma'am. Don't even think like that.

There was a pause. The eyes bored into the Navy man. 'If we get off the beaches with, shall we say, acceptable casualties, what are the chances of taking Stanley as originally planned?'

He looked down at his hands spread on the table supporting his weight. The wedding ring glinted in the diffused light filtering from the ceiling. Raising his hands, he began to twist the ring around his finger, a habit he was unable to control whenever he faced a difficult decision. He took a deep breath.

'I would estimate sixty–forty. No more.' The Admiral was aware of the uncomfortable movement, the occupants of the room shifting imperceptibly in their seats. 'Without the capital ships to protect the ground troops against air attacks, our chances are no better. And, knowing the effectiveness of the Exocet, we cannot risk the Carrier Group by bringing it further west. The Group must stay out of range of the Super E.' Realizing he was fiddling with the ring, he stopped, folding his arms as he spoke. 'You know from your earlier briefings that we lack artillery. The 105 Pack Howitzer, with all its advantages of mobility, is not heavy enough, its range limited, and accuracy is affected by high winds. If we are unable to spare ships to give naval gunfire support, because we are fending off air attacks—' The sentence was left unfinished. He studied her, noting the worry. 'We can, we *will* win, Prime Minister, and it need not be too Pyrrhic a victory. Time, however, is not on our side.'

The Prime Minister was very quiet. When next she spoke, the gathering in the room was shocked, the sharp intake of breath audible.

'It is unthinkable that we should be in danger of losing this war. It is a factor I will not contemplate. I want an edge. An advantage. A war-winner.' The pause was ominous. 'I want the ability to use tactical nuclear weapons. How you achieve it is a matter for you to decide. If this is to be an internecine conflict, then so be it.' The Prime Minister glanced around the table, meeting every eye. 'Spare me your cavils. See to it at the earliest opportunity.' The papers in front of her were neatly collected, then gathered, as the Prime Minister rose from her chair and left the room.

Field Marshal Sir Peter Beaufort was suddenly alert. Like the others, he was stunned by the shocking suggestion. However, the Army, after all, might suddenly be in the driving seat. The Joint Chiefs wouldn't recommend deploying the RAF with its ageing Vulcans. Too risky with the Argie pilots so close. And the in-flight refuelling was a nightmare. Maybe they could arm up Harrier, but they were needed for CAP. Polaris? That would be taking a pile-driver to crack a hazelnut. No. Something smaller, more mobile, that could be used conventionally if the nuclear option were not pursued. Tactical, the Prime Minister had said. Well, we've just the thing. Now, if he could just convince the others ... He glanced over at the Secretary of State for Defence who had removed his spectacles and was polishing furiously, the action agitated. His face was grey with worry. He looked older, more fatigued even than the rest of them.

Suddenly, altercation as the Joint Chiefs began to hatch a plan that would satisfy their Prime Minister and ensure that the Task Force was not to be defeated in the battle for the Falkland Islands.

MV *Viking* steamed slowly away from No. 4 berth in Bremerhaven docks. She was an old ship, inconspicuous, her paintwork flaking and rusty, her funnels belching filthy fumes as the Gardner diesel motors increased revolutions in response to the orders from the bridge. She was a STUFT, a 'ship taken up from trade', one of many plying cargo between Europe and the South Atlantic, in the early days of the Falklands campaign.

The vessel had been loaded the previous evening, under cover of darkness. The harbourmaster had been surprised when he had been told that the loading would be carried out by military personnel rather than the usual dockhands. But he had said nothing at the arrival, in olive-green coaches, of soldiers who had dismounted quickly in response to the orders from the officer-in-charge. He had noted from their cap badges that they were Royal Corps of Transport, familiar enough around the docks. But there had been a second squad of soldiers, aloof, standing apart, talking in quiet groups as the loading proceeded. When he had been close enough to identify the cap badge, the *Hafenmeister* had registered the shape of a big-wheeled cannon, with the inscription in Latin reading: *Ubique quo fas et gloria ducunt.*

He was no scholar, and knew no Latin, but his memory was good. When he was later able to inquire, he had discovered it to translate as: 'Everywhere honour and glory leadeth.' They were gunners from the Royal Regiment of Artillery.

The *Hafenmeister* was unable to discover the identification of the cargo which arrived a little later by massive Antar low-loader vehicles, their engines groaning as the diesel fumes spewed from vertical exhausts. The huge canvas-covered blocks were completely hidden from view as the cranes lifted them from the dockside and swung them inboard. Six long, cylindrical shapes followed and were lowered carefully into the holds before being lashed securely next to the bulkier items. The harbourmaster could not be sure, but he thought that he had seen a heavy track showing from under one of the tarpaulins, the type seen on a large tractor or piece of heavy plant.

Or a tank.

He wondered why the British would be sending heavy armour down to the South Atlantic. But the ungainly pieces of equipment were not tanks, although to an unpractised eye they could be mistaken as such. They were, in fact, three M110 8-inch self-propelled guns, called otherwise a medium-range cannon. Each was capable of firing a nuclear shell over a distance of 20 kilometres.

They were the Prime Minister's edge.

Her advantage.

The war-winner.

Capitan Antonio Begatti nervously scanned his instruments. The practice had become a habit. Airborne for 34 minutes, having left his base at Rio Grande, he had refuelled from an Air Force tanker, 127 miles to the east. Now, he was flying at sea-level, little higher than the white horses that broke on the wave-tops. This would keep him below the warships' radar, and he was again thankful that the British were unable to deploy an early-warning radar capable of looking over the horizon. Had they the use of AWACS, he would have been dead after his first mission. He let his mind dwell on it, remembering the thrill, the congratulations from his brother pilots when he had learned that he had hit a warship.

At the time he had not known.

The missile was fired as soon as his radar locked on to the target. Immediately the Exocet left the aircraft he banked steeply away without knowing whether he had hit or missed. With a worried eye on his fuel load, he had turned and headed for home, to his base on the Argentine mainland.

Now, he checked his instruments once more, dreading the high-pitched warning that would fill his helmet if an enemy missile system had locked on to him. It could be any number of missiles. Sea Dart, Sea Wolf, or a Sidewinder from one of the British Harriers.

He was most afraid of the Sea Harrier.

Shit scared.

'Whispering Death', they called it.

A wonderful, frightening aircraft, VTOL – vertical take-off and landing, unsurpassed in any air power in the world. The British pilots employed a technique called 'viffing', vectoring in flight, braking almost to stalling speed, the opposing aircraft overshooting in its attack, letting the Harrier turn inside its opponent, enabling it to lock its own missiles. It had proved a most successful tactic in the war. Some of his companions would not live to vouch for the effectiveness of the manoeuvre. Bitterly he recalled their losses.

Concentrating, he brought his mind back to the present.

He would soon be in range. The Argentine Neptune aircraft, with its outdated radar, had confirmed what appeared to be a pair of Type 42s, perhaps on picket duty, 70 to 80 miles south of Port Stanley. It was too good an opportunity to miss.

The capitan calculated he was some 25 miles from his target. Now, the most dangerous part of the attack. In order to verify the presence of a ship, he had to climb from sea-level to a hundred feet, then switch on the Agave radar to feed the bearing and range into the Exocet fire-control computer. To avoid detection, his radar was switched on but not transmitting. This prevented the British warships from receiving his signature. It was known as Rackets.

He held his breath, frightened, then climbed, bringing his aircraft from its relatively safe position skimming the wave-tops. Seconds later his radar gave him confirmation. He made slight adjustments, a brief touch on rudder and flaps. The missile was armed.

It was so simple. The French engineers had been right, confident in the weapon's capability. Already the British had lost HMS *Sheffield*, sunk before the crew had been aware of their enemy's potent weapon. He rechecked, scanning the bank of instruments, held the aircraft steady at 400 knots, then flicked up the safety switch on the firing button.

Steady, Begatti.

Steady . . .

He fired.

Once launch was confirmed, he banked sharply to his right, and made a long, gradual turn that would take him on a course for home. He felt elated. The Exocet would not miss. It would find a target. The BBC News would report the loss of another British ship. He began to hum 'La donna è mobile', Pavarotti's voice filling his mind. His head pivoted to his left, seeking his wingman. He sang into his headset, light-headed from the release of tension

10

that had been building in him since the mission had started. These were trying times for a pilot in the Argentine Air Force.

No! Please God, no!

Too late, he identified the warning pips of his anti-missile radar, the sound seeming to shriek into his helmet, deafening in its persistence. A Sea Dart missile struck his aircraft in the middle of the fuselage. The Super Etendard disintegrated in a white-hot ball of flame. There had been no time to eject.

For Capitan Begatti it was the end of his war.

Ronald Cooper, master of the MV *Viking*, stood hunched on the bridge, peering out into the grey expanse of the South Atlantic. His ship was in enemy waters, the crew tensely vigilant. Lookouts were posted fore and aft, nervous in the damp chill of the morning. The radar operator, green-faced from the reflection of the screen, watched the sweep of the beam as if his life depended on it. He knew that perhaps it did.

Cooper did not know where he was to deliver his cargo – only that he was to rendezvous at a certain latitude and await instructions. He would receive those instructions via a courier who would arrive by helicopter. Nothing was to be sent over the ship's radio.

Suddenly, tense.

A VHF walkie-talkie in front of him burst into life. The forward lookout.

'Skipper! Something coming! Smoke trail about six feet above the water line. Bearing two four zero. Moving fast.'

The master snapped the binoculars to his eyes, swivelling on to the bearing, twisting the focus, praying.

Nothing.

Just the sea, grey, flat, like a huge immovable slate. Visibility was three miles, yet the lenses stayed stubbornly empty. He was about to ask for confirmation from the lookout when he, too, saw it. His heart turned to ice. For a moment, he was too terrified to move, his mind numb, incapable of precise thought, his brain turned to porridge, cold, useless.

Exocet.

Instinct conquered his cataplexy, impelling him.

He screamed instructions, orders that would bring his ship about, presenting a smaller target, the stronger stern to the incoming missile. But even as he threw the control lever forward he knew he was too late. A few seconds, time to yell instructions to the crew, before the missile hit.

The Exocet struck the *Viking* exactly where its designers had intended. It tore a hole in the side just above the water line, below the bridge, the rent 15 feet in length. The ship's radio and navigation systems were destroyed in the orange ball of flame, tumbling through the ship, a dragon's breath, burning everything. The missile irrupted into the bowels of the ship with the equivalent energy of an 80-tonne diesel train decelerating from 60 mph to zero in less than 30 feet. She had no chance. Her plates buckled like aluminium cooking foil, letting the sea pour into her at a rate of 2000 gallons a second.

The armoured vehicles in her holds groaned on their lashings, and as the ship lurched to her side, broke loose and slammed into the starboard bulkheads. In less than four minutes she had sunk. Even had the radios been working, there would have been no time for Cooper to send a May Day.

The sea closed over the hissing, bubbling cauldron of water, once more turning it into a flat, grey slate.

A hungry swallowing.

A few bubbles.

Then, nothing.

The MV *Viking*, crew and cargo, had vanished without trace.

Belfast, then

It was untidy in the darkened room, the only light a low-powered, naked bulb glowing from a lamp in the centre of a group of tables arranged in an untidy square. The cramped, fusty quarters reeked of stale cigarette smoke. Condensation had formed on the inside of the windows, running in rivulets forming small puddles on the rotten wood of the sills. Three men and a woman, all wearing headphones, sat in folding chairs at the tables. Each set of headphones was attached by cable to individual scanning receivers. The group smoked or read from dog-eared paperbacks. Occasionally one would glance up to check the radio on the bench in front or hurriedly put down the book and hold the earphones tightly against the ears, as if fearful of missing something. Depending on what had been heard, a tape-recorder would perhaps be started.

Each scanner was fed by a co-axial cable into an active multi-coupler, connected to a co-linear array UHF dipole, an omni-directional broad-band antenna capable of receiving frequencies in the 940 to 960 MHz range. There was, in addition, a broad-band discone antenna, its distinctive outline hidden in the loft above the interceptors' seats. They were crudely monitoring the mobile telephone channels used by Vodafone and Cellnet.

The woman sat bolt upright, the movement sudden, as she ripped the headphones from her radio, letting the reception broadcast into the room direct from the speaker. Now, they could all hear.

'A Brit.'

She spat the word, showering spittle, the fine spray iridescent in the naked light from the bulb. Quickly she adjusted the volume, twisting the knob savagely, eager to hear.

'Someone see if they can get the other side, the second

channel. I've just the one of them. Try and pick up his party.'

The three others busied themselves, waiting for their scanners to be captured by the more powerful transmission coming from a repeater station, high in a distant tower.

A harsh English voice was amplified into the room.

'Is that Patrick Donnelly?'

Silence.

'Your executioner.'

A pause, perhaps an answer.

The voice, coldly inimical, went on, a judge delivering sentence.

Death.

'Donnelly, shut up. Your time is short. Don't waste it talking. Just listen. November, last year. You gunned down a soldier when he was out on the streets doing his job. A young officer. He was twenty-three years old. He loved life. The life you took. You chewed him up with an American M60 machine-gun. You hit him three times. Three fucking times, Donnelly.'

The woman, frantic, screamed at them.

'Find who he's talking to! We mustn't lose this! For Christ's sake, find him!' Shaking, she snatched up the earphones, clamping them to her head.

'Maura, if he's there, the scanner will pick him up. It's all automatic. There's nothing else we can do.'

'The hell there isn't! Switch on the other sets. Get everything searching. Quickly now!' They did as she bade, crouched over the scanner as it interrogated the frequency spectrum, coloured lights flicking across the front panels.

Nothing.

Then, suddenly: *'How do you like it, Patrick Donnelly? Terrorist. Back-shooting murderer. Pissing ourselves, are we?*

A pause, then, at last, an answer: *'I hope the fucker bled real bad!'*

There followed a vicious hissing, crackle, a sound none of them at first recognized. The room, silent now, save for the sound of strained, careful breathing. The woman raised a warning finger as one of them made to speak.

'Shsh!'

A grimalkin's hiss.

A match scraped, sputtering noisily into life as one of the men lit a cigarette. With a backward swipe of her hand, the woman slapped it from his mouth, too preoccupied to notice his anger flaring, then dying like the flame from the match seconds before. Like the cigarette, now burning a hole in the threadbare carpet, the man's anger smouldered.

It was quiet in the room.

The four stared at the radio.

The woman thought she had heard something, a faint sound she was unable to identify. Certain that no more conversation was to follow, she rewound the tape to listen to the replay, holding the earphones tightly against her ears, screwing up her face in concentration. Her eyes were bleak, dangerous, devoid of expression. None of the men could hold her gaze.

She listened, rewound, and listened again.

A moan.

Definitely a moan.

The agony in the sound made her faintly uncomfortable. With a sigh she removed the padded headphones. They had flattened her usually wiry hair and it lay damply on her cheeks.

'You'd best be getting a copy of this over to Command.' Ejecting the tape, she passed it to the youngest of the men. 'It sounded to me like a fucking Brit took one of ours. If that's the case, there'll be no rest till there's been vengeance.' She pursed bloodless lips, distorting an already ugly mouth, her eyes staring into space. Finally she refocused on the group.

'Be careful with that,' she warned as the young man

thrust the tape into his pocket and opened the door to leave. 'We don't want to lose that. No bloody way. That's some bastard's death warrant, that is.'

As he left, the remainder once more took up their stations. They listened, paused, sometimes recording unknown, alien voices, invisibly carried on the airwaves. One picked up a paperback, rubbing his mouth where the woman had slapped him.

Belfast.

Another night.

CHAPTER ONE

Late spring, now

The runner was moving well.

Two men watched him critically through powerful field-glasses as he jogged rhythmically along the muddy path bordering the wood. The watchers saw how the runner breathed easily, regularly, his breath punched from his mouth into clouds of condensation in the crisp air of the early morning. The runner inhaled as the left foot thudded on to the track, drawing in air over three paces, then exhaling over the next three. Even, steady, controlled. Footprints formed in the frosty grass as he reached the end of the track and continued across the open field. Later, when it was warmer, the spring sunshine would obliterate the tracks. One of the watchers pressed the button of a stopwatch, looked critically at it and grunted approval.

Without speaking, they watched him bend into an uphill section, now breathing every second pace, ignoring the rucksack as his work rate increased. The observer in the driver's seat swept his glasses to the right, refocusing quickly on an old farmhouse perhaps a mile distant. He looked at his wristwatch, assessing when the runner would arrive there. They would soon lose sight of him, but they lingered until he turned right at the top of the field, swallowed by a privet hedge. Only then did they put away the field-glasses and start the car. The suspension squeaked, wheezing unhappily, as the vehicle bounced along a narrow track leading out of the wood and on to the road.

They drove fast along the country lane, deserted at this early hour, seeing without noticing the cock pheasant strutting majestically across their path. A rabbit, perched inquisitively on its hind legs, hopped reluctantly into the hedgerow as a pair of finches, disturbed by the noise of the car, lifted fussily from the branches. The men were too preoccupied to register such niceties of nature this beautiful spring day. The passenger whistled tunelessly, a habit that no longer annoyed his driving companion. His hand went to the pocket of his suit, where his fingers played lightly with the cassette tape in a plastic case. He had listened to the tape on countless occasions and knew its contents by heart. He wondered at the reaction of the runner when he heard it. A smile settled at the corner of his mouth but did not reach as far as the eyes.

He felt good, better than in a long time. His body ached from the exertion of the early-morning run, and the T-shirt under the dark tracksuit was soaked in sweat. He had been punishing himself like this for months, feeling that his efforts were at last beginning to pay off. The big double gates were still 200 metres away when he gritted his teeth and broke into a fast sprint, not stopping until he was inside the courtyard. Legs apart, he stood, breathing deeply, drawing air down into his lungs, the sun beginning to warm him as it came up over the house. He dropped to the ground, taking his weight on his hands and toes and completed fifty push-ups as fast as he was able, straining, trembling as he went into the last ten. Shrugging out of the rucksack, leaving it against the door of the garage, he strode towards the house.

He smelt the coffee as soon as he entered the big kitchen. In the warmth from the Aga, he felt the sadness begin to envelop him, pushing the earlier good feelings away. The house was empty, where once it had been shared. The things around him looked the same but were not. He had changed nothing since she had gone, feeling that he owed her this small debt.

She had so loved this house.

He shook himself, pushing the sombre thoughts out of his mind, concentrating instead on his plans for the day. Holding a mug of scalding black coffee, he ambled into the hall, heading for the wide stair that would take him upstairs into the shower. The somnolent tick of the big clock in the hall was the only sound in the silence of the house. It was quiet, as he liked it. His foot was balanced lightly on the bottom step.

The doorbell rang.

He stopped, head to one side, listening.

It was too early for social callers, too soon for anyone to be calling other than for a very pressing reason.

'Mr Norris? Mr Richard Norris?' Two men stood in the porch, their faces withdrawn behind the shaft of light that probed through the small window at their left shoulders. It was done so that he could not make out their features. Silhouetted against the light behind, they observed him through the bright ray of sunlight, shadows, without detail.

Gunfighters, their backs to the sun.

The hair on the nape of his neck shifted as if someone had blown sensually across the back of his neck. He sipped coffee, not answering, refusing to cock his head, to squint, in order to see them better.

Dominate your subject.

Make him ill at ease. Keep him guessing.

Richard Norris had seen their type before.

Unafraid, he turned on his heel, sensing but not hearing them follow him into the hallway. The clock seemed louder, beating its slow methodical tick, a metronome left to run after the orchestra has gone, the silence, ominous. Norris led the way into the big drawing room, ducking under the beam across the door. At the window he turned to face them, the light behind him, the bright sun shining into their faces. They didn't squint. The one on the left looked sad, almost as if he were weeping. Tears welled in the corners of his eyes. He refrained from blinking.

Instead he walked to the low coffee table in the centre of the room.

Warily Richard watched as a portable tape-recorder was placed onto the top. Weeping Willie held out a hand. Without looking, the other passed him a cassette tape which he inserted into the machine. They stood looking at Richard Norris, one with a nicotine-stained finger poised over the play button. The delay was for effect, deliberate, designed to get him wondering, to take the initiative, and put him on the defensive. At a disadvantage. The yellow finger stabbed down on to the machine.

Richard Norris listened.

The voice from the tape exploded into the room.

'Donnelly's Motors.'

'Is that Patrick Donnelly?'

'Who is this?'

'Your executioner.'

'What the fuck you talking about? Just get the—'

Richard cringed at the orinasal tones, flat and harsh with the sounds of the Falls. He was shaking.

'Donnelly, shut up. Your time is short. Don't waste it talking. Just listen. November last year. You gunned down a soldier when he was out on the streets doing his job. A young officer. He was twenty-three years old. He loved life. The life you took. You chewed him up with an American M60 machine-gun. You hit him three times. Three fucking times, Donnelly.'

At the sound of his own voice, Richard ground his teeth, hiding the expression in his face, hating the two intruders for taking him back, for tormenting him.

'I don't know what the hell you're talking about.'

'He was my son. You bastard. My son.'

There was fear in Donnelly's voice, pleasing him.

'Look, mister, I don't know who the hell you are—'

'You're going the same way, Donnelly. With an M60.

20

Except you're going to know. Not like my son. I can see you now, behind your desk, everything. The hair up your nostrils.'

Richard, surprised by the savagery, listened to himself.

'Oh, you won't see me, Donnelly, but every move you make, I can see. Pick your nose, scratch your arse. I'll see it.'

Neither of the men looked at him. One whistled tunelessly, staring out of the window. The other studied his fingernails.

Uninterested.

'I've got an M60. You've used one enough. You have no place to hide in there.'

Richard remembered how exposed Donnelly had looked in the harsh lights of his own showroom.

'Drop behind your desk and the gun will eat through till it gets you. Try and move from your desk and I'll cut you down.'

He closed his eyes, seeing the plate-glass window down the dark street. The musty carpet in the room where he had positioned himself behind the gun. The peeling paper.

He hated the two intruders.

'This is what it's like, Donnelly. On the receiving end.'

The gun had juddered into his shoulder, the window shattering into a million pieces, a waterfall of broken glass cascading out into the street. Through the mist of the nightmare he heard his voice again.

'How do you like it, Patrick Donnelly? Terrorist. Back-shooting murderer. Pissing ourselves, are we?'

For the rest of his life, Richard Norris would remember the last words Patrick Donnelly spoke: *'I hope the fucker bled real bad!'*

Richard had not noticed the tape stop. Instead, he heard the yammering hiss of the silenced machine-gun as he had fired the rest of the belt at the moving figure, indifferent as the body had spun sideways as the burst caught him.

Then the Royal Mail van trundling across the line of fire . . .

He'd tried to forget the killing, push it into the back of his mind. And now these two had intruded into his private world, taking him back to the empty house in St James Crescent, Belfast. To the night he had taken revenge for the murder of his son. The coffee, cold now, tasted bitter. He sipped, not looking at the pair, keeping his face blank, standing so that the window was behind him and they would have to squint to see the untidy, expressionless features. Weeping Willie, the whistler, spoke.

'You should have known better than to use a mobile phone. Your call was picked up. That's it. On the tape. A man with your technical know-how should have realized that we'd intercept a call from a mobile.' Smug, pleased with himself. Richard had known the risks when he had chosen to talk to Donnelly, knowing there was a good chance of his call being intercepted. Anyone with a commercial radio could have done it. Courtesy of the Land of the Rising Sun. But it was a gamble he had been prepared to take. He had wanted the bastard to know what was coming to him.

He said nothing, his mind alive. What were the two men doing here? They had not come to arrest him, or if they had, there had been no caution. They were not the police. Richard Norris was certain of that. He pushed his hand through the damp hair, feeling it fall back over his forehead immediately afterwards.

The second man spoke.

'You're wanted. In London. An invitation to a meeting. Except you have no choice. It's not a case of RSVP, regrets only. You're to be there Friday, at ten. You can claim expenses.' The smile stayed on the mouth. 'Best to be on time.' He recited an address, a building off St James's Park. He didn't write it down. Richard Norris would remember it.

'Keep the tape, Mr Norris. We've plenty more.' Dismissively he glanced knowingly at his companion, gestured towards the door with his head, then preceded him out of the room and into the hall. Neither man looked back. The tuneless panpipe filtered back into the house as they crunched across the drive to their car. It whined into life, a spurt of gravel as the driver let out the clutch too quickly, an ugly scar left where the car had been. Richard watched from the window as the car turned at his gate, grimly satisfied as the driver wiped tears from his eyes.

The tape.

He looked at it, reliving the shooting all over again. He had felt the release, the satisfaction at the completion of his nemesis, after it was done. It had taken months to track the IRA man, Patrick Donnelly, but they had done it. With his brother-in-law, Alex Howard, he had gone to America and stolen an M60 machine-gun, then brought it back so that Donnelly would die as Johnathan Norris had. And Richard, the father, had avenged his son's murder. He had slept easy with his conscience, knowing that justice, *his* justice, had been done.

He no longer dwelt on the killing.

Until now.

He mulled over what the two men had said, trying to establish who they might be, although he had a pretty shrewd idea. Bending to the table he picked up the tape, holding it between forefinger and thumb as if morbific, that he might catch something. At the fireplace, he looked briefly at it again, opened the doors of the wood-burner and tossed it in. He stabbed the logs into life with a heavy poker, then watched as the tape burned with a blue St Elmo's flame. It crackled, hissed, hell's harridan, thrashing in death and consumed in the unforgiving fire.

The basement room was windowless.

Stale air.

Neon lights left no shadows, everything stark, bright,

exposed to the hard harshness. The main wall was hidden by a curtain, mustard-coloured, with a pair of draw cords to its right. The other walls were covered by charts and cork boards with pieces of paper, or notices pinned to them. Dog-eared pamphlets hung from string attached to one corner, next to a notice telling anyone who might be interested what to do in case of a fire. Prints of battles long past, forgotten by all but a few, hung haphazardly; Blenheim, he noticed, inclined towards the floor, balanced by Dettingen tilted towards the ceiling. An unfriendly room, functional without comfort, efficient without being tidy. Ill at ease, he rebelled at the stuffiness, the central heating, the lack of clean air.

A long table stretched in front of him. Three men sat behind it, note pads and pencils in front of them, a carafe of stale water in the centre, three dusty glasses surrounding it. There was no telephone. A small work station was set to one side where a stenographer, her PCW in front of her, sat waiting; the blue screen reflected her expression. Delicate fingers played nervously with the keys as she looked up briefly to catch his eye. One other occupant, a burly MoD policeman, his expression truculent, stood with his arms clasped behind his back, gently bouncing on the balls of his feet. It was impossible to leave the room without first passing him.

Richard Norris was uneasy. Now, he regretted coming here. Already he missed the warm spring sun, shining so benignly as he had walked around St James's Park from Green Park underground, Buckingham Palace, solid in its warmth, the Guardsmen already uncomfortable in the prickly heat of their scarlet uniforms.

He sat in the proffered chair, crossed his legs, hands lightly in his lap.

He waited for the leader to talk.

'Nice of you to turn up, old boy.'

Norris ground his teeth, knowing that the movement of his jaw muscles would be noticed, annoyed, still, that he was unable to control the habit. He stared at the man across the table, paying no attention to the other two. He was conscious of the woman's eyes on him, her fingers picking idly at the key pad. A pianist about to play a recital. He said nothing, his anger under control.

Barely.

'You'll be wondering what all this is about.' He was stating the obvious. He would not hold Norris's stare, instead looking quickly away, turning to the man on his right. 'Colonel, perhaps you'd be kind enough to put our friend in the picture.'

The Colonel's voice was dry, Wellington boots scuffing through dead leaves in the thick of a wood, the words hissing out economically, no effort wasted. Talking was painful. He tapped his pencil lightly on the pad as he spoke, a schoolmaster lecturing.

A glass eye looked at him, unmoving in its socket.

'They have a gun.' He wasted no time on preliminaries. 'The Iraqis. They've developed a prototype of their Supergun. It's almost ready for operation. Worse, it has a nuclear capability. We know that Saddam Hussein is preparing to use it. We want you to find it, pinpoint it so that it can be destroyed. We know you have the technical know-how. Any comment?'

'Fuck off.'

Unambiguous.

Richard stood, ready to leave. There was a lazy, imperceptible nod of the leader's head, and he sensed the policeman unclench his hands from behind his back. The stenographer had blushed, looking down at her hands. She might have been smiling.

'There is the matter of the tape—' Richard stopped, about to turn, head for the door and into freedom. 'It will send you to gaol, old boy. For a very long time. You won't see the outside of your cell this side of eighty.'

'Bollocks. A recorded phone tap isn't evidence in this

country. Not yet, anyway, much as your people would like it to be. Stop bullshitting.'

The eyes closed, opened, gleaming. Richard tensed, knowing now what was coming. He should have realized. Stupid of him.

'You're absolutely right, old boy.' The voice was tired, almost indolent. 'But you, you'd be extradited and tried in the USA where it *is* admissible. Ask any of the gun-runners or drug-dealers now serving time. No unbiased jury over there, chum. The FBI, the Justice Department will come down on you like Jericho's walls falling down. Uncle Sam doesn't take kindly to terrorism, someone pinching his hardware to do foul murder.' He waved, condescendingly, showing a frayed cuff peeping out from under his jacket. 'Sit down, there's a good chap, and let's talk about this sensibly, like the mature fellows that we are.'

Richard stared long and hard, features haphazard in his anger. He began to notice more about him, the penetrating expression in the reptilian eyes, bright, alert, a grey flecked moustache hiding a weak mouth, thin hair combed across his head to hide advancing baldness. It hadn't worked. The scalp shone through pink and vulnerable. A slight protuberance rounded his shirt over the waistband of his trousers. He wore an untidy suit, shiny at the elbows from a sedentary life behind a desk, a silk handkerchief hanging foppishly from the breast pocket, a nearly matching tie, slightly askew at his throat. The man had nicked himself shaving, leaving a small fleck of blood staining his collar. It went with the frayed cuff.

He looked tired, the world of intelligence-gathering a dreadful bore. He would be happier out tending his roses. But there was a no-nonsense confidence about him, a knowledge he held a winning hand. A royal flush, in hearts. Better than Richard's unfilled straight. Norris returned to his chair. He sat. The dry leaves rustled.

'You know about the second Supergun, the one that

26

got all the publicity. You'll have read about it in the press, seen the coverage, the pictures of the barrel on TV. Parts of it were being manufactured legitimately in various countries all over the world, but mainly in Europe, Germany, Switzerland, Sweden and, of course, here in the UK.' He paused, then sighed deeply. 'The individual sections of the gun were then moved to Iraq under the guise of being components for their oil industry. Damned clever. The West would never have known had it not been for a sharp young operative in the CIA, who accidentally stumbled on two parts of the gun, in two different countries.' He paused, scratching his chin. 'By chance he had been studying heavy ordnance in his college days, and was able to put two and two together. That was in the mideighties. He passed his suspicions on up the chain, but nobody paid any attention until we found the barrel. Damned fine operation by HM Customs and Excise.'

Richard remembered the scandal, the DTI issuing the export licence, hoodwinked by the plausibility of the story. He had felt sorry for the innocent driver, held in Greece, pending inquiries, then finally released when it was discovered that he was not part of a conspiracy. He looked at the man who was called the Colonel.

He was as tired-looking as his voice, yet wore his rank like a mantle. The glass eye stared unseeing from the left socket, unblinking, vaguely disturbing. It would have been a bullet wound. Someone had shot him from a high angle, the bullet passing through the eye and exiting through the back of the neck, probably damaging the larynx on its way. That would account for the voice. Richard tried to assess his age, finally concluding that he had bought it in the Mau Mau campaign. Some Simba terrorist, hidden in a tree. That would account for the angle. Was he that old, this Colonel? He would be from MI5, Norris thought, detached or seconded to MI6 as an ordnance specialist.

He listened.

'You are aware that what I am about to disclose is

27

covered by the Official Secrets Act. You'll be required to sign the necessary papers, a form E74, before you leave today. It goes without saying that anything you hear remains in this room.'

Norris bit on his smile, jaw muscles working. Ridiculous, Military Intelligence and their stupid little secrets. Enter the world of James Bond. The Colonel went on, absorbed. 'Two high-ranking Iraqi diplomats defected. You will have heard. It was on the news recently. They were poisoned. Saddam was trying to prevent them spilling the beans. He almost succeeded. But he was too late. They told an interesting story.' The Colonel, worried, conscious of the knowledge he held, went on. 'We have them, in a safe house.'

Richard Norris found it difficult to believe. He sat expressionless in the chair, like an applicant for a new post sitting before an interview panel. The dry, injured voice whispered on, and Norris learned about the secret assembly of the Iraqi Supergun, almost under the noses of the UN observers, hurriedly despatched to the area at the end of the Gulf War. He felt a cold fear gnawing at him, the story frightening him.

The Colonel stood tiredly, moving to open the curtains covering the wall in front of him. As if unveiling a commemorative plaque, he tugged at the draw-cord. The drapes slid back silently, to reveal a large-scale map of the Middle East, predominantly north-west Iraq and a section of the Turkish border. The single eye stared balefully.

'The gun is somewhere in here.' He gestured vaguely with his hand, a circular motion, describing what the military call a 'goose egg'. The egg covered an area of about 50 square kilometres. 'It's in an underground site, completely hidden below the surface. That's why it has never been picked up by any spy satellites. It is, according to our defectors, a huge complex, almost a town, completely self-supporting, built underground. The cost has been enormous.'

Norris was intrigued. The Colonel sensed it, pressing on, not wishing to lose his thrust. A tiny bubble of spittle had formed on his lips as he warmed to his subject.

'There is a door. An enormous sliding door,' – he paused, finding it difficult to describe the engineering that had gone into this project – 'which is opened electronically when the gun is ready to fire. It was tested last month, for only a few minutes, but long enough for a US satellite to pick up spurious radio emissions from the complicated electronics. That's how we got the approximate fix. It confirmed what our defectors had already told us.'

'You mentioned a nuclear capability? I thought the UN teams had all but destroyed the Iraqi effort, after the war.' Richard posed the question. The Colonel glanced over his shoulder at the leader, who was smoothing his hair across his scalp. He looked embarrassed, uncomfortable.

'Ours, old boy. We think he has three warheads.'

'How big?'

'Big enough to turn Tel Aviv into a desert. Make it look as it did before the Pharaohs let the Israelites escape across the Red Sea and trudge off looking for the land of milk and honey.'

Richard Norris felt the cold, as if an icy draught had blown in through a window left open on a winter's night. Iraq, with a nuclear capability and a man whose sanity was questionable with his finger on the firing button. He kept his mind blank, not letting himself think of the consequences, the nightmare of international blackmail. They told him then of the loss of the MV *Viking* all those years ago, during the Falklands War, and how a Dutch salvage vessel, searching for a treasure ship, presumed lost in the early part of the eighteenth century, had found it.

It was sheer chance that the *Viking* had been there instead. The Dutchman had beaten the British to it. When the Royal Navy diving teams had reached the hulk, the nuclear shells for the 8-inch cannon had been discovered. Three were missing, spirited away and smuggled into Iraq through a complicated, sanctions-busting, drug-dealer route.

The Dutchman was rich from his extraordinary fortune.

'Is it possible to convert these shells to be fired from the Supergun?' Norris knew the answer but asked it anyway.

'Easily done, old boy. The Iraqis persuaded a Russian – CIS now of course – to go over. He had been employed at their atomic research plant at Alma Ata in Kazakhstan. It was easy to do. The offer of a lucrative salary and a lump sum was guaranteed to win him across. Poor bastard was only on a tenner a month, since glasnost.' The movement with the flat of the hand on the nearly bald head was beginning to irritate. 'Besides, any competent ordnance man, even a garage mechanic, could do the job.' He looked at Richard directly. 'You could manage it, old boy.'

Garage mechanic.

Rude bastard.

The dry rustling of the Colonel's voice made Richard want to cough. Resisting the temptation, he listened instead.

'Your company, Norcom, has developed a radio direction-finding device. You call it Seeker. We know it is sensitive enough to pinpoint a radio transmission to within a few feet, provided of course you can get close enough. It's better than anything we've got.'

'It's all in your promotional literature, old boy.'

Colonel Oliver ignored the interruption.

'I said earlier that we'd like you to find it for us. Once you've done so, we, and the Americans, will do the rest. The gun must be destroyed at all costs.' The Colonel had probably not meant to sound so melodramatic. Back in his chair, he stared from his good eye.

'If Hussein is able to fire it against Israel, you know as well as us that they'll retaliate with a strike of their own.

They've had a nuclear capability since the Yom Kippur War. Then as sure as—' He shook his head like a sad Labrador missing its bone. 'One of Saddam's Islamic buddies will toss one back at Israel – it might even be Pakistan. Then, the proverbial excreta in the fan. Israel lets loose at Pakistan, the radiation drifts into China—' He looked away, unable to conceal the worry in his good eye. 'Does this alter your outlook?'

'Fuck off. Rude letter follows.'

Richard saw the leader open a drawer and take out a transparent plastic case. It had a cassette in it. He placed it carefully on the table in front of him, caressing it with little-girl fingers. When he spoke his voice was a low hiss, angry, spitefully menacing.

'Don't be such a pigheaded arsehole, old boy. I'm sure you are intelligent enough to realize that this is serious, that we mean what we say.' Spinning the tape, end over end. He held it up. 'This is your passport to prison. You won't pass "Go", nor will you collect your two hundred quid. Straight there, old boy. And' – he paused – 'there won't be a "Chance" or "Community Chest" you can draw on to get out. They'll toss the key down the can and crap all over it. Nobody's going to put his hand down and search around for it, even with rubber gloves on. Believe me. I can arrange it.' The eyes were hard, unblinking, venomous, watering a little.

Like the two at the farmhouse.

He meant it.

Every word.

Norris controlled his anger, grey-blue eyes, glacier ice. The muscles jumped in his cheeks as he ground his teeth, not daring to speak. He controlled himself, biting back the retort that had been on the tip of his tongue. The girl coughed gently, afraid of drawing attention to herself. He looked at her, her fingers flying over the pad, the keys clicking softly like a pair of dachshunds scampering across

31

a lino floor. Smiling grimly, he wondered how this conversation would transcribe.

'What's wrong with your people, your Sandbaggers or whatever you call them? Or the SAS? They must have specialized thugs just raring to go on a job like this. It must be right up their street.'

'No way, old boy. HM Government can't be seen to be involved. Terrible repercussions from the UN if our chaps were taken. And it would destroy the co-operation of the Arab states, what is still loosely referred to as the Coalition. It would be – ah – difficult if relations with Syria and Iran were to worsen at this moment. Wouldn't hear of it.' The hand went back to stroking, irritating Norris.

'And if I go? What if I'm taken?'

'You won't be taken, old boy. You're good enough to piss all over the Republican Guard. Anyone who is resourceful enough to do what you did in Belfast—' He hesitated, debating, not wanting to give too much away, show his hand. 'And we know what happened in America, in Boston and Fort Lewis. It didn't take the FBI too long to put the pieces of the puzzle together. Had it not been for us, the Americans would be applying for your extradition even now, without us pushing them. You're in the shit, old boy. No doubt about it.'

'How many will you need? In your team?'

Richard did not look in the direction of the voice, the third member of the group. When he did, he saw the leanness of the man, the hardness in the eyes and at the corners of his mouth. He had too much hair that should have been grey but wasn't.

'Three,' he said without hesitation. 'I'll need three.'

'Then get them together,' said the third. 'When you're assembled, we'll get you into shape, get you fit, hone up some of those old skills that might be a bit rusty. You'll do specialized training out of the country. But we'll get your team fit in the UK. I know just the place.'

'You'll be paid of course.' It was the leader speaking. 'You'll draw the equivalent salary had you stayed in the Army. At today's rate. I will make arrangements for—'

'Bollocks.'

Norris was not interested in what the leader was going to make arrangements for. He stood, controlling his anger, stepping forward to lean across the table to make his point, drive it home. His hands were screwed into tight fists. He glanced at the girl, in time to see the smile die quickly from her eyes.

'Make damn sure you get this. All of it.'

He looked back at the trio, then took a deep breath. Speaking slowly, deliberately, so that they would miss none of it, he started, checking off points on his fingers.

'OK. If you want me to carry out this hair-brained scheme, this is what happens. And it's going to cost. Plenty. First. The tape—'

The trio listened in silence to Richard Norris's terms.

The girl tried to hide her smile. She chuckled inwardly as her fingers pecked delicately at the keys. She had watched him, throughout, studying him critically, the untidy face, strong mouth, occasionally twisted into a sneer, spoiling what might have been a smile. Tense, yet he appeared relaxed and could give as good as he got. She knew what they were forcing him to do, and felt sorry for him. But they would not pin him down, nor dampen his spirit. Carefully she recorded the terms exactly as they were dictated. She felt she owed him.

The guy had balls.

He excited her.

Her sort of man.

Take cover, Mr Richard Norris. Keep your head down, and your belt buckled.

But it was a pity. There was no way this was going to succeed. Of all the operations she had heard conceived in this room, this one had the least chance of success. She listened carefully as they discussed the outline details of the plan, accurately recording what was said, memorizing the important factors, dates, times, places. The more she heard, the more convinced she became.

You're a dead man, Mr Richard Norris.

A shame.

She really liked his eyes.

Confused, thoughts crowding into his brain, he was unaware of the journey back to his hotel. Later he would remember the uncomfortable heat of the underground, the press of people as it swayed erratically on its way to Holborn. He had to admit it. They had him by the balls.

Thankful to leave the stuffy confines of the carriage, once more in the bright sunshine, he turned right on Kingsway and walked north, crossing High Holborn into Southampton Row. The sun was warm on his back, lunchtime, and he was hungry. He turned right onto Theobold's Road, crossing at the underpass. A small pub on the corner, just before the Cable and Wireless building, looked inviting. He turned into the dim interior. At the crowded bar, he ordered a small Budweiser, enjoying the sharp cold taste.

He tried to think.

Maybe he could take his chances, tell them to piss off, go to hell, do with him as they wanted. But in his heart he knew he could not. There was too much at stake. After Johnathan's death, his life, his being, had gone into his company. He was on the verge of a major breakthrough, lucrative contracts were lining up and he was making it. They would not take that from him.

He had done it for Johnathan.

He shook his head, for the first time looking about. The place was small, decorated in tasteful, neutral shades, with a pleasant clientele, mostly office workers, pretty secretaries and friends. The music was good, blending into the background, heard without having to strain. Chuck Mangioni, playing his arrangement of 'Maui Waui', the notes from the horn, cool, clear, easy to listen to. He let his thoughts drift, forgetting the basement in St James's Park.

A touch at his elbow surprised him. He turned, noticing a woman, his mind rapidly trying to recall where he had seen her before. There was a vague familiarity about her, for the moment not placed. He waited for her to speak.

'Hello. I'm Annabelle Sad. The stenographer at the meeting. I'm sorry, but I . . . I followed you here. I got changed then waited outside while they were debriefing you. I nearly lost you on the underground.'

He realized, then, why he'd not recognized her. She had been a rather dowdy girl, wrapped in a baggy, shapeless dress, hair drawn in a tight bun behind her head, large spectacles perched on the end of her nose. She had not worn make-up. He was certain of that.

But the woman who now stood before him was attractive without being beautiful, dusky, not wholly European, incredibly dark hair falling almost to her waist from a centre parting and eyes, in startling contrast, of the deepest blue. He had never seen eyes like them. The lisp came from the slight misalignment of her front teeth. Realizing he was staring, he raised an eyebrow, waiting. She disturbed him. He could smell her, the drift of her scent.

'I'm sorry. Can I get you a drink? Or are you due back?'

'A Martini, very dry. Ask them to make it with Tanqueray. One olive. Thank you.' She was looking at him intently, making it difficult to look away. 'And no, I've finished for the day.' They made small talk as they waited for her drink. Suddenly, he was enjoying her company. He picked up her Martini, handing it to her, her fingers light against the back of his hand. She sipped, licked the olive with the tip of her tongue, twisting the stick between finger and thumb, the olive rolling between the wet O of her lips. The gesture made him vaguely uneasy, excited.

'Um . . . that's good.' She paused, then looked at him directly. 'The tape. You realize the one they've given you is not the master? They still have it. What you have is only a copy. You could never be convicted using that as evidence, even in the USA. In court, the master tape has to be produced, sealed and annotated with the date and time of recording, then verified by an independent witness, another operator who was present at the time. I'm no lawyer, but I heard them talking, after you left.'

The anger returned, spoiling the present.

'Why are you telling me this?'

'Because I don't like what they are doing to you. It's underhand and illegal, getting you to do their dirty work for them. They shouldn't be allowed to get away with it.' She stared into her drink, then raised her eyes to look at him again. He saw an expression he was unable to read. Anger, hatred maybe. She nibbled the olive, smiled impishly, played absently with the cocktail stick, then snapped it neatly before placing it carefully in an ashtray on the table beside her.

'Look,' she said quietly. 'I think I can help you get the tape, the master. But it may take a little time. I know where it's kept and sometimes I'm left alone in the office where the safe is located. Would you want that, if I could?'

Richard Norris didn't answer at once. She must have seen his hesitation, the uncertainty.

'You don't have to make up your mind straight away.' She twirled the cocktail glass, staring into it, then, looking into his eyes, said, 'Look. There's a pub, in Uxbridge Street, just across from Notting Hill Gate underground. I've a flat in Pembridge Gardens. I use the place as my local. Could you meet me there at about seven, tonight? We could talk some more.' She inclined her head, the dark hair hanging vertically like a shiny black waterfall. 'Perhaps I could cook you a meal, later. I'd like that. I really would.'

36

He sipped his beer, this time without tasting it. He nodded.

'All right,' he told her. 'I think I would like that too. Seven o'clock. I'll be there.' He saw her smile, her tongue flick over the front teeth, one pushed slightly out of line by the other. Her lisp was more pronounced, perhaps deliberately. It put sex into her voice.

'Wear something casual. Don't come like an advert for Daks.' She indicated with her chin the wool blazer, the silk tie knotted neatly at the collar. Red-nailed fingers adjusted the handkerchief in his breast pocket. Placing the cocktail glass on the bar, she made to leave, stopping suddenly to rummage through a big, shapeless handbag hanging by a gold chain from her shoulder. It was a habitual, unthinking action, for her hand came out empty. Not wanting her to leave, he spoke, the first thing that came into his head.

'What do you do? In your spare time, when you're not working?' It sounded banal, and they both recognized it. There was mischief, deep in the blueness of her eyes as she looked up at him, his glass empty, awkward in his hand.

'Fuck,' she said.

Turning to leave, she looked over her shoulder, lips parted. He grinned suddenly, his face relaxing.

'You seem to know what you want from life.'

'Yes,' she said. 'Life lasts no time. No time at all.'

She strode to the door, the shape of her neat in the briefness of her dress. For the first time he noticed long legs, accentuated by the high heels.

'Seven o'clock then, Annabelle Sad.'

'Yes, Richard Norris. Seven o'clock.'

Briefly silhouetted, she turned out into the sunlit street. Annabelle Sad.

What the hell is going on here?

37

'He'll do it.'

'You seem pretty sure. Can you be certain?'

'Positive. I know the type. Not because he's afraid of prison. He *wants* it.'

The Colonel coughed.

'I'm not sure I approve of your methods, Adrian. Threatening him like that.'

'We have to be sure, keep him worried.'

The third man spoke.

'A hard case, that one. You won't find many who'll do what he did. Line some Provo up while chatting to him on the phone. Nice touch. But you're right. He'll do it. He looks pretty fit now, so there should be no trouble when he gets to Aldershot.' The hard man stood. 'Any idea who the other two might be? Anything on file?'

The others shook their heads.

'If they're anything like him, I wouldn't like to be in Saddam's shoes when they start causing mayhem in Iraq. Shit's going to start flying, that's for sure. I'd best warn Aldershot.' He shook his head and left.

The leader followed.

The Colonel stood and stared at the map, then pulled the curtains across, hiding its secrets.

'I hope you're right,' he said.

A woman stepped quickly along the pavement, not once looking behind her, hearing only the sound of her own footsteps tapping on the warm slabs. Crossing Russell Square, she stopped at a public telephone box, searching through her purse for coins. Glancing behind her, she leafed through a small notebook until she found the numbers she needed, then stabbed impatiently at the keys on the instrument, talking rapidly into the mouthpiece. She spoke, in turn, to five daily newspapers.

The woman did not give her name when asked.

Finally, she put the notebook away, dialling a final

number from memory. A casual pedestrian would probably not have recognized the language, had they paused to listen.

When next she spoke, it was in Arabic.

The room was dark.

A feeble light filtered through the thin gauze curtains as they floated inwards on the light breeze. It was cool. A man sat naked on a double bed centred against the wall, his legs crossed at the ankles, uncomfortable unless practised frequently. The air in the room was thick with the pungent odour of the weed as he dragged deeply on the loosely rolled joint held between finger and thumb. His eyes were dreamy, relaxed, as he listened to the woman talking to him on the telephone. Not once did he speak, until she had finished. Only then did he grunt an affirmative.

He replaced the telephone and continued to sit motionless on the bed, the joint now held between his lips, the smoke curling into his nostrils. Her voice, a picture of her, was fresh in his mind. Letting his head tip back into the headrest, he considered what was wanted of him, a slow, sensual smile rippling briefly across his lips, curving his mouth. The joint had burned out.

Yes.

That was how he would do it.

On the table under the window, an expensive camera bag. Turning his head sideways, he looked at it lazily, nodding dreamily. It would be easy that way, done before anyone would be aware of what had happened. Quick and clean. His thoughts returned to the woman, of how she had looked, felt, sounded as they had done it. Now, his penis stood out stiffly from him. Quickly, he stood, uncoiling from the bed.

He walked unhurried into the shower.

CHAPTER TWO

Alex Howard was unhappy with his lot. Worse, he was pissed off. The zip had gone, the excitement, leaving him feeling empty, embittered. And he was broke. Flat. Scuppered. There had been another affair, tears, damning recriminations, from peak to trough in one short week. The apartment was empty now, the room untidy with the things she had left in her hurry to be gone. Make-up, an ear-ring, found unexpectedly to remind him of where she had been.

The day had been foul from the moment he kicked off the duvet, the sun cheerfully mocking him. The work-out in the gym had not been right, the weights feeling heavy and not pushed with his normal ease. It was one of those days when nothing had gone right. Now, looking sightlessly out over the city, he tried to understand what had gone wrong with his life. Another account, the third that month, had gone down the tube as a client, chickening out, had wanted his money more secure. This damned, endless recession was now affecting the insurance business even worse than the rest of the economy.

He hunched his shoulders, tight, hard under his shirt, his forehead pressed against the warm glass of the window. The sun, at least, was trying. It was a beautiful day. How come this filthy mood?

To hell with it. He decided to go out for a drink, find a pub on the banks of the Thames, somewhere he had not been before, a place where he might drown his sorrows and perhaps meet new people. He felt like a change, needing excitement, maybe another woman. In the Stag he'd leave the top down. The fresh air would blow the cobwebs away.

Maybe.

The decision made, he felt better. Shrugging a suede jacket over his shoulders, he turned to look for his wallet and car keys, wondering vaguely where he had left them.

The telephone rang.

Business was the farthest thing from his mind and despite his cash-flow problem, he had no intention of involving himself with a client, especially in his current mood. He was interested only in leaving the flat and getting out into the fresh air. Ignore it. But the warbling persisted, on and on. He walked to the low rosewood table and looked down at the offending instrument, wondering. It was annoying him. Half turning, determined to leave, he suddenly changed his mind, snatched up the receiver and snapped into it. Unable to control his irritation, he spoke, his voice harsh.

'Howard.' Sounding churlish, he softened his tone, making amends, repairing damage. He needed the money. 'A. H. Financial Services. May I help you?'

'Alex?' The voice was American. It took him a few seconds, then: 'Jimmy? Jimmy Jamieson?' He looked at his watch. It was mid-morning in Seattle. 'Great to hear from you. How the hell are you? You coming over to England? You need picking up?' Suddenly, Alex was brighter, the grey clouds evaporating. He hadn't seen the American since his last visit to Washington State, when he had helped steal one of Uncle Sam's machine-guns. How long?

A pause, ominous.

'Alex, old buddy. I . . . I don't know how to tell you this.' The American was hedging, uncertain. 'You know we've had riots. In LA? All hell seems to have broken loose there. Crazy, man. Alex, Jesus. It's Carla, Carla Nicholson.'

Alex held his breath, frightened, the telephone tight in his fingers.

Carla Nicholson.

41

'Alex, God, oh, man ... She got caught up in a mob, on her way home from the airport. A bunch of nasties. She—' Another pause, longer than the first. 'Alex, she's dead. I heard it on the local news. If she hadn't been so big with Boeing, I never would have known. The local news, it's shit. Alex, I'm sorry, man.' The voice was distant, echoing over the satellite link. 'I know you two were really close, once. We all thought you would end up hitched. What can I say? Only that I thought you would want to know. You still there? Alex?'

Alexander Howard looked through the picture window without seeing the spires, the angled rooftops, the hazy outline of the city. He had loved her. Once. Maybe he still did, during those maudlin times when a tune that they had both liked was played on the radio, the Scotch in his head making his mind fuzzy, or when glimpsing a familiar figure, running eagerly across an airport lounge only to see a stranger turn at his call. God, now this. The rush of air was loud in the receiver, the sound a sea shell makes when it is held against the ear. His fingers hurt from his grip on the phone.

The voice was persistent, niggling, annoying in its repetitiveness. He came back.

'Alex? Alex? Talk to me, man!' The American was shouting, anxious.

'Jimmy.' The big man took a deep breath. 'I'm OK. Shaken up a bit, but OK. It was good of you to call. I would never have found out. Perhaps that would have been better.' He knew he was being unkind, hurtful, hating himself for what he had said. 'I'm sorry, Jimmy. It's just that I had never really given up. The two of us making it together. Deep down, I thought one day, she'd come over. Or maybe I would come over there. God, what a waste of life. Was she ... I mean did they—' Unable to bring himself to ask, he knew anyway that the question would be evaded, an excuse made, hiding the lie. He clamped his teeth together, his forearm trembling from holding the telephone.

They said their goodbyes, Jimmy awkward, glad it was done.

Alex dropped the telephone back into its cradle. He stared at it, half wishing that he had left a few moments earlier, letting the bloody thing ring into an empty room, with nobody to hear. But it had been told. Now he knew.

He walked aimlessly around the furniture, fists punched together, head buried. The shock, the real pain, would come later. Finally, he slouched into a chair, full of remorse and self-pity, remembering, all of it, with no dimming of his memory. They had last been together just after he had left the Army. He had told her everything was going to be fine, now that they were together. It had been a wild affair, both hungry for each other, wanting, needing, sometimes demanding.

Like yesterday in his mind.

They had gone to Spain where they rented a small apartment in Mijas, a white-painted little village in the foothills below the Sierra Blanca, long before the tourists found it. For them, it was solitude, unaware of the world of other people. It was going to be fine. Then, the rain in Spain. They had laughed as they watched it fall vertically from a windless sky, with Carla opposite, in a small *venta* where they had stopped for lunch, in the hills north of San Pedro. Sipping wine, she had looked at him as only she could, as if he were the only person in the world. Talk was of the future, of the things they would do together. How they would spend the rest of their lives. Together.

He squeezed his eyes shut, blotting out the vision of her, the memory of the afternoon. The last time.

As they drove back through the rain, the wipers had slapped across the glass, inefficient from not being used enough. Running in, hair plastered to their heads, clothes soaking, they undressed in the unfamiliar cold. Creeping,

shivering under the covers on the rickety bed they had
made love . . .

The telephone rang again.

He stared at it, coming back, unscrambling his thoughts.
At last, holding it close to his ear, he listened. No words
came.

'Alex? Alexander?' He recognized the voice, clipped,
businesslike as ever. His brother-in-law, Richard Norris.

Good old Richard. Solid. Always there when he was
needed.

'There's a job. No details on the phone. It's dangerous,
but not impossible. I need two. If we pull it off,' – he
paused, mischievous – 'there's a bag of gold at the end.
Fail, we're dead. Are you game?'

Alex paused briefly. What else was there? Now?

As he spoke, he wondered if his friend would detect
the sorrow, the bitter loneliness of his loss.

'What time do we leave?'

He listened.

The rucksack was heavy on the man's shoulders, his back
warm from the sweat running into the wool shirt he wore.
He seemed unaware of his burden, such was his concentration and the effort he was putting into his climbing.
Boots crunched on the gravel of the track, loosely scattered, the ascent made even more difficult by the scree.
The angle was steep, enough to deter the average fell-
walker. Few casual climbers would know of this remote
part of the Lakes. Even had they known of this hidden
footpath, not many would venture into this wasteland of
rock and stone. It was a remote place, scary, lonely.

Like the Radfan. Aden.

He tried not to think about when he had been in the
desert, that time on the *jebel*, with just him and the
Lieutenant.

Nobby Clarke bent to his task, pushing himself ever

harder whenever he felt himself slowing. He needed to hurt. The headband, a large checked bandanna, was soaked in sweat. Still he laboured upwards, grunting, the effort telling. The drizzle came out of the low clouds, cooling him, a wet sheen spreading on his ruddy face. There was anger, worry, and frustration, all mixed in, tearing at the mashed features, so that there was no peace in them. The big man was not at ease.

At each step, he swore out loud, words formed on the condensation, the rhythm monotonous with the sound of the heavy mountain boots as they thudded into the track, kicking the stones.

'Damn it. Fuck it. Damn it. Fuck it. Damn. Damn. Damn.'

He strove upwards into the mist.

At last he reached the summit and stood with hands on hips, unable to see the breathtaking view which, for once, was hidden in low, swirling cloud. In any case, he would have paid no attention. He shrugged out of the rucksack, lowering the great weight of it to the ground, balancing it against a rock. Reaching into his breast pocket, he found the old pipe and jammed it into his mouth, almost snapping the stem as he clamped his teeth on to it. He stood, sad in his loneliness. The depression weighed on him, a heavy burden, pressing down and subduing his spirit.

He had been coming into the hills for months, punishing himself, frightened and not wanting to think of the future. Without compromise, he had been unforgiving, allowing himself no rest. The guilt was shifted when he was here in the clouds but, once back in the valley, it returned to gnaw at him. Nor did his coming here solve the problem.

What the hell was he going to do?

He sat in the rain, perhaps for an hour, the cold unnoticed in his worry until the drizzle soaked through his shirt and spread the cold across his chest and shoulders. He shivered once, violently. At last, the chill eating into him, he stood, looking briefly about him. Heaving the rucksack on to wet shoulders he turned down the hill, running, leaping down the uneven slope, sure-footed as a chamois, his downward charge controlled. At last, chest heaving, he came to the road, to a battered Land-Rover parked on a grass verge. He felt better for the effort of coming down the mountain so fast.

He climbed into the cab and started the engine, listening with a practised ear to its regular beat. Holding the steering wheel in big calloused hands, he let his head fall forward on to it, only the sodden bandanna preventing him hurting himself.

What the hell was he going to do?

He reversed out on to the road, his mind full of worry. Turning in the direction of Ambleside, he drove automatically, his thoughts enmeshed in the problem which he could not solve. His big features reflected his despair as he reached up to remove the bandanna from his forehead. Dark curls tumbled into his eyes, rain falling from them. He drew his fingers through the wetness, feeling the small bald spot at the crown. Definitely bigger. Fuck it.

He saw the cottage through the mist, less thick here than it had been on the high fell. At once he felt better, forgetting some of his worries, if only for a while. Millie was in the garden busy with the trowel, weeding. She heard the engine, recognized it and looked up as he turned into the gate, waving as he got out of the Land-Rover. He took in the plump figure, at once sad again, knowing that their happy times in this place were to end. The cottage was, as always, a picture, the extension he had built last year blending perfectly with the original slate.

They were going to lose it.

All this.

Redundancy.

Repossession.

There was nothing he could do. Twelve years he'd been with the security firm. Twelve bloody years. Twelve, when he could have stayed in the Army earning the Queen's shilling, maybe making warrant rank. And the bastards had made him redundant, the money all but gone. He had tried. He had really tried to find work. Tramping between Job Centres in Keswick and Kendal, even as far as Barrow-in-Furness. Labouring, casual, anything to earn a few bob, keep the bastards away, keep the fucking bailiff out from the house.

There was only the cottage. It was all they had, him and Millie. The letter had come that morning, old Charlie Makepeace, in half a postman's uniform, trudging tiredly up the path with it. There had been the smart logo on the crispness of the envelope, the typeface dark, bold, so that there could be no mistaking the address. He had hidden it from her. From his Millie.

Andrew Clarke, Esq., it had read. Esquire, my arse. They were coming to collect, call in their marker because the mortgage payments couldn't be met. Six months in arrears, and the odd jobs bringing in only enough to keep them in food, the occasional ale. They hadn't been out for months.

He hadn't the heart to tell her. Let her tidy the borders as she had done on every fine day since they'd bought the cottage. Now it was to be repossessed. Taken from them. Sold to some smart-arse from London who wanted a place for the summer. Not even to live in like Millie and him.

Over his dead body.

'Nobby.'

He loved the way she spoke. Devon, up here in the wilds of Lakeland. Her accent never quite blended with those of his Cumbrian mates, theirs broad from time spent in the hills, or slurred from the beer that lay heavy in them. So soft it sounded, when she was amongst a group of them crowded into their front room, or in the Torver Bar at the Church House Inn.

'There was a phone call. While you were out. That nice Mr Norris you used to be in the Army with.' She pushed a wisp of hair from her eyes. It was always there, when she was in the garden, the combs never holding in all the ends. Dirty fingers in the gloves left a smudge on her forehead. 'He said something about a job. He said it was right up your street. You're to call him back straight away if you're interested. The number is by the telephone. I wrote it down, in case I forgot it.'

Nobby Clarke suddenly grinned.

'Nobby.' She looked at him as she always did, when she knew he was afraid, when he was hiding something. 'Does this mean it's all going to be all right?'

He kissed her, surprising her, bringing a flush to her face.

Lieutenant Norris.

'Bloody bandit,' he said. 'You bloody bandit.'

He ran into the house.

London, a sleepy, balmy afternoon, sunny without the oppressive heat that normally descended over the city like a warm, damp blanket, making life intolerable for those who lived and worked there.

A day for cricket at Lord's.

Richard Norris strode on the warm pavement, he thought in the direction of Victoria. The dry rustling voice of the man beside him told him more of what he knew about the Iraqi Supergun, the prototype they'd finished before Mossad had done for Gerry Bull, its designer, who had been clinically assassinated as he'd been entering his flat. Norris no longer felt angry. Committed, he could see no way out and had now resigned himself to going along with it. Shuddering, he remembered what the leader, Kronk, had told him, that he would face trial in the USA. He knew. With an unfriendly jury, no proper defence, they would nail him.

Colonel Walter Hadrian Oliver.

What parent would inflict such a mouthful on an offspring? Walter Oliver's had. Richard smiled, the rare touch of humour coming from the man as he had recounted a tale from his early days in the Army, as a young second lieutenant, appointed Assistant Adjutant while waiting for his platoon to become available. Green, he had discovered the pitfalls of regimental life.

An urgent letter had arrived from Brigade, very important and requiring a rapid response from Battalion. Young Oliver had signed off in the correct place with his initials, as he had been shown, and then passed it to the Commanding Officer through the little sliding door connecting their two offices. It had been forgotten in the flurry of the day.

Later, the intercom had sounded. It was the CO.

'Mr Oliver. This letter from Brigade. Did you pass it in?'

'Colonel?' What the hell had he done wrong?

There was a pause. To young Oliver, there had been the sound of stifled mirth.

'Mr Oliver—' Definitely mirth. He could hear it in the background. Someone else had been in the CO's office, a bunch of them, it had sounded like.

'Who's WHO?' The guffaw had exploded from the intercom.

After that, the regiment had called him 'Doctor Who'.

Norris was beginning to like the man.

He listened.

'Our two Iraqi defectors have been holed up in a safe house. We'll meet them there and they'll tell you as much as they know. Ask them anything you want. There won't be a second chance. They've asked for asylum in the USA, thinking, after the attempted poisoning, that it's not safe here.' He tugged an ear lobe. 'Can't say I blame them.'

They were early and had slowed their pace, their shadows leisurely preceding them. The houses flanking him were nondescript, short on decoration, some needing repair. His briefcase, loose in his right hand, bumped his knee. The Colonel stabbed, pointing the umbrella.

'There's the place. On the corner. Nothing special, so it

won't attract attention. They are expecting us at ... What the ...? Press! What the hell is ...? How the devil did they find out? My God! Our chaps are coming out. There, on the steps.' There was irritation tinged with panic in the scratchy voice, the spittle back on his lips.

Richard looked up, unnerved by the urgency, wondering what could have alarmed Walter Oliver.

The Arab drove quickly across London.

He used side roads and narrow back streets known only to experienced cabbies, grown familiar with the labyrinth through years of the knowledge. He drove meticulously, staying within the legal speed limit, careful not to commit a traffic offence. It would not do for him to be pulled over by the Law.

The camera bag was on the seat beside him, carefully sealed, the Velcro fastener tight down. He was proud of the contents, which he had designed, then overseen its manufacture by the best expatriate instrument makers in Baghdad.

He slowed as he approached an unfamiliar part of the city. At a red light he snatched up an A-Z of London, and quickly checked his route, head ducked below the windscreen to read the road name high on a shabby, peeling wall. Confirmed, he drove on, cautious now. Soon, he would be there. Right at the next lights, over the crossroads, then a left at the second junction. Closing the small atlas, he shoved it into the door pocket out of the way.

He slowed at an intersection, turning into a road of unimposing houses and small hotels. Already, he could see the knot of pressmen at the far end, cameras held casually, some occasionally checking a light meter or shutter-speed setting. He parked opposite the house on the corner and looked to left and right. Clean.

He got out of the car, leaving the engine running. Once

across the road, he stood a little behind and to one side of the group, a camera loose in his hand, held casually, as though he had done it before. He looked bored. Another Nikon was slung around his neck, ready when the first was finished.

It would be soon. The road, deserted, save for two men walking slowly along the pavement in the direction of the corner, the sun behind them making it impossible to make out their features. A taxi, its diesel clattering, turned into the road from the opposite end.

Raising the camera, he squinted through the viewfinder, focusing on the peeling paint of the door at the top of the steps. His pulse quickened at the expectant murmur. The doors swung inwards.

Two Arabs hurried out, looking worried, initially without noticing the group at the bottom of the stairs. Overnight bags were clutched nervously in their hands. They stopped, suddenly alarmed, surprised, at the gaggle of photographers jostling below them.

They made to hurry down the steps.

The camera came up swiftly to the eye, aimed at the man on the right, the sleeve of the lens twisted as if focusing. Now, if the subject would just keep still. It would be a perfect shot . . .

Norris looked up, alert.

There were two men with their backs to him standing hesitantly on the top of a flight of steps leading to a wide door from which they had just exited. At the foot, a group of about five or six press photographers jostled for the most advantageous position. Cameras rose and fell, flash-guns already flaring, despite the brightness of the early-afternoon sun. Flash for infill, thought Norris. The sun behind would make the subject badly back-lit.

One of the photographers was slightly to one side, behind the rest, just beginning to raise his camera. A spare was hanging from a strap around his neck. He was dark, swarthy and looked like an Arab. A shiny black hatchback, a Golf GTI, was parked a little to his left.

The engine was running, the exhaust bubbling quietly.

There was something odd, not quite right. Richard tried to place it but nothing would gel. He looked again at the swarthy photographer. The camera, its long telephoto lens probing outwards, was pointed up the steps.

Richard stared. The camera hanging from the strap around the man's neck was also fitted with a long telephoto lens. Probably a zoom.

It wasn't right.

Two telephoto lenses? At close range? The other photographers had shorter focal length, wider-angle lenses on their spare cameras. He saw it all at once. There was no reflection from the sun like the others. It wasn't a lens, but a hollow tube, aimed at the Iraqis.

A faint puff of smoke spurted from the barrel as the man depressed the shutter. One of the Iraqis at the top of the stairs flung a hand to his chest and staggered backwards. He would have fallen, but the other steadied him with an outstretched hand.

Already the second of the cameras was coming in to aim.

Shit. A weapon. Silenced. Small calibre, single shot, probably a poisoned projectile. There was no other explanation.

Instinct.

The clatter of yesterday's gunfire. NCOs shouting at him on the drill square, the gruelling, punishing sessions in the gymnasium, when to survive was to avoid the screaming obscenities in his ears. It was no longer today.

Aden.

Borneo.

Belfast.

The past crashed over him, a wave, pebbles leaping as the power slammed inshore. He felt himself propelled forward, adrenalin pumping, the excitement wild in him. Norris started running, already yelling, waving a hand. But his warning, if it had been seen, was ignored. The Colonel was beside him, gasping.

'What the—'

But he was gone, sprinting hard, his breath held as he dashed to the corner. Feet pounding, Norris knew he couldn't get there in time. The assassin was down on one knee, for a better angle, a better shot. Without thinking, Richard Norris swung the briefcase in his hand, hurling it like a discus, at the kneeling man. It spun away in slow motion, never getting there. It seemed to hang suspended for an eternity until it hit the cameraman hard on the chest, thudding into him. The camera clattered on to the road.

Confusion.

The would-be assassin fell backwards on to his haunches, cursing, the tongue foreign, the movement comical. Hands on the Tarmac, he made a vain attempt to save himself from sitting on his backside. At the top of the steps, the uninjured of the pair dragged the other to the bottom and into the crowd where they were swallowed in the mêlée. They pushed through the group of photographers.

A taxi pulled into the kerb. A woman, her arms full of bags, began to get out.

Richard Norris arrived, charging.

'Here! This way.'

Thrusting out an arm, he grabbed the uninjured of the two, dragging him, barging his way through. Richard took no notice of the protestations, not even hearing, his reaction automatic. Escape. Get them out. Recriminations could come later. Just get them out of the line of fire.

'Come on! Quickly now!'

The urgency, the sharp authority, were recognized. They stopped struggling and allowed themselves to be guided, hauled, towards the vehicle.

The driver, open-mouthed behind the wheel.

The woman, fussy, was searching for money, deliberate, oblivious to the commotion. Her fingers picked through her purse, the parcels awkward in her arms. Norris unceremoniously shouldered her out of the way. She gasped, indignant, staggering from the open door at the rear of the cab. Coins scattered, tinkling on the pavement, bouncing and rolling away.

Norris fell into the cab, smelling the newness of the upholstery. One of the Iraqis was foaming at the corner of his mouth, which hung slackly open, his breath coming in sobbing, irregular gasps. His companion crouched over him, speaking in rapid Arabic, close against his ear, so that Richard did not catch what was said. He turned to pull the door closed and, as Colonel Oliver ducked into the interior, wrenched the door shut.

'Go!' Norris was yelling.

'Where to?' The cabby asked the needless, inevitable question.

'Anywhere. But get us the hell out of here. And fast!'

The taxi was gone, diesel engine rattling from the unfamiliar demand put on it. The hatchback in front tore away with a screech of tyres. They followed, with no chance of catching, but hoped to see which way it went. Already it had turned at the intersection, ignoring the red light, the clamour of horns and screech of brakes as other vehicles swerved to avoid a collision. Gone, before they even reached the junction.

'Did you get a number?' asked Oliver hopefully, trying to steady his breathing.

'No. But I saw CD plates. Clear. Embassy car.' Richard too was panting from his exertions.

'Welcome to the world of espionage, Mr Norris.'

The Colonel turned to the two men, concerned by what he saw, then spoke to them in fluent Arabic. The second of them nodded. Oliver gave instructions to the cab-driver, telling him to drive to a private hospital in Chelsea. The wounded man coughed. Oliver told the driver to get a move on as he tugged a mobile telephone from a pocket and stabbed quickly at the keys.

But it was too late.

They turned into a shady drive and sped up to a set of imposing doors. The Iraqi twitched violently, his back arched, out from the seat. There was pure agony in his eyes as he coughed pink blood on to the cleanness of his shirt. His sightless eyes rolled upwards into their sockets.

The white-coated attendant opened the door and looked in, impersonal, uninterested. The man was dead. Eyes, like opaque marbles, stared at Richard Norris.

He wondered what had happened to his day.

It was his sort of place, the pub on Uxbridge Road. Noisy without being loud, and he was comfortable there. He stood, savouring the sensation, liking what he saw. Dressed in a casual Pierre Cardin sports shirt, moleskin jeans, pale blue in colour, dark loafers on his feet, he hoped he didn't look like an advert for Daks.

He wanted her to like him.

Absently he pushed the thatch from his forehead as he stepped into the interior, irritated when it tumbled immediately back into his eyes.

Impossible to miss, he saw her at once. A group of three young men surrounded her, laughing, enjoying each other's company. He was angry, jealous, not sure of the reason. Now, he was uncertain. Shrugging, he made to leave, half turning towards the door.

'Richard! Richard Norris. Here. Over in the corner.'

He hesitated, awkward, suddenly uncomfortable, the room full of strangers. But she strode towards him with long strides. On reaching him, she kissed him unblushingly on the mouth, leaving her taste there, so he would know and would want more of her. He grinned, the afternoon forgotten, the tension falling from his body like leaves shed from a tree in autumn when a breeze blows suddenly through a copse on a bare hillside.

'I promised you dinner. If you want, we can have a drink here and then leave. My place is just across the road.'

They were away from the crush at the bar, somehow finding a corner where they were able to talk, voices low in the clamour of conversation as the crowd roistered. Richard spoke of his plan in Iraq, she about nothing in particular but interesting him. It was his third Scotch. Her Martini glass was empty. He felt as if he had known her for longer. Her hand brushed him, then took his, her own warm, squeezing his fingers gently.

'Don't worry too much, Richard Norris. You can pull this off. And as soon as I can, I'll try to get the tape. Everything will be all right. You'll see.'

He felt the closeness of her, smelt her, liking her. She looked at him, the message clear. It was in her eyes, the blue of them.

'Get me out of here, Richard Norris.'

The telephone call had surprised him. It had been years since he had heard the accent so strong, grating, harsh, devoid of humour. A sinister, menacing voice that had made him feel uneasy. He had not been in Belfast since his late teens, leaving the Province to study at an English university. Now, in his late twenties, he had hoped never to go back to the city. The dismal streets, the derelict buildings, the despair etched into the faces like grime on an urchin. Here on the mainland there were no Army or RUC patrols, restless, suspicious, in amongst the population, untrusting and unloved. A man could move freely here. He had studied hard. Now, there was only a year left before finishing his university course. He had been reading Political Science.

Then, the telephone call.

Sometimes, when things were good, he almost forgot

that he was a member of the Movement. But never quite. The vow was with him, the oath, still remembered, burned into his subconscious, the scar deep and irremovable.

I, Joseph Thomas Fallon, promise that I will promote the objects of Oglaigh na hEireann. No, he had never forgotten. Nor would he. Ever.

He had been told to meet a visitor who would tell him what he was to do. The visitor had been a stranger, surprising him by being dressed in a bespoke suit. The general demeanour of the man was not a bit like he expected a terrorist to be.

But Fallon had smelled the Falls on him.

The damp.

The suit, he was told, was good cover when travelling from the Province, the expensive leather briefcase adding credence to the lie. Bad guys travelled in dirty jeans and grease-stained anoraks.

Fallon took the underground, then a taxi to the address he had been given. It was a chic apartment in Leinster Terrace, better than his own cramped digs. Here there were plush furnishings, Regency wallpaper, elegance. There were crystal decanters in the tantalus on the sideboard, all filled. He looked around him appreciatively. The stranger seemed at ease there. Fallon accepted the drink, then sat awkwardly in the comfortable armchair as the man told him what was required of him.

His days as a sleeper were over.

There was a job to be done.

Puzzled, he watched as a cassette tape was inserted into the music centre in the corner. The amplified voice boomed out into the room and the man moved quickly, nimbly, to adjust the volume.

Fallon listened, a nerve throbbing in his temple.

The tape was played twice, so that he would miss none of it. The stranger twisted up the volume at the end and Fallon was able to hear the agonized moan faintly through the thump of the telephone banging against a desk or table.

'Patrick?' he had said. '*Patrick?*'

'Ay. Patrick. One of our best. A fucking Brit took him out.'

Fallon could not comprehend, unable to make a connection.

'But I thought it had been sectarian, the killing. All the papers had said so. *Our* people said so.' Fallon looked confused, unsure. 'He was found on waste ground not far from the Shankill. I don't understand.'

'We all thought so.' The visitor's eyes glittered like tiny diamonds in an eternity ring. 'But a Brit got him. You heard. And Patrick was supposed to be clean. When they found him, Patrick, he was a hell of a mess. He was hit bad. Shoulder, head, and' – there had been a pause, for effect, to fan the embers of hatred that were beginning to glow in Joseph Fallon's heart – 'his bollocks had been shot away. His dick was gone. Just a squashy mess where it had been. That's no way for a man to die, Joseph.'

Fallon came quickly from the chair, the fine crystal glass tumbling from the arm, spilling Jamieson's on to the thick carpet. He had no desire to be involved, not then. He thought he knew, now, why they had contacted him and he was afraid of what was expected of him. Shrugging, he turned to leave, looking for his coat, wanting out, to have no commitment. He was afraid. He had never expected to be called upon to fulfil his vow. Turning, he headed for the door, but stopped when he saw the big automatic in the man's hand, appearing suddenly from behind his back, like a conjuror producing an egg from someone's ear. Fallon felt the cold hardness against his forehead. The barrel was twisted, savagely, drilling into the skin, making him bleed.

'Yes.' The voice hissed. 'You're afraid, shit running scared like we all are to start. When they're hounding you, bursting into your home, waking the wee ones and

tearing the place apart. Every time you stop for a check-
point with some fucking snotty-nosed Brit kid of a soldier
bending into the car, wrinkling his nose at the smell of
you.' He straightened his arm, pushing with the gun. 'But
you'll learn. Like us, you'll learn to let your hate overcome
your fear, Joseph Fallon. Let hatred, pure and undiluted,
drive you on. Command wants its revenge for the taking
of one of ours. You're nominated.' The smartly dressed
terrorist looked at Fallon contemptuously. 'You've had it
easy over here, safe on the mainland. Good boys been
dying over the water, while you've been pissing around
with your school books. Oh yes.'

He turned and slipped the gun into a drawer, then faced
Fallon once more, his eyes devoid of life, the expression
hard, uncompromising.

'Listen, Joseph Fallon, and listen good—'

Fallon, all ears.

He was told how he would be given access to a TV
video recording of the aftermath of a funeral held in a
village not far from Cheltenham. He was to study it, get
familiar with the place. Fallon was to be the tool of
revenge. He listened as the courier gave him detailed
instructions where he would find the Kalashnikov AK74
assault rifle and the ammunition for it. He continued listening as he was told that the soldier who had been killed
was Johnathan Norris. The father, Richard Norris, had
taken out their man Patrick.

Their man.

His cousin.

Patrick Donnelly.

They had eaten, then talked some more. He felt comfortable, enjoying her. Relaxed, brandy and coffee in the dim,
cool half-light of her flat, woman's things surrounding
him. He sighed. They sat together, close in, touching, then
lying, her nakedness soft next to him, her mouth wet. He

did not remember their clothes coming off. She rolled on top of him, staring, her tongue washing across her front teeth. She dipped her head, kissing the dark hair that lay across his lips.

'I make a lot of noise. When I fuck.'

He felt the guilt, and could not respond. She straddled him, reaching behind her, breasts tilted upwards as she felt, finding, fingertips gently on him.

There was puzzlement in her eyes, those oh-so-blue eyes.

'I'm a slow starter.'

It happened, without his trying.

Hard, deep into the lubricious warmth of her.

'Bull's-eye,' he said.

Her mouth smothered their chuckles.

She was wild, noisy, obscene. Assaulting him, leaving him spent.

They slept then, as lovers do, close together, feeling the warmth of each other, their bodies entwined. In the depths of his sleep, he thought he heard her crying. Dreaming, he had kissed the wet cheeks, tasting the salt of her tears. He was too contented to pay much attention, feeling the softness of her thigh against his own. But his shoulder was wet from the tears that spilled from her. He murmured in half-sleep, pushing against the softness of her hair, feeling her hot against him. He dreamed, hearing her speak, her voice tormented, unforgiving, muffled, whispering, through her tears.

It sounded strange, foreign to him, and he didn't understand, until, in his subconscious, it came to him. He didn't care, then. It had been so long and she had been so good. He held her gently against the wetness of her cheeks.

Annabelle Sad.

Sad Annie.

The noisy fucker.

He smiled in his sleep.

*

At first, the stranger did not recognize the village. It looked different from his previous visit. But this time he had entered from the opposite end and as yet had not found a familiar landmark with which to orientate himself. A pretty place, with white-painted cottages, neatly juxtaposed, with warm thatch or lichen-slated roofs, diffused in the early-evening sun, casting deep, purple-blue shadows in the narrow lanes. A picture-postcard village, he thought, the sort seen on chocolate boxes.

Once he had found the square, granite tower of the church, he knew where he was. He stopped the car in front of the narrow lich-gate leading into the churchyard and peered through at the neatly tended gravestones standing in precise patterns in the short grass. Tired from the long drive, he got out of the car and stepped through the narrow entrance, eyes closed, the video of the TV interview clear in his mind.

Yes. There was no mistaking it. This was the place.

Languidly, without apparent haste, he walked along the gravel path which took him past the memorial cross. The grave he sought was a little beyond it, in a more private part of the cemetery. Breathing deeply, he approached the spot and stood staring down at the polished marble of the simple headstone. Inscribed in gold, the Gothic lettering stood out boldly, easy to read:

JOHNATHAN RICHARD NORRIS

1967–1990

SO YOUNG IN DEATH

Definitely the place.

He spat, watching the lazy path of the spittle as it slid slowly down the polished surface of the headstone, weaving into the indented characters. Turning, he strode from the cemetery. Not once did he turn to look back.

Now to find the house.

He drove back into the village, to the pub on the edge of the square. Under the shade of a horse chestnut, its buds just breaking, he switched off his engine, left the vehicle and strolled casually over to the wide doors, held open by an old millstone propped against them. He ducked through the low door into the dim interior, letting his eyes adjust to the darkness, looking about him, a casual visitor taking in his surroundings. Despite the warm, evening spring sunshine, a fire burned brightly in the grate, the crackling logs overpowering the silence, absorbing the hollow tick of the grandfather clock in the corner. A nice pub, with shiny horse-brasses adorning the blackened beams, the bowed ceiling so low in the corner, they had needed to dig out a groove in the yellowed plaster to accommodate the tall clock. Better than the smoky dives in London.

There were two other occupants, country types, one with pieces of straw clinging to the old Army sweater he wore. Obviously local, at home in this friendly place, they leaned at the bar drinking cloudy cider with studied concentration. They looked at him over their shoulders but said nothing as he walked across the faded carpet towards them.

'Evening,' said the stranger. 'A nice day outside.'

He wondered if they would notice the accent.

He paid no attention to their mumbled reply, instead studying the sanguine character who now stood behind the bar having entered from a dark wood door with a latch recessed into the wall. The epitome of a village pub landlord, to look at him, one wouldn't imagine he regularly finished the *Times* crossword in under fifteen minutes, even on an off day. Leaning on the bar with both hands, he looked at the stranger questioningly.

'Sir?'

'A pint. Any one as long as it's real, not one of those plastic beers.' The landlord sniffed, looked at the two drinkers knowingly, then reached above him and drew down a pint mug, holding it up to confirm it was preferred to a straight glass. The stranger nodded.

62

'Fine.' The beer hissed into the glass as the pump was worked. Satisfied, the barman placed the drink on the bar where it left a wet circle on the shiny wood. He took the proffered money and rang it into the till.

'Have one yourself.'

'Thank you, sir. I'll have a small one, of the same. Cheers.' The glass was raised. The stranger waited, quietly sipping his drink. He spoke, his voice casual.

'I was looking for Richard Norris's place.'

The three looked at him, one with a piece of straw hanging from a thread caught on the elbow of the military sweater as he held his glass quivering on its way to his mouth. 'We were in the Army together, and I've lost contact with him, although I know he lives around here somewhere. Been a long time since we left. We served in Cyprus.'

That should be convincing enough.

The barman paused, looking archly at the other two. Reluctantly, he said, 'It's the big old farmhouse. On the right, at the far end of the village. You can't miss it. Take the Cheltenham road. He comes in sometimes. If I see him, who shall I say was asking?'

Ignoring the question the stranger ordered another beer and walked over to a table by the window where the sunbeams sliced through the dust particles into the dim room. Sitting in an old wheelback, he drank slowly. Finally, as more customers entered the bar, filling the room, he got up and left unobtrusively.

But the landlord had seen the leisurely exit.

He left the bar and walked quickly into a small office at the far end of the building. There, he lifted the telephone, dialling quickly.

'Constable Atkinson? Look, Trevor, this may not be important, but there's a stranger in the village. Odd accent, which I couldn't place. He said he was an old Army buddy of Richard Norris. He wanted to know where he lived.' He paused and took a deep breath. 'Well, no

63

way could he have been in the Army with Richard, he's been out too long. This fellow's too young. What . . .? Yes. I gave him the address. I shouldn't have done, I s'pose. As I said, it's probably nowt to worry about but I just thought it might be important, with what happened to his boy. Over there.' He hesitated. 'Yes . . . yes. Of course. If I see him again, I'll let you know.' He hung up, thoughtful, remembering the stranger.

There had been something odd, the look in his eyes.

Bright, obsidian, like Flossie the sparrowhawk's, hunting the voles and the fieldmice in the meadow at the end of the garden. Deep in thought, he picked up the newspaper, folded to expose the crossword, except for 16 across, neatly completed in red ballpoint. It came to him now, the clue that had been swirling in the tumble-dryer of his mind before being summoned to the bar.

'Feathered hunter or apt liar to give this appearance.'

Nodding, he printed RAPTORIAL in bold red letters.

Flossie and the stranger both.

No expression in the eyes.

Even when killing.

CHAPTER THREE

Major Peter Ashworth strode briskly up the gentle slope and turned into the building in which his office was located. For once, it was a beautiful day, and Aldershot, with no claim to fame other than that of being home of the British Army, was basking in warm sunshine. Feeling good from the effort of the early-morning run, there was a spring in his step. He was looking forward to the week.

As always, his mood was cheerful, his enthusiasm infectious. His Regimental Sergeant Major, bright as a button, stood in the corridor, dressing down a junior NCO who did not look at all happy and who had, no doubt, incurred his superior's wrath over some misdemeanour. The Warrant Officer looked up at the approach of the Major, his expression neutral, guarded. He never quite knew what surprises the old man had in store for him and the Squadron. Always keeping them on their toes.

He reflected, ruefully, that it was all part of being in the Army's only Parachute Signal Squadron. *Keep 'em lean and mean.* The phrase had almost become the unit motto. But the Major didn't have that wicked twinkle in his eye and the RSM knew that there was enough paperwork in the office to keep the boss pinned to his desk for at least another week. There would be no surprise deployment today.

Besides, there was the visitor.

A big, athletic-looking bastard, he reflected. He was ex-military too. There was no way a man could hide the fact he had been a soldier, even in the scruffiest clothes, unshaven and with his hair worn like a heavy-metal artist. There was something in the way a man bore himself. It was stamped on him. This one had been an officer. He would have put money on it.

'Morning, sir. You've a visitor. I've put him in your office with a cup of coffee. Believe you were expecting him? We had to have him escorted up from the gate. No ID,' he added unnecessarily.

'Thank you, Mr Dukes.' Ashworth hesitated and, because he was interested in the plight of all his soldiers, he asked about the problem with the junior NCO.

'A bird. In the block after the Squadron do,' said the RSM.

'Well, at least it wasn't a little boy.'

Ashworth chuckled, then entered his office, the grin staying on his face, creasing his features. He thrust out a hand as the big man uncoiled from the only armchair, reserved for visitors.

'Colonel. It's good to see you again.' The Major studied the athletic figure before him. He'd filled out a bit, thought Ashworth, probably worked out on a multi-gym. He had to admit, his ex-Commanding Officer looked as fit as he had ever seen him; if anything, better than when he had been in the Army. Ashworth had been a young lieutenant in those days.

'Good to see you too, Peter. And by the way, it's Alex.' Smiling again, he punched the Major lightly on the shoulder. 'I can see, without your telling me, that you're in your element here. Life seems to be treating you well. You look in great shape.'

Peter Ashworth gestured to the chair, then sat down behind his desk. They made small talk, laughing together as they recounted past adventures, the good times and sometimes the bad. There came the inevitable pause, the brief silence stretching into long seconds. The former Colonel was uncomfortable and, for the first time since Peter Ashworth had known him, he appeared uneasy. The Major waited, spinning his coffee mug absently on the blotter with his fingers. At last Alex Howard took a deep breath.

'Peter. I can't say too much at present, not much more than I could on the phone. It's all a bit ... guarded. Yes, I suppose "guarded" about describes it. I, we, that is, have been given a job, three of us. We've been ...' – he hesitated, searching for the right word – '... sort of called up for a special mission. I can't tell you any more than that.' Alex looked embarrassed. He coughed into his fist.

'But they need to get us fit, fitter than we are at present. And it has to be done fast. The ... they, ah, also want to be sure we're up to the job. Peter,' – Alex let a crooked grin twist his features – 'they're putting us through P Company. Your Squadron is to sponsor us as Territorial Army applicants. You'll be getting your instructions from the MoD in the next day or so.' He looked at the Major lamely. 'We're all a bit long in the tooth to look like Regulars.' Then, for a moment, he appeared serious. 'I'd appreciate your telling me as much as you can about the system, the personalities, and perhaps give me some advice on how the hell we survive.'

Peter Ashworth had gulped his coffee, sputtering as the scalding liquid burned his lips.

Shit.

P Company.

You poor bastards.

Grimacing, he breathed out slowly, almost a sigh of resignation. He shook his head disbelievingly, then chortled mischievously.

'The first thing you must understand, is that the P stands for Pain—'

Alex felt slightly uneasy as he listened to his former Lieutenant.

Major Simon Endercote, Officer Commanding P Company,

Depot of the Parachute Regiment, felt elated. Today was going to be different, better. Things were looking up. At last, his prayers had been answered. He was to leave this bloody lot and get out and do some proper soldiering. Running P Company was OK, he reflected, but it wasn't *soldiering*. It was just bloody routine, day after day, putting the applicants through their paces, bullying them, seeing if they had the balls to be airborne soldiers. He didn't mind those that wanted to be *proper* airborne men, those that would wear their head-dress, the coveted red beret, with pride. It was the other imitation Paratroopers he despised. The bloody engineers, signallers and sodding blanket-stackers in the Ordnance. And as for the transport pukes, well that was another time of day.

But today was *the* day. He had learned that he had passed selection for the Special Air Service, the SAS. There was only this one last course, and he would be on his way.

Hereford.

He rolled the name around on his tongue. At last. His dream had come true. All the hard work, the fitness training, the pain and the suffering, had been worth it. The pain, the degradation, were behind him now. He was going to Hereford. If you bastards out there think P Company is hard, just try SAS selection. No fucking comparison.

Turning right as he left the Officers' Mess, he climbed the short grassy bank and strode over to the Trainasium. This was where it all started. It was here that you proved you had balls big enough to be an airborne soldier. Fail on the Trainasium, and you were sent packing. Back to your pissing radios, plant and stacking fucking blankets where you all belong.

The latest group stood nervously in three ranks listening to the instructor as he briefed them on what was expected of them. They were dressed in coloured PT vests, white for the officers, red for the soldiers, and wore helmets

68

with numbers painted on them in white. The officers had the lower numbers, the higher the rank, the lower the number. At the front of the squad, Major Endercote stood with hands on hips, unable to keep the contempt from his eyes.

His instructors told the squad how they would be given three lives to lose, three failures only. After that, it was the ignominy of Return to Unit, the dreaded RTU. His eyes swept over the group identifying the more obvious individuals from their profiles which he had studied the previous evening. The three TA soldiers stood out immediately. They were older than the others, although for the life of him he could not guess their ages, and anyway he had been sceptical of the date of birth shown in their files. They had probably lied anyway.

He looked at Number 1. That would be the Lieutenant Colonel, Howard. He looked huge, like an athlete, a javelin-thrower, or a man who could chuck a discus right out of the stadium without trying too hard.

Number 2, the smaller man, had to be Major Norris. There was something menacing in the untidy face. Everything was jumbled and irregular with the mouth set tight. A hard man, Endercote thought.

And the big ugly bastard with the squashed face, looking as if someone had hit it with a sledge-hammer, Number 15. Corporal Clarke.

The rest of them looked no different from any other motley collection of aspiring Paratroopers. Their hair would be cropped short under the helmets, and Endercote was quick to notice the apprehension in their faces, the fidgeting as they stood listening to what was expected of them. He felt a twinge of disgust at the faded tattoos, stark against the white flesh of their forearms, the emaciated bodies overly lean from pre-course training.

As for those three middle-aged berks. Those . . . Territorials. Not even regular soldiers. Sent for special selection. We'll see about that. He almost spat, but refrained in time. Well, well, you three part-time fairies. We'll soon see if you've got balls or cherries hanging between your legs.

He felt the flush in his cheeks, remembering the nickname he had been given. The bastards had been sniggering as they gulped their beer in the Pegasus bar. Resentful, he shuddered.

Endercote the entrecôte.

Tenderloins.

So be it. Now was the time of reckoning, to pay the piper.

Tenderloins.

You bastards. You ... you ...

Airborne!

Constable Trevor Atkinson thought for most of the morning about the telephone call he had received from the landlord of the White Lion. It probably wasn't important, but still he debated what he should do about it, not wanting to waste police time, yet ever conscious that the report could be important. The landlord had said something about an odd accent. That could have implications. And everyone in the village knew what had happened to Richard Norris's boy, over in Belfast.

The Constable shrugged, sighed, then picked up the telephone. Let somebody else decide if it were important or not. It wasn't his problem, and he wasn't paid to make decisions of this sort. He'd pass it on up the line and let them sort it out. The Sergeant answered at Division.

'Sarge? Atkinson here. I've received a report of a stranger in the area, making some odd inquiries. It may not be important, but in such a close-knit community, they notice anything out of the ordinary straight away. Pardon? Yes, he had an odd accent which couldn't be identified for sure ... Irish? No, he didn't say. Just that it was odd, didn't sound right. OK, Sarge. I'll keep my eyes open when I'm in the area. No, there's nothing else. Yes, and you too, Sarge.' Atkinson was about to put the telephone down when a thought came to him.

'One other thing. He was asking where an ex-Army bloke's house was. Yes, that's right. A Mr Richard Norris. His lad was killed by the IRA, over in Belfast. You think there might be a connection? OK. I'll leave it with you. I'll check in as normal. I'll let you know if anything develops. Bye now.' The Constable hung up, scratched his chin, and stared down at the telephone. Nodding to himself, he made up his mind to have a look around the village that night.

You never know, he told himself.

They had finished the entry fitness test.

It had been less difficult than they had anticipated, a gentle jog for a mile and a half around Queen's Parade, followed by the same distance at best speed. They had achieved the nine and a half minutes qualifying time, although Alex, with his greater bulk, had needed to dig in at the last. Richard had found it easier than the others, probably because of his daily run with the rucksack. But they finished in the middle of the group, the place to be, Peter Ashworth had told Alex. There had been one failure who dejectedly disappeared to report to the Sergeant Major.

Now for the Trainasium.

Richard studied the scaffolding construction in front of him as he listened to what was expected of them. He was not overly concerned for any of his team. They were all climbers, so he knew that the height would not worry them. He was less convinced about the remainder of the selection. Alex had told them to expect pain. So be it. Pain never killed anyone. Surprised to hear his number called first, he ran forward quickly and climbed a sloping ladder up on to a narrow platform. He looked across the gap he would be required to jump when the instructor yelled.

Shit.

It looked impossible. Suddenly there was doubt. Although only about 12 feet up, it seemed higher and the plank across the gap, covered in rough matting, looked desperately narrow. It had to be possible, he reasoned, knowing that this whole contraption had been designed to make them overcome psychological as well as physical problems.

He saw the deception then. Being higher than the plank across the gap, the height advantage on his side would get him over.

Wouldn't it?

He tensed.

'Go!'

Impossible.

He leapt, the gap stubbornly wide. Suspended in space, he felt a brief moment of panic before his boots thudded on to the plank opposite. He almost pitched forward on to his face, but was able to prevent it. His mouth was dry.

Shit.

Thereafter, it was a matter of keeping the momentum going, not stopping to think about the height or the exposure. Frightened, he climbed on to shuffle bars, the highest of the tests, two parallel bars set about 18 inches apart, with cross-pipes, off set, so that the foot had to be lifted over them. Richard was reluctant, full of doubt, feeling the fear of lifting one foot from the relative security of the bar and placing it back on the parallel beyond the crosspiece. Although it required a lift of only a few inches, it seemed as if he had been balancing on a high wire up in the big top of a circus.

Dizzy with apprehension, he was reliving the nightmare, the fall from the limestone of the Kaisergebirge. Drifting, floating into the dark chasm, weightless, the brilliant stars in the black soot of the sky accelerating away from him.

Then the dreadful sickly fear he had felt on the roof in Boston, below him the narrow pipe, which he knew he would eventually have to cross. Alex, then, had needed him. He had thought of Donnelly, focused on Johnathan and taken the first tentative step. Then . . .

That had been another adventure.

Richard relived those awful moments as he stood balanced at the end of Shuffle. The sweat ran from under the rim of his helmet and settled on the line of his eyebrows, before trickling down his nose on to his upper lip. He flicked it away with the tip of his tongue, tasting the salt. Thrusting his arms out like a tightrope walker, he concentrated on the far end, his target, which seemed miles away.

He took a faltering step.

Boston.

Donnelly.

Johnathan.

He shuffled awkwardly, hesitantly, along the bars, shiny from countless feet that had preceded him in this delicate manoeuvre. Nothing to it. Once you got moving. Then the cross-piece. He would have to lift his foot to negotiate it. His boot was glued to the bar. It stayed there when his brain ordered it to lift. Come on, Norris. A couple of inches. Come on, foot. Lift.

Bastard foot. Lift!

In an instant everything co-ordinated, and it was done. Once this tricky bit had been negotiated, he was required to bend down and touch his toes and yell out his name, rank and number. Norris almost blew it, feeling exposed, standing level with the roofs of the buildings around him. It took all his nerve. From where he stood, he seemed level with the spire of the Church of St Michael and St George in the distance over his left shoulder. Had he not realized at the last moment that there was a safe platform only 10 feet below him, he probably would not have done it.

Anyone falling would land safely on the platform.
Wouldn't they?
It was only 10 feet.
Wasn't it?

Four of the squad, including a young officer, failed at the Trainasium, despite the incessant, strident yelling from the instructors on the ground. The shouting, the obscenities, constantly in their ears, were beginning to jar. The young officer was almost in tears.

At least he was to miss the pain.

The pain started on the first TAB, a Tactical Approach to Battle. Richard stood with the rest outside the accommodation block, his rucksack at his feet. He read the name of the building: GRAYBURN VC.

Richard knew the story of Lieutenant John Hellington Grayburn, 2nd Battalion, The Parachute Regiment, and his heroic action in attacking the Arnhem Bridge during the fierce fighting of 17–20 September 1944. Grayburn, too, would have completed P Company, or something like it.

The rucksacks were weighed on a spring balance. Each had to be a minimum of 35 pounds. Those under this weight had stones added, picked up where they stood, until the spring balance read the correct weight. Their water bottles were checked for fullness. A meniscus had to show when the cap was unscrewed. Those that didn't suffered the discomfort of emptying their water bottles over their heads, an unpleasant start to a forced march if the weather was cold. Seeing his did not have the requisite little bulge of water, Richard stooped, picked up some small stones and dropped them into his bottle, raising the level of the water to form a perfect meniscus.

The real pain started.

74

The pace was fast, almost running, out over a sloping bridge where the planks rattled under the pressure of the rubber-soled boots, along the path at the edge of the canal to an iron suspension bridge. The iron struts hurt, cutting into the feet through the soft leather uppers of their boots as they climbed, ready to cross a narrow girder. Voices screamed at them not to look down, not to bend and grip the hot iron with sweaty fingers to steady their trembling legs. Nobody wanted to fall, even into the relative safety of the water.

Long Valley lived up to its name, never ending, going into infinity. Officers were kept at the rear where it was harder to settle into a regular pace. Nobby dropped back so that the three of them could stay together, giving quiet encouragement, forcing the pain into the back of their minds. They had wrapped neoprene padding around their waists, preventing the rucksack frame rubbing them raw. As some of the group began to fall behind, there came relentless, high-pitched screaming from the instructors, drowning the sound of the safety vehicle as it ground along, just behind, tempting them.

They were surviving, keeping up, lungs heaving, legs straining, ears constantly assaulted by the incessant yelling.

'Dig in.'

'Stick with it.'

'Don't jack now.'

The man in front of Nobby when down, tumbling on to a shoulder.

The gasp was audible as Nobby Clarke tripped over the tangle of arms and legs, twisted on his ankle and almost went down too. The one who had fallen first was up on his feet, running again. But they were on Nobby like a pack of baying wolves, snapping, snarling venom, mouths close to his ear as his head fell forward in agony. Richard and Alex eased their pace, staying with their injured companion. Nobby was limping, favouring his good ankle, still moving, still keeping up. He looked done in, as if he could not continue.

'The Jack Wagon's behind you. It'll be a life gone. Two to go.'

There was a sneer in the voice. Nobby Clarke held on, running through the pain, his teeth clamped shut as he drove himself along. Richard was beginning to hurt and knew that big Alex would be feeling it even worse than he.

They reached Flagstaff Hill, leaning into the slope, bodies protesting, forcing straining leg muscles that felt like jelly. Nobby groaned, swore and went down on to all fours at a place where the track had narrowed into a thin, stone-filled gully. Their feet were propelled backwards as fast as they strove upwards, a task to torment Sisyphus himself. With Nobby's big body blocking the track, the rest were forced to skirt around him. Those that were able offered gasped words of encouragement. But it was plain to see. He was done for.

Richard reached him as the others pushed on up the track, dodging the stones cascading about them as they were dislodged by those above. Nobby had rolled on to his back and was gripping his ankle, his head shaking in pain. They were yelling at him, pointing to the Land-Rover idling at the bottom of the hill.

'Number 15. You gotta kick shit. Dig! Don't jack now! The top's fuckin' there!'

Nobby Clarke stared at them balefully, his eyes pure hatred. There was murder, mixed with the pain.

'Come on, Nobby. We can hack this. Between us.' Richard spoke quietly, feeling for the man whose life he had once saved. 'It's a piece of piss, really.'

With a huge effort of will, Nobby Clarke rolled back on to his hands and heaved himself up. Hesitating, balanced delicately, he gingerly tested his weight on his ankle. With an animal grunt, he pushed on up the hill. Richard came up behind, supporting the weight of Nobby's rucksack whenever it looked as if the big man might falter.

Richard felt the strain in his legs, and tried to force the feeling into the back of his mind, letting his thoughts drift into neutral, floating into a diaphanous, dreamlike world in which he was part suspended, seeing his body from afar, distanced from the suffering, trying to ignore the rucksack as it bounced on his shoulders, hurting his spine.

He tried to remember at what age Johnathan had been when he had taken him on his first Alpine climb. They had started early, before the sun had risen above the distant peaks, and Richard had led his young son along the track from the Amberger Hutte in the Stubai Alps to the foot of the Schrankogel, a steep ice climb that would serve as the boy's induction. Their breath had formed into fine condensation in the clean crispness of the early morning.

A fine dawn had turned into a lovely day.

Their crampons bit into firm ice as they made good time up the steep slope, not cutting steps, but using the front points to give them the slight purchase they needed. Richard kept a careful eye on his son, secretly pleased that he was able to move with such smooth confidence, unworried by the steep angle and the ever increasing exposure. Yes, damn it, he was proud.

It was going well. Richard was balanced in a small stance he had cut with his axe, belayed securely on to a 'dead man'. Suddenly he tensed. Johnathan had hitched the point of a crampon into his breeches as he drew up his foot. He was off balance and, without even a cry for help, tumbled backwards down the mountain. Richard held him easily enough on the rope, and looked down the slope, initially unworried.

The dark pool of blood oozing into the snow alarmed him. Johnathan's ice axe had pierced his leg. Richard reached him, tiptoeing fast down the ice, comforting him as the effects of shock set in. The storm, which he had hoped would miss the mountain, then broke upon them.

His son had begun to shiver violently as the wet snow drifted silently out of the sky, soaking them.

Emptying his rucksack of all but the bare minimum he would need to survive, he threw things down the mountain, then pulled it over the boy's legs. Somehow he heaved Johnathan up on to his shoulders, telling him quietly, with a confidence he did not feel, that everything would be fine. The slope above him was never ending. Each step was agony as he dragged one painful foot after the next. Ten steps and rest. Seven steps. Then rest, bent over the axe, lungs searing with the effort. Five steps. God. Three. Rest . . . OK, son. Dad'll get you off the hill . . .

They reached the top.

They had not been the last. Alex was standing with his hands on his hips, sucking air into his straining lungs. He lurched over to the other two.

'You OK, Nobby?' Alex looked at him in concern. 'It doesn't matter. If you want to call it a day.' He tried to grin. 'It's all a fucking game.'

They shared water from one of their bottles during this brief stop, waiting as the last of the group made it to the top of Flagstaff. Sweat ran from red faces, stinging the eyes and making it difficult to see. They moved off again, into a blur of pain which none of them was to forget. In the dimness of their agony they heard the names of their places of torture. Heartbreak Hill, steep and unforgiving, Zig-Zags, Spiders, Seven Sisters and Round the Mulberry Bush. Most of all they hated Round the Mulberry Bush.

Days flowed into weeks.

Weeks flowed into pain.

Pain flowed into numb agony, which in turn became despair. More was to follow. In the gymnasium. On the assault course, and in the Milling.

Nobody on the course would ever forget the Milling. How could *anybody* forget that day?

*

Milling is the test, according to the lore of P Company, of a man's 'bottle'. His ability to deliver and absorb punishment from his fellow man, preferably one of approximately equal size and weight. Skill does not enter into the equation. A pair squared up, the big 16-ounce gloves heavy on their fists, then tried to beat the shit out of each other until they were told they could stop. It was inevitable that Alex would be paired with Nobby. They were the biggest of the group, and were to fight last. Alex had stood silently watching as soldiers, NCOs and officers tore into each other. Richard had survived. Just.

Major Endercote entered the gym.

'Right. Number 1 and Number 15. Ready?' said the CSMI.

'No,' said Alex.

'Beggin' your pardon, Number 1?' The instructor looked incredulous.

'I said "No",' repeated the big man. 'I'll not fight him.'

'This is Millin', Number 1. Everybody does Millin' in P Company.'

'No.' It was final.

Endercote called him over. Alex walked, defiant. Endercote spoke, quietly, so that the squad would not hear. 'All of us do the Milling. You don't mill, you don't pass. You're off the course. Failed. RTU.' He looked at Alex contemptuously.

'I don't give a shit. I'll not fight Clarke, Number 15. So shove it.'

There was pure hatred in the Major's eyes. 'Got something going with your little chum, have you, Number 1 . . . Sir?' It was spat. 'All right then. But you'll do your Milling, Number 1, whatever. But you won't be wanting to give a blow job to the feller I have in mind for you. He's TA too. Does a bit of boxing in his spare time. CSMI!'

'Sir?' The PT instructor ran over to the pair.

'Get Blake,' he said. 'Get Driver Blake here. Now!'

There was a cruel smile on the Major's face. The CSMI looked uncertain.

'Major Endercote, begging your pardon, sir . . . Are you sure about this?'

'Do it!'

The gymnasium had gone very quiet. An air of expectancy had fallen over the assembled soldiers. Something was on. Something was coming.

Oh, shit.

A soldier had come through the doors and was walking slowly, purposefully towards the group. He was stripped to the waist, wearing boxing shorts, the light reflecting from the dark skin, where the muscles were knotted, rippling as he moved. He was bigger even than Alex, and the cumbersome 16-ounce gloves were tiny on his fists. He looked cruel, evil.

A pro.

Walking directly to Alex he stood in close, bearing down on him, eyeballing him, to make him afraid. He said nothing, staring, his eyes full of menace, lacking humour, devoid of mercy. He spun on his heel, then walked over to the Major. Alex did not hear the words but read the hatred in the expression.

'Hurt him,' said the lips.

Alex knew his opponent was a pro and that he trained in a gym somewhere in London. Some of the lads had talked about it. And he could tell, just from watching the way he moved. Alex had boxed in his Sandhurst days, when he had represented the Academy at light heavyweight. But that had been at Army standard, carefully controlled and refereed. This would be different. There would be no quarter given here.

'Come on, Mister A.' Nobby had stepped up to Alex's side. 'We can mill about a bit. No point in letting this bastard beat you half to death. He's a fucking pro. Anyone can see that.'

'I'll not fight you, Nobby. I'll not give them the satisfaction. They're trying to break us up. They've been trying ever since we arrived. I'm not going to let them do that. I'll take my chances here. But thanks.'

It was very quiet as the two men squared up and circled warily around each other, Alex crouched, losing the advantage of height. He stabbed out a tentative left jab at the dark, bobbing, weaving head, as his opponent moved around him. The punch was slipped with contemptuous ease, and Alex gasped as a fist that felt like a frozen leg of lamb slammed into his belly, hurting him. The man began to beat him, purposefully, systematically, adopting a rhythm to his punching as if working out on the heavy bag.

Alex had no chance. He went down for the third time, his head bowed, his chest heaving as he knelt on all fours on the hard wooden boards. The blood trickled from between open, smashed lips and lay in an ugly pool between his hands. Alex tried to raise his head, but could barely focus beyond his opponent's feet. He concentrated on the smart boxing boots.

He dragged himself upright.

The blows rained on Alex Howard, the movement of the red-leather gloves blurred to those watching. He did his best to cover up, to protect his vital organs. His shoulders were red, sore from the incessant pounding as the gloves thumped into the muscles of his arms. Despite his efforts, many of the blows got through to find their target, thudding on head and body. Alex went down again. Incredibly, he got up.

There was an angry growl from the watching men who were moving uncomfortably from foot to foot. This wasn't right. Nobody should have to take a beating like this. Not even an officer. Alex got up, staggering as his opponent closed in for the finish.

Richard felt a deep anger. This wasn't proper. This wasn't necessary. This was spiteful. The CSMI, too, looked across at Major Endercote, who stood with arms folded, his face impassive apart from the brightness of his eyes, and the flush, high in his cheekbones.

Damn it, the man's enjoying this.

Alex was retreating, his head tucked under his powerful forearms, shuffling awkwardly backwards as his opponent came after him on the balls of his feet, throwing punches with a monotonous rhythm until Alex reached the wall and could retreat no further. If anything, the boxer had increased his work rate. The end must come soon. When Alex went down again, he wouldn't get up.

Alex Howard was hurting. He was also very angry. He was outclassed and knew it. But he was damned if he was going to roll over and let this man walk all over him. If he were to survive this savage beating he would have to act fast, before the last of his strength went. Already his arms felt weakened from the hammering they had sustained from the massive fists that continued to slam into him. A long way away, he heard old Dusty Miller, his second, who had stood in his corner during his bout in the all-important RAF Cranwell match. He saw him clearly, the pudgy, pock-marked face, the boneless nose, the missing teeth as he had expounded his theory on how to get out of a tight corner.

'When some big bastard's beating the shit out of you, an' you gotta cover up to stop 'im spattering your brains all over the canvas, you 'ave to look at 'is feet. 'Is feet'll tell yer wot direction the next punch is comin' from. Watch wot 'is feet's doin', an' you can ride 'is punches, take the sting out of 'em. Then,' – Dusty Miller gave a wicked, cunning grin – *'when 'e next wellies you wiv a right 'and, just try this little move. You won't find it in no instruction manual—'*

Alex watched the feet in the smart boxing boots, the tassels flying as the man swung punches with all his body weight behind them. He was working to a set rhythm, and

Alex rolled with the blows, waiting for the next right hand. It would come after the two quick successive lefts. Alex felt his buttocks against the wall bars.

It was time.

The right hand swung in a vicious hook. As it thumped into his shoulder, Alex pushed his left hand out, under his opponent's arm. Instinctively, he was caught and held there. Alex felt the elation.

Got you.

He heaved mightily on his trapped fist, punching hard with the other. The combination spun the boxer like a ballet dancer, very fast, so that in an instant the two men had changed position, Alex no longer with his back to the wall. The chin was exposed as the element of surprise stayed in his favour.

Just the one chance.

Now.

Alex hit him with all his power, the upper-cut starting somewhere down by his right knee. It sliced upwards towards the unprotected chin, now exposed because the man still, instinctively, gripped Alex's left fist under his arm. Even through the padding of the gloves, Alex felt the satisfying force of the blow as his pain, anger and frustration were poured into the punch. The head snapped violently back, and cracked against the wall.

Eyes rolled up into sightless sockets as the boxer went from consciousness to oblivion. Feeling the pressure on his fist released, Alex stepped quickly back, watching through pain-filled eyes as the huge boxer tipped forward like a felled tree. His chin smashed into the hard floor.

The gymnasium was silent, save for Alex Howard's laboured breathing. The man on the floor started snoring. Alex fell to his knees, shaking his head in bewilderment, the blood and mucus flowing from his mouth staining the polished boards on which he knelt.

The men had held their breath. They too were quiet.

Then it started.

The singing.

One soldier first, joined by another, then a third, at first hesitant, then growing to a crescendo as more joined in. The whole group picked it up, now singing with a gusto that told the Establishment what they thought of the spectacle that they had just witnessed. There were no words. Nobody knew them anyway. But the tune was unmistakable.

'Rocky'.

Dah-dee dah, dah-dah. Dah-dee dah, dah-dah.

The group sang, the noise louder and louder. Faces that had earlier been badly beaten were grinning wildly. Hands were clapped above heads, feet thumped on to the floorboards, as bodies swayed with the rhythm of the tune.

The Kop End.

Soldiers.

The CSMI smiled to himself.

No way anyone on that course would ever forget the Milling.

'Do you remember that time when—'

But Major Simon Endercote had murder in his heart.

At last, it was over.

The Stretcher Race was finished. None of them had fallen off. Wales was behind them, where Nobby Clarke, with his experience in the mountain-rescue team, had left everyone, including the instructors, standing. At the end of each march, he would be sitting on a boulder with an old pipe clamped in his mouth. Nobody ever saw him smoking it. He had seemed at peace in the wildness of the Welsh mountains.

They had drunk beer in the 'Peggy' bar, and most now lay on their beds, dizzy from the ale. Tomorrow they would learn their fate, whether or not they had passed or failed. A comradeship had developed between them, inevitable with a group that had suffered such hardships and come out of it in the end, survivors.

Alex Howard was spent. Stretched flat on his back on the narrow bed in his room, he was still dressed, lying in a fuzzy limbo of part wakefulness, letting the fatigue wash over him, unbelievably glad that it was done. A few hours' kip, ready for an early departure in the morning. There was a tap at the door.

It was Number 6, a young fresh-faced captain. He swayed slightly as he entered the room, the grin lopsided on his mouth. He looked uncertainly at the big athlete stretched out on the bed trying unsuccessfully to prop himself up on one elbow. At last he gave up and fell back on to the pillow.

'Pissed,' was all he could manage.

'Colonel . . . I . . . we . . . the officers on the course. We wanted you to know—' He sat heavily on the foot of the bed. 'Pissed,' he agreed.

Alex looked at him, trying to focus.

'Whatever the result tomorrow, Colonel, I'd like you to know that I feel proud to have done P Company with you. I . . . Don't know how the hell you did it. You're old enough to be my father. No offence meant. You showed 'em. And as for fucking Tenderloins . . . oh, shit. The look on his face when you laid their man out in the Milling. I wish you could have seen it—' The Captain was laughing, tears streaming from his eyes. 'I thought he was going to . . . to . . . oh, shit!'

Alex started laughing too, as the door swung open and Richard pushed his way in to see what was causing all the mirth.

Norris, too, had drunk too much.

The Captain went on, unable to control his mirth.

'The bastard would have eaten his hat . . . oh, dearie me, his *head-dress*, if it hadn't been nailed to his head. I bet he sleeps in the fucking thing.' He wiped away the tears streaming down his cheeks.

Alex was still chuckling when he fell into a drunken sleep.

It was raining, out on the square.

Now they would know. Pass. Or fail.

Major Endercote stood in front of the group, a board with the results typed on it held loosely in his fingers. It was covered in plastic to keep off the rain.

'Number 10.' It started.

'Sir?'

'Failed.'

'Sir.' There was no expression in either voice.

'Number 6.'

'Sir?'

'Pass.'

'Sir.' The young Captain with the fresh face grinned inwardly.

'Number 1.' Endercote was looking forward to this. Really looking forward to it.

Silence.

'Number 1?'

'Gone, sir. I had instructions from "up the top". They left at oh five hundred. They had their own wheels.' The Sergeant Major sounded apologetic.

'All three of them?'

'All three of them, sir. They were up and ready, like they had been expecting to move early.' His face was expressionless. 'Pass or fail, sir?'

Simon Endercote felt the deep anger. He stared at the Sergeant Major, wanting him to know his displeasure.

'They'll *never* fucking know.'

Anyway, he didn't care.

He was going to Hereford.

Airborne!

CHAPTER FOUR

The place is called the Hönnetal.

Straddling Route E65 between Iserlohn and Hemer in the German Sauerland, it is a smooth limestone cliff, the rock formation soaring skywards from the edge of the roadside. The vertical cliffs of smooth, brittle rock, no more than 400 feet at their highest, brood sulkily, staring haughtily down at the road below. To a climber, an irresistible challenge.

They had been sent here to learn.

On this early summer day the place seemed deserted, except for four men standing in a small knot on a bridge spanning the river that roared, tumbling over jagged rocks beneath. The sound, amplified in the confines of the gorge, forced them to shout in order to be heard. Each stared up at the cliffs. At last, one pointed. The rest followed the line of his outstretched arm until they too saw the small specks of colour, other climbers, high on the face. There was a sign, black lettering on a white background, fixed firmly into the earth at the edge of the road: BE-STEIGEN DER FELSEN BEI STRASSE UNTERSAGT.

'What the fuck does that mean?' The Cumbrian accent was broad, the expletive pronounced 'fook'.

'Roughly translated, Nobby, it means keep your arse off the rock.' The biggest of them spoke.

Norris hid his nervousness, remembering the fall from the limestone of the Kaisergebirge, when Alex had been injured. He had needed all his skill to get them off the hill. He shuddered, looking at Alex, relaxed beside him, envying his calm as he stared upwards, assessing routes, gauging difficulties. It had been so bloody long. Nobby Clarke slipped the empty pipe into his mouth, sucking on it as he gazed benignly about him. The fourth member of the party was apart, not one of them, though he too was dressed for climbing. He did not fit, excluded from the cheerful banter, the occasional laughter. Slightly apart, he kept his own counsel, searching through a heavy climber's rucksack at his feet.

'Right, gents.'

Richard winced.

'Maybe we can get down to our reason for being here, get some serious training going. We don't have long, and there's a lot to do.'

He was the Instructor.

They knew him by no other reference.

Nobby tapped the empty pipe needlessly on the palm of his hand, looked at the others, then heaved a heavy rucksack on to his shoulders. He led the way across the road, scrambling up the steep, rock-strewn bank on the other side to the base of the buttress in front of them. The Instructor followed.

'Right, gents.' The expression was becoming a habit. 'I'm going to sit back and see what you can do. I dunno what the climb above us is like, but I want to see you all in action. I'll know then what needs doing. Bring you up to date so to speak. Anybody see a route, from across the road?'

'There was a crack, going part way, leading into a flake, then up on to a ledge. There's not a lot from then on, maybe a traverse out to the left, linking into a narrow chimney. It looks like it might go from there.' Richard was staring upwards, his jaw muscles working.

The Instructor looked unconvinced.

'Go up a few feet so's I can get an idea what you can do, see if you're bunnies or tigers.' He smiled at the comparison. 'You want a top rope?'

The three looked at him.

'I've brought a whole pile of kit. Help yourselves, gents.' With that, he upended his rucksack, letting the contents spill on to the ground. In the pile, the most up-to-date climbing gear. Nobby Clarke stirred with a toe, then stooped, picking out a perlon climbing rope and heaving it at Norris.

'We'll be needing at least one of them.' He grinned as Richard caught it, uncoiling it and letting it fall at his feet in a neat pile, in the shape of a Catherine wheel.

'I've not used half of this stuff before.' Alex, hunkered, picked through the brightly coloured pile. 'Better than the junk we used to use, Richard.' He examined a Moac on its loop. 'Nuts, the thread filed off, is the best we had.' Norris picked out a length of 5-mm cord, wrapping it around his waist, before clipping a lightweight D karibiner into it. He spun the screw-gate open and clipped in the climbing rope.

I don't believe I'm seeing this.

The Instructor shook his head. The biggest of them tied the rope around him, a method he'd never seen before, looped around the chest, tied off over the shoulders, done without looking, by feel, fingers quick, efficient.

'A Bulin harness. No one uses it any more.' Alex was matter of fact.

The Instructor looked away.

'You lead, Richard.'

Norris glanced briefly at the others, then at the Instructor, who said, 'You sure you want to try this, in them great clodhoppers? There's composites, your size, in the pack, like his.' He pointed to Nobby's feet. Norris looked down at the Vibrams, then at Alex.

'Damn. Forgot to bring the Tricounis.'

'And the hemp ropes.'

'And the battered trilby. Can't climb without the hat.' Nobby too, saw it funny.

They laughed, three of them.

Norris, his grin nervous, shrugged at the Instructor.

'We know what you're doing for us. No offence. This stuff,' – Norris pointed – 'to Alex and me it's too new, though Nobby uses it all the time. We'll stick with what we know. Then you can sort us out. Old dogs, new tricks. You know what I mean?' He looked up, to where he had to go. 'It's been a long time. A hell of a long time—' The Instructor nodded, sweeping the shoulder-long hair from his eyes, tying it out of the way behind his head with a tear of rag.

'Here we go then.' Standing close, Norris shut his eyes, remembering the climb as he had seen it from across the road, picturing the route. Licking his lips, for a moment uncertain, he placed his hands on to the rock at shoulder height, kicking the mud from the cleated soles. He raised his knee, then his foot, on to a small projection.

He stood.

Back on rock.

Jerky, tentative, he started, his mouth dry and his tongue sticking from the apprehension in him. The same, always, on a new route when out of practice. Gradually, the rhythm, long forgotten, returned. Moving more easily, searching the rock above and to the side for holds, he felt the height from the drag of the rope at his waist. Alex called anxiously. Engrossed, Norris had climbed higher than intended. It had been difficult, testing him, and he was reluctant to reverse the pitch. Committed, he climbed on until all the rope was used.

You've done it again, Norris. Don't you ever learn?

A ledge, he thought, at the top of the crack a few feet out of reach. Afraid. The fall. The Kaiser Gebirge. The exposure caressed his heels, fingers tugging gently, reminding gravity to do its job. He picked his way upwards, suddenly wary, anxious, fighting the last few feet. A hold, just one, for the fingers of his right hand, above his head and too high to reach safely. The rope, tight from his waist, suddenly slackened. Gingerly, delicately, he stretched for the hold, fingers digging into the tiny flake.

Then, unorthodox. Gripping his right wrist with the fingers of his left hand, hesitating, doubt impinging his thoughts, he shook his head, expelling the reluctant uncertainty. He heaved. The tips of his boots scuffed the smooth limestone as he walked upwards. Head level with his hands, he paused, forearms protesting, fingers hurting, his body trembling.

Something up to his left which might be a hold, the only imperfection in the unblemished surface. There was nothing else. Friction was all that kept his feet in contact with the rock, his body weight supported by the fingers of his right hand. Breathing hard, he tried to control the trembling. Move, or fall. Squeezing, right hand, toes braced, he took a deep breath. Releasing his right wrist, he twisted upwards.

Fear.

Briefly, then gone in the moving.

A jug.

Euphoria.

The Instructor had been unable to watch. The whole 40-metre run-out used up without a single protective runner. Then, his second started climbing before the leader had belayed. It had been too much for him. Unheard of. Yet these two arseholes had just done it. He shuddered. The Instructor didn't even know their names. Ex-military. He could tell by the way they talked, the way they held themselves. Again, he wondered why they were here. He would have been happier on the granite of north Wales, rather than on this loose, flaky limestone. But he had been told that this shit was what they were to get used to.

The rope came in quickly, feeding through his hands, falling away from the narrow ledge on which he stood. It stopped as Alex reached the crux. He grinned.

'Nasty!'

The powerful body pulled up on to his stance, the ledge just wide enough for them, shoulder to shoulder, touching, a team. Norris let Alex get his breath, then spoke, his voice casual.

'There's nothing above us from here. It's as smooth as your arse, not a hold in sight.'

'I thought from below there was another crack over to our left.' He blew out. 'Buggered if I can see it now. Must be round that bulge, about fifteen feet?'

Norris looked, out to his left.

'You may be right. Bring up another rope. We'll make a tension traverse.'

'You're enjoying this.'

Norris grinned, the nervousness gone.

Alex hauled up the spare rope.

'Anchor it off.'

'I'll bring Nobby up before I come over.'

Richard Norris already moving, shuffled across the holdless rock, leaning against the tension of the rope to keep himself in balance. He eased his way carefully across the cliff, delicately balanced, feet tiptoeing on the smooth limestone. He disappeared from sight.

The Instructor was mesmerized.

A *Dulfer* traverse.

He'd heard about it, read about it in old climbing books, but never thought he'd see it used. He nodded. These guys were good. With the leader secure, they brought up the third who moved with surprising grace for a man so big, every movement flowing into the next, wasting no energy, the rhythm taking him higher and higher, until he too was on the ledge. They climbed on until the last of them scrambled over the buttress.

*

'Gents, that was fucking awful. You couldn't have done it worse if you'd practised.' He hid his humour from them. 'Climbing's different, now. Nobody goes at it like that no more. There's protection, stuff to stop you falling. Christ, if you'd come off—'

'I didn't.'

'No, but if you had—'

'But 'e didn't.'

'You had no runners in—'

'I forgot.'

'In the excitement.'

'Shit—'

''E nearly did, I 'spect.'

'What the fuck am I going to do with you lot?'

'Teach us to climb.'

'You willing to learn? About chocs and camms, and Friends. Rerps and bongs, about cold and hot-forged Krabs. Thermo-forged harnesses, sport climbing, rehearsing a move, falling if necessary, the lot?'

'Bongs?'

'Yeah, they go—'

'Bong, bong, bong . . .' They sang it, a carillon.

'— when you hit them with your hammer . . . You bastards!'

They laughed, four of them.

They became firm friends. Days went by, spent climbing harder and harder routes. Each time they improved. But he was puzzled, the Instructor. Not once had they asked his name, nor offered their own.

Then, when it was finished:

'I can't teach you nothing else.'

'You can.'

'Tell me.'

'We have to keep it quiet. No noise at all. Quiet as mice farting in a graveyard. No ironmongery jingling, and no yelling to each other. We have to move as quiet as shit oozing down the inside of a shiny crapper. Can you do it, show us?'

'You'll need UHF radios. Single ear-piece and whisper-activated bone mikes. That leaves your hands free for climbing.'

The three looked at each other.

'Fancy a beer, John, at the *Gaststatte* down the road?'

How the hell had they discovered his name?

For a week the man had sat on a grassy ledge on the far side of the road watching the rocks opposite through powerful field-glasses. He made notes in a small leather-bound book as he studied the four men. The weather had been fine all week. It had been a fun assignment. He produced a mobile telephone from the small day-bag at his feet, keying in the 00 44 digits for London while watching them drive away. He spoke briefly, then stood and ambled up the slope to his own car. Once on the road, he drove in the direction of Düsseldorf, where he would return the rental and catch the first available flight.

He was humming to himself as he drove.

They might make it.

They just might pull it off.

CHAPTER FIVE

It was quiet in the lane bordering the old farmhouse. He waited until the cloud passed across the moon, obscuring its whiteness. A breeze fanned his cheek, sensual, like a lover blowing warmly on him. The darkness around him deepened still further until he could no longer make out the shapes around him. He stood in the shadow of a large holm-oak, which on a sunny day would provide deep, purple shade under its spreading boughs. Now, in the night, the branches above his head hid him.

Striving to control his breathing, he cocked his head to one side, listening intently. There was no sound other than in his imagination, small intrusions which he was unable to identify that crept into his mind. Uncomfortable, out of his depth, he fretted in this alien place. Still the man did not move, remaining motionless for long minutes. Finally, satisfied he was alone, he stepped softly forward, placing his feet to the ground using the outside of his foot, wincing as the fine gravel, scattered on the surface of the lane, crunched against his soles. Stealthily he moved forward, hesitating each time he heard a noise he was unable to recognize. As a town-dweller, the eeriness unsettled him and he would have been happier in the bustle of the city, listening to the sounds with which he was familiar. Here, in the country, he was fearful, out of his normal environment.

But it was necessary.

There was a dark shadow in front with no diffused light beyond it. Stepping delicately forward he found a hedge growing above the high bank surrounding the property. At its base, he waited, uncertain, before turning sharply right, moving more confidently now that he had established his bearings. Again, clouds scuttled from the moon.

He followed the line of the evergreens, keeping close into the deep shadow thrown by the moon behind them. At the end of the hedgerow it was brighter, exposing him, where open fields stretched to a line of hills bathed in moonlight, the grass fluorescent, like a skating rink once the lights have been extinguished at the end of the day.

He stopped. Quiet, except for the sound of his breathing. His heart beat in the depths of his chest and for a moment he was unable to breathe properly. As he climbed the short bank, he slipped in the damp grass. Cursing quietly, he regained his balance and walked along the fence which he could touch with the fingers of his left hand. Brambles caught his ankles, snagging his socks.

He reached the gap sooner than he had expected, and stopped once more to orientate himself, looking back the way he had come. There would be no problem finding his way out. The house, clearly visible, its dark shape etched against the background of the lighter sky, the tall chimney stacks sharply formed in the moonlight as the clouds again drifted away from the moon. Looking to left and right, then cautiously behind him, he ducked carefully under the wire fence into the garden.

He waited, listening.

Nothing.

He began to walk across the lawn, counting the paces to himself as he went, forming the words with his lips, until, with his breath coming in quick, irregular gasps, he reached the patio. Five more strides took him to the side of the house where he was once more hidden by deep shadow. Head pressed against the cold stonework, he strove to control his quickening pulse, dreading a light from an upstairs window. Finally, when he had steadied himself, he reached out with his left hand. Glass, ice cold to his touch.

The french windows.

Seventy paces from the gap.

Fifty metres, give or take.

Nothing to it.

He could do it from there.

The man turned, feeling the rough stone of the house against his back. He listened once more, holding his breath. Then, with the utmost care, keeping his back to the wall, he shuffled to his right across the patio, carefully avoiding the ornamental firs in the terracotta pots, until he reached a narrow pathway. The mirror surface of a small swimming pool reflected the image of the moon, magnifying it into a huge portrait, framed by the low wall surrounding it. Its sudden appearance startled him.

Gathering himself, he followed the line of the path until he came to a small lodge or outhouse. In the darkness he could not be sure. There was another dilapidated building, moonlight in narrow beams showing through holes worn by nature and time in the corrugated iron of its roof. It was of no interest to him, probably housing old machinery. He turned into the dark gap between the lodge and the main house hoping to find another vantage point that would better serve his purpose. This done, he would leave.

His heart stopped.

A security light had come on, the unexpected brightness startling him. For a moment he stood transfixed, unable to move, suddenly exposed in the brilliance of the light, his shadow stretching away from him, crisply formed against the gravel of the driveway. He had time to register a wood pile under a lean-to, a double-headed axe embedded in a heavy log, before he panicked.

He ran.

The branches in the hedge tore at his face, hurting, bringing tears to his eyes. He slid down the bank, his only thought to be away from this unfamiliar place, to get back to the security of his car and to leave.

Fucking country boy.

Once in the lane he slowed his pace, then turned away from the house. He walked, faster now, the job done. Left of the junction, the lights of the village winked in front of him, the car another half-mile away. He lengthened his pace, ever closer to the friendly glow of the lights. Soon he would be there, knowing what he had to do. Just wait for the bastard to show.

The shout behind him was loud, authoritative.

Joseph Fallon started running.

PC Trevor Atkinson shivered.

It was not cold, but a sudden breeze had caught him unawares and now he regretted not wearing the bright yellow fluorescent jacket that would have kept him warmer. But it was more important not to be seen. Yawning, he looked at his watch, squinting in the moonlight, trying unsuccessfully to make out the luminous figures in the dim light. Curling his fingers into a tube, he circled them around his watch face, lifting his wrist to peer down the improvised tunnel at the face of his watch. Too close to his eye, it was out of focus, but he could see it was just gone 3.15 am. Five more minutes and he would be away. Beginning to feel the chill, he shivered again.

Time to go.

No point in hanging about here to catch his death.

He swivelled his eyes sharply to his left. A faint light suddenly appeared from the Norris house in the distance, probably a security light. Division had told him that Mr Norris, who owned the house, was out of the country for a week or two although God knows how they had known that. Division had ways and means far beyond him, a mere community Bobby.

But the light shouldn't have come on.

Not unless there was a fox.

Or a prowler.

Trevor Atkinson started walking quickly in the direction of the Norris home, then broke into a lumbering run; his heartbeat quickening, his breathing heavier. Already the sweat had broken out on his forehead under his cap.

Tugging it off, holding it in his hand, he ran along the lane in the direction of the white gate illuminated by the bright security light. Suddenly, the light went out. The timer. Blind now, he stopped to let his eyes adjust to the darkness. Then, a sound from the hedgerow at the corner of the garden as someone forced their way out into the open without caring about the noise. The Constable raised his flashlight, searching for the switch, cursing as the torch fell from his fingers on to the road.

'Sod it.'

Unable to find it, Atkinson ran on, out of breath, his legs feeling the strain, wishing he hadn't skipped the fitness training being introduced in the Force. At the junction in front of the house, he stopped, listening. For a moment, nothing, then, to his right, the sound of hurried footsteps, fading in the direction of the village. He turned to follow the figure silhouetted against the distant lights.

A man, moving quickly, away from the house.

Atkinson set off in pursuit, trying to steady the asthmatic wheeze of his breathing. He shouted, only to see the figure break into a run, easily outstripping him, gradually fading into the half-light. A car door thumped shut, followed by the sound of a starter and an engine revving. Atkinson cursed again.

The policeman turned and ran, faster now in the direction of his own vehicle parked a few hundred yards further back along the lane. At the gate of the Norris house, he turned left, lungs straining as he forced himself up the incline towards the gap in the hedge where he had parked. At last, the white outline of the patrol car. Atkinson, hurting, reached the gap, fell against the bonnet, then wrenched open the door, gasping as he fell in behind the wheel. The keys thankfully still in the ignition.

The engine wouldn't fire, just the high-pitched whirr of the starter.

Bastard car.

Don't panic, Trevor boy. Keep calm, try again. The

headlights of his quarry flashed past the junction at the bottom of the hill he had just climbed. At the same time his own engine caught. Atkinson was no fool. The man would make for the main Cheltenham road, turn right and head for the motorway. In that case, he'd have him. Smiling grimly, he rammed the car into gear, yanked the wheel to his left, turning uphill instead of down in the direction of the valley road. Atkinson steadied his breathing, so excited he forgot to call Control.

The T-junction. Foot hard on the accelerator, he drifted into a hard right turn. To his right, at the bottom of the hill, the headlights of the other car as it drove on a parallel course to his own, the stroboscopic effect of the lights as they rushed past the trees at the side of the road hypnotic and distracting.

He was going to catch him. Right when the bastard would be least expecting it, as he came round the long left-handed bend just short of the hamlet. Atkinson laughed to himself, keeping the car in third, driving at the top end of the engine's performance. Branches whipped against the bodywork in the narrowness of the lane as he tore down the tunnel cut through the night by the halogen beams. He winced as his engine sputtered, the regular high-pitched beat faltering briefly. Come on, baby. Don't let me down now. Fucking motor pool. Don't even service them properly any more. Bet this bloody heap of shit hadn't even passed its MOT test. Come on, baby. Be kind to Trevor. Just till we catch this bastard, then you can fall to pieces, go to that happy scrapyard in the sky. See if I care. Then.

The junction with the main road was in front of him at the bottom of the hill, the gap closing fast. Foot pressed hard on the accelerator, he flicked the gear lever towards him, taking the car into top gear. He had gained half a mile on the car in the valley, forced it to follow the longer bends, unable to take his direct line. Atkinson had now lost sight of the car below and wondered if the driver could see his lights. He didn't care. He knew, now, that he would reach the junction first.

Right. Got you, mate.

This'll teach you to piss around on my patch.

With consummate skill, Atkinson changed into second, maintaining his engine revs throughout the change. His car slewed across the road, blue light flashing, dust settling on the roof and bonnet. The other vehicle was approaching fast. Third gear at about six thousand five. Bugger was in for a right shock when he cornered and came face to face with the police car. Atkinson again smiled grimly. He picked up the microphone of his police radio, about to call in to Control, when a dark-coloured car rounded the bend and hurtled towards him, engine howling. He dropped the mike back on to the seat.

The driver of the other vehicle jammed on the brakes the instant he saw the police car blocking the road. A screech, the smell of burning rubber, and the car slammed to a stop, no more than twenty yards away. Holding both hands up in the air, palms facing the direction of the stationary car, Atkinson waited.

The Law.

Solid.

Immovable.

The other vehicle had stalled, the driver making no attempt to restart. In the silence, Atkinson stood with his back to his own car, the police light flashing its regular message out into the night, a blue beacon of respectability. Blinded by the headlights of the other car, unable to use his own because of the angle of his car across the road, Atkinson thought he saw movement behind the lights, a shadowy figure standing at the side of the driver's open door. Squinting into the brightness, he cocked his head to one side, trying to see better. He was about to speak.

It was a strange noise.

For a moment Atkinson couldn't identify it. Familiar, but unusual. A noise like ... he tried to think. Like ...

Christ. A weapon. Some bastard cocking a weapon. Atkinson felt the fear rise in his throat, feeling sick, light-headed, frozen in cataplexy. It happens, he thought. It really does happen. When you're shit scared, your knees tremble. My bloody knees are knocking. Jesus. Not me. Please God, not me.

He half turned, uncertain, not sure what to do. Get back to the car, try and talk some sense into the man. He could think of nothing else. His brain was paralysed with fear. He made to turn.

Flashes, spitting at him.

A fire cracker going off that he couldn't hear.

The unbearable agony in his chest felt as if somebody had hit him there, three times in rapid succession with a ball-peen hammer. Numb, arms not moving. Thrown back against the door of his car, he struggled to stay on his feet, instead sliding into a sitting position. The surface of the car was slimy, sticky, he supposed vaguely from the blood and pieces of his back that had spattered on to the shiny white paintwork as the bullets passed through his body. He coughed, hurting, feeling the blood running down his chin on to his uniform jacket. He tried to raise his hands to stem the bleeding, to keep in the blood that would keep him alive. His hands were heavy with no feeling in the fingers.

A shadow passed in front of his eyes, blocking out the headlights of the other car. A man stood in front of him, the halo of light around him making it impossible to identify who it might be. Held loosely in his right hand, a weapon. Curved magazine. Russian. Kalashnikov, AK74. Atkinson knew his guns. A lot of good that will do you now, you daft bastard. Funny. He had only been thinking – Christ, how long ago? – that this was a hell of a night to be out and catch your death.

The squelch circuit from his radio hawked loudly, the voices on the set a long way away, muffled through the thickness of the car door. He thought of reaching up to open it, take the mike and report in, but was afraid to take his index finger out of one of the holes in his chest. Finger in the dyke. Got to stop the flood. The water coming in from the sea felt warm. Odd.

Shoes. City shoes. Cow's shit on them. He could smell the cow's shit. The radio, Trevor. Get to the radio. Another hole...? His fingers probed. Middle finger should plug it ... not what the middle finger is for ... He tried to keep his mouth closed, but couldn't prevent the barrel of the gun forcing his lips apart, the metal hard between his teeth. He shook his head sadly, feeling the foresight protector ripping the roof of his mouth.

Oh shit, Atkinson.

What have you gone and got yourself into this time?

He hurt too much to try and move. But he did not want to die.

Not like this.

Never like this ...

Henry Fielding, driving too fast, had drunk a little more than he had intended, and thought uninterestedly that he was probably over the limit. But it had been a damned good party. The Young Farmers' Association annual do, with plenty of champagne, good ale and a country-and-western band. It had been a bloody good night all round. And, finally, he had made it with Teresa Sharp, laughing and giggling outside the marquee where they had fallen on to the damp grass.

What a fuck.

He shook his head in amazement. Someone had once told him sagely that the hardest ones to screw were the mini-skirted little tartlets outside a disco, nipples like generator starter-buttons, looking for all the world as if they would eat the first dick that went by. If you want an easy bonk, his acquaintance had said solemnly, find yourself some high-society bird.

The daughter of a judge.

One very salacious chick.

What a fuck.

Leaping about under him, she'd been moaning almost before he had it in, his penis weeping all over her thighs in his eagerness. Not caring about his ineptitude, she had rammed her hips up off the wet grass and squeezed him into her, then, bucking wildly, screwed his brains into scrambled eggs. They never did find her knickers. He blew through pursed lips, reliving the moment, her teeth drawing blood from his ear lobe, her fingernails hurting his scrotum.

Wow.

Fielding came out of his reverie. From the corner of his eye he suddenly noticed the blue police light flashing, as he left the hamlet and headed for the fork that would take him off the main road into the minor lanes. Once there he would be relatively safe from a casual police check. Now this. PC Atkinson, overly keen all of a sudden. What the bloody hell was he doing up at this hour instead of being stretched snoring under the duvet? He tried to think of an alternative route, perhaps by turning in through Joe Thursday's yard then out across the open field to Jenny's Cross. From there he could cut back on to his original route and still be home before dawn.

Still procrastinating, he arrived at the police car angled across the road. His headlights picked out the dark scars of the tyre marks where it had come to a sudden halt from the lane on his right. Now it blocked the road from both directions, ominous, its blue light flashing monotonously. There was no sound, and Fielding began to think that the car had been abandoned. Nothing moved in the uncanny silence.

For a moment he thought about reversing and driving back the way he had just come, which would at least save him the ignominy of arguing his way out of a breath test. But there was something unreal, sinister, in the way the car was left, its light flashing persistently, as if crying for help. He felt uneasy, suddenly sober.

Stopping, he switched off, leaving his headlights illuminating the car in front. Quiet as death, he waited, listening, looking for the policeman who must surely soon appear from the far side. Finally, when he still saw no movement, curiosity got the better of him. He got out of his car and, leaving the door open, walked slowly forward.

The first thing he saw was a pair of legs in dark trousers thrust out from the side of the police car. He took a few more uncertain steps, until, at last, he was able to take in the whole scene. Everything was in deep shadow, difficult to distinguish detail. He leaned forward, fearful, curious. The shape of a figure sitting in the road, its back to the car, legs at right-angles to the body, as if someone had just felt tired and slumped down.

Fielding reached into a pocket for his cigarette lighter, trying to steady his fingers to spin the wheel against the flint. The lighter trembled in his hand, almost uncontrollable. Shaking his head, concentrating, he finally managed to create a flame. Bile filled his mouth, the champagne, beer and finger buffet a perfect emetic. Coughing, retching, he spewed helplessly, feeling the hot dryness in his throat when the last of it was up from him. He fell forward on to his knees, almost pitching into the body of the constable propped up against his own patrol car.

Fielding knew the policeman was dead.

Most of his chest had been shot away. In the flickering, uncertain flame of the cigarette lighter, he could see the soggy mess where his jacket had soaked up most of the blood, not yet congealed. And if that hadn't been enough, most of his brains were smeared on to the paintwork of the car door, the blood splashes as high as the driver's mirror.

The cigarette lighter was shaking so badly in his fingers that it finally fell to the ground. In the dark he threw up again, trying to think where the nearest telephone might be.

Nobby Clarke felt uncomfortable.

The flat in Reading was like nothing he had seen before and he envied his two companions their casual acceptance of these luxurious surroundings. He shrugged, partly from habit, but mostly to hide his embarrassment. Alex, quick to see the uneasiness, spoke quickly.

'Nobby. A beer?'

'Ay,' replied the big man from the mountain-rescue team, 'I'll take one of your ales.'

'Richard, what about you?'

'Scotch,' said Richard Norris. 'Plenty of ice. No water.' Richard, too, had seen the disquiet, but knew that Nobby would soon recover and revert to his normal extrovert character as soon as he had a few beers in him. It had been inevitable that the three of them would get on so well. Their individual characters seemed to blend as is so often the case with such diverse personalities, their strengths complementing their weaknesses. Seated around the big pine table in the kitchen, they talked of nothing, remembering everything, each aware of the others' capabilities. For the first time Richard began to think that there was a chance they might pull this off. Each of them had a purpose for being there, driven to embark on this venture for reasons that they had chosen not to disclose. But the determination was strong in all of them. They had proved that already. Failure was unthinkable. It was not in the equation.

Richard realized that he was the only one with the advantage of knowing the other two, the common denominator. Nobby and Alex seemed to have established a mutual respect, each recognizing the qualities in the other. A fine officer identifying a good soldier. Norris had considered telling Nobby that it had been Alex with him when they had heisted the security van belonging to the firm that had employed Nobby. They had needed a lot of money to finance their operation when they had hunted down the IRA man, Patrick Donnelly. Nobby, on the promise of no one being hurt, had provided vital information on the security firm's schedules.

He decided against it. Nobby anyway would guess, long before this adventure was over. He wondered how Nobby Clarke felt, now that the firm had made him redundant. Probably that it would have done the bastards good. Shaken them out of their smug complacency. No. Best leave it be so that they could finish as they had started.

Alex and Nobby listened without interruption as Richard told them what he had learned from his visit to London, not only from Colonel Oliver's team, but from the surviving Iraqi dissident. Richard, sipping Scotch, could not conceal his apprehension as he told the story. Both whistled in astonishment at the account of the assassination attempt. There had been nothing substantial in the papers, despite the presence of the photographers and the numerous pictures that had been taken. Richard could only assume that Oliver had arranged a D-notice.

'How the hell did the press know where to go?' Alex was incredulous. 'You said the Iraqis were in a safe house. Tip-off?'

'Had to be,' said Nobby.

It had been worrying Richard more than he cared to admit. Ever since... He shook his head slowly. 'I don't know. I just don't know. Something in the back of my mind, something below the surface, that keeps wanting to pop up, like a bottle with air in it. But it can't break its way out. It'll come to me. Eventually.'

Richard continued, telling them in short, simple terms what was required of them. Alex looked at Nobby. This was serious. Richard finished, his eyebrows pushed up into his hairline in a look of mild inquisitiveness, as if asking them to join him on a trip to the pub rather than embark on a dangerous mission into the unknown.

'Well, I'm buggered,' said Nobby Clarke with feeling.

'Bloody hell.' Alex, equally reserved, didn't look up, instead, cleaning his nails with a small stainless-steel knife he always carried. 'I understand what you're saying, Richard, but just how do we pull this off?' He spun the knife in his fingers, palmed it, then slipped it back into his pocket.

'We use my new piece of kit, Seeker, a radio direction-finder. We'll need to get in quite close – maybe to within five miles – so that we can get three fixes on his control radio. As soon as each of us gets him located, we feed the data into the computer on the set which automatically checks the figures. Then, zap, press the tit and the information is sent back here, all in one short burst. The equipment will even send back confirmation that the message has been received.' Norris looked pleased. 'Then, we fuck off. Out to the RV, and it's all over. The Americans do the rest with a Stealth aircraft.' It was quiet around the table. Then:

'Well, I'm buggered.'

'Bloody hell.'

This time, said in unison.

The woman crossed one ankle over the other, adjusting her position on the floor, making herself more comfortable. At ease, relaxed, she put the telephone in her lap, the handset held against her shoulder by her chin. Her fingers picked delicately at the keys as she tapped in a series of digits. There were thirteen in all: 010 96 26 623 175.

It was the Iraqi Embassy in Amman, Jordan.

While waiting for the connection she played idly with the telephone cable, glancing without interest around the dim room. At last, the telephone was answered, although she had to listen carefully through the crackling static on the less than perfect circuit. Her Arabic, when she spoke, was fluent. She talked for perhaps five minutes, finally replacing the receiver with a thoughtful, worried look.

Finally, she shrugged and got up from the floor, letting the robe fall from her shoulders as she did so. She walked into the bathroom, already steamy from the full tub. Wiping the condensation from a full-length mirror hanging from the wall, she stood looking at her reflection. Briefly, she cupped her breasts, feeling the perspiration already forming on them. She stared at herself, her body, her face, liking what she saw.

Fearful of what she might see there, she could not bring herself to look into her eyes. Instead, she guiltily slipped into the steaming, soapy water, hoping it might ease some of the worry from her mind.

Perhaps.

Somehow, she doubted it.

CHAPTER SIX

The room was the same, the water, the dusty glasses. Now, the three of them were together seated in a shallow semicircle in front of the table. The air was stale, constricting; claustrophobic if it hadn't been so brightly lit. The leader, as uninterested as before, leaned back in his chair. His stare, meant to be unnerving, missed nothing. If he had hoped to find nervousness or anxiety, he was disappointed. The man's hair was plastered even more greasily across his skull, either from the action of his hand or from the application of an unnecessary hair lotion. The reptilian eyelids reminded Norris of a crocodile basking leisurely on a mudbank in the Florida Everglades, lying in ambush, the jaws ready to open and snap down on him. The thought amused him.

Richard avoided looking at Annabelle Sad. On entering, he had caught her eye briefly, before she looked quickly away, different, more withdrawn, perhaps regretting what had happened. Some women were like that, he thought, wildly libidinous in the heat of the moment, only to be filled with guilt and remorse the following morning. He hadn't thought that she was that sort, and for some reason he could not explain, had believed their relationship might be more permanent. He pushed the thoughts away, concentrating instead on what was required of him. Perhaps, when this was over, he would find her and the two of them could remember how it had been.

Wild.

Noisy.

Colonel Oliver's glass eye stared at him sightlessly. Richard nodded briefly, acknowledging his presence before looking at the leader, who had at least changed his shirt. Adrian Kronk. Christ, a name to match the jejune suit, the unfashionable brogues. Kronk the Croc. Norris almost smiled.

'So far, so good, old boy,' said Kronk. 'I'm glad you've made it this far. I'm told that you caused quite a stir with the Paras. We ... ah ... heard about your attendance at P Company.' He looked at the trio, letting his eyes flick from one to the other. 'You're looking ... ah ... fitter, if I might say.'

Richard controlled the desire to grind his teeth. He was getting better with practice. Returning Kronk's indifferent stare, he concealed his dislike. Oliver, whom he had grown to respect, looked at him with a benevolent expression. That, and admiration.

He had seen Norris in action.

'We need nothing more than your outline plan; where you intend starting, your approximate route, and most importantly, an RV from where you can be easily extracted. When it's all over,' he added unnecessarily. Kronk, at last, seemed to be taking an interest, the lids not drooping to cover the eyes, an antique roll-top closing.

Richard, at the map, pointed with his finger: 'We'll start here, in Riyadh, Saudi Arabia. My kit is still there. I was giving the Saudis a demonstration of Seeker when—'

For a moment he was unable to speak. It was Oliver who noticed the distant look, suddenly vacant, unresponsive. Norris was somewhere else. Both Alex and Nobby knew the reason.

Richard remembered learning of Johnathan's death, from a Saudi officer somewhere in the desert north of Kasm al Am. He relived the moment, the warm air blowing on to his face, the sun burning through the thin cotton of his shirt, uncomfortable on his shoulders, the metallic ticking of the hot engine as it had cooled. The Saudi officer walking slowly through the heat haze, the red and white *ghuttrah* flicking in the breeze, sadness in the dark eyes. He had taken the note handed to him, focusing on the unfamiliar, childish writing, the wind picking at the flimsy paper, fluttering like a trapped butterfly in the man's fingers. Just a telephone number and a message telling him to call immediately. His home number.

He shuddered, coming back.

'There is a British military team in Riyadh who can prepare everything we need, as long as your people authorize it. And', he added, 'you provide the funds. This isn't going to be cheap.'

Richard Norris looked at the group. Alex and Nobby were listening carefully, although he had gone through the details a dozen or more times with them. 'I've sent a fax, telling them exactly what we need. I'm assured they'll have the equipment ready for us.'

'You'll get their full support. Everything you need. Documentation, maps, customs clearance, the lot,' Oliver said and then asked, 'How will you move?'

'From Riyadh, we'll drive north, taking the Buraydah road as far as it goes, probably to Hail, then due north to Ar Ar. There's a National Guard post in the town which will be our last friendly port of call so to speak. Any last-minute snags, and we'll call in from there.'

Lawrence country. Norris pictured the arid wastelands. Vast empty skies. Wide horizons as far as a man could see. Nothing. Empty, hot, dry.

'From there we'll follow the Trans-Arabian Pipeline, south of it, skirting the desert of An Nafud.' He hesitated, weighing his words. 'In two days, we'll reach Al Jalamid, a group of buildings, a few shops and dusty streets.' Richard paused, looking at his audience, holding their attention. Everyone was listening.

'Then,' – Richard shrugged, an ironic smile twitching the corner of his mouth – 'we just turn right into Iraq and keep going. There's a small village called Qis'aam – it's not even shown on the large-scale map, but it's about' – he scanned the map, then stabbed a finger – 'here – where we're to meet our guide. He'll take us to the escarpment, to a fault, a crack. We can climb it from there. There is a narrow fissure, Al Shuk fee Sakr, which should give us a relatively easy route on to the plateau. Because they'll never expect us to come that way there won't be such a heavy guard force deployed that side. It's a natural obstacle.'

Richard wasn't sure if he had convinced them. He didn't care anyway. Just as long as they fulfilled their part of the bargain. Unless they encountered difficulties with the guide, getting there shouldn't be too big a problem. Their troubles would start once they arrived.

'What about disguise?' It sounded melodramatic.

'Just local clothing. Nothing special.'

'You've light eyes. Except for—' Kronk gestured with his chin, at Nobby.

'Clarke,' said Nobby. 'Mr Clarke.' The anger was concealed, but barely. 'Mine are brown, 'cept when I'm pissed. Then they look more like an AA road map.'

'Indeterminate colouring.' It was Alex, paring his nails with the little stainless steel knife.

Oliver smiled, looked away.

'We wear sun-glasses,' said Richard, simply. 'With a head cloth, a *shimargh*, wrapped around the lower face, no one will tell us from genuine Bedouin. To add a bit of authenticity, we might even tie a camel or a few sheep in the back of the truck.' He grinned without humour.

Oliver at least was amused.

Kronk then outlined his part of the plan. On the surface, it sounded good. An in-and-out job. Nothing to it. Richard wondered how the others felt. Nobby was sucking on his pipe, annoying Kronk with the sound. Alex was looking down at his hands, seemingly uninterested, but missing nothing. He put away the knife.

Annabelle Sad still hadn't looked at him.

They confirmed details: frequencies, call signs, radio schedules. Richard would use his own equipment. Kronk would arrange for the frequency to be anchored and permanently monitored as soon as he received a coded message from the Embassy in Riyadh. From that moment there would be an operator listening as though his life depended on it.

They would use burst techniques, keeping transmission time to a fraction of a second. That way it would be almost impossible for them to be intercepted, even with sophisticated monitoring equipment. Kronk told them what Richard had known anyway, that the Iraqis had no such technology. Kronk was looking puzzled. Finally, unable to contain himself, he asked, 'How will you know you are listening to the right people?'

'The guard troops are the best of the Republican Guard. They have the most up-to-date equipment. Our dissident confirmed that their radios use a speech encryption device. When they transmit, they can't be intercepted by an unauthorized receiver, can't be understood. It's like a scrambler, for want of a better description.' Richard drew in his breath, scratched the side of his face, then went on. 'This is what will give them away, identify them to us. They're using French equipment, purchased before the Gulf War, in the days when End-User Certificates were less important than now. The sound is distinctive, a low warbling note with high-pitched whine on top of it – a bit like a motor boat with its exhaust bubbling below the surface. It's quite unmistakable. We've listened to recordings of these transmissions a hundred times. We hear the sound in our sleep. If they're there, we'll find them. The control station and the gun will be located together. Bet on it. If we find their control, we find the gun.'

'And once you pick them up, you can pinpoint them accurately?'

Oliver shifted uncomfortably. They had been through all this before. He knew that Kronk was aware of Seeker's capabilities, that he was just being pedantic, trying to rile Norris.

'If we can get in a position where he's triangulated, we'll

nail him to within a few feet. The more of an isosceles, the better. But in the worst case, we can do it from a straight line. We may have to lie up for a while, waiting for him to transmit.' Richard looked at Alex, Nobby, seeing that they understood. 'In your terms, right on the nose. Just to be safe, we'll take a small, portable laser-designator. If the worst comes to the worst, and Seeker fails to live up to my expectations, or we pick up someone other than their control, we'll light the target, and the Stealth can zero in on that. For the designator to be effective though, Seeker has got to get us in close. Otherwise we'll be pissing over the windshield of a Tiger Moth at 80 knots. But I'm confident of the kit. It'll work.'

He was unable to resist it.

'It's all in my promotional literature, old boy.' Alex's impersonation of Kronk was perfect.

Richard looked away, hiding his smile. Nobby the same, coughing into his hand, choking on the pipe. Oliver turned and looked at the map, his jaw muscles working. Kronk, for his part, appeared not to have noticed. Instead, he and Oliver spoke together in low voices, preventing Richard from hearing. He tried again to catch the girl's eye, but she stared stubbornly at the equipment in front of her, uncomfortable, fanning her face with a stiff piece of card. He remembered her when her hair hadn't been tied in a bun, flying like a kite in the wind as she had straddled his sweating body, her breasts bouncing as she cawed obscenities . . .

'Right. It seems we've covered everything. I have no real wish to see you again until you've succeeded. Nevertheless,' – he looked down at his fingers, uncomfortable – 'good luck.'

It sounded patronizing.

Kronk was dismissive, wanting to be out of this unfriendly room, reposing comfortably in his club, sleeping off an after-lunch brandy. Richard stood, relieved it was over. Nobby carefully put away the pipe into the breast pocket of his shirt where he could find it easily. Alex, uncomfortable, too big for the stuffy room, rolled his shoulders, stiff from being too long in one place.

Annabelle Sad still would not look at him.

It was all over the news.

He heard it first on the early broadcasts on the car radio as he reached the outskirts of London, too early for the commuter traffic at the end of the M4. Listening carefully, he searched the words for any indication that the police might have a lead. He was calmer, now. The panic welling up in him when he had seen the police car blocking his escape had been almost too much for him. He had thought that he had been safe, no cars following, the road behind him empty of pursuing headlights.

Where the hell had the Law come from?

Standing there like he was on bloody point duty, directing traffic at a busy junction, his hands up in the air like King Canute trying to stop the fucking tide coming in. Oh yes, he'd panicked. So badly, he'd been paralysed, his brain a mess of jumbled thoughts and tangled ideas, each superseding the other as soon as one formed in his mind. Gradually, he calmed and started to think. He had remembered the gun on the floor in the driver's well, taken just in case that bastard Norris had shown.

And the look on the pig's face when he loaded it.

The inimitable sound of the cocking handle, snapped back, sliding forward and carrying a live up into the breech. It felt good in his hands, heavy, comforting. See what your fucking truncheon can do against this heavy artillery. The policeman had to die. It was the only way to ensure escape, to prevent his being taken. It was his first time. For a moment, just before he fired, he was elsewhere, at the training sessions in the tunnel range, huge concrete pipe sections, buried in the south Armagh countryside, deadening the sound of the gunshots as they zeroed the weapons. Now, the target was real. Bathed in the white brightness of the halogen lights, helpless, a dark figure with shiny buttons outlined clearly against the white backdrop of the police car.

He relived the moment of pressing the trigger.

He had meant to fire only the one, but after the first something snapped in his mind and he pulled the trigger twice more. Even then the bastard wasn't dead. Quickly he searched and found the four empty cartridge cases, alarmed until the last was discovered in the long grass at the edge of the road where it spun on ejection. They nestled warm in his pocket. Remembering, he walked around the police car to look for the exit hole in the passenger door, torn through the metal by the last of the bullets. Yes. There it was, jagged, shapeless. Otherwise clean. The mess would be on the inside of the door panel.

No clues. None that he could see. The bullets clean through, miles away in a ploughed field, a hayrick somewhere. Alert, he picked up the sound of a car's engine coming from somewhere in the direction of the small hamlet. It had appeared suddenly in the distance, someone driving fast, a couple of miles away. He had been able, just, to make out the faint glow of its lights from beyond the dark buildings. Going quickly to his car, he'd restarted and driven left up the lane, assuming that the police car had come from there and that it must lead back into the village.

And now, there was nothing on the news that could link him to the killing.

Carefully he thought for a few minutes. The gun, the AK74, was safe, hidden in the lock-up he'd rented by telephone, paid for in advance, as they had told him. The car had been put through a Californian-style car-wash, the wheels, chassis and bodywork scrubbed clean. Asking such a low price, it was sold almost immediately, to a dealer in north London. He'd remembered to haggle, a hard-up student, down to his last few pounds, needing the money.

The last he had seen of the car, two industrious young men were steam-cleaning it, giving it a full valet service. The works. By the time they finished, it looked almost brand new. A bargain, he thought. A real bargain. To be certain, and in case there had been a change of plan, he decided to call the emergency number he had been given, a number he had memorized and then destroyed, never needing to use it, until now. In a callbox at the end of the street, he dropped coins into the slot and dialled the Belfast number, looking casually about as he waited for the connection. He recognized the high-pitched, continuous tone.

Number unobtainable.

Frantically, he redialled.

Again, number unobtainable.

The sound was distant, mocking him. He called the operator, confirming his worst fears. It had probably been disconnected. She was helpful, offering to report the fault. Was there a number where he could be reached? Cursing, he slammed the instrument back into its cradle, frightened.

Panic. He tried to think what had happened. His lifeline, gone. Cut off, nowhere to turn to for support. Out on a limb, up the creek without a fucking paddle, just because he'd blown away a copper. He was afraid of being taken on the mainland, convicted and gaoled away from his own kind. All of them in the Movement hated the thought of being taken away from home. He ground his teeth. Right, you bastards. See if I give a shit. I'll get your target for you. Then maybe you'll show me the respect I deserve. The respect I've earned. Anger, betrayal and resentment bubbled in him. The mark on his forehead, where the man from Belfast had twisted the gun barrel, throbbed painfully.

Joseph Fallon was fighting mad.

*

118

Walter Oliver looked again at the flimsy message in his hand. He read it for the third time. It had been received by special despatch from the Scotland Yard Anti-Terrorist Unit, SO13. He rubbed his good eye, feeling the strain of working with the Middle East desk on the Supergun project, giving it all his energy. Now, he was heartily tired of it. Since its presence had been confirmed, he had lived in constant fear of the Iraqis firing a nuclear shell at Tel Aviv. It didn't bear thinking about. By all accounts the gun was not yet ready. Two months, the dissidents had told him.

Two months.

Then?

Oliver shuddered. As if he did not have enough on his mind. Now this. A report from the Gloucestershire Constabulary informing Special Branch that a stranger had been noticed in the area of Richard Norris's village. They in turn had passed it to MI5. The police had been warned of the importance of Norris and his team and were doing as instructed. What the hell was he supposed to do with the information?

Norris had left. They were safely in Saudi Arabia, that much he knew from the British Embassy in Riyadh. But once Norris was on his way, they would not hear from him again until he had found the gun. Unless there was a disaster. Then Norris would be up on the emergency frequency, demanding the extraction team to go in and pull him out.

Walter Oliver read the signal again. It might be nothing, a tourist, or holiday-maker, renting a cottage for the early summer. Perhaps it was an old Army buddy, as the signal implied. That was more like it. He doubted if there was anything to worry about. He was much more concerned with the content of the second signal. A shooting. A policeman, in the same area. That was too much of a coincidence. And there had been something, about an accent. It could be important. Sighing, he picked up the telephone, dialling a number in New Scotland Yard, which, from constant use, was filed permanently into his brain. For the moment, the Supergun project, codenamed CHARLATAN, was on hold.

He listened as the distant telephone rang.

The heat was painful, striking them a physical blow, wrapping around their bodies like hot, dry towels. Leaving the comfort of the air-conditioned office was like opening a door and ducking into an oven. The heat was dry, devoid of humidity, making it impossible to sweat. As soon as the moisture broke out of the body, it was immediately evaporated by the scorching wind, leaving the surface of the skin hot and dry to the touch.

The four men descended the short flight of steps and crossed a small courtyard. They passed through a stout iron gate which led to the road. The engine of the 4WD had been running, the interior mercifully cool from the air-conditioning.

The British Army Major wore civilian clothes, cool in a short-sleeved, light-blue cotton shirt, linen slacks and open sandals. Richard remembered Tony Meredith from his previous visit. Now nearing the end of his tour, he would soon be packing his house ready for his next posting, once he had seen Norris and his team safely away. The constant moving in the Army was one of the reasons Richard and Felicity had decided to leave. Twelve houses in twenty years had been enough for them both.

They drove in silence through the wide, empty Riyadh streets, the shops and the banks and the undeveloped building sites with their gaunt ugly cranes, unnerved by the absence of people. It was only when Meredith reminded them that Friday equated to Sunday, that they understood the reason.

'They'll be at prayers,' Meredith said conversationally. 'The place will liven up in an hour or so. They take their religion very seriously. Occasionally, you'll see the religious police, the *Metahwah*, ordering some of the younger Saudis off to the *masjid*. It's almost entirely voluntary though, and only a few will miss prayer call.' He grinned. 'Mind you, there may not be a lot of takers for the early-morning shout. They like their kip as much as us.'

They had arrived at a contractor's workshop, and Tony Meredith turned off the road into a compound at the rear of the premises. He greeted the foreman, dusky, a mouth full of gold, grinning, as he shook hands. Two Filipino workers closed the heavy iron gates behind them. Again the sun burned them until they were under cover in the shade of the work area. In the dim interior, it took a few minutes for their eyes to adjust to the unfamiliar gloom.

Four men dressed in light cotton overalls were working on a vehicle in the centre of the workshop. The firm's logo, AL HASSEEM, was printed on the back in English and Arabic. The men worked, quiet, except when a tool clattered to the floor from careless fingers, the sudden noise echoing in the huge cavern of the room.

The truck looked a mess, the bodywork dented, scratched, covered in dust, thick mud on the sills. Closer inspection showed a chassis that was immaculately clean. Richard bent to inspect the underside, impressed to see what had been achieved in so short a time. The vehicle was a Toyota four-wheel-drive pick-up truck, the workhorse of the desert, fast replacing the camel as the favoured form of transport for the ubiquitous *bedoo*. This model had the expanded cab and could seat five in comfort. Meredith pointed.

'We've made it look like a heap of junk, as you asked in your fax. Mind you,' – he gave that piratical grin – 'poor old John here went ape-shit when he had to lift off the deluxe body and replace it with this wreck. It broke his heart.'

Meredith led them over to the vehicle so that they could inspect it more closely. He pointed out the special features

121

fitted, joking that it was the best set of optional extras they would find anywhere.

Nobby Clarke looked rapt. This was going to be his baby. He listened attentively, noting everything. High-profile cross-country tyres, oversize wheels, additional long-range petrol tanks, extra water containers and the Loran C navigational device hidden in a concealed compartment between the two front seats. It could be pulled out on an expandable arm when it was required, then hidden again. He looked lovingly at the heavy-duty springs, shock-absorbers and modified suspension, the armour-plating behind the cab. But it was the engine that drew and held his attention. The sort of engine that Nobby could only dream of. It was the 4-litre 165-bhp direct-diesel, fuel-injection with turbocharger. Nobby had the pipe in his mouth. He extracted it with a big hand and pointed to the pick-up.

'Lovely wagon, that. It'll go like greased weasel shit off of a shiny shovel. Can't wait to try it. Bloody good job it's got harness safety-belts. You two'll need them when we're tanking cross-country. With permanent four-wheel drive and diff-lock, she'll top the ton, that one. I'll be OK, hanging on to the wheel, watching the pair of you bouncing about like a fat lady's tits.'

Alex grinned, then asked, 'Weapons?'

Meredith led them over to an office out of sight of the working men, straight to a steel cabinet, its door secured by a large Chubb padlock. Opening the doors, he showed them the guns lying on the shelves. Oiled, stubby, deadly, Heckler and Koch MP5K, one with a fat silencer fitted, the other two, the MP5KA1, with the smooth upper surface, no sights to catch in clothing when it was pulled out in a hurry, small enough to fit into a briefcase. Or the glove compartment of a vehicle. Nine-millimetre. Parabellum. Death-dealers.

Richard Norris shook his head.

'No hardware. If they get that close to us, we're done for anyway.'

'Are you sure about this, Richard?' Alex, puzzled, was fondling one of the guns as he might a lover, caressing it with strong fingers, squinting along the barrel.

'I'm sure.' With that he left the office. Alex followed. Tony Meredith shrugged, and went back to the truck. Nobby Clarke scratched his chin, looking at the weapons, oiled, gleaming in the dim light.

Deep in thought, he hefted one in his hands.

Colonel Zaydn sat relaxed in the passenger seat of the big off-road Land-Cruiser, staring into the night as the halogen headlights cut a corridor as bright as day in the otherwise impenetrable darkness. Insects spattered against the windscreen, noisy in death. He let his mind dwell idly on the future, not really concentrating, his thoughts meandering. He was surviving. That was what was important. His future was assured. One of the chosen few, he would continue to survive. Zaydn was not clever. It was his cunning, his cruelty, that made him a survivor.

The Colonel was Chief of Security for Operation SLING SHOT.

The project was their revenge. Revenge for the humiliation at the hands of the Zionists and for defeat by the American-led Coalition in the short war that had ended in such ignominious defeat for the Iraqi Army. Zaydn felt the shame, remembering the Republican Guard, their élite troops, crumbling before the onslaught. The Russian armour had been no match for either the American Abrams tank or the destructive power of the Apache attack helicopter. He winced, recalling the mutilation of his brigade. A flight had come at them, out of the sun, a swarm of angry killer bees, the clattering of the rotors drowned only by the sound of the chain guns, the roar of the rockets, as they unleashed their death on the armoured

123

vehicles scattering in panic in the desert below as they tried to escape the slaughter.

But it had not always been so. There had been glory in the early days, when they had ripped through the weak defences and rolled triumphantly into Kuwait City. He flushed at the memory, the crack of the 120-mm. tank gun as it destroyed the street along which he and three other tanks had driven. Beautiful marble and stone buildings had disintegrated, collapsing into heaps of rubble as he delightedly, laughingly, told his gunner to reload, fire, reload, fire. Nor would he forget rounding up the British hostages. He hated the British, with their supercilious, condescending attitude, even more than he did the Americans.

The villa had looked cool, inviting, in the late-afternoon sun, the lawns neatly tended, the bougainvillaea cascading in a riot of magenta over the spotless white walls. He had felt the potent power as he'd climbed confidently from his jeep and lit a long King Size JPS from the elegant black pack, drawing on it through an ivory cigarette holder which he'd held effeminately between finger and thumb.

Their dog, a small breed he did not recognize, had approached him, at first quizzically, its nose twitching as it tried to identify the unfamiliar smell of cordite and engine oil. It had sniffed the desert boot then the leg above. The growl, low in its throat, menacing.

Zaydn nonchalantly pulled his pistol from the shiny leather holster and shot the dog through the brain at close range, laughing as the animal's head had been torn from its body. The woman began to wail, the man trying to comfort her, his arm around her shoulder. She stopped her crying when he pointed the gun at her, indicating the dog, still twitching on the marble patio, a pool of dark blood where the head had been.

His men went quickly into the villa and rounded up the

children, hustling them out to join their parents. They looked frightened, despite the air of bravado the man tried to display in an attempt to reassure his family. They were herded into buses at the end of the street, leaving Zaydn free to enter the house after the last of his men left. He did so partly from curiosity, but also to see if there was anything left worth stealing. Walking through the silent rooms, he opened closets and picked idly through open drawers. About to leave, he heard a noise coming from a closet in the kitchen. Standing by the door, he listened, curious, a cruel smile beginning. Crying. A woman, crying, the sound a whimper, frightened, forlorn. He put his hand on the door knob, waiting, eager.

He wrenched it open.

At first he saw nothing, only the darkness of the interior. Then, a shaft of light fell across the paleness of her, partially hidden by the things in the closet. Her eyes were wide open, afraid, as she gaped, transfixed, like a young desert hare fascinated by a sand viper. Her legs were drawn up to her chest, as she tried in vain to force herself further into the dark interior.

She saw his smile, and was afraid.

Zaydn pulled open his fly, exposing himself, without taking his eyes from the woman's face. He saw her fear, the dread in the dark eyes, and felt the eagerness coursing through him. He let her see the stiffness, his moving hand, and know what was to come. Throwing both hands up to her face, she covered her eyes, tears flowing between her fingers as she rocked back and forth in the dim light. The Colonel had laughed, then crammed himself back into the camouflage-pattern trousers, the hardness pressed against the material. Standing, he'd closed the closet slowly so that the shape of her was swallowed gradually by the closing door. Turning the key in the lock, he'd put it carefully into the pocket of his desert fatigue uniform.

Yes, little Filipino handmaiden. I will come back for you later.

*
125

He was almost asleep. Memories of the woman were as a dream, the present, happening now. He snapped his head up, alert, his thumb poised on the wheel of his lighter that shook in his fingers. A few more miles and they would arrive at the barrier across the road, the road leading to the tunnel entrance in the side of the mountain. Another night of boring duty.

Closing his eyes again he let his thoughts drift back to the woman, her struggles as he had dragged her from the closet, quietening only when his hand had left ugly marks on her face as he slapped her brutally, a back and forth motion. The knife had kept her silent. He'd dragged her whimpering to the sink, tying her wrists to the taps with a clothes line he found wrapped in crisp Cellophane. Bent over, she had been exposed, helpless.

He stripped off his dusty desert uniform, the floor tiles cool on his bare feet as he padded across the kitchen floor. Not wanting to slip when his feet began to sweat, as they always did when he was aroused, he put the desert boots back on. Zaydn was skilled with the use of a knife. Finely honed, he used it to cut off her clothes, watching them fall to the floor as he worked with deft, delicate strokes, sawing through the stitching of the seams, slicing through the thread that held the buttons in place, his excitement intensifying as her pale flesh appeared. As the blade cut through the straps of her bra, the elastic of her panties, he fought to stay in control. Finally, when she was naked, parts of her clothes hanging at her wrists, collapsed at her ankles, he stood back to admire his handiwork, liking what he saw. Then, he walked quickly from the kitchen, into the lounge where he poured a large glass of the Englishman's whisky. It was gulped, greedily, his eyes watering at the burning, unfamiliar taste.

He had walked back into the kitchen, unsteady, his eyes never leaving her pale figure. Reaching over her, feeling

126

her softness as he leaned against the back of her thighs, he had torn from the roll of kitchen paper, stuffing it into her mouth, making an improvised gag. Shaking, eager, he'd stood behind her, mesmerized by the darkness of his flesh against the paleness of her, a tarred rope end, hard, hurting him. Too briefly, the warmth, the dark heat, so quick he was angry with her for denying him. Whisky had slopped out of the glass, spattering over her naked back. In his rage, he had hit her.

He let his mind remember the sudden pumping thrust . . .

A bullet slapped into the windscreen.

Two more followed almost at once, neat holes appearing in the glass, eyes, with veins running out from the pupils. His driver sat upright, motionless, his face a bloody mess where his features had been a few seconds before, eyes sightless in the ragged flesh, hands clamped tight on the steering wheel, immovable. The vehicle veered, careering at alarming speed towards the edge of the road. Zaydn afraid, yelled, hurting his throat. He had no idea what had happened. Only that someone was shooting.

He tried to keep the vehicle in a straight line, to hold it on the road, away from the ditch at the side of the highway. The dead man was immovable in the driver's seat, impossible to budge. Zaydn yanked at the wheel, desperate, yet even in his fear he recognized the flashes coming from the automatic weapons firing at him. He felt the numbing shock, hit, high up in the left shoulder, paralysing, preventing him using his left hand to steer. From the heavy feel, lack of response, he knew that a tyre had been shot out. Now, he could no longer hold the vehicle steady.

In a slow-motion chimerical dream, he felt the front wheel hit the ditch, wrenching the steering wheel from his grasp. The fingers of his left hand were sticky, blood oozing down his arm on to the seat. Now the pain, as the vehicle, normally so dependably solid, leaped the gap at the top of the ditch. It smashed heavily into the bank at the far side. His forehead thumped into the side window, an agony exploding in his head, concussing him.

He was conscious, still, as his vehicle rolled majestically on to its side, then cartwheeled, nose over tailgate, until it hit the rough surface of the desert with a spine-jarring crash. The truck came to a stop finally, in a twisted heap of groaning metal, the body mangled, unrecognizable. But the reinforced cab did not collapse, leaving him upside down, hanging from his safety straps, barely conscious.

He identified the smell.

Gasoline.

The cab was thick with fumes as the liquid flowed unchecked from a fractured fuel line, making him light-headed, fearful. Dimly, through the noise of the wreck, he heard the crunch of footsteps. A pair of boots came into view, blurred in his peripheral vision. There was dust on the boots, different from his own. The legs in the boots bent at the knees. A face came into view. The head wore a helmet, but not like his own. Even with the camouflaged netting disguising the shape, Zaydn could see it was not an Iraqi helmet. He tried to think where he had seen the helmet before, but his mind was confused from the concussion, the mad tumbling of his vehicle.

American, British, maybe.

Israeli!

The soldier looked in at him, turning his head to see into the cab, his nostrils flaring at the strong smell of petrol. The soldier looked away, speaking to someone off in the darkness, his Arabic faultless.

'Hey, I need a cigarette. Bring me a pack. And a lighter. Over here by the truck.'

The Arab sweated in his fear, even more than when he had run from the Apaches, diving for cover, his face burrowed into the dirt behind a rock as his tank brigade was slaughtered in the open desert. The soldier worried a cigarette from a packet held loosely in dirty fingers.

There was a picture of a camel.

The soldier delicately placed the cigarette between his lips, the movement deliberate, casual. He held it lightly by the filter tip between his bared teeth, the grin impish. Raising the lighter, he cupped it in his hands, his thumb on the wheel, ready to make the spark, unaware it seemed of the danger, and that he too would be consumed in the fireball if he lit the flame.

It was a shiny Zippo lighter.

The soldier blew on the wheel through pursed lips.

'Perhaps I'll wait awhile or join you guys over there, away from this wreck. Come to think of it, there's a stink of gas coming from the truck, so strong, I can't even smell the pig hanging in there.' The eyes were blue. Zaydn could not see them. He just knew them to be blue.

The legs straightened. The boots did an about-turn, then disappeared from his view, leaving him alone in the silence, which was broken only by the occasional creaking from the damaged vehicle, groaning like an animal in pain. He turned his head from left to right, seeing nothing as he fought unsuccessfully to loosen the safety harness. But it was jammed. He struggled, sweating, even in the cold of the desert night. His arm throbbed, blood running into his left ear. For a moment he thought he had passed out, drifting dreamlike to the kitchen of the villa, the girl exposed invitingly before him.

A tiny firefly landed in a shower of sparks, bouncing across the ground towards him, finally coming to rest a yard from his head. Staring at the cigarette, the smell of petrol vapour thick in his nostrils, he shook with uncontrolled fear. A cold desert breeze fanned the tip, sparks rising lazily from it, the pattern haphazard as they were caught and borne upwards by the movement of the air. The breeze seemed to strengthen, spinning the cigarette like a compass needle pointing at his face, blowing to fan the tip once more. He was conscious of nothing, save the red glow, the strengthening wind and the sickly smell of the petrol.

'No!' he screamed, the veins thick parachute cords in his neck. He began to tear at the restraining harness that prevented his escape, breaking his fingernails as he kicked feebly with his feet at the floor of the cab. The dusty boots crunched in the gravel as the soldier came back into view.

'God be praised!'

The soldier bent and picked up the cigarette. He squatted on his haunches like an American Indian and bent to squint into the cab.

'Does the Colonel want to talk, or do I drop the butt and walk out of here?'

'Yes! But get me out! Cut me loose. I'll tell you anything. Please—' He hated begging. 'In the name of God.'

'Yours or mine?' The soldier was biding his time, the cigarette hidden.

'Please—' The Arab was weeping shamelessly.

'You'll talk, Colonel. No matter.'

Zaydn caught the flash of the blade in the faint light from the stars as it sawed roughly through the nylon straps. As they parted he fell out of the harness and landed whimpering on his wounded arm. The soldier dragged him roughly from the cab and hauled him to his feet, where he was left to stand unsupported, swaying drunkenly as he tried to prevent himself from falling. Through half-closed eyes he saw four Israeli soldiers standing in a small group, unconcerned, but talking quietly, heatedly, in their own tongue which the Colonel could not understand.

He knew, though, that they were discussing him.

Gradually he regained his composure as he realized that the immediate danger had passed. He looked carefully about him, assessing, calculating his position in relation to the road barrier.

Five miles?

If he was more than ten minutes late, a patrol would

come looking for him. That was the regulation. It was *his* regulation. After all, he was Chief of Security. He composed himself.

Bastards.

Camel-shagging bastards.

Suddenly, his new-found confidence evaporated and he was afraid again as the group approached him. No one spoke. They stood around him in a small circle preventing him seeing the four of them simultaneously. He felt the sharp pain of a weapon as the barrel was ground into his spine.

'Move. Over to the jeep.'

He stumbled forward, pushed roughly by the weapon at his back. The Israeli jeep was hidden in a rock outcrop, a light camouflage net flung over it. One of the soldiers tugged it away and lifted the bonnet, supporting it with a metal stay. The Arab could smell the heat from the engine, oil mixed with the pungent odour of coolant. There were rocks behind the jeep, their shapes distorted by the engine's heat haze. The vehicle looked old, well used, efficient. A radio was fitted in the back behind the rear seats, the antenna bent forward and tied down to the front bumper. A dim red light glowed from the set.

They questioned him in faultless Arabic.

What did he know about a Supergun?

Afraid, Zaydn's brain worked fast as he calculated how late he must now be. In the guardhouse beside the dusty compound outside the underground complex, they would be worrying. Already a crew would be hurriedly mounting its Russian-made BTR armoured personnel carrier, ready to leave as soon as the officer of the guard gave the order. Then, the high-pitched whine as the engine burst into life, followed by another and another. There would be three. It was the regulation.

Zaydn began to feel more confident. The Israeli soldiers seemed to sense it. The questioning stopped as they once more went into a sinister huddle. The speed with which they moved took him by surprise. With his arms pinned to his sides he was bundled over to the jeep, screaming in agony from the pain of his wound. Already he had lost a lot of blood, his whole side, his uniform trousers wet from the continuous seepage from his arm and shoulder. He fought against the light-headed weakness, the dizziness and the cold enveloping him. They dragged him to the front of the jeep, where the soldier with the knife placed the blade under his belt and sliced quickly upwards until the leather parted. Zaydn tried not to look, feeling the fear as another of them pulled on a pair of thick leather gauntlets. He yelled as his trousers were wrenched over his hips and pulled roughly down to his ankles, the desert wind cold on his genitals. Exposed, he felt foolish, embarrassed.

In an instant he realized what they were going to do to him but could do nothing to prevent it. Three of the soldiers lifted him bodily, laying him across the radiator of the jeep. He screamed as the heat seared his naked belly. They asked him again, questions he was afraid to answer. But for the moment, he was more afraid of what they were going to do to him. The Colonel whimpered, the rough leather of the gauntlets ripping his pubic hair as the soldier savagely unscrewed the radiator cap a quarter of a turn. Superheated steam hissed out of the loosened cap, then, as the cap was unscrewed a little more, coolant splashed and bubbled under immense pressure on to his genitals, turning them instantly into a yellow mess of blistering flesh.

Colonel Zaydn had never known such pain could exist. His whole body was immersed in it, so dreadful that it permeated every muscle, tissue fibre and nerve end. He longed for the sweet innocence of death. But Death, unforgiving, stayed stubbornly in the shadows, refusing to come forward and release him from his agony. The pain continued its remorseless advance into the inner privacy of his mind. Here in the darkness, it cast its bright, penetrating light, leaving him no place to hide.

Sobbing wretchedly, he told them what they wanted to know.

About SLING SHOT.

Weeping bitterly, he babbled the details of the Supergun, with its nuclear capability, and which was now aimed at Tel Aviv. And he told them of the team the British had put in to find the gun. Screaming, the words they wanted to hear spilled from his lips.

He died before he could tell them where it was.

The soldier who spoke Arabic with such fluency looked at the body of the dead Arab lying in a crumpled heap on the ground where he had landed on falling from the jeep. It reminded him of an abandoned scarecrow he had once seen in the wheatfields of his homeland. At least the darkness hid his humiliation. Turning away, he fanned the wheel of the lighter with the palm of his hand, dipping the cigarette into the oily flame and drawing the smoke deep into his lungs.

He spoke one short sentence into the radio.

They left the Colonel near his vehicle. With a cursory look around them, they scrambled into the jeep and drove off into the desert. Already the Huey UH8 helicopter was throbbing out of the western sky towards them. In the dim light of the early dawn it would hover above the sand, then settle like an anxious bird of prey, awaiting its young.

Then, it would bear them away.

He read the signal again.

It shook in his fingers, making it difficult to read. Looking up at the man with the glass eye, he gulped, the Adam's apple bobbing in his neck as if he had swallowed something too big to go down his throat. He bent his head to read it again shaking his head in disbelief.

'Mossad? How the hell—?

The one-eyed man shrugged.

'God knows. Perhaps one of their patrols stumbled on something—'

'You know what this means?'

Oliver nodded sadly.

'Compromised. They've been compromised.'

'What now?' Oliver knew the answer, but asked it anyway.

The reptilian eyes closed, opened.

'They're on their own. That's what it means.'

The signal was screwed into a ball and tossed into a basket for classified waste. The saurian eyes closed again as the man from MI6 spoke. 'There is nothing we can do now.' The word, when it came, was short, whispered.

'Abort.'

The one-eyed man from Five looked away, preventing Six from seeing the sadness in his good eye.

CHAPTER SEVEN

The barbed-wire fence was crossed without pause or slowing of their speed. It lay rusty, twisted, an ugly, untidy skeleton in the sand. They ignored the warnings painted on small black boards nailed to posts at intervals along the broken fence, the Arabic not understood, the grinning death's head of the skull and crossbones scorned. They travelled as *bedoo*, paying scant heed to international borders, free to roam, nomadic, as their forefathers before them, until the signing of treaties, the lines on charts, which prevented men from roaming free.

They drove fast across the desert, a dust plume streaming from the rear of the vehicle. The well-engineered highways, the Tarmacadam rivers, lay behind them in Saudi Arabia. Now, desert, scrub and rock, strangely beautiful in the evening sun, the colours diffused, indistinct, softening the harsh outlines of the distant, shimmering mountains. The going was firm on this stretch and they had made good time, seeing no one. The dust plume did not concern them, for here, in western Iraq, and northern Saudi Arabia, it was a sight common enough.

Nobby Clarke drove, relaxed, at peace, hands lightly holding the wheel. Norris, beside him, occasionally checked their position from the Loran navigator, calling instructions to the man driving who made a correction here and there, following a direction that would take them closer to the escarpment, which they could see faintly in the distance. The biggest of them dozed in the rear of the cab. He was to drive next.

The flat gravel of the desert was changing, the terrain rougher, broken, requiring more concentration, more effort from the man at the wheel. The sleeper grunted his displeasure, the truck now bouncing along a rock-strewn track. Nobby Clarke drove expertly, the terrain not unlike his homeland where he had driven on many occasions worse than this, when he had been out with the mountain-rescue team. The angle was steeper, the engine revs increasing as Nobby shifted through the gears. He spoke, the first real conversation since leaving Saudi Arabia.

'Reminds me of a time when we had to go and pull someone off of Scafell.' He grinned into the roll of the headcloth covering his mouth, keeping out the dust. 'He'd broke his leg coming down in the middle of the night. Silly sod. God knows why he didn't bivvy up and wait for rescue. We'd been on the ale in the Sun Inn in Coniston when we was called. Pissed as rats.' He looked at Norris, grinning, his face disintegrating, suddenly a mass of creases. 'There we were, in a single file, charging up the Band out of Langdale, trying to find our way in the dark, farting pure Theakston's. Bloody dreadful it was. They reckoned you could smell us from down in the Old Dungeon Gill. Never forget that night. Dead easy finding our way down, with this poor bugger bouncing on the stretcher. We just headed for the stink. Still hanging about on the way down. No problem.'

Norris grinned, seeing the humour.

'Ten more minutes and Alex can spell you. Get your head down for a while.' But Nobby Clarke wasn't listening. Instead, he gestured with his chin. Lyncean, he'd seen something moving, way out on the horizon.

'Dust cloud. Right. One o'clock. Converging.' If he felt worried, he hid it.

Norris looked, then, turning, spoke over his shoulder.

'Alex. You awake? Best buckle up. This could be rough.'

They were tense, watching the dust spewed up from the wheels of a vehicle not unlike their own. Nobby had been right. It was converging. If they took no evasive action, they would meet two miles further on, perhaps on the ridge line.

'You want I should lose him?' Nobby, calm, watched the other vehicle's progress, gauging where he should start to take evasive action to miss the intercept.

'Leave him be for a while. We don't want to cause a stir. Let's watch what happens. Put your foot down. See if he stays with us.'

'Music to my ears. Been dying to try this baby.' The gear change was smooth, practised, as Nobby rammed the lever forward, taking the vehicle up the incline faster, concentrating hard now, steering around the boulders strewn across their path.

The distant vehicle followed, keeping to its course, driving at them into the sun, the advantage with Norris. The vehicle was outlined clearly as the two converged. Open topped, a group in it, three, maybe four. Sunlight flashed from the windscreen, the reflected brilliance momentarily hiding the occupants as the gap between them closed. He had been right. Four men, a large-calibre machine-gun mounted on a tripod. Norris could see the uniforms now, the dusty berets on their heads, the glint of a brass badge or button. Anxiously he watched as one of them climbed into the rear behind the gun and stood swaying, hanging on to the firing handles as he tried to steady himself.

Suddenly, flashes, pinpricks of bright light. Roman candles as the tracer bullets curved lazily towards them, not hitting, not even close, yet making them duck, instinctively hunching their shoulders. They watched the trajectory, the ricochets in slow motion. A warning burst, or the gunner was a poor shot. Norris hoped it was the latter.

'Go, Nobby! Lose the bastard!'

Now they were motoring, bouncing over rocks that could no longer be avoided. Nobby wrenched the wheel, crossing the ridge and turning sharp left down an incline away from their pursuers, the engine howling as the turbo kicked in. The gap was closing, not from the other's greater speed, but from the obtuse angle at which the two vehicles were approaching and the terrain that was forcing them closer together. At the bottom of the ridge, open desert, hard, flat gravel and good going. The big off-road tyres hummed over the surface, stretching them away, the dust hiding them, making them a hard target, difficult to hit.

'He's stopping, I think. Can't see too well.' Alex was looking over his shoulder, through the rear window of the cab, straining to see through the dust that spewed from under their rear wheels. 'Either he's given up or . . . shit! He's firing!' More tracer crackled overhead, this time closer, now that the gunner was static, not bouncing around over the rough terrain. He was positioned part way up the ridge, shooting down at them, a target going away fast.

Suddenly, the gunner found them, the heavy bullets thudding into the armoured plate at the rear of the truck. Nobby spun the wheel in a wide arc across the cab, weaving now, irregular zigzags, stirring up as much dust as possible, making them harder to hit. A longer burst and the Toyota swerved alarmingly, Nobby steering as best he could.

'Tyre! They've hit a tyre.' Nobby, yelling, fighting to keep the truck on a straight course, strove to prevent it turning over. 'I'll have to stop. It'll wreck the suspension, else.' They slewed across the track, Nobby caressing the wheel, still not gripping tight, instead, letting it flow through his fingers. Then, still, dust settling on them in open desert with nowhere to hide. Already in the distance, the ominous sound of the approaching Iraqi vehicle, louder as it drew nearer. First Richard, then Alex, got out of the truck. Nobby hesitated, bending forward in the cab, reaching under the seat. Richard guessed he would be hiding the Loran, the evidence that would prove they weren't as they appeared. They waited, despairing, wondering.

The Iraqi jeep stopped in a swirl of dust about thirty metres from them, the gunner watching warily as the other three climbed out and approached them. There was a caginess about them, nothing casual nor left to chance. The three advanced, rifles up in the shoulder, leaving a clear field of fire for the gunner in the jeep. They had fanned out.

None of them answered when the patrol shouted. Instead they watched apprehensively, letting them get in close. Seeing Norris and his party were unarmed brought a confidence to their step. Rifles, once aimed, were lowered. They stopped, ten metres away. One, the leader, spoke, the Arabic too fast for Norris. He stood his ground with Alex and Nobby, waiting, tense, the sun warm on his shoulders as it dropped down the sky, stretching their shadows.

Two of the patrol had lowered their rifles, careless, resting the butts on the ground, hands over the muzzles, feet spread, relaxed, confident now that there was no danger. One took out a packet of cigarettes, fidgeting to get one to his mouth. The leader watched them, uncertain, his rifle still up in the aim, but half-hearted now. The one with the cigarette dropped his rifle.

He spoke in Arabic, remonstrating with himself.

It was a typewriter, Norris thought afterwards. An old Olympus model. Somebody typing at forty-odd words a minute.

Clicketty–clack–clicketty–clack.

Strips of Nobby Clarke's desert coat flew into the air like butterflies seeking a resting place, the cloth flowing out like streamers on the front of a fan. The three men staggered, thrown backwards as the bullets cut into them, dark marks appearing on their chests, pieces flying off as if handfuls of raspberries had been scattered. The soldiers crumpled, slumping to the ground, rifles falling from their fingers.

It was suddenly quiet.

Nobby had the gun out from under his coat, the silencer, fat, ugly, a thin stream of smoke curling from its end. He snapped it up into his shoulder to take the one behind the gun in the jeep. Horrified at the carnage, yelling, frightened, the gunner leaped from the vehicle, not using the big machine-gun to chew them into minced meat. Instead, he ran into the desert away from the vehicles, towards a gully behind and to his right.

'Shit.'

The gun in Nobby's hands, empty.

Alex, galvanized into action, bounded forward, heaving a body aside, shifting it from a weapon, then snatching it up into his shoulder, about to fire at the running soldier. Norris watched, holding his breath. Nothing, no shot. Alex cursed, tearing at the cocking handle, trying to free a jam in the breech. Too late. The fleeing man weaved away and leaped into a deep *waadi*. Alex flung the weapon away.

'Come on!'

Already, Norris and Alex and Nobby were running in pursuit, spreading out, a net to catch the fleeing soldier. Nobby with his shuffling run, deceptive in its speed, breaking off to the right while the less agile Alex went left. Norris took the direct line into the gully, pausing briefly to listen at the entrance. He jumped in.

Immediately he picked out the sound of footsteps, uneven, tripping, stumbling in their eagerness to be gone. He followed into the depression, unable to see or hear the others above the high bank. Alone, running hard, not yet breathing heavily, he drove after his quarry. Rounding a bend, he saw the soldier looking behind him as he ran, afraid as Norris gained on him, knowing that to be caught was his death. Norris ran on, faster now, concentrating on the dark sweat patches in the uniform shirt as the Iraqi ducked round a huge boulder thirty metres on. He would catch him now.

He sprinted past the boulder, ignoring Nobby's warning shout.

Suddenly, the exploding pain, a blackness in his head, dizzy, sick with the agony that grew in him, spreading numbness to his arms. He tried to breathe, impossible without air to keep the body functioning, a tightness in his throat. Blackness, turning to a haze of dizzy red. Now, his mouth open, he gasped for air, frightened at the roaring in his ears. He swam lazily away from the sunlight, into the darkness, knowing it was into death.

Nobby Clarke, running hard along the lip of the gully, tried desperately to keep Norris in sight. He could no longer see the soldier, now some distance in front of them. Following the line of the gully, he suddenly saw Norris, then Alex, on the far bank, slightly behind him. The soldier was nowhere, vanished, not running any more. Alarm bells clanged in Nobby Clarke's head as he searched the gully below, now splitting into two, forking to the left, the main course bearing straight ahead. Watching, he saw Norris hesitate then take the left fork, choked further on by a large boulder broken away from the wall.

At the boulder, suddenly, a figure stood, arm drawn back.

He yelled a warning, too late, as Norris skirted the rock. The Iraqi, hidden until now, had appeared from deep shadow as Norris passed, a stone held in his hand ready to throw. The thud was heavy, audible, the rock hitting Norris in the back of the head, felling him. Norris collapsed on all fours, head hanging, as the Arab soldier leapt at him, holding him in the sand with a knee jammed into the small of his back.

Nobby, desperate, lunged forward, knowing he was already too late. The lock was on Mr N., the soldier heaving backwards and upwards, using all his strength as he had been taught in his unarmed combat training. The neck, then the spine, would be broken. He cursed at not having picked up one of the rifles back at the trucks, angry he could do nothing to save the man who had once saved him. Running on, he leapt, hurling himself forward, feeling the strain, the tightness in his legs preventing him going faster.

The screaming obscenities. He could not go on with the agony of his ankle. Still, the NCOs driving, cursing, mocking him through the pain.

P Company.

He had done it all, everything that had been demanded of him.

The 'tabbing'.

Milling.

The fucking Trainasium.

Go!

He leapt from the bank of the gully, yelling, not thinking, feet thrust out from him, crashing into the Arab soldier who was so intent on killing his lieutenant. Now, in the sand and dust and the gravel of this unknown place, he fought, with no other idea than to kill. Fist, elbow, boot, anything that would do the job. The soldier fought desperately but could not match the strength of the bigger man. Nobby Clarke, the wild light of madness in his eyes, beat huge fists into the face and head, stopping only when the mess of his hands told him it was over.

He stood from straddling the soldier, chest heaving, arms weak from the hammering. The body, forlorn, lay broken in the sand. Nobby looked up at the crunch of boots, as Alex jumped from the far wall into the gully. He too, was breathing hard from running. Not, like Nobby, from killing.

'Shit, Nobby. That was close.' Alex was sucking in air, looking down at the body. 'How's Richard? I thought he was a goner. God knows how you were able to reach him in time. Hell of a leap. I didn't think you could make a jump like that.' Alex thumped him on the shoulder. 'You OK?' He paused, grinning. 'I'm bloody glad we never did do the milling, back in Aldershot. I would hate to end up like that poor bastard.'

Norris was lying close to the rock that had hidden the

soldier. Alex dropped to his knees, concerned for his friend, lifting his head, gentle, unusual in such a big man. He loosened clothing pulled tight in the fighting. Norris coughed, once, then again, as the air was sucked back into empty lungs. At last his eyes opened, surprised to find himself alive, not dead as he ought to have been. He put his hands to his throat, massaging the back of his head and neck and rolling his shoulders, easing the pain.

'Shit.' He was coughing, the sound rasping in his throat, hurting him.

'Thank God. I thought I might have had to give you the kiss of life. No knowing what Nobby would be thinking if he'd seen that. Seriously, you OK?'

'Yes, at least I think so. My throat feels as if I've been eating barbed wire with acid dressing.' He hawked again, then, holding his head in his hands, shook it wearily. 'I'll be all right. I shouldn't have let him take me like that. I wasn't thinking. I just wanted to stop the bastard, although God knows where he thought he might be going. Out here.' He motioned with his chin, indicating the wasteland.

Turning, he looked again at the dead soldier, shapeless, crumpled in untidy death, flies already encrusting the congealed blood of his features where his face had been, before Nobby Clarke had beaten it to a pulp.

'I see old Clarke's not lost his delicate touch. Thank heavens he reached me in time. Where is he? Nobby?'

'Back at the truck, fixing the wheel, calm as you like. Do we bury them? The Iraqis?'

'Yes, but away from their vehicle. Far enough to prevent their being found in a cursory search. Who knows, maybe their unit will think they've deserted, or gone AWOL.' Norris was pensive. 'It beats me how they were on to us so damned quickly. It's not like them, even the Republican Guard, to open up on a vehicle just on spec. They were trying to waste us, no doubt about it.' Thoughtful, he turned, walking back in the direction of the truck, where Nobby, stripped, was changing the wheel. Norris stopped, hesitating. He bent for one of the weapons, staring at it in his hands.

'Something he said when he dropped his rifle. I just had the feeling . . . something that's been bothering me.' Norris frowned, trying to think, dredging back through his mind. 'My Arabic is a bit rusty, but I heard him say, "*aysh 'amalt*". Something odd about it. I . . . oh, I don't know. The bottle. Trying to pop up to the surface. I mentioned it, way back, when we were in the flat.' How long ago? He shrugged. 'It's probably nothing.'

The two walked back to the truck and Nobby working with the jack and base-board. Shoulders pale against the sunburned forearms, he looked sadly at the wheel with its fat cross-country tyre, now in shreds.

'Bastards.' They heard him, clearly.

'Nobby, you bloody crook. Where did you get the gun?'

Nobby Clarke looked up, grinning, then back at the wheel.

'Bastards,' he said again.

Dusk, quiet, eerie, the engine cooled and no longer ticking. They huddled, grouped around the map spread on the warm bonnet of the Toyota. The middle of them looked at the other two, first one, then the other. Both shook their heads, understanding what was required of them without the need to ask questions. The map was folded and thrust into a pocket under the shapeless desert coat. They looked about them, then pulled a camouflage net over the truck, hiding it amongst the rocks. Shouldering their packs, they turned up the slope heading for the faint line that marked the top of the ridge.

The village would be beyond it, in the valley.

Qis'aam.

The schoolmaster, their guide, lived somewhere in the village. They would lie up, watching the place, all day, and the next if need be, then go in and find him.

It was decided.

Alex Howard would go down into the village, find the schoolmaster and bring him back. The schoolmaster knew where to find the Great Crack, the fissure which they would use to find a route up the face of the escarpment and on to the plateau. There was no other way up.

They needed the knowledge of the schoolmaster.

Alex would bring him out.

They slept in shifts, hidden.

The noise was not unusual, a big truck, a long way off.

Norris, awake, paid no attention.

None at all.

A new day, a greyness merging with the dark, a gradual paleness, softening the harsh lines of the buildings, hiding those still in shadow on the dark side of the street. The smells of the village came to him, assaulting his senses, heavy in the still air, spoiling its crispness. Yesterday's cooking, drain smells, clung to the stone walls of the rude buildings that surrounded him.

He shivered, cold in the new morning.

He wondered where everyone was. It was deserted, much too quiet, nothing moving. No people, no sound in his ears but the scuffing of his sandalled feet on the compressed dirt of the road. Suddenly he was worried, the boarded-up shops, the deserted houses, creating an unreal, ghostly atmosphere. Only the tumbleweed was missing. He reached a corner, stopped, and peered carefully around it, scanning the street on both sides. Empty. He spun quickly, the noise alarming him. The dog, emaciated, its ribs standing out from the mangy hair, loped away from the overturned can in which it had been searching for food, lazy with its movements, resenting the intruder. Otherwise, silence.

Turning into a narrow street, he walked flat-footed, stooped to disguise his height, the *thawb* hiding the exaggerated bend of his knees. Again, he wondered why he could see no people, no early-morning workers hurrying to tend the meagre crops struggling to grow at the entrance to the village. They should have been there before the sun came up, as they had been the previous day. He turned another corner, angry at his carelessness, annoyed he had forgotten to look first, checking it was clear. He saw the reason for the emptiness.

At the far end of the street, in a small square, a pantechnicon was parked, its ramp open, resting on the dusty ground. The men of the village were sitting crowded together, where they would be in the sun when it came up fully, later in the day. A group of soldiers in dusty uniforms guarded the group. Rifles, ready for use, were held across their bodies.

Alex stopped, alarmed. But he had been seen, immediately he had turned the corner. He hesitated, made to leave, then changed his mind as the four-man patrol came from the far end of the street. Indecision. Not like Alex Howard. Briefly he wondered if he might outrun them, then knew that he could not. Not the Kalashnikovs. They were shouting, waving their rifles. The soldiers by the furniture van looked up, two of them detaching from the main group. They came for him, spread, one each side of the road, limiting his options, cutting off escape. The four from behind closed in. He was taken, worried, wondering what Richard and Nobby were doing, and whether they could see him from their position up on the ridge.

He said nothing, shaking his head when they spoke to him in a tongue he did not understand. He tugged the *shimargh* over his mouth, drawn tight across his face, squinting to hide the greyness of his eyes, the fear that was in them. Weapons menacing, gesticulating, pointed to the van, sinister in the centre of the square. He approached it, fearful of what it might contain, seeing others ushered into its dark interior. Suddenly he realized what was to happen. They would be taken, God alone knowing where, questioned, discovered. The torture would follow, then death. In his alarm, he tried to remember if he was carrying anything. Papers, maps, identity. He was clean. Except for the knife, the lucky charm which he carried everywhere, and was never without. Less than an inch in length, stainless steel, a picture of a Challenger tank etched into one side, the other with the words: R.O.F. LEEDS 16 MARCH 1983; it was a souvenir, a company handout, given to all those attending the factory demonstration of the tank's capabilities.

He had carried it in his pocket ever since.

Norris would have been mad, had he known. But it had been so small, so insignificant. Now he knew he must be rid of it. Hands in pockets, he ground his fingers into the material until he forced it out through a split in the lining. He felt the warm metal hit his thigh and calf as it fell down inside the baggy trousers he wore under the *thawb*. He shook his leg.

In the middle of the group, he filed up the ramp of the van, already full, it seemed, with men from other villages. He almost panicked, breaking away, wanting to run from this evil place. A soldier, grinning, barred his way, rifle held up, a barrier he could not cross. Alex hesitated, remembering to stoop, disguising his height, the mass of his body, angry as the rifle butt thumped into his shoulder, hurting. Fearfully he looked inside the truck, feeling the heat coming from it, smelling those already there.

It was dark.

He shuffled in, the sun left outside.

More from behind were forced into the mass, already packed tight, making it impossible to move. He bit hard into his lip, afraid that some small sound might betray his fear. Unafraid of heights, able to stand physical pain beyond the threshold of most men, knowing little fear of death itself even.

Alex had never told anyone.

He was terrified of the dark.

*

The war had not long been won. He had been nearly five years old and England was a mess from the bombing and sweets were still on ration. Depressing for grown-ups, fun for a child, with so much to explore. They had lived in Waterlooville then, and one Saturday he had gone with his parents into the smashed city that had once been Portsmouth, its harbour and naval facilities prime targets for the Luftwaffe. They had taken Johnny Stevens, Alex's friend, someone to keep him company while his parents examined what had been left of their house, wrecked by a V1 rocket. Alex, years later, was to remember his father's imitation of the Doodlebug droning overhead, the engine cutting out to let the rocket tip and fall to earth and explode, wrecking someone's home, their life.

The two boys, eyes sparkling, had laughed at the impromptu demonstration, then stopped, sensing the sadness as the parents had turned into what had been their road to stare at what had once been their home, now a pile of rubble, jutting beams and broken floorboards. He had reached up and taken their hands, one in each of his own, trying to understand what it all meant, and why they had to stay with Aunty Eileen, instead of in a house of their own.

He shouldn't have let go of his father's hand and chased into the ruins after the puppy. It was only a stray, probably looking for food. Especially he should have heeded the anxious, alarmed shouts from both of them. But the puppy was there, just under a pile of twisted wood and rubble, through a hole that he was just small enough to squeeze into.

Come on, boy, there's a good boy.

But the pup, perhaps frightened at his eagerness, evaded him, moving further into the dark tunnel. He could see its eyes glinting in the thin shaft of light behind him, hear it whimpering. First on all fours, then flat on his belly, he squeezed after it, trying to coax the animal to him. Very dark now; his shoulders brushing the walls of the tunnel, he could no longer see the bright eyes shining. Just the whimper, a little further into the dark. Then, at last, he reached it, groping then holding it by a furry front leg, a soft pink paw, trying to tempt it to him. He gathered it, tugging it into his cradled arms.

It was then he realized he could not turn. He tried to shuffle out backwards, but his foot caught against something. Faintly he heard the alarmed shouts at the entrance to the hole, a long way away. He tried not to be afraid, tugging, trying to free his foot. One final heave and it moved, bringing the tunnel down on him, filling his mouth and eyes with thick acrid dust. He could see nothing. Nor could he hear. Just the dog, yowling, louder the more frightened it became.

He tried to move but could not.

Something heavy, sharp, dug into the small of his back, hurting, trapping him.

Panic, wanting the light, the air, the cleanliness of the day that he had left behind. He yelled, his voice piping, trembling in his fear, worse as the time passed. Where were his parents? What were they doing? Why hadn't his father dug him out? Dad! Mum! I'm here. Don't leave me. Please don't leave me. He let go of the puppy. He could move nothing other than his hands. He began to tear at the bricks and the wood and the blocks that held him, but could not move them, only dislodge more dust into the darkness of the hole, filling his mouth and nostrils. Crying, screaming, he yelled for them to come and get him.

Head rested on his forearms, he wept.

He had no idea how long he had been there. An hour, an afternoon, a day. A lifetime, an eternity. For ever, sometimes sleeping, always crying whenever he was awake. The pup was nowhere and he could only suppose it had found a way out, further along the tunnel. Tell them where I am, little puppy dog, that I'm stuck and afraid and don't want to stay here. I want my mum, my dad . . .

He slept and dreamed and cried and slept.

Shaking, sobbing, terrified he would be there for ever

and that the terrible Jerries, those bogey men who started the war, would come for him, even though England was supposed to have won . . .

Noises. Rumbling. Light.

He thought people were shouting, calling his name as the weight was at last raised from his back. Gentle hands lifted him, the rough serge of the fireman's coat against his cheek, a shiny button pressed into his face. Someone – the fireman, his father – carried him to an ambulance, its big shiny brass bell ringing as it rushed him away. Someone putting a mask over his face, terrifying him until he tasted the delicious sweetness of the oxygen. His father, leaning over him, his mother too, her face streaked from her tears and anxiety. He tried to smile through the mask but could not. Light-headed, flying through the air . . .

The memory of it faded with the passing of the years.

Then later, at his prep school, finding with the others an old wooden locker lying on its side behind the sports pavilion. They had been playing hide-and-seek, and this was the perfect place. Lifting the door, he lowered himself into it, missing the stealthy approach of the other kids as they crept back to it. He lay in the box, a coffin, not hearing the pranksters outside in the sunlight, the sound of a peg as it was fitted through the hasp and staple of the doors.

It was quiet, dark as he lay in the box. He was not, at first, worried. Just a game of hide-and-seek. Until he tried to get out. Finding the door jammed tight, he pushed, heaved, kicked and threw himself at it. But it would not budge, not even to let in a chink of clean sunlight. The memories of the tunnel, the puppy, rushed into his mind, filling his head. Blubbing then, unashamedly, he screamed at the top of his lungs, beating with small fists on the wooden door, a small boy, afraid in the dark. His fingers, raw from scrabbling at the rough wood, were blistered, bleeding, hurting him. Still he scratched at the door.

In the distance, the ringing of a bell, summoning them back to class. He was alone.

He did not know how long he lay there, trapped like an animal, before he heard someone outside. The cheerful whistling stopped suddenly at the sound of his yelling. Finally, the lid was raised, as old Thompson, the groundsman, peered worriedly in, bending to help the weeping, frightened boy, lifting him from the place of his anguish. The man had held him, comforting, the smell of damp grass about him, smoke from the bonfire thick on the leather of his jerkin. Alex, angry and afraid, had soundly beaten the leader of the group who had locked him in the box.

He had never gone into a dark, confined place since.

Until now.

The strip of sunlight climbed the far wall as the ramp was raised, the clang of bolts loud in the stillness of the morning. He could not move. Pressed into the men around him, he listened to the gasping moans and smelled the reek of bodies close to his face. He had no idea of the passage of time. It grew hotter as the sun climbed into the sky, making it unbearable inside the van. Those around him whimpered, some openly crying or praying aloud in high singsong voices. He too prayed, as he had in the box behind the sports stadium. Some slumped, fainted or died, prevented from falling by those around them. His brain swam as he sucked for air that was not to be found, not to be shared. Sweat burst from him, soaking his clothes.

Alex, almost crying, barely conscious, prayed silently to his God who had forsaken him. Hallucinating, he dreamed of white beaches, high mountains in the crisp air of an early dawn. Paddling in the lake at the Academy, the June ball, laughing with her as she pulled the long dress up over her ankles. He could feel the cool wetness on his own feet.

He shook his head, coming back, keeping alive. The heat, the smell. Worst of all, the dark. Shaking from uncontrollable spasms as the fear spread through him, he wondered at the pain in his ankle, the cool at his feet. His ankle. The cool . . .

'Jesus.' Barely breathed.

Faintly whispered, yet noticed.

'*Ingleeze?*' The voice was beside him, close, or he would not have been heard. He held his breath, controlling the shaking.

'English?' It came again, the accent educated, polished. 'We are in this together, my friend, whoever you may be. Are you one of the Englishmen? One of those they are seeking?'

The voice carried no menace in it.

'Yes. English.' Alex gasped, searching for air, feeling the cool, the pain in his ankle. It was definitely cooler, lower down by his feet. He turned his head a fraction, seeking the man. He spoke, fighting to keep his voice calm.

'Listen. There's something. Low down. Talk to the others, get them to give me room, so I can get down on the floor.' Alex wondered if he had been understood, if he had been believed. But the man spoke softly to those closest to him, then, low voices as the message was passed, mouths pressed close to ears. Alex, obsessed with the feeling at his ankle, fought against the rising panic, wanting movement, freedom to find the cause. Gradually at first, almost indiscernible, came the shift. The pressure on him eased, as the men moved fractionally away from him, giving him space, air, freedom. At last he could move an arm, then two. He could bend at the knees.

'Listen out for me. Relay my instructions.'

The mass of men moved, forcing the dead or fainted

out of the way. Those who could squeezed up on to the shoulders of those beside them, making room, space for Alex Howard to find out why his ankle felt cool. He was being trusted but would never find out why. Gradually he bent his knees, forcing through the press of bodies to the floor.

The crush of men closed in over his head.

He wondered if he had imagined it all.

The glasses, tight in his fists, shook.

Unable to hold them still, he fought to control his anxiety. He had seen the van, parked up, hidden from anyone coming into the village from the south where it would be out of sight until the first rays of sun picked it out. He cursed, knowing it was the engine he had heard the previous night. Now he knew. Alex had not been up on the ridge with the glasses and had not seen it. He had been taken. Norris swore. Nobby Clarke, his expression quizzical, heard the worry in Richard's voice. The two looked at each other.

'They've taken Alex. Locked him in a furniture van with a few hundred others. Poor bastard. It'll be like an oven in there as soon as the sun comes up for real.' He looked again through the field-glasses.

'Can't do owt till it's dark.' Nobby spoke, his voice wary. He knew Norris, knew he would be working the angles, assessing their chances. Mad bastard. Nobby would follow him though, no matter what. Norris was like that. Men followed him without asking why. Nobby Clarke knew the reason. He would not forget, ever. The Radfan, Lieutenant Richard Norris killing, to keep Corporal Nobby Clarke alive. Yesterday, in the gully, at least, he'd balanced the sheet.

They spelled each other watching the village. All through the day the van stood in the square, starkly outlined in the harsh glare of the sun. It was hot, even with

153

the cape for shade and with a breeze blowing up the hill to cool them. God alone knew what it was like inside the van. Norris dozed on and off, when it wasn't his turn to stare through the lenses at the village below. They watched, timing the change of sentries. When it was dark, he and Nobby would go down into the valley to see if they could pull Alex Howard out of the shit.

At last, dusk.

There was no movement in the village, but moving lights as the guards patrolled around the van, vehicles coming and going. At last that, too, stopped. Now, except for a dog barking in the distance, it was quiet, the village a dark mass down on the plain. Time to go. Neither man spoke. They left their gear, hidden, then turned, crawling down the hill. Once off the skyline, they could stand and walk like men.

Norris led, not hearing Nobby Clarke behind him.

Alex could move, barely.

Feet stood on him as the men moved to fill the gap, the space he had left when he slid to the floor. They were heavy, hurting his legs, his belly and chest. He heaved, moving them enough to turn on to his front. The weight was on his back now as the mass of men above him sought relief. He lay, unmoving, wondering what was to become of him now that he could not stand, could hardly move for the weight pressing down on him.

He let his head fall to the floor of the truck, tears mingling with the sweat on his face. He was desperately afraid of dying, hidden in this awful hole with a hundred more destined to a similar fate. Alex prayed, as he did, when he was afraid, yet seldom thinking of his God when things were good, when there was no fear in him.

He remembered why he was on the floor, not standing

as he had been. He felt it then on his cheek, insignificant if it had not been so important. Air. Air that was fresh, not stinking, fetid like that where the men were squeezed together, dying as they stood. His air. Alex Howard's air, fresh, clean, filtering through the small hole in the floor of the truck, taken greedily, guarded jealously. He clamped his mouth over the tiny hole, sucking precious life giving air, clean and sweet in the stench of the truck.

He had felt it on his ankle. That and the pain. The pain was the knife with the Challenger tank on it, now caught in the baggy trousers, bloused and tied with a strip of cloth. The pain had come from the knife where it stuck into him at a sharp angle.

He began to explore the hole, no more than a few millimetres across. It was a screw hole without the screw. He gulped in the fresh air, a greedy secret, for the moment protected from the others. Heaving at the heap of men pressing down on him, he made sufficient room to be able to drag an arm up to his face. Probing, searching, he found the line of screws holding the thick steel plate of the floor to the chassis of the truck. He counted three small round headed screws. Stretching out his hand, he squeezed it down his body, through the mess of feet and legs, then bent his leg until he could touch his ankle. He worried the knife free, afraid lest he should drop it and lose the precious tool in the feet that shuffled about him.

Carefully he worked it up to his face, tugging at the narrow screwdriver blade with a thumbnail, relieved when he felt it snap open. He worked in the dark, alone, stopping to take in air, knowing that some were dying above him. The blade was too small for the job, slipping and burring the screw-head. It took all the strength of his fingers to hold it in the head of the screw as he twisted, trying to tease it out from its rusty lair.

It would not shift.

He tried the second, searching until the blade slotted into the head. Again the gradual twisting, with all the strength of his fingers, hurting from the pressure, sweating with the effort, unable to get a proper purchase. Then, suddenly, it moved. A tiny, imperceptible jump. Concentrating, grinding his teeth, he worked assiduously at his task. Sweat streamed from his chin on to his hands, making the knife slippery in his fingers.

A quarter-turn.

A half.

One full turn, easier now as the screw worked out of the hole, a machine doing its job. He worked, steady, unhurried, painstakingly slow, avoiding burring the head of the screw. He heard it quite clearly as it fell on to the metal floor. More air, this time from a second hole. He sucked, tasting it, like clean water from a spring. Two holes. He went back to the first, slow, easy, slotting the blade into the soft metal. Stubborn, it remained unmoving, defying him, mocking him. He tried, he really tried.

The screw would not shift.

Alex dropped his head on to his forearms, rubbing the sweat from his eyes, his big body shaking in fear and frustration. Sweat that might have been tears. In the darkness he worked his fingers along the line, through the heat of the sweating ankles crowded around him, eventually finding another he had missed when he had looked first. This one came out, easy, almost as if it was oiled. But not the first, the one he had found initially. Stubbornly solid, nothing he tried would shift it. Despair gnawed at him, knowing he was so close. Had there been room, he might have beaten his fists on the steel plate.

Not wanting to give up, he probed, searching along the line of the floor. He could get his fingers under the sheet of metal, feeling it sharp against the flesh. He pulled. It moved, a fraction, but definite movement. Desperately he sought the English speaker.

'The men. They must move, give me room. Tell them to shift. Away from me.'

Alex had no idea how long he had been working on

the floor of the truck. It might have been an hour or a day. Breath held, he listened for a reply, terrified, praying the man had not died in the crush. Then, he heard the gasp of the unseen man's voice above the moaning as the mass of men moved away from him. As the weight lifted from his back and shoulders, he moved until he could squat before the press of bodies was back on him.

He squeezed his eyes shut.

Feet flat, back straight, the classic position of the weight lifter. He let his mind drift away, to the work-out room in his Reading flat in the cool green of an English spring.

He pictured the weights heavy on the mat, the bar gleaming, except where he had smeared it with chalk for a better grip. The sun poured in through the open window. He had never done it. Not 180 kilograms. Gripping the bar, feet shuffling for better purchase, he blew the air from his lungs, concentrating, as Norris told him he would never press 180 kilograms. Not even you, Alex. He stared at the bar, scrubbing his hands around its roughness, a circular motion, picturing the bend in it when the weights came up off the floor.

He heaved.

Nothing, only pain in his hands as the rough metal tore at his fingers. Gasping, he rested, his head hanging, the men trying to give him the room he needed. He cleared his mind of everything except the sight of the weights, then squeezed his fingers tighter under the metal sheet.

Breathe out, hard.

Hold it.

Concentrate.

Alex Howard pulled upwards with all his strength, tendons, muscles, tearing at the effort, panting, grunting with the strain. An age, suspended from his fingertips, hurting, pulling. Nothing, still. His teeth hurt as they ground together, veins proud from his neck as he applied the relentless pressure to the floor. He wanted to scream, but knew he could not.

Then, suddenly, the ripping, tearing, of splintered wood, the floor bending up in his hands. Sighing, he gasped, as the air, clean, fresh with the smell of the night on it, poured in through the hole he had made. The crowd, those that were still alive, scented it too, animals penned in like a herd smelling water at the end of a cattle drive.

He listened. Nothing. He had not been heard.

Slowly, Alex peeled up the floor of the truck, making a gap big enough for him to squeeze through. He stood his full height, a broad back keeping the mob from the hole. Breathing deeply, he turned, squeezing through the press and leant against the wall of the van. He pushed with his feet to widen the hole, feeling the air rushing, tumbling cleanly into the confined space which had been their prison.

Heaving the men away from him, he dropped to his knees.

In the dim light he could see the chassis, road springs, and smell axle grease.

He could see the ground.

Norris had never understood how a man as big as Nobby Clarke could move so quietly. He had not heard him as they had come down off the ridge and would not have known he was there until they stopped and he came up beside him. The rough track was widening as they drew closer to the village. Cautiously he moved off its surface, creeping instead along its edge. A shape loomed out of the darkness, square, ugly, the house of dirty stone which they had seen from the ridge. The village was close.

They stopped, waiting in its shadow, peering into the darkness, alert for anything out of the ordinary, any sound that they could not identify. A dog barked, the same one they had heard earlier. Otherwise, quiet, their breathing the only sound. There was a gap that had to be crossed before they would be swallowed in the shadows of the buildings of the village. There was no moon to break the impenetrable blackness of the night. Fast, the only way, not creeping like a ghost in the night.

He took Nobby's hand, bending the fingers into a fist, then jerked it rapidly up and down, like wanking. But it was understood. Double, go like the clappers. A deep breath, and Norris was away, sprinting on the balls of his feet, upright, not crouched, which would only slow him. He reached the wall, deep in shadow. Turning, he looked for Nobby, seeing nothing, but hearing his breathing when he got close to the wall. They turned into the dark street, moving quickly now that they were in deep shadow. Leading the way, Norris pictured the village layout, trying to remember the location of the van. The van with Alex in it. If he was still alive.

There was one sentry, sitting with his back resting against one of the wheels. They hoped he was asleep. Norris searched the square, feeling the tug at his arm. He looked in the direction Nobby was pointing, seeing at once the jeep with the machine-gun mounted in the back, not heavy calibre like the one in the desert, but smaller, probably a Russian PKS, 7.62 mm. The only light to see by came from an open door in one of the buildings close to the van. It was probably being used as a guardroom.

Tugging gently, he led Nobby around the buildings that made up the square, keeping into the shadows. They moved crabwise, shuffling sideways, keeping their backs close to the wall. An alley appeared suddenly, another obstacle to cross. Norris, about to move, felt the tug at his coat. Nobby was pointing upwards to the roof of the building. A set of rough stone steps led up on to it.

This time Nobby led, silent, skimming the ground, almost as if he were not in contact with it. Norris followed, tiptoeing up the broken stone steps until they reached the flat roof. They rolled over the parapet, then lay with hearts beating, pulses quickened with the tension in them. They crossed the roof, moving slowly, quiet on hands and knees, to the low wall at the other side. Together they peered over the parapet. The van was across the square, maybe fifty metres, the jeep directly below with two men asleep in the front seats.

They sat, backs to the parapet, as Norris tried to work out what to do. They had to get the gun. The gun controlled the square. Whoever had the gun controlled the village since all routes led into or out of the square below.

Tapping Nobby softly on the shoulder, he held his hands up as if firing a machine-gun, then pointed over the parapet, jabbing his finger downwards. Nobby Clarke nodded, understanding. Kneeling, they looked at the jeep ten feet below them. They climbed slowly up on to the low wall, crouching, gathering for the leap that would take them down and carry them once more into battle.

Norris looked over at Nobby, his thumb in the air.

Like Alex, on the roof in Boston . . .

Nobby Clarke nodded, his face invisible, but grim. Norris knew.

Without warning a sudden curse broke the silence as the sentry at the pantechnicon scrambled to his feet, bending to look under, then yelling something in Arabic. Norris saw the rifle, the curved magazine, the dull glint of the bayonet in the light from the door as the soldier raised it in the classic position for a sharp, downward thrust.

Horrified, he watched as the soldier drove downwards.

A killing stroke.

Clean air, like water, gushed into the truck, washing over him. He gulped the freshness, feeling the stirring as those closest to him tried to find the source. Sensing the beginning of panic, the madness that would soon start, he whispered hoarsely, seeking the man who spoke his language. Using his great strength to hold the mass back, away from the hole, he gasped.

160

'Speak to them. They must give me room. I have to find a way out and see if there are any sentries. They *must* keep quiet.' He heard the man's voice, urgent, angry, perhaps pleading. But the pressing against him stopped. They waited, tense, quivering. Alex could feel the restlessness. It would take nothing to start the stampede. Again, he was reminded of a thirsty herd at the end of a long, dusty cattle-drive, the water gurgling.

He bent, ducking his head into the night, savouring the clean dampness, looking, listening, hearing only a dog in the distance, barking half-heartedly. There was something else he could not identify, animal noises, snuffling, close to the truck. Snoring. A sentry, asleep. Alex held his breath, alert, listening for other sounds, but hearing none.

He squirmed, shifting a little into a position from which he could get out through the hole feet first. But, in the crush, there was not the space. Head first, he leaned out, reaching for the prop shaft below him. He stretched for it with fingers still hurting from heaving up the floor, feeling the tightness against his shoulders. He squirmed until he could pull himself out as far as his waist. There, he waited, suspended, the edges of the hole holding him.

It could not last inside the vehicle, where the heat would still not let them breathe. It was too much to expect. The panic grew, endemic, a disease that spread as the fear grew in them. He felt them on his legs, tugging, tearing, twisting, as those closest tried to force him out of the hole. Desperate, he tried to hold on to the shaft, to prevent himself spilling untidily on to the ground. But the pressure was too much, even for him.

He fell, thumping hard on to his shoulder. Cursing, he heard the others, those that had bundled him out, gasping, as they too sought the freshness of the night. Twisting, he looked for the sentry, seeing instead the light filtering from an open doorway across the square. He tried to picture the geography of the village, but could not remember it. He rolled, away from the hole, towards the edge of the truck where it was less dark, where there was light and more air.

A pair of feet danced comically as someone tried to get up in a hurry. Behind him he heard the noise of a struggle as men fought to be free from the stink of the truck. He rolled quickly from the vehicle, wondering where the hell the feet had gone. Out into the night, still rolling, he suddenly saw the sentry above him, blotting out the faint glow from the stars. Momentarily, his face was reflected in the light from the open doorway, illuminating the features, highlighting his expression of surprise, perhaps fear.

Already, the rifle was being raised, into the classic position for a downward, killing thrust.

Alex rolled, away from the truck, desperate to avoid the bayonet. His shoulder struck the wheel, jamming him, preventing further movement. He looked up at the man who was to kill him. There was no shine to the bayonet, dirty, black gunmetal, but he could see it in the dim half-light. The sentry lunged, hard, angled down towards him. He twisted sideways, into the wheel, feeling the pain as the blade pierced the flesh of his buttock, worse as it was withdrawn for a second attempt, a boot thumped into his thigh as the soldier wrenched the bayonet free. Despairingly, he reached up, catching the muzzle of the rifle as it was pulled upwards away from him. Grimly he clung to it, knowing that to let go would be the end of him. The sentry was shouting, summoning help, surprised at the strength of the man who twisted and turned below him, gripping the end of his rifle.

Concentrating hard, Alex scrabbled with his fingers, trying to locate the release catch for the bayonet, to free it from the rifle, wondering what the hell he had to do to get it off. The soldier, panicking, could not bring the weapon up and was heaving, twisting, shouting as loud as he could.

More men spilled out of the van, not stopping to help him, instead shuffling into the night, freedom their only thought. But there was more on his mind as he fought to stay alive.

Suddenly, the bayonet was loose in his hand, a weapon, to kill with if need be. The sentry reached down to the cocking handle, snapping it back, letting it fly forwards to carry a live round up into the breech, the sound louder than the running men, the shouts of the sentry. Done for now, and Alex knew it. He fought to stay alive, forcing the barrel away from him so that he would not be shot. But the soldier, with the greater leverage, would win the uneven tug-of-war.

Growling, primeval, Alex slashed with the bayonet, feeling its bluntness glance off the sentry's leg. He remembered to stab with it, higher this time, a short, savage jab, yelling his exhilaration as he felt it bite into the knee cap, the force of the blow jarring against his fingers, driving the blade through to the back of the patella. A piercing scream sounded from above him. Before Alex could pull the blade free, the man fell, writhing in the dust of the street, gripping his leg with both hands, twisting, bucking, close to the truck wheel where Alex lay. Alex scrambled to his feet, wincing as the pain stabbed through his buttock. Now, he must kill the sentry, to stop his yelling, to prevent his summoning the others.

From nowhere, a machine-gun started yammering from across the square, the noise coming without warning, as bullets punched into the side of the van. Screaming, moaning, came from the inside as those closest to the walls were hit. The bullets, their copper jackets ripped from the soft lead core as they drilled through the walls into bodies still pressed together, brought terrible carnage inside the van. But more men were spilling out of the hole, shouting, running into the shadows, away from the vehicle, into the security of alleyways and side streets.

Feeling the tightness of his wound, Alex rolled back under the truck, away from the screaming man, into the darkness behind a wheel. He felt a sudden fear as he watched the fairy lights of the tracer bullets curving towards his hiding place. They were aiming at the fuel tank. The whole truck would go. Gasping, he rolled out, the opposite side from the gun, and started running away to safety.

The whoosh of the explosion almost flattened him and he stumbled, losing his balance, the heat burning him as the petrol ignited. Terrified screams came from those still trapped inside. The sentry who had tried to bayonet him leaped and spun in a macabre death dance, his uniform burning. Alex turned to watch, ignoring the heat, smelling the burning, the cooking, in the truck. The gun stopped firing as suddenly as it had started. It was quiet except for the crackling from the fire and the dreadful intensity of the screaming. He ran, limping, as fast as he could, away from the inferno, shadows leaping, his own a devil's dance on the walls of the buildings.

Then, above the wailing, someone yelling his name.

'Alex! Alex! For God's sake. Over here, in the jeep. Quickly, man!'

Norris was standing in the jeep, waving, Nobby Clarke crouched over the gun, pivoting it on its tripod, looking for a target. There were two bodies lying near the jeep, not moving, dead, he supposed. Norris and Nobby must have taken them out as soon as the Iraqis had started shooting at the van. The dancing flames made the scene grotesque, unreal, as the gun spat a stream of tracer, not at the truck, but at the lighted doorway. Men were running, spilling untidily from the door, some half dressed, blinded by the light from the fire, confused at the noise of the machine-gun, dying as they came out into the square. Men fell, bodies crumpling like discarded puppets as they folded untidily on the ground, yelling, moaning, some trying to jam magazines on to their weapons, others coming up into the aim, before the gun chopped them down. At last, no more came through the door. Instead, they took up firing positions inside the building, shooting through the window. The gun turned, finding them as the bullets chewed through the soft stucco of the walls.

Alex looked over his shoulder at the burning van, hearing the terror of their despair. Richard and Nobby called him again, but he turned, and without thinking, sprinted back across the square towards the fire, no longer feeling the pain of his wound. One chance. He knew he had the one chance, that he must get it right first time. He felt the heat, still yards from the truck and knew that to hesitate would be the finish of it. He would never start to run again.

Hot, the air sucked from his lungs burned as he breathed. But he was at the van, behind it, searching for the bolts that held the ramp in place. Finding them, he twisted, tugging, screaming at the fucking things to move, the hot metal of the bolts burning his hands. One clanged free, the other, stubborn, refusing to move. He grunted, almost sobbed, heaving at it, knowing that he could not move it, that it would not open. The screaming coming from inside haunted him. He tried one last time, the flames and smoke licking at his forearms, his coat smouldering. He heaved, muscles bunched, the veins thick in his arms.

The bolt would not move.

A voice, calm in the chaos.

'Here, Mr A. Give us a go at it.'

Nobby Clarke, his big hands joining his own as the two of them heaved, bellowing with the effort. Suddenly, the bolt clanged open and the ramp fell with a clatter to the ground. Men poured from the smoke, coughing, gasping, those with their clothes alight rolling on the ground to extinguish the flames. No one stopped to help those who had been caught in the fire, instead, running out of the Hell, away into the night.

The two of them ran from the heat, towards the jeep.

Nobby Clarke, disgusted, spat on the ground.

'Bastards,' he said.

'Don't be too hard on them, Nobby,' Alex gasped, his

chest heaving. 'It was bad in there. We all thought we were done. You can't blame the poor sods for legging it as soon as they got a sniff of freedom.'

'You OK? Me and Mr N., we thought you'd had it. We saw them take you when we was up on the ridge. We 'ad to wait till it was dark before we could come down. Here, drink.' Alex, away from the fire, took the canteen, drinking greedily, letting the water run down his chin into the sweat-stained shirt. He passed the canteen back, guilty, forgetting it was Nobby's water.

'There's a well. On the edge of the village. Don't worry about it.' Nobby Clarke missed nothing.

Norris was yelling, eager to be gone. The flames could be seen for miles. They made to leave, suddenly seeing a figure in the shadows, almost invisible in the dancing light from the fire. He came forward, tentative, almost shy. Alex recognized his voice.

'I will thank you, Englishman, even if the others saw fit only to run off into the night, without thought for who had saved them.' The man brushed at a smouldering sleeve, grimacing from the pain of the burn. 'If I am able, I will assist you in any way I can.'

'The schoolmaster. You can tell us where to find him, if he is still alive. Where will he go, if the village is no longer safe?'

'I am the one you call the schoolmaster, although I am no longer allowed to teach. I was captured with the rest of my village, and many more besides. Tell me how I may be of service to you.'

Nobby Clarke took him by the elbow.

'Come this way, sunshine. There's this place we're looking for—'

Chance.

A fine thing.

They would never have found the fissure, the Great Crack,

without the guide. East facing, the sun low in the sky, it had been almost invisible. Even with the schoolmaster pointing, Norris had had to stare hard through the glasses to see it. From a distance of two miles it looked like a pencil line drawn on weathered parchment. He passed the glasses to Alex, heard him whistle through his teeth, muttering as he in turn gave the binoculars to Nobby.

'That's it?'

'That is the place. The place which is called Al Shuk fee Sakr, the Great Crack. It is the only way to the top of the escarpment for fifty miles, maybe more. No one will expect you to come from this side. My cousin,' – the schoolmaster was quiet, sad, unable to conceal the pain in his dark eyes – 'in London, before he was killed, did well to tell you of this place. We found it as children, one day playing, following our father's herd. That was before we grew up, going our different ways, he to the Diplomatic Service, while I followed a career in education.' The schoolmaster looked into the distance, remembering carefree days as a child, happy times. Before the Revolution, the killings and the war.

'I know nothing of what you seek at the top of the escarpment, not even by rumour. We know that there are many troops there, the best, the Republican Guard. They are well armed with Russian armoured personnel carriers, helicopter gunships, everything new, well maintained. But this is rumour. I have never seen them.'

'What will you do, now that the village is all but gone? They'll raze it, you know that? After what happened back there? It won't be habitable, when they've done with it.'

'I know this.' Again there was sadness in the dusky features, a resignation. 'I will go west, head for Jordan. I am a teacher. My skills are needed. I have no family, so I leave without regret. My country has not been the same, since—' The man looked away, as if ashamed to speak.

'Here.' Norris threw him the keys of the Toyota. 'There's plenty of water, gas and, if you don't mind it, infidel food.' He grinned, showing that it was not meant to offend. 'Enough to get you to where you want to go. When you've done with it, the truck, torch it, sell it if you like, if you can get over the border with it. We don't need it now.'

Nobby and Alex had unloaded all that they would need. Everything was in their packs, little enough it seemed. They had discarded the clothing that had effectively disguised them until now, changing instead into camouflage combat suits, the colour, pattern, nondescript and untraceable. Now, dressed as soldiers, they felt the better for it. They shook hands with the schoolmaster who would never teach in Iraq again, watching the dust cloud climb higher in the sky as the truck disappeared into the distance. Nobby Clarke looked sad.

'Lovely wagon that. Bloody lovely. Shame we 'as to lose it.'

The sun was going, one minute balanced on the edge of the escarpment, the next diving into oblivion. Heaving the packs on to their shoulders, they turned in the direction of the cliff. They would be there before midnight, lie up and kip until the sun came up. Then, they would sort the gear and climb the escarpment.

Richard Norris tried not to think about that.

That was for another day.

That was for tomorrow.

It was the third time he had come to the house, in the night, with no one to see his doing so. Now, as before, it was dark, this time with no moon to see by. It was quiet, no sound at all since he'd disturbed the pigeon, roosting in the oak tree in the corner. He thought the bloody thing had probably been bonking, judging by the clatter its wings had made when it had taken off. He could not remember how many times he had told himself how much he hated the country, hated being away from the sounds he found familiar in the friendly lights of the city. A comfortable oppidan, that was him. Fuck the countryside.

He stood with his back to the tree, holding the rifle loosely in his fingers, the butt resting on the damp grass. He yawned, feeling the stretch of his features, the tightness in his jaw. In the distance the church clock struck. He counted. One. Two. Three. Christ, what a time for a man to be out, when he should be at home under the covers, a good woman held in close, smelling the loving on her.

Fuck this.

Another half-hour, then he would leave, using a different route to that coming in. He was tired from being there half the night, waiting for the man to show. A drag. Not cut out for this, he had never wanted to be a front-line soldier. It was his brains they should be wanting, not his creeping about like a ghost in the night, waiting for some ex-army bloke to show. But the bastard had done for Patrick. So he'd get him. Fallon wondered where the hell Norris was. Vanished it seemed.

Not for the first time he wished that someone in the Organization would contact him, give him fresh instructions, telling him what to do. There had been no word since the killing and he no longer worried about being picked up by the police. Again, he told himself he would never let them take him on the mainland to rot in an English prison, miles from his homeland. Better to die than be captured in England. But he was in the clear. There was nothing to link him to the shooting of the policeman.

He heard the clock again, striking the half-hour.

Sod it.

Let's be away from here.

He picked up the rifle. Careful with it, he released the magazine, heavy with its forty 5.45 mm. bullets, and dropped it into a pocket, the weight tugging his jacket out of shape. Quietly, he turned and walked along the line of the hedge back to the road.

*

They sat in a cluster of boulders, the camouflage cape covering them, the tasteless high-energy food eaten without pleasure washed down with tepid water. Nobby Clarke prepared to take the first watch, spreading his bag so that it would be ready, easy to find in the dark when he came off watch. Alex looked at Richard Norris, seeing the worry in his features, as if he was trying to solve a problem that had no answer.

'Something's on your mind. I've been watching you. It's not like you to keep things to yourself. What's bugging you?'

Norris, his back against the rock, jabbed a heel into the sand, digging an ugly scar, almost as if he were angry. He looked up, his expression giving nothing away. But the hint of worry was obvious, impossible to hide. He took a deep breath, then looked from one to the other.

'It's been too much of a coincidence, all of it. Ever since we entered Iraq, they've been one step ahead, almost as if they had been expecting us, waiting.' He threw a pebble, aiming at his rucksack. He looked up at Alex and Nobby who stopped work on his sleeping place. 'Look at the facts.' He held up his hand, one finger extended, counting on it. 'First, our brush with the patrol. How the hell did they know we would be there? Coincidence? I doubt it somehow. And the bastards let fly at us without so much as a by your leave. Christ, Alex. We could have been perfectly innocent *bedoo*, even Saudis.' He looked away into the darkness before continuing. 'Second,' – he held up another finger – 'how come they rounded up the villagers, then herded them into that van for no apparent reason, unless it was a trawl, bringing in everyone for questioning? And then thirdly, the schoolmaster. What was it he said to you, Alex?'

'He asked me if I was one of the Englishmen, one of those they were seeking. I won't forget that in a hurry. Even though I thought I was dying in that hell-hole, it seemed odd.'

'And don't go forgetting the two Iraqis, in London, getting clobbered on the steps.' Nobby had the pipe out. He pointed with the stem. 'There's summat not right. Buggered if I know for sure, but it stinks of a leak. Somewhere.' He stood, placing a booted foot on one of the boulders that hid them, resting his hands, palms down, on the rough surface, staring out into the night, away from the escarpment. He shrugged his shoulders.

Norris stood, spreading his sleeping bag, scuffing pebbles from the place he would lay it, then pushing his rucksack into position for a pillow. Dragging off his boots, he threw them into the bottom of the bag. He climbed in, and lay with his hands behind his head.

'It's late.' He yawned, hurting the split on his lip. 'No good our playing Poirot at this time of night. We've an early start in the morning. There's that bloody crack to think about. We'd best turn in.' Alex too slid into the lightweight bivvy bag, hunching, seeking comfort on the rough ground, wishing now he'd bought a kip sheet. It didn't weigh much.

Tonight Norris would sleep, trying not to think about climbing the crack. He dozed, dreaming, seeing the flat with the woman's things about him, her clothes scattered on the way to the bedroom, wispy exciting things that she had worn and thrown off in her hurry to start the lovemaking. He remembered, drifting into sleep, the wild noisiness of her, then, after, the wetness of her tears on his chest, as she had cried.

He had heard her saying . . . heard her say . . .

He slept.

CHAPTER EIGHT

'What do we know, so far?'

The Chief Constable looked pensive; weariness, tugging at the corners of his eyes, made him appear older than his fifty-three years and even more like a tired basset hound. He craved a cigarette, wishing now that he had not decided to quit at such an inopportune moment. Maybe one of the little cigarillos he kept in his drawer . . .

'Not very much.' Chief Superintendent Flaxby shrugged, hunching into his shirt, feeling the material tight across his shoulders, knowing he should heed the medical officer's advice and lose some weight. Some other time. 'We've the report from MI5, telling us that the man Norris, who seems to feature in this, is quite an important honcho. He's out of the country at the moment, and they don't know or, more likely, won't say when he is due back.'

'And the connection? Between Norris and the suspicious character seen in the village? Where's the tie-in?'

'PC Atkinson, before he was foully murdered, reported to Division that someone had been asking questions about Norris, where to find his house, that sort of thing. The stranger had implied that he and Norris had served in the Army together, in Cyprus, I think he said, although it was felt that the fellow wasn't old enough.' The Chief Superintendent looked down at his fingernails, choosing his words, wanting his boss to understand the importance. 'Atkinson was killed a spit from Norris's place, two nights after he reported. As yet we've got nothing on the murder, despite the most extensive inquiries. A mediocre photofit, assembled from a description given by the landlord of the local pub, and a couple of drunks who were in the bar at the time. One, the landlord, said words were his inspiration, not faces.' He did not look optimistic.

The Chief Superintendent knew his superior would not like what was to follow. Nevertheless he went on.

'Ballistics think, only think, mind you, that the weapon was a Kalashnikov, maybe the AK74 version. That's a Provo gun. But the holes in the car door—' He paused, angrily bitter that one of his men had been so easily butchered. Flaxby was one of a growing number of senior police officers advocating arming the police. If young Atkinson had had a .357 Magnum shoved down the back of his trousers or stashed in the glove compartment, then maybe the killer would have been spread all over the road instead of one of his best protégés. Oh yes, there would have been an inquiry, the press baying for the policeman's blood. But at least the poor sod would have been alive to argue his case in court.

'What concerns the Intelligence people is that the Provos, the IRA, may be after Norris. They wouldn't give their reasons, of course, nor would we expect them to, but they were pretty damn sure there is a connection.'

'Are you telling me, George, that the Provos are stalking someone, over here, on the mainland? It seems a bit far-fetched. I could understand it if it were a Minister, or an MP, but not a low-key target like Norris.' He searched through his drawer, looking for the cigarillos without finding them. Irritably, he slammed the drawer shut. 'A Major, didn't you say he was? Hardly seems worth their while.'

'Norris's son was killed by the IRA, in Belfast, end of last year, I believe. Maybe that's the connection? Could that be what this is all about?'

'Perhaps.' The Chief Constable looked at his watch, trying not to appear impatient. He was due to chair a meeting of the Emergency Co-ordinating Group, followed by a briefing to the Public Protection Committee immediately after. Not for the first time that day he reflected that a copper's lot was not always a happy one. 'George, I have to leave soon. Do whatever is necessary. Stake out the Norris home, and have a Firearms Team put on standby, ours, not from SO19. Establish Silver Control if need be. You have my full backing. If he's the one who killed Atkinson, I want him.'

'Overtime? Will you authorize overtime?'

The two senior police officers chuckled.

Overtime.

My arse.

Flaxby gathered up his Filofax and made to leave, content to have got what he had come for.

Authorization to deploy a Firearms Team.

This time he did not stop at the gap in the hedge, instead going directly to the edge of the house where he stood hidden in deep shadow, listening, confirming what he knew. The house, as before, was empty.

Where the hell was Norris?

Had he gone, packed his bags and left for good? He did not understand. Each time he had come here the house had been empty, even when he had watched from the hill in the daytime. No milkman, no paper delivered, no tradesmen calling. Only the postman, whose van had stopped outside the gate as he walked across the drive to deliver the mail.

Knowing the place was unoccupied, he moved more confidently, skirting the wall and stopping opposite the french windows. He waited, listening, looking over his shoulder before pulling out a slim pencil torch. Face pressed into the cold glass, he shone the light into the big sitting room, letting it play on the furniture, the TV, the stereo in the corner.

He was looking for the telephone.

Finding it on a small table close to the window seat across the room, he smiled grimly when he saw the answering machine beside the instrument, a light like a green eye glowing from it. He walked around the house to an opposite window close to the table. He shone the light. The number was written in bold figures on the telephone, ex-directory, but he had known that already, from trying to trace the number through Directory Enquiries.

It was memorized.

He played the beam of the torch over the answering machine, squinting through the refracted light until he could identify the model, then made a mental note of it. Satisfied, he pocketed the torch, looked quickly about him and walked rapidly back across the lawn. He had everything he had come for. The rifle was where he had left it against the tree. The solid weight of it comforted him, reassuring him of its power and what it could do. Hefting it into his hands, he walked along the hedge, down the bank into the lane, deep in the darkness of the night.

Joseph Fallon did not turn to look back.

On a hill overlooking the house, a man lay prone, close to the dark hedgerow. Dressed in black, invisible, he had not moved, not once, in the four hours he had lain there, other than to shift his hips to alleviate the discomfort as cramp attacked his lower legs. The night observation device gave him a clear picture of everything in the fields below him, greenish-yellow ghostly images swimming in the lens. Nothing moved without him seeing, noting it.

This was his second night of duty in the hide, the first that he had seen anyone. He had been about to call in to Control, to report another frustrating night, when he had caught the sudden movement. Too big for an animal, too methodical in its approach, he had watched, waited, needing to be sure.

This animal was human.

He watched as the man, now in the garden of the house, skirted the lawn, peering into the windows. The image he had been watching was suddenly punctured by the flare from a flashlight, for a moment distorting his vision. He noted everything the man did.

He whispered into a recorder, logging the prowler's actions. The man in black moved a fraction, hot now in the bullet-proof vest, the beret tight on his forehead. At first he had thought the man was a common burglar, but knew that burglars, even the worst kind, did not carry rifles.

Not the AK74 like this one.

Maybe it was an AK that had done for Trevor Atkinson.

If it was you, you bastard . . . well, next time I'll be up here with you balanced on the cross-hairs of telescopic image-intensifying night-sight.

Then, try shovelling your brains back into your skull before they spill down your shirt front.

The policeman whispered into his radio, listening to the reply from Silver Control in the single earpiece, glad to get orders to come in. They would not try to take him. Not yet. The man had come for Richard Norris, so Division said, and Norris was out of the country. When Norris came back, so would the prowler. Then, they would take him at their leisure.

Dead or alive.

Stiffly, he crawled out through the hedge, carefully taking his equipment with him. He left it, neatly stowed at the edge of the track, then turned and walked up the hill in the direction of the van.

He made his inquiries of a young man walking the floor of the electrical goods store. The assistant was helpful, pointing out the section where he could find the things he sought. There were six of them, arranged neatly, identical except for the colour coding on the stiff plastic of the packets. Satisfied, he selected one of each colour, then walked with them in a wire basket to the cashier's desk, where a sign indicated payment should be made. He placed his purchases on the counter, curbing his impatience as the sales girl skimmed the bar coding with an electronic pencil, recording the sale.

He paid with notes that were new, crisp from the cash dispenser in the High Street, irritated when the girl held each under the ultra violet detector set to the side of the till, checking for counterfeit notes. A mistake. He should not have paid with new money. It might be noticed, remembered later. It was only when he was outside, on his way to the car, that he realized he should have made his purchases in separate stores. It had not occurred to him that it would seem unusual for one person to buy six pocket tone-dialling equipments without arousing suspicion. He shrugged. So what? Who noticed anything unusual these days?

The girl at the cash register watched him leave, innocent enough, apart from his expressionless, bird-of-prey eyes. She had been more than a little puzzled about why he had bought six tone-diallers, designed to work on a particular make of answering machine. A young man approached her checkout with a compact disc in his hand and she shrugged.

He was good looking.

And he liked Crowded House too.

The girl smiled as he approached the counter, forgetting the man who had gone before.

The crack, Al Shuk fee Sakr, was narrower than Norris had expected, dark, no sun coming in, keeping them cool, almost cold. He could touch both sides when he extended his arms, the surface rough against the palms of his hands. Raising one foot, then another, forcing each on to the walls, he applied pressure to keep himself balanced.

'We can bridge it. Provided it gets no wider, it'll be a doddle, all the way to the top.'

'That's a relief.' Alex was busy sorting the ropes and

the rest of the equipment, Friends and rerps and camms and chocs, all sizes, neatly arranged on their belts, easy to hand when needed. The karibiners were wound with rubber tape, preventing their clinking together. With these, they could climb silently.

They roped up, Norris leading, Alex middleman, Nobby coming up last. They had stripped to shorts and light-weight rock slippers, Norris with a chalk bag. They tested the short-range, UHF radios, each nodding to show they were receiving.

Norris's mouth was dry, worse than it had been at the Hönnetal. This was real. A new route, a climb up to hell, as far as he knew. With no instructor standing below him to call advice, Norris began to doubt. Could he do it, now, when it mattered?

The hold, breaking away in his hand, floating . . .

'Right,' he said softly.

Again, momentarily, the fall from the face in the Kaiser-gebirge jumped into his mind, frightening him. He paused, not wanting to start. Knowing, neither Alex nor Nobby looked at him, instead letting him struggle with his private fear. He had done it, training, and would do it now. While he waited, Alex re-dressed his wound, then picked up the rope, feeding it through his fingers. Nobby sucked on the pipe, looking out through the crack at the bright sun of the desert.

'Right,' Norris said again. 'Here we go then. See you at the top of this pitch.' Lips dry, he was suddenly thirsty. He pushed the desire to drink into the back of his mind. Bridging, feet and hands on each side of the crack, he pushed out, working his way upwards, hesitantly at first, then more confidently as he got higher and warmed to it.

'Twenty feet.' A whisper from Alex, acknowledged. It was easier than he had expected, and he worried only that the crack would widen and that he would have to transfer to one or other of the walls, fearful of choosing the more difficult and not being able to get back on to the easier if things got too tricky. Instead, the crack narrowed. Now, with his back jammed against one wall, feet on the other, palms flat on the rough surface, he squeezed upwards.

A ledge.

'OK,' he whispered hoarsely. 'Come on up.'

Norris stood on the narrow ledge anchored on to a choc, feeling secure. Alex, there in no time. Norris, without speaking, went straight back into the climbing, knowing that as soon as he was at the next stance, Nobby Clarke would come up to join Alex. Hauling up the packs took a long time, even with Alex's great strength and Nobby pulling tirelessly, hand over hand as if his life depended on it.

Norris, with no real idea how high the crack was, climbed on, biting back his worry. It was dark now, damp in the chimney, and Norris had no idea what insects might be lurking in the nooks and crannies. He hoped they preferred the sun. But the crack was narrower still, Norris now using his back and knees, his helmet scraping against the rock in the darkness. There was no light anywhere and he struggled, inching his way upwards in the darkness. He had to see.

Taking a calculated risk, knowing there was little chance of it being seen from beyond the crack, he switched on the headlamp attached to the helmet, the rock immediately more friendly in the warm, yellow light. But the crack was narrower still, worrying him. If it got tighter there was no way the bigger men would squeeze through. The helmet, a nuisance now, jammed in the narrowness of the fissure. Norris, vertical, was almost able to hold himself in by the friction of his clothing.

Bugger this.

'Ten feet.'

Alex, assessing the amount of rope.

Come on, gap. Widen out, give us a chance. He could no longer see the narrow strip of sunlight to his left, so climbed by feel, with just the glow of the head-lamp to guide him. He had gone five rope's lengths, 600 feet, perhaps more, not knowing how far they were from the top. Norris had thought the whole climb was about 1500 feet. That had been a guess, when looking at it from the outside where the sun had been.

He wondered how far from the sun he was now.

He gritted his teeth, climbing ever upwards, worried they might be in the dark for ever.

In the dust and dirt of the compound outside the tunnel in the mountains, the armoured personnel carriers, APCs, the jeeps and the helicopters were constantly on the move, entering and leaving throughout the day. Foot patrols, weary from trudging across the ash-fire heat of the desert, came in to divest themselves of dirty uniforms and equipment, tired, bored from the constant patrolling. There was no relief, no let-up.

Colonel Zaydn, Chief of Security, had been found dead in the desert, his body, mutilated, bloated and left to rot in the sun by his unknown killers. His driver had been shot to death. Neither had been buried.

Every day the patrols had gone out looking for the men who had done the killing. The increased activity meant nothing to the average soldier in the guard unit, nor the incessant coming and going. The commanders, those who knew, were much more worried. Zaydn had been tortured. It was assumed that he had talked. The soldiers had heard the rumours filtering down from the officers. They had no idea what went on inside the mountain, only that it was most important, vital to the security of the Iraqi people. Those higher up the chain of command, those in positions of importance, knew what the project was.

SLING SHOT.

The Supergun, aimed at Tel Aviv, the vipers' nest, lair of the hated Zionist enemy. The gun would destroy the nest for ever. Revenge, so long awaited, would be sweet.

Now, they had heard, the project was to be brought forward. The firing was to be in two more days. The Great One would be there to witness the firing. He who had made it all possible. The West would learn of the greatness of Iraq. Once more, the Arab world would look to her with admiration and devotion, knowing that the great enemy, the Zionists, were destroyed, that those who survived would walk in constant fear of what could be done to them.

'The Sword of Damocles,' one of the officers said.

Glory and rejoicing would follow.

There was only the problem of the British team that had been put in to find and destroy the weapon. It was known that they were in the area. They had been seen, shot at. They would be found sooner or later. It was impossible for them to avoid detection for long. Eventually, they would be taken.

The air waves were alive with the passage of messages, as the APCs and the helicopters and the jeeps and the foot patrols went out into the desert, seeking the Englishmen.

They would be caught and brought in for questioning.

And torture.

It was only a matter of time.

Alex Howard was afraid.

He would climb anything, out in the sun.

In the dark, the fear cloaked him, cloying, stifling.

He moved reluctantly upwards as the fusty darkness closed in, the smoothness of his climbing deserting him. He shook in the holds, his fingers sweating in the cold damp of the crack. Occasionally, a light, bright, friendly, as Nobby came up to join him on the stances, a few muttered words of encouragement to each other, then on, up into the darkness.

He knew that the crack was getting smaller, could feel it as he squeezed his big body between the two walls, forcing himself up to Norris somewhere above. He had to bite his bottom lip lest the animal sound of his *Angst* betray him to the others. But he was moving, slowly, deliberately, careful in his fear.

Up.

The sun was there, somewhere.

As he moved, tentative, nervous, he felt his helmet scrape the rock as he tried to look up to see where he was going. It was tighter, and he could hardly fill his chest to breathe. He reached up with a hand, groping for a hold, something to pull himself over this tight section, sucking in his chest, collapsing his lungs. He whispered into the mike, asking Norris for tension on the rope, help to pull him through where the rock was at its tightest. Fingers digging into the rock, he heaved, driving with all the strength of his powerful legs. The crack was tighter still, constricting, forcing against him. He tried to move sideways, searching for space. Nearly there. The tension began to leave him. He wanted to draw in a great lungful of air, but could not. A frightening image of getting stuck formed briefly in his mind, and he had to grit his teeth and force himself on. One last push with his feet . . .

His left foothold broke, rattling down the crack.

With a gasp he slid helplessly down into a narrow fissure.

His body rammed into the funnel like a cork hammered into a bottle.

Suddenly, darkness, all around, pressing in on him, the loud metallic clatter telling him the head-lamp had been torn from the helmet. Jammed tight, he was unable to see the light as it fell away from him.

In the darkness, he smelt the bodies in the van when it had stood in the square, hot, afraid, pressed in to his face. He felt the tightness, the stuffy confines of the tunnel that had trapped him when he'd gone for the puppy. The box behind the sports pavilion, feeling the pain in his hands as he had fought to be free. Metal cutting his fingers as the

182

floor of the truck had been heaved up to let in the sweetness of the night air, the damp smell of the dew on it.

He could not move. The crack held him.

The rope was tugging, as Norris heaved, perhaps wondering what the hell was up, why Alex had stopped climbing. It did nothing other than to jam him tighter. Struggling, caught, unable to move, he gasped, into the mike, seeking the presence of the others, wanting to be reassured, to hear Nobby, Richard, and know that they were close by. Alarmed, he heard no side tone in his ears, the set dead, a lead broken, probably when the head-lamp had been ripped off.

Screaming, terrified, not caring then that he might be heard.

The echo rolled up the crack, bouncing off the dankness of the walls, mocking him in his fear of the dark. He beat his fists on the wall, hurting himself. Sweating, trembling as the fear in him grew, he tried to move but he was held in a huge vice of damp stone. The panic grew poisonously from his belly, and he knew that his struggling was doing nothing, only exacerbating the situation. He let his head fall against the crack, striving to keep the moan of fear that rose in his throat. There was movement below him, something touching his feet, perhaps a hand, he could not be sure, then scrabbling, the sound cloth makes when dragged over rough stone. Then a body, hot, gasping, a little below him. Somewhere.

'You OK? Mr A.? I saw your lamp go. It hit my helmet on the way down.'

He tried to see the light below him, to feel the reassuring presence of Nobby Clarke. Unable to prevent it, Alex trembled, the movement magnified in the flickering light below his feet. He could not stop it, and was ashamed that his fear was showing. He could not see Nobby, just the light, bright in his eyes, blinding him as Nobby moved below and to one side of him.

'Stuck. In this fucking crack. Can't move.'

'You 'ave to, Mr A. We can't stay here for ever. Where are you jammed? Can you move anything? Anything at all?'

'I told you, damn it. I'm stuck. Held fast. I can't move sod all. Can't you get up to me? I . . . I can't see.' Angry in his fear, he shouted at Nobby Clarke, who was strong, calm, and unafraid.

'Try, Mr A. We're done for else. There's no way I can get past you.' The light, bright in Alex's eyes, hid Nobby's face, his expression.

'You bastard, Clarke. I told you. I'm stuck, done for. There's no way I can move. Not a damned muscle. If only I could see—'

The light from the head-lamp hurt, preventing him seeing the man behind it whenever he looked down between his feet. Again the voice, annoyingly calm, as though talking to a petulant child who had pissed itself at a birthday party and would not go and change.

In the vileness of his fear, Alex hated him.

Silent, Nobby Clarke listened to Alex gasping, understanding, knowing how he had suffered in the van. He spoke, slow, deliberate words, intending them to be heard, clearly understood, so that Alex would know of his contempt.

'Fucking officers. You're all the same. Full of piss and wind when the going is good, then collapsing like a pricked johnnie when it gets a bit tough. You make me puke. Mr Norris is the only decent officer I've ever known. 'E in't blubbing like a fucking schoolgirl when her first period's started, thinking she's going to bleed to death. He's up there, climbing, leading from the front.' Nobby, behind the head-lamp, spat the words. 'You going to stay here, till you lose enough weight to move? Well, I ain't got that amount of time to spare. Get out the fucking road. Mr Norris and me, we'll finish this.'

Alex Howard hated Nobby Clarke for what he had said, for what he was doing, cynical of his fear, not caring that he had needed to tear his way out of a truck full of stinking men, with no light to see by nor air to breathe, with only his strength saving him. He hated him for his lack of fear of the dark, the mocking voice, the jealousy of his loyalty to Norris. It was Norris's fault, all this. And Clarke. That bastard Clarke, close, despising him.

'You bastard, Clarke.'

'Piss off. Bloody fairy. You make me puke.'

Alex roared, part fear, part anger.

He lunged, sideways and downwards, swinging a booted foot in the direction of the lamp, aiming at his tormentor, at the sneering face. Every ounce of his power went into the movement.

He felt his body shift.

A fraction, but enough.

No longer held.

The lunge he had made at Nobby Clarke had been driven by his anger, fear and the madness in him as he had striven to keep his sanity. It had been enough to free him, sufficient for him to squeeze out of his rocky prison, the vice of cold rock that held him. He could move, upwards, where the crack was wider. Once out of it, he climbed fast, no longer heeding the dark, the faint glow from the lamp below him, the one above coaxing him. Richard Norris, standing on a ledge, took the rope in fast as Alex rushed up the crack. He joined him, saying nothing, hauling in the rope as Nobby, too, came up on to the ledge.

'Problems, Alex? Nobby? Thought you were never coming.'

'I 'ad a bit of trouble, in the narrow bit. Couldn't move for a while. OK now though. You did all right, Mr A.' Alex thought he might have been grinning behind the light. 'Your feet thrashing about down there nearly took my 'ead off. Another inch—'

Alex said nothing, understanding the bond that linked Richard Norris and Nobby Clarke, thankful that he, too, was part of it now. Norris, unaware of what had taken place, gestured upwards.

'Look.'

There was no mistaking the thin strip of sunlight, 200 feet above.

It was the most beautiful thing Alex had ever seen.

They came out of the crack, into the heat of the sun, moving quickly into the cover of a clump of scrub and rocks. Alex, at last, had lost the trembling that had stayed with him for the final part of the climb. Coming out had been like surfacing from a murky pool. He gulped the clean, dry air, as if it were pure oxygen, refreshing him. Norris saw the look passing between them and realized that there had been an incident in the crack, a problem resolved.

They buried the climbing gear. All of it, deep in the sand where it could not be found. Norris remembered the bodies back in the *waadi*, seeing the dead soldiers' faces, the flies gorging greedily on the dried blood too slow to fly away as the sand had been shovelled over them. A lifetime ago.

They lay up, resting, as Alex injected another tetanus shot into his thigh and replaced the dressing, torn off in the climbing. Norris hid his concern. The wound looked ugly, inflamed. But Alex had been moving well enough and would never complain to the others. He was not that sort.

'Need any help with that?'

'Richard,' Alex smiled tightly, 'if you think I'd bare my arse to you—'

The three of them laughed.

They went once more through the procedures as they waited for dusk, listening to the beat of the helicopter rotors as it hovered low over the desert, searching to a regular pattern. Far off, they heard the high-pitched whine of armoured troop-carriers, the sound carried to them on the cold of the night air. They tried not to think about who they might be searching for. The three of them slept, in shifts, through the last of the day, waiting for the darkness that would hide them.

It was time.

They checked their gear again.

They set off, the three of them, Nobby Clarke going due north, Alex and Richard angled off to his left and right, soon losing sight of one another. Alone now, each went his own way, with his own thoughts, his own fears.

None knew when they would meet again.

CHAPTER NINE

He came low over the ridge, off the skyline, the sun behind. The place he was looking for, perfect, in front of a small rock pile. Sitting, legs slightly bent, he shrugged out of the rucksack, placing it carefully between his feet. In the distance, the mountains, hazy, their shapes blurred, shimmering in the heat. He leaned against the rock, feeling its sharp heat through the thin shirt, wondering how long he would have to stay in this godforsaken place. Not once did he move, other than to raise the binoculars to his eyes. Quartering the ground, he looked, missing nothing. Movement, over to his left as a bird rose lazily on a thermal, the trailing wing feathers spread like fingers, stabilizing its flight. On the ground, a desert hare, cautious as it tested the air with a quivering nose. Otherwise, emptiness.

This place would do.

From the straps on the outside of his pack, he took a short tool, its blade folded against the handle. He opened it quietly, then, with painstaking care, began to scrape a narrow trench in the hard gravel. He worked, kneeling, without causing dust. That way he would not be seen.

Satisfied, he went once more to the pack, taking from it a piece of nylon netting, used normally to protect fruit from greedy blackbirds in early summer, from an English garden in the Lake District. He used small aluminium pegs to hold the net taut across the pit, then laid a camouflage cape over it. Sand and gravel were scattered over. Once more he rummaged through the pack, economical with his movement. He dragged the pack close to the hide, then slid into the dark hole. The pack was tugged down to cover the narrow entrance, the cape spilling over it.

He had disappeared.

Wondering again how long he would be here, he shrugged, indifferent.

It was cooler in the hide, where the sun could not reach him directly. He sucked at the straw, drawing the tepid, brackish water into his mouth from a bottle still almost full. It did nothing to quench his thirst, only supplying fluid to his body. Resting on his elbows, he shifted slightly to avoid the stone that dug into his thigh. He stared through the glasses, eyes watering as he searched the ground to his front, watching the shadows stretch away with the approach of dusk. Suddenly, dark, and nothing moving.

He slipped out of the hide, low on his belly, pulling at the pack. There was much to do before he was to sleep. The collapsible antenna was unfolded and carefully erected, hidden in a clump of sparse scrub. The cable, a dark bootlace against the ground, was connected to the equipment that lay unattended in the front of the hide. With deliberate care, he scuffed out the footprints around the low antenna. The cable was buried. Finally, he turned down the hill and walked a hundred metres, where he lay on the ground and looked up at the place where he had been working.

Invisible.

Slowly he walked back, below the skyline, stopping every few yards to look critically at his handiwork. Minor adjustments were made here and there, a little more sand, scuffed with his fingertips, the cape tugged gently. Done, he slid back into the hole.

He would not come out again. Not until he got the signal.

Unless he had to kill someone.

Nobby Clarke hoped he would not have to do that.

Now, at last, he slept, head resting on his forearms, listening to the faint hum from the earphone fitted to his left ear. He hoped to hear a noise like a motor boat, its exhaust bubbling just below the surface, the sound Norris had made him listen to until he would recognize it in his sleep. Then he could be gone. Not yet.

The quiet buzz in his ear.

Peaceful.

Awake suddenly, stiff, cold, even with the down waistcoat. Immobile, he felt the beat of his heart, his breathing loud in the confines of the hole. Something had woken him, not the hum from the earphone, but another sound close by. Again, a faint noise which had intruded into his subconscious. Now his breath was held in his chest, ears strained, hearing only the roar of his fear.

A stone.

It had been a stone, dislodged from its place where it had lain through the heat of the day. Now it had moved. The sound had come from his left, down the hill. Lifting the edge of the cape, light in his fingertips, he peered into the darkness.

Nothing.

He smelt them. Unmistakable. Gun oil, making his nose twitch as the smell wafted up the hill. Something moving, dim, shapeless, shadows within shadows. No moon to see by, but light from the stars, glinting on something shiny. Then voices, pitched low. The movement stopped. Silence, then muted conversation in Arabic that he was unable to understand. He picked out several voices in a tight huddle, a patrol, resting up, not doing its job. Not finding Nobby Clarke.

Jesus.

No weapons, Norris had said. That close and we're dead anyway. Where the fuck are you now, Mr N.? He did not breathe, but listened, frightened, hopeful the patrol would leave. Instead, they moved closer, unbuckling their webbing equipment, the belts and ammunition pouches, rifles dropped carelessly into the gravel of the desert. They sat, grouped close against the cold of the night, yards from where he lay. One, then a second, stretched out on the hard surface, heads rested on the crumpled mess of their equipment. The other two lay down, snoring within seconds. Committed, he could not move. Lie still, Nobby Clarke. Breathe, and the bastards will hear you.

The night stretched, interminable, bringing the cramp and the cold. He lay, unmoving, the luminous watch, close to his face, recording the slowness of the night's passing. He dozed, not sleeping, jumping each time one of the patrol turned in uncomfortable sleep.

Dawn came slowly, a dimmer switch controlling the roseate glow that spread across the stage. He could see them now, ten yards to his left, shivering in the early day, not yet awake. One sat up, the movement sudden, looking nowhere in particular, down the hill into the desert where he had been the night before. Into Nobby's world. The soldier stood, stretching the stiffness from his shoulders, hugging his arms across his body to warm himself. He scratched his crotch, the fart loud in the still air. The Arab turned half left and began walking up the hill, towards the rock pile.

Nobby watched, slight spurts coming from the desert boots as the feet scuffed. He did not move, not even to blink, lest he missed a change in the stride, the faltering that would tell him he was discovered. He held his breath, heartbeat faster than it had been. He stared at the boots, very close now, the sweat marks clear against the dusty suede. Two more paces and the soldier would step on him. The boots held his attention. He missed the other movement close to his face.

He forgot the boots.

The scorpion, suddenly, was more important.

It was too close, the image blurred, the shiny black gunmetal reflecting the sunlight. It seemed that it was looking at him.

Lie still, Clarke. Don't even think about moving.

The boots. The insect. Eyes wary, flicking from one to the other. He heard the boots, but watched the scorpion.

The crunching, suddenly loud in the loose scree around the entrance as the man prepared for his morning ablutions. The sound of the urine splashing, like autumn rain in the stillness, was close to where he lay.

The scorpion scuttled from the warm shower, seeking security in the darkness of the hole. For a moment, he thought it might shake itself, like a dog caught in the rain. Instead, it crawled on to the back of his hand, against the thick hair, resting. The warm liquid splashed into the entrance of the hide, wetting his hands, the acrid stink filling his nostrils.

The insect moved. It turned right, looking, then picked its way delicately along his forearm, the scratch of its feet light on the surface, as it moved through the stiffened hairs. Fear, growing as the thing advanced in the direction of his sleeve. The Arab had stopped pissing and was shaking himself, the action magnified in the bend of his knees.

Slowly, Nobby pulled his right hand from under the left, inching it along his arm until it was opposite the object that was frightening him. He looked at the tail, not remembering if it should be up, or down, in preparation for stinging. Concentration, aligning his right hand, middle finger bent behind the thumb. Shaking. Ink balls aimed at the kid in the row in front, the smart little sod who could do fractions. Aim at the back of his neck. Miss and the pellet would fly out to the front of the class and earn a walloping from the maths master, old Moggie Morrison. Crusty old bastard.

He flicked with his finger, the movement hard, sharp.

The scorpion was gone, his arm tingling at the place it had lain on him. Out into the sun, on its back, legs dancing, it tried to roll over. It never made it. The desert boot drove down on to it, grinding into the gravel. Squashed into death. Better you than me. The boots turned down the hill, gone, now back in the group, kicking at the others still sleeping with no more feeling than had been shown the scorpion.

Power, usurped.

The patrol stood, sheepish, confused at waking, looking to the pisser for direction. They grouped around him sullenly, looking at the crumpled map taken from a pocket, then flattened on the ground. He pointed with a dirty finger, tracing a route, speaking words Nobby could not hear.

The men bent to their equipment, tugging at it, stiff from the dew, resisting fingers clumsy in their awkwardness. Rifles were collected, casually checked to see that each had his own. They turned up the hill, formed into a rough file. The leader grunted, the sound harsh, catching in the back of the throat as he gestured with his arm. Forward. They were gone, shuffling, not having done their job, missing finding Nobby Clarke.

Breathing more easily now, he drank, gulping from the bottle, a long pull so that his rationing schedule was spoiled. No drink at the first lie-up for Nobby Clarke. Fuck it. He'd needed the water. Forearms hot against his cheeks, he lowered his head, shaking still, a big man afraid of something so small.

The day stretched, hotter as the sun rose into the haze of the sky. The mountains, once clear in the cool of the dawn, now vague, shimmering in the distance, the sharp outlines merging, like rain on a watercolour, frustrating its creator. Occasionally he would look through the glasses, once seeing a dust cloud far away, not intruding into his solitude, not threatening.

The listening was more important. He must not miss the signal. Into the night, the day gone by, half sleeping, he heard it. Like Mr N. had said. Just like the tapes he had listened to in the darkened room.

He studied the olive-green box, the small illuminated screen, saw the receive light, a dim glow in the entrance to the hide. The motor-boat sound, warbling more frequently now. He tapped a switch locking it, pressed the reset button, watching the digital figures tumbling in their hurry to stop. Finally, only the last number was blinking, before it, too, was stabilized. He stored them into memory. Fingers, dirty, awkward in the confined space, picked at the tiny keypad, the entry confirmed automatically against the memory setting. He read the message again, rechecking as he had been taught. The habit never forgotten.

It was correct. He had checked. Bearing, position, his base line. Nothing else required of Nobby Clarke. Gently, breath held as he pressed the transmit button. A pause as the set looked for a favourable receive condition from a distant receiver, a hole in the ionosphere. Then, gone. Fingers crossed. Wait for the green, the confirmation that it was received. A quiet noise in the earphone, three short pips. Relief. Right, Nobby. That's you finished.

Now, get the hell out of here.

In the communications room, Century House, an operator, detached for special duty from GCHQ Cheltenham, sat in front of a console, a pair of earphones clamped to his head. As is the universal habit, he read from a book, barely conscious of the faint static that filled his ears. Bored, he had been sitting on this pattern for days without hearing a squeak from it. And so he read, as do all operators when sitting on a dead frequency. Occasionally he would look up, checking a read-out, making a tiny adjustment to a control switch better to hear the signal when it came. If ever it should. It was cushy work, better than when he had been in the Army, as a signaller, sitting out his shift in a Land-Rover in a damp wood or smelly German barn, everything linked by remote cables down into the staff vehicle, leaving him sod all to do.

Suddenly, the book was laid down as his fingers hovered over the array of switches. He held the earphones in against his ears, sure he had heard the tones, three, low pitched, faint, in amongst the static. Again, three soft pips, the receiver, drifting to look for the transmitter, finding it, then locking. The operator held his breath, eyes flying over his equipment, checking the receive light, dull then bright green, LED lights glowing, the recorder running.

A red lamp glowed, faint, then bright, just for a fraction of a second. Now it was there, in the set, stored, memorized, confirmed automatically, the sender relieved. Technology. Some poor bastard holed up somewhere, poking at his keypad to get this back to him in the communications room in a basement in the middle of London. He had no idea, then, who had sent the message, nor from where it had come.

Waiting, he listened, fingers tapping at a keypad. The message contained in that one short burst appeared on the VDU in front of him. He read it, puzzled, then understanding as he tapped ENTER then ESCAPE, hearing the brief hum from the laser printer. He tore off the message, checking the time of receipt at his port, then logged it.

He read the message again.

It was a position, given in latitude and longitude, and a bearing, measured in mils.

Standing, he walked to a map of the world, covering one wall, where he ran a finger up, then across the map, laying it down gently in the position printed on the signal. He tapped a finger, gently.

He stared, whistled quietly, then shrugged.

His finger, where it had lain on the map, had been in western Iraq.

The message was carefully folded into a buff envelope and sealed with clear tape. There was a rubber stamp which he pressed into a red inkpad, then carefully on to the envelope, rocking it so the letters would stand out clearly. He read the words in bold lettering. OO – IMMEDIATE. No one could fail to see the urgency.

At the wall he opened a sliding panel, then dropped the envelope into a wire basket. The panel slid shut. Back at the console, he put the earphones on, once more picking up his book.

He read, listening.

'Good God.'

Kronk looked at the signal that had been brought up from Communications, disbelieving. Oliver looked at him, knowing.

'They're going to do it. This is just the first of them. Two more and we have a fix. We'll know where the Gun is. We can deal with it, get the Americans to go in with a Stealth bomber.' Oliver looked pleased, relieved. 'Thank God. I knew they'd find it.' He noticed Kronk's evasiveness, the uncomfortable shiftiness as if something was kept hidden. Alarmed, he stepped forward, leaning across the desk.

'Adrian. For Heaven's sake. They're going to do it, find the Supergun. They've done all we asked of them, and more besides. We've *got* to pull them out, cancel the order to abort. We can't leave them. Not now.' The spittle was thick on his lips in his agitation, the good eye bright with realization. He had been shouting.

'It's too late, old boy. We ... we couldn't get anything laid on in time. It's just not possible.'

Oliver exploded, the first time Kronk had ever seen him angry, his face red, a vein pulsing in his forehead. He slammed his hands on to the table, the thump loud in the room, making the pens and the pencils and the paperclips jump. He looked at Adrian Kronk contemptuously.

'You bounder.' Oliver never swore. It was un-officer-like. 'You absolute bounder. There never was a plan to pull them out. You had always intended leaving them there, even if they had been successful. Damn you, Kronk.' Oliver paced the room, looking disgustedly at the other, hunched over his desk, his head held in his hands. 'I'll go above your head, Kronk, to the PM if necessary. What you have done is despicable. An insertion is *never* left on a mission, deserted, to fend for itself. It's against all the traditions of the Service.'

'They're not an insertion in the true sense, not one of ours. A bunch of over-the-hill has-beens, wasters, soldiers of fortune, in it for the money, with no thought for the security of the nation. Mercenaries, nothing else. They won't be missed.' Kronk was defiant. 'By anyone.'

'You're forgetting the blackmail. You all but forced him, Norris, to go, threatening him with the tape. I'm telling you, Kronk, I'll not let you get away with this. It is unforgivable. Not the sort of things soldiers do.'

'Soldiers!' Kronk exploded. 'You've had your time, Walter. It's over, the Cold War, and everything that went with it. Options for Change, or maybe you hadn't heard. Your time is gone, creeping about the woods with a gun in your hand. Wise up, man. It's over. Finished. In ten years we won't need, won't have, any Army.' He paused, softening his tone, appeasing. 'We get the fix, the Americans can go in and destroy it. But those three are for the birds. Forget them.'

Walter Oliver turned away, the anger thick about him like a mantle, all but visible. Kronk had never seen such anger in the man, not in all the years he had known him. He cared not. CHARLATAN, their part in it, was over, finished. If they're so resolute, so damned good, they could bloody well get themselves out. But he knew they would not. Not even those three. There was nothing to link the operation to his desk. Only Oliver knew. And Oliver would never tell.

It was against the traditions of the Service.

Just not the sort of thing a decent chap did.

He would have preferred to move at night, in the friendly darkness that would conceal his movement. But there was no time, no time to lie up and wait for the sunset. Instead he moved during the day, in the heat of the sun, when it was easy for him to be seen. But he was careful, moving in the hollows and depressions that abounded, keeping in shadow whenever he could, following the line of gullies rather than ridges. Not once did he cross the skyline, unless flat on his belly.

He was difficult to see, even when he was moving, the outline of his body and pack broken up by pieces of ragged cloth, torn into strips and tied about him. His face was smeared with dark cream, yellow and pink and brown and black, leaving no defined shape or pale colours. A dun-coloured bandanna was tied around his head, knotted, the ends hanging from behind his neck, keeping the sweat from his eyes. That way, he could see.

He moved quickly, covering the distance rapidly with a loping, economical stride, pausing occasionally to glance at a compass which he carried in the palm of his left hand. Every few miles, he stopped and took a bearing on a distant peak, glancing down at a folded map before continuing his journey. He knew he was almost at his destination. Soon he could lie up, rest and take stock. Only then would he allow himself to drink.

He had seen no one, not since the patrol. Eight of them, making enough noise for him to have heard them from a long way off. He had lain, hidden in a hollow, watching them through squinting eyes as they had crossed the desert towards him. If they had been warned, or had known of his existence, the patrol had given no sign of it. Rifles were slung from shoulders, not carried with intent. They talked and laughed, too noisy for disciplined soldiers.

Richard Norris had wished he had been home designing electronic equipment.

They had passed to his front, not pausing in their hurry to be gone, neither seeing him nor detecting his nearness. He was contemptuous of them, wondering again why the British media had seen fit to call them élite. But that had been before the war. Before the Coalition had got in amongst them, sorting them out.

He dismissed them from his mind.

The ground was rising more steeply now, and he bent to his task, feeling the warmth of the sweat on his back where the pack pressed against him. It was lighter than it had been since burying the climbing gear near the top of the crack. Now, all he carried was what he needed to survive, and the electronics, the kit he would use to get his bearing on the control radio. That and his water. Most of the weight was the water.

He knew he was right. They had been compromised. There had to have been a leak. Too much was moving in this remote part of Iraq. It should have been empty, desolate. Yet there had been almost constant troop movement, from the time they had exited from the Great Crack and started moving their separate ways across the plateau.

He had seen too much for it to have been coincidence. The patrols, the vehicles, the jeeps, armoured troop-carriers and the helicopter, moving, looking, searching constantly. For them? To Alex and Nobby, he must have looked worried, almost guilty when they had sat and talked about it, as if he had known something which they had not. But he had kept quiet, saying nothing. He determined to tell them, when next they met.

If.

Just below the ridge line he stopped, dropping to his knees, glancing up at the sun to see where his shadow would be. Crawling forward, careful not to make dust, he stopped behind a boulder, shapeless, anonymous on the top of the ridge. He peered round it, surprised at the close-ness of the mountains. Raising the binoculars to his eyes, he searched, foreground, middle, then far distance. For once, nothing. Dusk, another half-hour. Down the slope to his front, a small scoop in the desert, just the place, needing the minimum of digging.

That would do.

The crack over his head was sharp, sudden, frightening him. The thump that followed told him it was a weapon, fired from about 400 metres. Again, but this time he saw the strike of the bullet, ten feet to his left, the dust spurting into the air as it ricocheted away, moaning forlornly in its lonely journey.

Cursing, he rolled back down the ridge, wondering how he had been seen. He had been careful enough, not crossing the skyline, looking round the base of the rock and not over it. An observation post, a spotter with powerful binoculars and a marksman with a telescopic sight. It had to be. They would have radios, even now calling their base. Soon they would be out looking for him. His only salvation, distance. That and the night. He looked again at the sky. Fifteen minutes. He rolled back down to the bottom of the hill. Once below the skyline, he got to his feet.

Again, he cursed.

He hefted the pack to make it more comfortable on his shoulders.

Richard Norris started running.

'Why was I not informed of this. Earlier?'

The man from Intelligence shrugged, uncomfortable in the company of the Prime Minister.

'It was thought best not to involve HM Government officially. If things had gone wrong, we could have disclaimed our knowledge of the operation, insisted that it had been privately funded, mercenaries, anything to hide the truth. At the time, it seemed, ah . . . well, appropriate. In retrospect, however—' Walter Oliver did not finish.

'And they are going to find it, this Supergun?' The Prime Minister looked intrigued. He had, of course, been aware of the Supergun project, but not that there had been an insertion. A group, an irregular group, it would appear, sent in without his knowledge, to find it so that it could be destroyed.

'We need one more fix.' The single eye stared balefully

as the damaged voice whispered painfully on. 'Two have been received. We don't, of course, know which two of the three have so far been successful and it doesn't much matter anyway.' The Prime Minister noticed the spittle at the corner of the man's mouth the more agitated he became. He tried not to look at it but found his eyes drawn there. The Colonel continued.

'The Americans have a pair of Stealth aircraft standing by from their base in Saudi Arabia. They can take off in minutes and hit the target with pinpoint accuracy as you saw when they were putting their bombs down ventilator shafts during the Gulf War. They'll use 2000-pound, laser-guided high-penetration bombs, probably GBU–27 Pave-way III, which will slice through anything. Standard practice for a high-leverage target. Pentagon jargon,' he said when he saw the Prime Minister raise an eyebrow. 'You know the effect. The Iraqi Command and Control bunker, taken out during the Gulf War.'

The Prime Minister looked pensive. At last he looked at the man sitting opposite him, still vaguely disturbed by the lack of expression or movement in the glass eye.

'This has been most irregular. I cannot say I am impressed with your handling of the situation. There are, after all, professional . . . This could well backfire, and cause the Government untold embarrassment.' The Prime Minister looked rueful. 'You will understand why the Opposition and, indeed, some of my Cabinet colleagues would like to see your organization made more account-able. This could be most embarrassing.' He paused. 'How-ever, it would seem that it could prove a successful operation, and credit to you for that.' He looked away, then, his decision made, said positively, 'Pull them out. Get on to Hereford, and tell them to lay something on. You have my full authority. Thank you, Colonel Oliver, for bringing this to my attention.'

The one-eyed man stood, made a slight bow, turned and left the room. In his office, he picked up the telephone, placing a call on the secure circuit to Sterling Lines in Hereford, to the operations room of 22 Special Air Service Regiment, listening as the telephone rang.

Damned civilians, especially those in Six. Five would never have done such a thing.

He was thinking of Adrian Kronk.

Colonel Charles A. Stone Jnr, of the 37th Tactical Fighter Wing, sat in the air-conditioned comfort of the operations room of the Forward Tactical Air Group, USAF, at the Khamis Mushait air base in Saudi Arabia, sipping his third cup of coffee in an hour.

FORTACAGSAR.

Shit, what a mouthful. Only we Americans can dream up non-speak crap like that. He read, pulling out the centrefold of a soft-porn magazine so he could see it better, pursing his lips as he studied the size of the girl's breasts, the expressionless smile on her overly pretty mouth, pouting sexily at him. Staring at the breasts, he shook his head, then let his eyes wander to the pubic region.

'Fuckin' unreal, man. How come I never get to meet a broad with tits like that? An' look at that snatch. Some love-box. Man, oh, man.'

'You say somethin', Chuck?' The Major, his number two, looked up from the letter he had been reading which had arrived from South Carolina that day. 'You still looking at those dirty books, Colonel, sir?'

'You know me, Earl. Like you, I'd fuck a bush if I thought there was a snake in it. Plenty snakes out here. All we need is the fuckin' bushes. Goddamned sand and more sand. Worse 'n Tonopah. At least they got golf courses in Nevada.' He looked into the distance, for the moment seeing the small white ball, dimpled, flying away in a perfect parabola, hearing the thwack as the persimmon head of the driver smashed into it. He shook his head.

'Yeah. They got bushes too.' The Major laughed. He looked serious. 'Chuck, you hear any more about the mission?'

'Nope. Only that we got to have a pair of birds fuelled up and ready to go, quicker 'n you can jack off, Earl. Yours 'n' mine. We pulled the short straw, again. They're in Number Three hangar, wired and ready. No change in the status we got from the ops brief, shit, a week ago.' The big Air Force Colonel scratched his crotch, thinking about yet another coffee. Two more hours, and the relief crews would come on standby duty. He decided to give it a miss, turning his attention back to the magazine, flicking the pages absently, not really looking. He glanced at his number two, his expression conspiratorial.

'I did hear, Earl, unofficial, that the Brits put a team into Iraq on some kind of seek-and-destroy mission.'

'Yeah.' The Major was sarcastic. 'They do the seeking, we do the fuckin' destroying.'

'You got it, Earl. I was beginning to think you didn't understand the mission here. Glad you realize what is required of this crew.'

'I guess we shouldn't be too hard on the Brits,' said Earl. 'All I got against them is what the Pilgrim Fathers did back in sixteen-something. They really screwed up. If they would've shot a wild cat, 'stead of a turkey when they landed, we'd all be eatin' pussy at Thanksgiving.' The big Colonel laughed.

'Now that would really be somethin' else.'

A captain, their maintenance engineer, looked in through the door.

'Birds are ready, sir. Fuelled, armed, programmed and we just resprayed both with a good covering of RAM, case you guys get caught out in the daylight and some bogies come looking for you.' He stuck a thumb in the air. 'All you gotta do is fly 'em there. Where is it, "there"?'

'Need-to-know basis.' The Colonel was grinning. 'Colonels and majors only. Not for the likes of grease-monkeys like you maintenance pukes.' The Captain grinned back. ''Tween you and me,' the Colonel went on, 'I am reliably informed that it, our target, is in Iraq.'

'Eye-rack?' The maintenance engineer sounded incredulous. 'Old Saddam H. getting too big for his breeches again?'

'If he is, you can bet a used rubber to a Scud missile, that we'd be the last to know.'

The Captain from maintenance grinned, turned and left the room.

Eye-rack.

Damn.

Well, if there's a target needs hitting in Saddam country, old Chuck A. Stone was the man to hit it. Right on the nose. He walked off in the direction of the PX whistling.

Eye-rack.

Goddamn.

CHAPTER TEN

Richard Norris ran, away from the ridge and into the darkening sky. He ran silently, light on his feet, the pack firm on his shoulders, nothing loose. Now, he could set his mind to the problem of opening the distance between himself and those who would soon come after him. He had never been a runner, hating the tedium of the sport, knowing he did not have the build to be good, that he lacked dedication. Not like the skinny fellows who entered for the marathons. Apart from the punishing sessions with the rucksack, Norris ran when he had to, for a bus, or, as now, to escape. A nightmare of being captured, imprisoned like Alex in the pantechnicon, flashed briefly through his mind.

He would not be taken.

They would not catch him.

He bent to the task of running.

The flat beat of the helicopter rotor thwacked dully from somewhere over his right shoulder, the direction of the shooting. The sky, his ally, darker as every minute passed, was still light enough for the pilot to offload a full brick on the ridge, then to come looking for him. They would not all set down in one place. Some, probably half, would offload in the area where he had been seen. The rest would go in the direction they thought he would run. Knowing where the Gun was, they would guess which way Norris would go. He was close enough to it to get his bearing, had been ready to prepare his hide and to wait for the motor-boat sound of the control radio when the rifleman had shot at him. He had told them, Nobby and Alex, that, at a push, the kit could be used on the move. He should know. It was his design.

He was late in getting his bearing, later than the other two in passing his information back to London. He wished he were there, attending a conference, afterwards a drink on the *Tattershall Castle*, moored in the sunshine on the Embankment. Instead, he was here in the desert running from a platoon of Iraqi infantry. Norris had had the furthest to go. All right then. Let's see if this kit is as good as you say it is, Mr Clever Inventor.

It had bloody well better be.

He stopped running and waited, quietly holding his breath, straining to hear the voices shouting in the distance, maybe half a mile away. Moving into a tumbled rubble of rock, he stopped, listened again, then shrugged out of the rucksack and began to sort out the electronics. The equipment was in the top of the pack, easy to get at, laid out neatly so he could find what he needed in a hurry, holed up in the dark, or running from an Iraqi patrol.

More voices, sounds, closer, threatening, equipment bouncing off a man's hips as he ran trying to hold it still, keep it quiet, so that he would not be heard. But Richard saw them, 50 metres to his right, clear silhouettes on the skyline as they passed across his vision, untidy in their haste, nobody looking properly. Again they had failed to find him as they ran raggedly away.

Quietly, he eased the antenna from the set, holding his breath as the last section pinged quietly, snapping into place. Angled slightly, it pointed behind him. He touched switches, caressing them with a lover's fingers, seeing the dim glow from the LED lights, hearing the low hum from the single earpiece, the other ear free to hear the Iraqis. Leaning against the rock, he listened. He took out the locator from its clip on the side of the set, then, holding it in his hand like a pistol, walked quietly forwards, sweeping his hand in an arc.

Listening.

Come on, you bastards, talk, so that I can get a bead on you.

206

A mile gone and nothing. Worrying. His watch told him he was even later than he had thought, from marching half a day longer than the others. Nobby, with the shortest distance to go, should have been the first, then Alex. He did some quick calculations. At a push, they could get an approximate location with two bearings. Three made it exact. The Americans would want that, to be certain of launching their ordnance in the exact co-ordinates. What had he told Kronk? Right on the nose . . .

The patrols were all around him. Norris could hear them moving, scuffing across the desert, noisy and ill-disciplined, equipment dropped, metal clinking as rifle slings rattled on pivots, water sloshed in canteens. But he could not hear the radio, the sound he most wanted. He made up his mind, gambling against their ineptitude, their inefficiency as soldiers.

Breaking from cover, he ran across the open desert, without worrying if he made a noise. A shout, guttural, somewhere behind him, excited voices, hounds baying as they sniffed the scent. They had heard him. They would be spreading out, extending a net to throw around his piece of desert, gradually tightening it, a trawler reeling in a big fish, thrashing as it came in sight of the ship. Its prison. Its death. They would lose discipline as the excitement took them and they yelled their exhilaration at his closeness. They would shout, call encouragement to each other, yelling order and counter-order.

Pleased they were close to catching him, they would toady, call in to their control on their radios, to say how clever they had been in finding him. They would ask their control what to do when they caught him. Their control would answer, transmitting from its base station, sounding to Norris like a motor boat, its exhaust bubbling below the surface.

Then, he would nail him, get his fix.

Provided the kit worked properly, used on the move, when he was running away from an enemy who would do unspeakable things to him if he were taken. He ran, fast across the desert, surrounded by their noisiness as he swept the air in front of him with the locator, willing them, any one of them, to talk on the radio. But mostly he concentrated on the running.

The running would keep him alive.

Alex sat in deep shadow, a large boulder hiding him. Tired, craving sleep, he felt it heavy behind his eyes, his head snapping back each time he dozed, only to wake with a start. He shook his head, licking the pads of his fingers and wetting his eyelids in an attempt to stave off sleeping. For a while it worked before the fatigue insidiously, luxuriously foamed into his mind. Finally, his head fell forward onto his chest. Not even the pain, the dull throbbing of his wound, could keep sleep away. He'd got his fix, there was nothing more for him to do, other than wait for the others. Finally, exhausted, he slept.

Awake, he tensed, wondering at the sound. Water sloshing, a sound of drinking, making him thirsty. A dark figure beside him.

'OK. It's me, Nobby. I heard you snoring. I knew I was at the right place.' He grinned, teeth showing in the darkness of his face where the cream had been spread. 'How's the arse? Any sign of Mr N.?' The canteen, back on his belt, the buckles of the carrier tugged tight.

'Not yet.' Alex yawned, stretching at the stiffness that was in him. 'I'm not worried about him. Yet. He had further to go than we did, over some pretty rough country.' Alex squinted at his watch. 'He should be there about now, as long as he doesn't run into any trouble. Did you have a clean run, Nobby?'

'Ay. But there's a lot of shit out there, troops, jeeps and a helicopter. I kept hearing the helicopter but only saw it the once. A patrol came close, when I was in the hide.' Nobby Clarke shivered. 'What now?'

'We wait, for Richard to get here, to the RV. We can't be far from the Gun now. I reckon it's a bit further north, over that ridge.' Alex pointed. Nobby looked, where they could see the outline of the low hills, perhaps ten miles away. In the dark it was difficult to be certain.

The two of them sat, Nobby chewing on a tasteless ration bar, trying to make enough saliva to swallow, finally taking a small sip from the canteen on his belt. He shook the bottle, guessing its quantity. If he was worried he gave no sign of it. Nobby Clarke carefully folded the wrapper and slipped it into the pocket of his pack, leaving the desert as clean as he'd found it, with no trace of his being there.

Alex spoke, awkward.

'Back there. In the crack. I never did get the chance to thank you for getting me out.' Alex, unsure why he was telling this, moved, easing the ache from his wound. 'The dark, it's always bothered me, frightened me, I suppose, since I was a boy. Something happened, when I was a kid, not long after the war.' He shuddered, remembering. 'I went into the bombed-out ruins of what had been our house, before a V1 demolished it. Daft really, I was trying to catch a young puppy. I must have felt sorry for it. Even now, I can remember exactly what it looked like, a little black-and-tan furry thing with huge paws and eyes, a tiny beard on its lower jaw.' He looked at Nobby, wondering if he was making sense to him. 'The tunnel caved in and I was buried under the rubble. My father told me later I was under for the best part of a day. The 999 service wasn't so efficient in those days. It took them hours to get to me and then to dig me out.' Alex rolled on to an elbow, watching Nobby as he stared at the distant peaks, now almost hidden.

'I'd just about gotten over it, but I suppose the fear had always been in the back of my mind. Years later, something happened at school and brought the whole bloody nightmare back again. It was a prank, some of the other kids locking me in a box during a game of hide-and-seek. You know what it's like when you're young, impressionable, your mind playing tricks on you.' He stared, into the distance, where the gun might be. 'I thought then that I was never going to get out.' Alex glanced at Nobby Clarke, wanting to know him as Richard did. 'Then, when those bastards hustled me into the furniture truck ... Well, I just couldn't think.'

'You was stuck. Where the crack got real narrow. You couldn't move. I knew how you was feeling, after the van. Me, I'm not too keen on bugs, insects and spiders. That's what scared the shit out of me, in the crack.' He grinned. 'If you couldn't get out, nor could I. No way did I want to 'ang about in there with a scorpion nibbling my nuts like a bloody squirrel noshing at 'is store, hungry after gonking 'alf the winter. I think I'd have yelled, if it had been me.'

'How did I get free? I can't remember.'

Nobby Clarke dug a heel into the desert, drawing a ragged line with it, doodling, uncomfortable. He had done what he had thought was necessary.

'Got yourself out.' Nobby said it with finality. 'I didn't do nothing.'

Alex shrugged, unsure, liking him.

'You've known Richard a long time.'

'Ay. 'E come to the Squadron greener 'n bullfrog's piss. Always in the shit, 'e was. The other subbies loved 'im, all the extras he picked up from the adjutant. Hardly anyone else did orderly officer.' Nobby, remembering, chuckled. 'But 'e knew about us, his Toms as he called us. Always on the lookout to make sure everyone got what he was due, that no one was being done unfairly, that the blokes were looked after. Stood up for us.' Nobby knocked the pipe on his knee, as if he were emptying it. 'When we was out into the desert, the Radfan, he brought up the resupply, walking in because all the choppers were deployed on an operation. He brought up the mail to our rebroadcast site. There was a letter from Millie, telling me that young John Clarke had arrived in the world.'

Knowing, Alex listened. He started sorting through his pack, organizing.

'It was 'im who got me into climbing. Never done it before. Mr N. dragged a bunch of us down to Chamonix with some Frog Alpine unit. I was scared to start with, clinging on to some rock needle, nothing between us 'cept a piece of nylon rope. But we could see 'e loved it, and it seemed to rub off on us. I was hooked after that.' Nobby paused, awkward. 'He still climbs good, but not like he did. 'E don't flow like he used to.' Nobby stuck the pipe between his lips, sucking on it.

'He fell. In the Kaisergebirge. Getting me down after I'd peeled and done my head. It took a lot to get him started again. It's always in the back of his mind, that fall. I know.' Alex was in Boston, on a flat roof, the desert, for the moment, forgotten.

'I never knew.'

'He doesn't talk about it.'

'No reason why 'e should.'

Nobby hunched big shoulders.

'He was after a Provo, the one who killed his lad. I've never asked the outcome and he's never said.' Nobby looked astutely at Alex, suddenly pointing with the stem of his pipe. Nodding. 'You. Course it was. Said something about a partner when we was up in the Lakes, when 'e was setting me up to... But then you know all that.' Nobby grinned again, then yawned tiredly. 'Bloody bandit.'

'Yes, Nobby. Me. If Richard's never told you, then nor must I. One day you'll know how it all worked out.' Alex yawned, tired. 'We'd best try and get some kip. We can't do much until Richard gets here. I'll put the cape over us. I'll take the first watch. You get your head down.' Alex spread the net over them.

There was no reply.

Nobby, head back against the rough rock, snored quietly.

The pipe had dropped on to his chest. Alex took it, careful, and slipped it into Nobby's breast pocket.

He wondered why he never lit it.

Adrian Kronk read the letter again.

It was from a firm of solicitors in Cheltenham.

Couched in the most legal terms, it spoke of their client, a Mr Richard Norris, who had left instructions at their offices, that if he did not contact them by a specified date two weeks hence, they were to deliver certain tapes to *The Times* newspaper. The tapes, they understood, contained information received by radio signal from a location in the Middle East. The tapes were to be collected from an address which had been furnished to them by their client. When transcribed and compared with a letter, also in their possession, their client's absence would be explained . . .

'The bastard!' Kronk was white, part anger, part fear.

'Problems?' Walter Oliver looked at the man, despising him.

'Nothing I can't handle.'

But he had been worrying about the letter for two days.

Kronk was aware of the tension that stretched between him and Oliver. The relationship had not been the same since Oliver had learned that there was to be no recovery of the three in Iraq. He spoke, hesitant, looking at the Colonel, but avoiding his eyes. 'But ah . . . I've decided, to ah . . . pull them out . . . ah, Norris. It's not too late. Hereford will have a team on standby.' He reached for the telephone.

'It's done.' Oliver was contemptuous. 'I told you, Kronk, that I would go over your head. I've been to the top, the PM. He's authorized an extraction. They're alerted, although their key people are already deployed. It might be a second eleven. Better than nothing.' He thought he saw an expression in Kronk's eyes. It could have been relief. He was not sure, and did not care. Again he told himself that it was time he was out of this business. As soon as this was over, he would quit. But he'd see those three safe first.

Soldiers looked out for one another.

Damned civilians.

When it came, the inimitable sound burst into his earpiece. Clear of the patrols, there was enough time to spread the folding antenna, then transfer the data from the hand-held into the main computer. Looking nervously about, he keyed in the information, ever fearful that the patrol pursuing him might be closer. Staring at the screen, he tapped at the keys. He waited. There was nothing, a hum. No corresponding tones from the distant transmitter. Come on, damn you! Some bastard safe in a basement communications centre, probably reading his book, was missing the signal.

He rechecked the settings. Correct. He pressed TEST. A red light, angry, staring, unblinking. It should have been green.

Damn. And damn again.

What the hell was wrong?

Jesus, what is this piece of shit you've designed, Norris? He looked down at the offending radio, the combined mini-computer and direction-finder. Without specialized tools, spare boards, a meter, he was unable to repair it. He wondered what to do. The sound of the patrol coming towards him made up his mind. Gathering in the antenna, reeled in as best he could, he folded away his gear, then looked about.

He started running again, this time quietly.

'You should see this, from the Middle East desk. You won't like it. Not one bit.'

Oliver placed the signal on Kronk's desk, in the middle on the blotter, behind the green onyx pen stand with its matching cigarette lighter and paper knife. Oliver knew from seeing Kronk play with it when he was nervous that the lighter didn't work. Kronk picked it up now, pressing the lever. No flint. No spark.

Kronk read the signal.

He looked up.

'Does this mean what I think it does?'

'Heavy troop movement in western Iraq, units of the Republican Guard on full alert, a column of armour moving from Baghdad? Yes, I think it does.' The eye looked at Kronk accusingly. 'It means (a) our team is not yet taken, otherwise the troop movement would have slackened, and (b)' – he paused ominously – 'it means that they are ready to fire. The armoured column. It'll be an escort for some bigwig. Might even be for Saddam himself. If they're going to fire, he'll want to be there.'

'What about the Israelis? Are they planning a mass evacuation? Of Tel Aviv?'

'If they are, they won't tell us. They'll do it under the pretence of Civil Defence Training. They've been running small-scale evacuation exercises ever since they saw what the Scud could do.' Oliver paced the room, worried, trying to control his agitation, knowing that the spittle was on his lips. He'd never been able to control it, ever since he'd taken the bullet through his neck. His mind went back briefly to the woodlands, the flat plains of Kenya.

'So what do we do?'

Oliver leaned over the desk.

'You're the boss. *You* make the decision. This was your idea, or have you forgotten?'

'Recommendations?' said Kronk fractiously, dithering with the lighter. Realizing, he put it back on the desk. 'You're the military expert. What do you suggest?'

Oliver was laconic, businesslike.

'One: scramble the Stealth. Two: deploy the extraction

team. There isn't much time. They'll be pushed, even moving now, to get there in time. They'll have to fly civil to Cyprus and by RAF flight on to Turkey, then go in covertly by helicopter. At least there's a team geared up, not that *you* had anything to do with that.' Oliver stared at him, the good eye glittering. 'And, finally, three: kiss your job goodbye. Is there anything else you need to know?' Walter Oliver turned to leave. '*Old boy.*'

His Parthian shot had struck exactly where he had intended.

In the heart.

Adrian Kronk let his head fall into his hands.

He had been running a long time.

They were still coming after him, but a long way back. It was getting lighter, the sun beginning to appear as the day began. The sky, imperceptibly lighter over his right shoulder, told him he was still going north. It would not be long before it was fully light. He must be rid of them by then.

The sound of his pursuers was lessening. Each time he listened there were fewer, until he thought that there was perhaps just one. A solitary soldier, chasing him doggedly. They had shot at him too, wildly inaccurate in the darkness, causing more confusion with the other groups, who, in turn, had fired back.

He stopped, listening. Footsteps, methodical, regular, two or three hundred metres behind. Dropping·to the ground, he looked back from below the skyline.

One man, armed, still running.

Shit.

The captain of the unit cross-country team, maybe their 10,000 metres runner, or marathon man, training for the next Olympics. Norris began to run again, tired now, dragging his feet, his mind working. The information was stored in the computer. All he needed was a way to get it home. Other than to stop and try again, he could think of nothing else. If that failed, he had to get to the RV with Alex and Nobby, then use one of their sets to relay the information back. But that, he knew, was cutting it fine. Too fine.

Either way, he had to be rid of the soldier behind.

He jumped down into a narrow gully, following it into a Technicolor sky, knowing he must kill the soldier before it was light. Otherwise, out in the open, he would be cut down by the rifle. Easy.

Breathing heavily, thirstier than he had ever been, he stopped in an open space. He took off the rucksack and leaned it against the wall of the gully. The sound of the footsteps approaching was louder now, regularly thumping into the hard surface of the desert. The soldier, when he came, would see him as soon as he rounded a bend 20 metres away.

Richard hoped he had been right.

He hoped that the wildness of the gunfire had been to frighten him, to make him stop. Nobody shot as badly as they had done. They had missed him purposely, to take him alive. Hadn't they? Soon he would know, the approaching footsteps louder as the soldier got closer.

He stood, legs apart, arms folded across his chest.

He waited, listening to the footsteps.

'Earl, shift your ass. We got a "Go".'

Colonel Stone had come from the Ops. brief, wanting to run, but refrained, knowing it wasn't good for the troops' morale. Bad, to see a bird colonel running. Instead he had walked quickly back along the cool, neon-lighted corridors, the legs of his flight suit hissing as they kissed against each other. In the crew room he picked up his helmet, the unit patch, a shield with the yellow cross and the black night hawk with the red lightning flashing from its talons, bright against the shiny surface. He looked briefly at the centrefold fixed to the wall with thumb tacks and blew a kiss.

'You wait there, baby, till old Chuck A. Stone gets back on base. Don't you go forgetting me now, y'hear?'

He led his number two out through the sliding double doors and climbed into the electric golf-cart. The others were already moving in the direction of Number Three Hangar, to the Stealth airplanes. His baby. He smiled, grim.

'You guys at the target. Just pull your foreskins up over your ears an' start whistling "Dixie" up your pricks. Chuck A. Stone is comin'.'

'You say something, Colonel?'

'Nope,' he said to the driver. 'Nothin' you would want to be hearing.'

'Is there a fix, a target, from the Brits?' Earl was asking.

'They got a 90-per-center. Apparently they're one short. But there's a real flap on, from the Embassy in London, who's been talking to the Pentagon and the White House. This is heavy shit, Earl. They got cruise stood to from a warship in the Gulf. Case we fuck up.' He grinned at the Major. 'Do we *ever* fuck up, Earl?'

'Not so's you'd notice, Colonel.'

'I'll brief you soon 's we're airborne. No time to do a proper Ops. brief on the ground. AWACS is going to guide us in. We got to move, Earl. And I mean *move*.'

The golf-cart stopped in the hangar.

The F-117A Black Hawk, Stealth, with the maintenance men scurrying fussily around it, stood in the taxiing position. It was ready. Every time Chuck Stone saw his airplane, the thought came to him. It was beautiful, black, wedge-shaped, V-tailed just like a bat. This one, a vampire, going for the jugular.

He climbed the ladder into the cockpit and slid into the Aces 2 ejection seat which took up most of the tiny cockpit, waiting for the maintenance man to hook him up, then carry out the finals. It would not take long. He lifted a thumb and called across to his partner.

'Here we go, Earl. Shuckin' and a-jivin'.'

'Heavy on the shucking, Colonel.'

Soon the two General Electric F404–GE–FID2 engines would roar into life, catapulting him down the runway, bearing him into the skies.

Vampire.

He waited, impatient.

The soldier stopped, surprised.

He looked about, then behind him, realizing suddenly that he was alone. He had outstripped the rest of the patrol and now they were a long way back. Yes, Norris thought, you're all on your own, just you and me. The soldier was unsure, half bringing his rifle up into his shoulder, the movement half-hearted, lacking confidence. Norris began to think he might have a chance.

He spoke, the Arabic rough, but understood.

'Empty.' He pointed to the Kalashnikov. 'No bullets. All gone.'

The soldier looked at the weapon, twisting it sideways. Norris knew he couldn't tell, not from looking at it. A limitation of the AKM. There was no handle to hold the breech open. It was impossible to tell if there was ammunition in the magazine without first pulling the cocking handle back and looking inside. Or firing. That was a certain way to know. But the drill was to snap the handle back and look. Norris gambled on the soldier doing it.

The man stood, uncertain, as Norris walked towards him, slow deliberate paces, nothing fast, relieved at the indecision in the dark obsidian of the soldier's eyes, the fear, as the *Ingleeze* walked slowly towards him. Norris watched, the eyes, the fingers, seeing them shifting, the movement almost imperceptible.

'Empty,' he said again.

He watched.

Eyes.

Fingers.

The hand moved, gripping the cocking handle, snapping it back. The live round ejected, spinning out and lying shiny in the sand. The soldier stared at it, realizing.

Richard Norris was on him, leaping the short gap separating them, his hands grabbing for the rifle, kneeing upward as his weight bore the soldier backwards into the sand. Cardamom, thickly sweet on his breath. Norris wrenched the gun from the man's fingers, laying it across his throat and pressing all his body weight behind it, rocking so the killing would be quicker. Briefly, he remembered the pain when he had been in the gully, knowing how the soldier felt as Death queued for him. Norris too had felt it, until Nobby Clarke had arrived. Finally, the cawing stopped. Richard Norris hit the man with the butt of the rifle, very hard, on the forehead. He rolled away, then stood, shaking, gulping from the canteen at his belt till the water was gone. Chest filling and emptying, he looked at the man he had killed, then turned and went back to his rucksack.

He set up the electronics again and went through the procedure.

Nothing.

He looked at his watch as the sun burst suddenly into the grey of the sky, bringing the light, the new day.

'Bugger it!'

He picked up the set, the best piece of equipment he had ever designed, simple controls, made possible because the complicated electronics were inside. Easy to use. Anybody could do it with a couple of minutes' instruction. Anybody. Except Richard Norris, its creator. He held it, raised above his head, then, cursing, threw it to the ground.

He kicked it.

The red test light blinked out.

The green smiled benignly.

Elated, he punched a fist hard into his palm. His fingers flew over the keys as he transferred the data, the dim light from the tiny screen reflecting his expression. The figures stabilized. He touched the transmit key, waited, holding his breath, unbelievably relieved to hear the confirmation. Now it was up to Uncle Sam. Then, the RV, to the waiting helicopter to get them out.

But he had things to do, when they got back. He felt the anger, boiling in him, tingling at his nerve ends. For the hundredth time he remonstrated with himself. It had come to him, suddenly, as he had awoken, cold in the bivvy bag, hard from dreaming of her. In the dream, her voice, softly through her tears, sounding foreign to him.

'What have I done?'

The Iraqi soldier, when he had dropped his rifle.

'*Aysh 'amalt?*'

The same. Both spoken in Arabic.

What the hell is going on here?

When he got back, he would sort it out.

If ever he got back.

The aircraft, invisible to radar, hissed across an opalescent sky, guided unerringly towards their target by the Boeing E–3 Sentry AWACS that shadowed the pair from a position off the eastern coast of Saudi Arabia. All systems were go.

Chuck Stone loved this airplane. It was the best, worth every one of the billion dollars of its production and development costs. He could fly it with impunity, right up the Iraqi assholes, and they would never know he had been there, until his ordnance, the GBU–27 Paveway III, zipped up their shirt fronts. That, he thought, really made their eyes water. There had been the arguments whether or not the plane was more effective than a cruise missile. Well, there ain't no question. OK, this baby had plenty electronics on board, but if things went badly wrong, you could still *fly* the damn thing. Not your old cruise. Get the wires crossed in that baby, and it could end up in DC, in Abe Lincoln's lap, sitting there so stern in his Memorial, 'stead of in the Kremlin where it had been aimed.

Before the end of the Cold War.

He shrugged, comfortable in the familiar cosiness of the cockpit, everything constant, normal. He checked the controls, scanning the conventional HUD, the MFDs and the monochrome CRT and the bank of computers to the front and side of him. From the nose of the aircraft four spikes protruded, probing outwards, sensing then confirming air speed and altitude. The engines, without afterburners, burned quiet with no visible exhaust. Flying at Mach 0.81, he was waiting for AWACS to confirm the exact location of his target, the Brits having passed the coordinates to London, who would pass 'em to the Embassy, who would pass 'em to the Pentagon, who ...

Shit.

As long as somebody hauled ass and passed them to *him*.

And if the Brits had screwed up, and the electronics failed to respond, they'd try and put a mobile laser-designator indicator down on the target. If that was the case, he would have to wait for the indicator light to glow, confirming that the target was lit, ready to receive the high-penetration ordnance he carried. Something should come soon. It had better. Their fuel level was registering critical. The square orange panel was flashing. It would glow continuously, orange, then flash red. Then ...

'Earl, you getting anything?' His voice echoed in the radio's sidetone. He asked, knowing the answer.

'Quieter than a gopher farting in the White House.' A spark of worry, there behind the calm.

'C'mon, baby, talk to ol' Chuck. Where are you *at*, honey? We need to find him. Quicker than soon.' The

Colonel rechecked the fuel load, stroking switches with thinly gloved fingers.

'The computer is tellin' us somethin', man, like I am *empty*. One more pass, Chuck. Then it's home, with a big H.'

'I'm getting you loud and clear, Earl. This bird is flyin' on fresh air. If 'n we don't find him, get that third fix, like now, that maintenance puke will have to get his ass out here with a wrecker truck. Hoover the bits of this baby on to it from where it will be scattered all over the Persian Gulf.' He whistled into his helmet, pretending calm.

'You're the boss, Chuck.' He paused. 'AWACS just come through on the emergency push. They say we're outta gas.'

'Yeah, I heard. Tell me something I don't know already. Got your credit cards, Earl? We may have to put down on the highway, tell them to fill her up at the nearest gas station. I wonder if they got unleaded in Iraq?'

'You're the boss,' said the Major again.

'Yeah. One more pass—'

The operator in the communications room recognized the sound as soon as he heard it. It was the third time in as many days. He worked quickly, knowing the urgency. There had been a man from upstairs, the old boy with one eye, prowling about like a gorilla in a cage, as if his pacing would make the message come through any quicker. Straight away, he had been told. Call through, just as soon as you get it.

He read the message on the printer, ripping it from the machine, leaving a jagged end to the paper roll in his hurry to have it. Reading it again, he went to the map, where he picked up a protractor and a finely sharpened pencil. Laying the protractor on the map at the position indicated on the signal, he measured off the bearing.

He drew a thin line.

It intersected with the other two, already drawn there.

There was not the slightest triangulation error.

The three lines crossed exactly.

Somebody had found something. The operator wondered what it was. He looked at his watch, then at the time zones on the map. In Iraq, it was dawn. By going to the map, he had delayed the delivery of the signal by a couple of minutes.

A couple of minutes wouldn't matter, he told himself. Would it?

Not a couple of minutes.

Nothing was that important.

He picked up the telephone and dialled upstairs.

They lay, the three of them, grouped in close, looking down into the bowl where the gun was supposed to be. Somewhere. Norris looked through the glasses, searching, hoping to see something to confirm that the cross marked on his map was the gun's location. There was nothing, just desert, scrub and rocks. He was worried, doubting, afraid that one of them had got it wrong. Maybe Seeker wasn't as good as he had thought. He was tired, drained from the chase across the desert, the fight with the soldier, then the forced march to the RV and on to the ridge.

Nobby, as ever, was calm. Outwardly at least.

Norris opened the pack at his feet, pulling out the telescopic antenna. He plugged in the earpiece, switched on, cocking his head to one side, listening. He wrenched the earpiece from his ear, the movement sudden, as if it had been painful. He shook his head.

'Shit. That was loud. We're right on top of it.'

Alex had the glasses up, sweeping them to the left, to the line of the ridge. He stiffened, holding the binoculars steady, twisting the focus.

'What is it?' Norris had sensed the urgency, looking too.

'Across there. Follow the line of the ridge. The middle of those three humps. I saw something. Movement, the sun flashing off something . . . there! Do you see it?' Alex was tense, excited, Norris still searching.

Then: 'I see it. You're right, Alex. Something shining, in the sun, along the line of the ridge. Here, Nobby, take a look.' Norris passed over the field-glasses. Nobby stared through them.

'There's an antenna. Right in the middle, sticking up like the Eiffel Tower. I wonder you missed it.'

Norris and Alex were looking hard now, finally finding what Nobby had seen. Norris tensed, then exploded.

'Of course! That's a relay, their rebroadcast, or a repeater of some sort, up on the ridge in a good communications site, where it can broadcast for miles.' He dropped the glasses to waist level, looking at the other two. 'It's obvious. They'll be using that to relay from a lower-powered set down here, in the bowl.'

Richard Norris raised the glasses to his eyes once more, searching below them. 'Now we know what we're looking for. An antenna, down there. Find that and we'll have the bastard.' Excited, the three of them scanned the desert, looking for the tell-tale antenna that would show them where the gun was hidden, somewhere under the ground.

It was Nobby who found it.

A short stubby array, mounted on an elevated pole.

'You see why they've done it like that.' A statement rather than a question. 'Up on the ridge, they'll have an observation post, with radar, image-intensifiers, the lot. They'll be scanning through a 360-degree arc, covering the whole area. We were lucky. We were screened with our approach up the gully. Must have been a blind spot.' Relieved, he pointed. 'Down where the gun is they'll be blind, never knowing whether or not it's safe to open the door. They won't do so until they've checked with the OP. Dumb of me. I should have thought of that.'

'Trouble is,' – Alex was looking thoughtful, frowning, pointing – 'if the radio up on the ridge is the one we've been getting our fixes on, the co-ordinates we've been sending back to London will be way out. The OP is half a mile from the gun. The Stealth. It'll be programmed on to the wrong target.'

Nobody said anything.

'You're right, Alex. We've got a problem, but one we ought to be able to solve.' For a moment he was silent. He stared down into the bowl where the desert wind scuffed the tumbleweed across the surface of the sand, creating columns of dust, like tiny tornadoes marching drunkenly on parade. He sucked in a deep breath. 'In that case, we have to light the target with a laser-designator so the aircraft can lock on to it. Down there in the bowl. Then, the Stealth will splat it, seagull shit on the roof of the car. Here, give me a hand. We've not much time.' Quickly Norris rummaged through his pack, sorting out the equipment he needed, lifting out the small box-like instrument resembling a pair of binoculars. He leaned forward on to the rough rock in front of him and raised the designator to his eyes, focusing on the target, his fingers moving over the switches. For a long time he looked, fiddling, twisting. He swore, hammering the heel of his hand against the rough rock.

'Problems?' Alex, his voice worried.

'Damn it!' Norris cursed. 'I don't believe this is happening. The batteries in the designator. They're almost dead.' He stared at it, stabbing the TEST button. The readings told him what he feared most. Nobby Clarke took the instrument from him, double checking.

'You're right. Flatter 'n Twiggy's tits. Can you swap them, for those in the Seeker equipment?' Nobby, thinking as always.

'Wrong sort, wrong voltage.' Norris thought hard. He chewed a thumbnail. 'There's only one way. I'll have to get closer, get the target in range so it can be lit. It's a gamble, but I can't think of anything else, other than standing out there and waving a fucking flag.' He looked down the hill, out into the bowl. He pointed. 'There. That

rock pile, about a hundred metres away. I'll have to get
to it somehow and use the designator from closer in. And
it has to be done now, in broad daylight, under the noses
of the gunners up there in the OP. Any ideas?'

He looked at Alex, at Nobby.

They stared back, realizing.

CHAPTER ELEVEN

The convoy of armoured vehicles clanked laboriously along the dusty track towards the furnace of the rising sun. Battened down, it was difficult for the drivers to see, squinting through their periscopes, those at the rear having to cope with the dust as well as the glare. Once away from the Command and Control bunker complex, the line of vehicles moved north then turned west, the sun now behind them. Three helicopter gunships hovered overhead in arrowhead formation, the two rearward aircraft higher than the one in front, covering him, searching the ground to right and left. The engines of the armoured troop-carriers whined as they ground along in low gear, not driving at best tactical speed, but keeping pace with the armoured staff vehicles that contained the distinguished passengers.

The Great One sat comfortably in the air-conditioning of the middle of the vehicles, well protected, sipping Scotch whisky from a delicately cut crystal glass. He listened as those in the vehicle fawned about him, truckling, seeking his favour. Nodding, he received their reports on the readiness of the SLING SHOT project. This very day it was to be launched against their most hated enemy, bringing them the revenge for which they had waited with such patience. It would catch them at their most vulnerable, leaving their places of work, when the streets were at their busiest, people heading for their mid-morning break, with no thought of dying in the fireball.

He, the Great One, had made this possible.

The convoy clattered monotonously on its way. There were no windows in the armoured command vehicle. The weapons slits were clamped tightly closed. Had they been open, and had the Great One chosen to look outside, he might have registered surprise at the sight of a luxuriously appointed Land-Cruiser lying on its roof, twisted and mangled at the side of the road. Had he asked, he might have been told that the vehicle had once belonged to Colonel Zaydn Ibn Ismail, one time Chief of Security at the SLING SHOT project.

But without windows, with the weapon slits tightly clamped, the Great One could not see out. He was able to see only his senior officers, obsequious in their temerity. But he was enjoying the trip. Since the war, his travelling had been severely restricted. It was a change to be out, away from the underground bunker, even though it was necessary for him to be confined to the interior of an armoured staff vehicle.

SLING SHOT.

Contented, he sipped the Scotch whisky.

Two men moved quickly up the steep incline towards the top of the ridge, stopping only when they were in cover. They had not spoken since leaving the watching place, conscious there was now very little time. The plan was thin, but the best they could think of. Pressed against a rock, they waited at the side of the track, lungs straining from the mad dash along the ridge. There had been no gunfire. They had not been seen.

One peered around the rock. The observation post was closer now, no more than 200 metres. Movement, clearly seen as the soldiers inside shifted, restless behind the weapon slits, hot, bored, looking out into the desert, the opposite way from the direction in which the two men were approaching. They waited, breath held. The bigger of the two looked at his watch, holding up five fingers. The other nodded, his expression grim, tense, understanding.

The two men turned and looked back along the ridge. There was no sign of the other, still invisible. He would not move for another five minutes. It was what they had arranged. They looked once more to their front, the way they had to go. The big man, tense, held up a thumb. He tried to grin, knowing he had failed. The other understood, raising a hand in a gesture of waving, then checked the Iraqi rifle he carried.

'Go, Nobby. See you at the RV.' Whispered. He tried to grin again, failing as before.

Nobby Clarke scuttled off to his right, slightly downhill. He carried the rifle easily, loose in his fingers, wishing there had been more ammunition with it when Norris had brought it back to them. Removing the magazine, he had ejected the bullets on to his shirt where they would not pick up the sand, the gravel from the desert, and jam when he fed them back into the rifle.

There had been twelve.

They had lain, spread on his shirt, glinting in the sun.

Twelve only.

Not enough. Not nearly enough.

Best not to think about what would happen when the magazine was empty, when the gun stopped firing and he could no longer cover the other two, Mr A. and N. Sounded like a laxative, he thought, or a make of candy. He stopped procrastinating, instead moving off with a shuffling, sideways gait, down the hill, keeping in dead ground between the Iraqi position and the direction in which he was moving. There was a good place, between three boulders, the one in front lower than those on the side. He could rest on the lowest to steady his aim, important because it gave him an edge. Not much, but some.

He watched the big figure of Alex Howard as he moved up towards the OP, slow, cautious, keeping in cover, up on his feet, crouched slightly. The main radar would be looking out into the desert, to the west, so, with luck, no one would be looking this way. Despite knowing where Alex was, Nobby Clarke found him difficult to see. Even moving, he was a blur, a fleeting chameleon blending with the cover, nothing fast or jerky. They had spent a long time on their camouflage, the strips of hessian breaking up their outline, cream on their faces. It would prevent them from being seen, not protect them from a bullet.

He looked again at the position, the Iraqi OP on the crest of the ridge. It had been built, fused into the rock, invisible to the naked eye. If he, Nobby, hadn't seen the antenna they would never have found it. The construction looked solid enough from Nobby's fire position. But it had been built balanced on a pillar, one corner on a column of stone, manmade and not part of the natural rock. Its weak point, Mr A. had said.

Two men. A Russian AKM. And twelve bullets.

Thin odds.

And while they sorted the OP, Mr N. was going out into the bowl to get closer with the laser-designator so that the Stealth bomber could put a cluster of bunker busters into the Supergun.

Bugger.

He watched Alex Howard as he moved up the hill.

He rechecked the rifle.

Suddenly, he felt very alone.

'I make it we're over the target area, Colonel.'

'That's affirmative, Earl. Anything?'

'Nothing.'

'Last pass, then. Status from AWACS? We got a target yet?'

'Not definite enough to hit. Still waiting confirmation on the third fix. But they scrambled a refuelling bird, soon 's they registered we were critical. There's a KC-135E full of juice, just waiting to meet us. Sky's clear, no bogies about.'

'Thank God someone in the Head Shed is thinking. Here we go then. Cross everything, rub the rabbit's foot. Last pass—'

'You're the boss.'

The Colonel stared at the computer bank, the coloured lights flashing, iridescent.

Willing.

Alex picked a line from which he could not be seen should a soldier look out of the weapon slits cut into the sides of the Observation Post. He moved, slowly, carefully, back against the rock as he eased upwards towards the deep shadow cast by the construction. He was close, close enough to hear the talk coming from the box-like contraption, standing out from the rock, supported by the stone pillar at one corner. He waited, breath held, thirsty from the climb, wondering if Nobby could see him, worried about Richard when he made his dash out with the designator.

Cautiously he peered around the rock that hid him, scanning, looking for the dark shapes that would show him where the soldiers were located inside the OP. The slits were empty, no one looking this way. For the moment. He squinted once more at his watch, surprised that the time was almost used up. He looked over his shoulder, trying to see Nobby Clarke. Nothing. Just the boulder clump further down the hill.

He hoped Nobby was there, that he could see him, cover him when he made his dash to the Iraqi position. One more look at his watch, then up the hill, running before he had time to change his mind. It was only twenty metres. He counted them, each pace, as he rushed up the hill aiming for the deep shadow under the OP where he would be out of sight of the occupants.

If he made it that far.

He waited for the burst of fire that must surely come. The distance was shorter with each pace, the shadow, safety, closer as he ran. Fifteen ... ten ... he looked up at the weapon slits, transfixed, tensed as he waited for the

guns to start firing. Eight ... five ... a couple more ...
Throwing himself into the shadow under the OP, he tumbled into the darkness, out of the harsh glare of the sun.
He rolled over on to his back, sitting up, then ignoring
the burning throb of the bayonet wound, shuffled on his
buttocks into still deeper shadow, pushing with his feet to
propel himself faster.

Panting, he looked about him.

Above, the rough wooden planks of the floor, dust
filtering through the cracks where the soldiers moved restlessly. In the corner, almost hidden, he could make out
the building materials used during its construction, bags
of cement, tarpaulins, a plethora of tools, scattered untidily. He looked then at the pillar supporting the structure
above, wondering. Closer inspection showed it to be made
of blocks, balanced and held together with a crumbling
mortar. It was soft, powdery, flaking when he dug his
thumbnail into it. Thoughtful, he walked over to the tools.
He wrenched back the tarpaulin, elated at seeing what
was there. He looked at his watch again.

If only there was time.

He bent and picked up the sledgehammer. Hefting it
in his hands he drew in a deep breath, then walked to the
pillar. Briefly he closed his eyes, letting his mind dwell on
what he had to do. Again he looked for Nobby Clarke.
Still, he saw nothing.

Another shuddering breath.

Legs braced, deep breath, bellowing.

He swung the hammer.

Norris looked at his watch. It was time. He had no idea
if Alex and Nobby were in position, nor what they could
do even had they got there. Alex had been right. The plan
was bloody thin. Nobby as ever, silent, sucking the pipe,
nodding to show he understood what was wanted of him.
They were off to his left, up the ridge in the direction of

the OP, Nobby with the rifle with the twelve bullets in it, Alex with nothing. Bloody thin. He shrugged.

He had worked his way down the slope towards the bowl, now perhaps 300 metres from the antenna, the antenna that showed where the gun was. He let his mind go back over the briefing he'd been given in London on a sunny day in spring, when all this had seemed distant, unreal. Not any more. The dates, the times, the places, the margins of error. All remembered. It was close, maybe already too late. He hoped they remembered that the designator, if it came on, overrode any other target indicators. As fail-safe, last-ditch, it had absolute priority.

The Stealth aircraft were up, even now overhead. He looked, realizing then that he would not see them. He took stock, staring, eyes inflamed, lips split from the sun. Fatigue cloaked him. Now, he saw nothing except the rock pile where he needed to be, the clump of scrub that marked the antenna and the 300 metres of open ground between. His eyes were drawn back to his watch, the face scratched from the climb up the Great Crack, where he had jammed his fist into the holds, hauling himself up out from the dark and back into the sunlight.

Gathering himself, he crouched, like a sprinter in his blocks, the laser-designator in his hands, not heavy, but enough to upset his balance, spoil the flow of his running. He tried not to think about the dash across the sand, nor to worry about Alex and Nobby, somewhere up on the ridge. He stared out at the clump of rocks, the place he had to reach, wondering what he was doing here.

He checked the time again and looked at the rock pile.

Think of Johnathan.

Suddenly, a long way off, he heard a dull muffled sound, as if someone was hitting a brick wall with a hammer. He thought he could hear yelling. A rifle started firing, single shots, aimed so none would miss. He counted three. Nobby with his twelve before they were gone. The dull, flat reports of a rifle tumbled down the hill.

Three more.
Six left.
He started running.

Nobby Clarke, the gun supported on the rock, saw Alex appear from the shadow under the Iraqi OP. There was a hammer in his hands, big, heavy, purposeful in the way it was carried. Alex walked to the pillar, peered at it closely, then rested the hammer with the head on the ground leaning against the rough stone. Spitting into the palms of his hands, he rubbed them on his thighs. For a moment he appeared to be looking down the slope, to confirm that he, Nobby, was close at hand.

Alex raised the hammer, angled back over his left shoulder.

Mr A., even you can't knock the bloody place down with a fucking sledgehammer. I don't believe I'm seeing this.

Gripping the rifle, tighter now, he realized what Alex intended. Nobby had no idea what would happen when the first blow slammed into the pillar. He was soon to find out. Fascinated, he watched as the hammer swept forward, almost in slow motion, slamming into the stonework with a dull thud. A piece of brick flew off, spinning away into the shadows behind Alex. No sound came from the OP, until Alex had hit the pillar with four or five crashing blows. Then, the shouting, the alarm, as those in the OP realized. Nobby watched, listening, waiting for the first of them to appear in the doorway.

A soldier, bare headed, looked round the door, then stepped out on to the narrow gangway at the top of a rude stairway which led down to where Alex was thumping with the hammer. The man turned briefly inside, returning almost at once, rifle held up into the shoulder as he came out to investigate what was causing the OP to shake on its foundations. He looked over the edge, but could neither see nor identify the cause.

The soldier yelled back into the OP, guttural, threatening, gesticulating with the rifle, pointing downwards. He began to descend, cautious, looking nowhere except down into the shadow, where Alex Howard was trying to knock the OP off its foundations. At the third step, Nobby shot him. There was no sound as he crumpled, rolling in a tangle of arms and legs, down the steps to the ground, twitching momentarily before lying still.

Nobby waited.

Alex paused briefly in his work as the gunshot cracked from somewhere down the slope. Satisfied the firing had not been directed at him, he continued hammering. Two more soldiers came out on to the ledge, alarmed, frightened when they saw the body lying crumpled at the foot of the steps. They looked about them, seeking the shooter, not finding him as the front man took the next bullet in the chest. The last of them ducked back inside, another bullet slapping into the wall close to his head, spurting dust and debris into his eyes.

Three gone.

Nine left.

They rushed, the next time, three of them coming out together, tightly grouped, unable to spread out on the narrowness of the platform. Nobby hit two, one falling out over the ledge, down the short cliff, the other screaming, ducking to clutch a leg where the bullet had torn into his thigh. He was left, moaning. No one dragged him back into the OP. The thumping from the hammer continued, heavy, relentless, as it smashed into the brickwork. Nobby waited, tense, gripping the rifle, waiting for another target to appear, not knowing how many men had been in the OP. Surely not many more. He would know, soon.

A machine-gun started firing, not at Nobby or Alex, but down into the bowl. It could mean only one thing. Norris had started his run and had been seen. Nobby looked hard at the OP, seeking the weapon slit that hid the Gun. Not seeing it immediately, he knew it had been well hidden, back from the firing slit where the tell-tale smoke signature would be invisible. The gun kept firing, long irregular bursts, as if its target appeared briefly, fleetingly.

He picked out the smoke, coming from the middle of the weapon slits, spitting out into the clean air of the desert, plucked away on the breeze before it could linger. Nobby sighted, fired, three careful, aimed shots, into the slit.

The firing stopped.

Alex stood, legs braced, balanced on the flat of his feet, staring at the pillar, hating it. He swung the hammer, letting the big muscles in his back pull the heavy hammer head forward, allowing it to trail and accelerate into the target. He felt the jarring, through his fingers, hands and arms, the wrenching in the muscles of his shoulders down through his injured leg as the head slammed into the brickwork. Elated, he saw the large chunk as it flew off behind him. He knew then that he could do it, could knock the pillar down, collapse the OP and wreck the radar equipment inside. More important, it would prevent them shooting at Richard Norris as he sprinted across the desert with the laser in his hands.

It was imperative he stopped the machine-gun from firing.

Vital.

A rhythm now, as the hammer swung and thumped into the bricks, pieces flying off, cracks appearing where before it had been solid. Dust from the floorboards above his head showered down on him, sticking to the sweat pouring from him, clinging to the bandanna tied around his head to keep his eyes clear. He ignored the voices coming from above, hearing the urgency as one called to the others. The gun, one shot, Nobby firing, the sun briefly obscured as a body tumbled down the steps.

Swinging the hammer, he felt the thump through his body.

Pain in his hands as the rough wood of the handle, the friction from swinging, blistering his fingers and palms. His lower back straining, pain transferring upwards from his buttock.

Hands, fingers, bleeding.

He swung the hammer, harder, faster, driving it into the pillar. Hurting now, but he did not stop to ease the pain. Gunshots, two more, bringing cries from above, agony in the sound. Nobby Clarke doing his job, keeping them at bay, so that he could knock down the pillar. No pain now, swinging the heavy iron into the brickwork, singing.

. . . yeah, Lord, gonna . . .

He swung, thumping.

. . . die with this . . .

Lumps, chunks, flying everywhere, hitting him.

. . . hammer in my hand . . .

Movement, a slight rocking. Imperceptible, but moving. One more. One more good one.

. . . yeah, Lord, I'm gonna die with this hammer in my hand . . .

The hammer smashed into the pillar, already crumbling, teetering as gravity and the pounding won the battle. Alex Howard felt the dust, pieces of stone falling on his shoulders, the fierce pain as the first of the planks, one of the floorboards fell about him, hurting him. Dimly, through the pain and noise and the dust, he heard shouting, saw a figure charging towards him.

Ten metres and going well, running hard, then tripping in the light scrub, feeling it wrapping round his ankles pulling him down. It probably saved his life. As he lay, mouth and eyes full of sand, he heard a machine-gun start firing from the position up on the ridge. Clawing fingers across his eyes, he cleared them, enough to see the dust spurts as the bullets crept towards him. He rolled, first to his left, then immediately back to his right, hearing the vicious crackle as the burst clattered inches above his head.

He searched for the designator, not seeing it immediately. It had been flung from his fingers when he had tripped and now he felt the beginnings of panic when he didn't see it at once. But there, in a clump of scrub where it had jumped from his hands as he had fallen. A bloody fine time to knock-on. The thought amused him for a reason he could not explain. He rolled over to it without getting up, waiting for the next burst of gunfire. Then, quickly on his feet, he scooped up the small box-like contraption that would tell the Stealth bomber where to drop its load.

Fingers under it, now held under one arm, a winger going for the corner flag, side-stepping, avoiding the machine-gun, instead of a full back's tackle. But the gun was finding him, the spurts showing the line of bullets pecking across the flatness of the desert. Close, closer still. There was no way it could fail to cut him down, chewing first through his legs, lower, then upper body, as he pitched forward into its path.

He tried not to look at the strike of the bullets, creeping ever closer, but his eyes were drawn there, mesmerized as the line stuttered across the sand and gravel. He knew that despite the evasive action he was taking, the gun would find him, cut him down, slamming into him as he lay helpless, twitching in the sand.

Dear God, Johnathan, is this what it was like? When Donnelly got you? Were you this afraid?

He heard the flat report of the rifle, three quick shots, aimed, not squirted off anyhow, and knew that Nobby was doing what he could. He had even counted.

Nine gone, now only three.

But the machine-gun had stopped. Just the sound of his boots as they thudded across the hard pan of the desert, seeing the rocks where he would mark the antenna, closer with every pace. He tensed as he ran, waiting for the gun to start again knowing Nobby Clarke could not pin down the heavier firepower for very much longer. Vaguely he wondered what the hell Alex was doing, whether he was with Nobby, perhaps in the fire-fight he could hear.

He dived at the rock base, lying with the warm roughness pressed against his cheek, feeling the heat from being in the sun all day. He scrambled to the top of the pile. This close, he could see the guy-lines, the pegs that kept the antenna vertical in the sudden desert winds, the paint chipped from its base. The ground seemed artificially flat here, puzzling him. He scooped up a loose rock and threw it, watching as it bounced on the shallow covering of sand.

Solid.

Christ. He was nearly on it. He was almost on the door.

Through his body, he felt a faint vibration, growing in intensity. He heard the high-pitched whine of turbines, deep in the earth below him. The ground began to move, slowly at first, then more quickly. He realized immediately what was happening.

The door was opening.

An image of Oliver came suddenly to him, the spittle on his lips when he had tried to tell Norris of the complexity of the engineering. He had given up. It had been too much for him to grasp. The door spun slowly, Norris watching, feeling it revolve, clockwise, turning him so that he would soon be facing the sun. He was transfixed, feeling the power, his own inadequacy as he lay spread against the hot rock, gasping for breath, the laser-designator still in his hands. He knew, then, what was going to happen.

They were going to fire.

Quickly he set and locked the designator and checked it was transmitting.

He placed it carefully on the rock in front of him, aimed at the target.

Then, like a startled hare, he was running.

*

Nobby Clarke squinted through the sights, waiting for the machine-gun to start firing again, willing it to keep silent. He wondered, briefly, what Norris was doing, if he had succeeded so that the USAF could do their part. The thumping of the hammer brought him back. He took his eyes momentarily from the weapon slit to watch Alex Howard. Like the bloke at the start of the movies, he thought, but damned if he could remember the name of the studio. Some big bastard hitting a gong, but in slow motion. Of course. J. Arthur. Wank. Not like Mr A. up under the Iraqi position. Nobby thought he could hear him singing.

He wondered how the hell Alex was going to get out, if, when, the pillar was shattered and the whole structure collapsed about him like a house of cards. Suddenly, a deep, groaning rumble. It was going. Even from his position down the hill, Nobby could see the pillar rocking as the blows struck it with crushing, splintering force.

Silly, daft bugger.

He scrambled over the boulder that had sheltered him, and rushed up the hill towards Alex working with the hammer, tireless, massive in the shadow. Nobby carried the rifle across his body, knowing there were only three rounds left in the magazine, but feeling comforted, less helpless than he would have been without it.

He had no idea how he could help.

Pushing hard up the hill he saw where a great bite had been taken out of the pillar, in the place where the hammer head had been relentlessly slamming into it. Had he not witnessed this, he would never have believed it. But it was going. The whole structure was teetering, balanced finely now, the pillar wobbling, bringing frightened yells from those soldiers left inside, as they wondered what was causing the violent movement below them. Nobby watched, running, knowing he could do nothing, and Alex would be crushed under the rubble as soon as the pillar finally fractured. Not many more blows were needed.

It took just one.

Nobby Clarke, yards short, saw the dust and the stones and the rubble and the planks, all begin to tumble downward, covering Alex in a fine dust, one of the boards striking him on the shoulder. He rushed on, yelling, screaming at Alex to get out, to leave the bloody place, let nature, gravity do the rest. He hurled himself into the mess of tumbling masonry, ducking into the confusion, feeling his shoulder crash into the man with the hammer, the momentum of his charge carrying them through the mess of falling timbers and stonework, out into the sunshine, coughing, gasping as the dust was sucked into their lungs.

Collapsing, gagging, spitting the mess out of their mouths, crouched on all fours, they stared balefully at the carnage they had created. They waited for the jumble to settle, to tell them it was over, that their work had been done. It was quiet, eerie now, only the occasional rattle as a piece of stone fell from the top of the heap, or a pile of dust slipped between the floorboards, stacked like an untidy bonfire. The dust settled, clearing slowly in the still air, lingering, preventing them seeing the damage. A hand, dust covered, bleeding, spurting blood from a severed artery, the arm sticking awkwardly from the pile of rubble, was the only sign of what had once been life.

They stood, shaken, Alex looking at the damage to his hands, rubbing a shoulder where the plank had hit him. They walked, Alex limping badly now, over to the remains of the OP, at what had once been a place where men had lived, breathed, shared their lives. Amongst the cooking pots, weapons, technical equipment, tattered newspapers, letters from home, and the magazines, lay the bodies, men who would never fight again.

For whatever cause.

Alex shook his head.

Nobby Clarke, head cocked, was listening, screwing his face in concentration.

'Listen.' He held a finger to his lips, as Alex was about to speak.

They stood together, trying to identify the sound, a high-pitched whine, a humming, down in the bowl. Alex, suddenly excited, pointed, his finger bleeding from his gripping the hammer.

'Look!'

'What the—?'

The two men watched, stunned, seeing the hole appear in the desert below, hearing the noise of the enormous turbines working to move the tonnes of steel and sand that covered the entrance to the Supergun complex hidden under the ground.

'Well, I'll be ... Shit. It's huge. Nobby. Just look at the size of it.'

'Where's the Gun?'

'It'll be there, somewhere.'

As if in confirmation the ugly snout of the Gun appeared at the entrance, like the blunt nose of a cobra as it peeps from the charmer's basket. Driven by a complicated system of hydraulic ramps, the barrel, telescopic in construction, rose into the bright sunlight, enough that when fired, it would be clear of the complex and not fill the underground chamber with poisonous fumes. Speechless, they watched, each finding the magnitude of the project difficult to comprehend. Nobby was about to speak when suddenly, inexplicably, the barrel stopped elevating, the whine of the turbines dying with a tired sigh. Almost at once, they restarted, the pitch higher, more urgent than before. The Gun began a lazy, majestic withdrawal, like a giant glans retreating under the cover of its protective prepuce. As it vanished into the dark hole, there was absolute silence. For a moment nothing moved.

'Nobby, they're starting to close it! What the hell is going on?'

'Don't ask me.' There was a puzzled look on Nobby Clarke's features. 'And what about Mr N.? Where the bloody 'ell's Mr N. got himself to? If they fire when he's still in the bowl, he can kiss his arse goodbye. He'll have no chance. Do you think he got the marker down? For the bomber? D'you think he laid it, Mr A.?'

'If he did, Nobby, we'll soon know.'

None of them wanted to tell the Great One.

There was a last-minute hitch.

A report from the OP up on the ridge had told them to hold.

The task fell to the General, the Project Director, a technical man who had qualified for his engineering degree in the United States. A conceited, arrogant man, who had not been so pompous when he had entered the briefing chamber to inform the distinguished audience of the last-minute hold-up. Truckling, dry-washing his hands, he had approached the hallowed position where the Great One sat. The Director had leaned forward, first the obsequious touching of the coat, then speaking, his lips almost brushing the ear, letting none in the chamber hear what had been said.

There was anger, barely concealed.

The firing had been cancelled. There had been no communication from the OP on the ridge since the initial panicky call telling them it was not safe to open the doors and lift the barrel out into full view. The door had been hurriedly closed. Suddenly, they had lost contact with the radar, even on the emergency frequency. The procedure was to close down, then wait until it was safe to open. The others, the infantry and the artillery and the tank officers, breathed a sigh of relief because it had not been their duty to tell of the postponement of the SLING SHOT project. They were glad that they had no responsibility. None at all. Later, when they told of their inability to find and capture the British team, they, too, would feel the wrath.

Everyone in the chamber watched as he stood to leave. Looking neither to left nor right on his hurried way across the polished tiling of the room, the Great One swept through the airtight doors. The sigh was audible. Gradually, the group dispersed, back to their tanks and guns and infantry units.

The British team was proving elusive, difficult to find.

But it was only a matter of time.

Then, the project could continue as before.

As if nothing had happened.

'There it is, Chuck, confirmation, the third fix.'

'I got it, Earl.' The voice, crystal clear over the airwaves.

The Colonel carried out pre-delivery checks, speaking briefly again on the radio to his wingman.

'All ready.'

Silence in the airplane.

Suddenly, a green light, flashing intermittently, demanding attention.

Pips, high-pitched, filling his helmet.

'What the . . . Shit. The designator, the override. Compute, confirm it for me, Earl.'

'Wait, come *on*, baby.'

Fingers tapped buttons, threw switches.

'Different target, Chuck.'

'How come?'

'Fuck knows!'

'Deviation, alignment?'

'Three thousand, two hundred twenty-four feet. Coupla inches. Same azimuth plus one eight point two three, right.'

'Yeah. That's what I'm getting. Miles out.'

'Tell me,' the wingman asked, tense now. 'Which one, Chuck?'

'The designator is supposed to override. Whaddaya think?'

'Iraqi counter-measure? ECM? We know the team's been compromised.'

'By the goodies, not the bad guys.'

'That's what they said to Custer—'

Shit.

Chuck Stone pondered, weighing the options. Whatever else, his Ops. brief had said, if the auxiliary designator light came on, act on it. But supposing the Brits had been taken, talked, and been made to set the beacon as a decoy? What if . . .?

'I'm goin' round again. We overshot.'

'Chuck, we're flying on vapour. You sure about this?'

'Here we go, Earl. You ready with the load?'

'Soon 's you tell me what to shoot at.'

'Lemme think. Eenie, meenie, minee . . . Shit, I just don't know, man!'

Agonizing.

'Colonel—?'

Chuck Stone made his choice.

He told the other airplane.

He called the AWACS, impressing them.

'Do it, Earl!' Colonel Stone stretched out a hand, finger pointed, to the F\DLIR laser-designator system, hesitating only briefly, his finger circling the switch, then settling reluctantly on it.

'Colonel—?'

'I'm sure. Do it!'

'You're the boss, Chuck.'

It was quiet in the cockpit. Then the quiet whisper of hydraulics. Below the aircraft the wings on the Paveway snapped open as the missiles fell from the pods, hesitated, suspended, then fell away from the aircraft and dropped earthwards, seeking a target.

'All gone.' The voice tight. 'Jesus, I hope we got the right one.'

'Let's go home, Earl.'

'You're the boss,' said the Major again.

The two aircraft banked majestically, levelled, flying to a programme that would bring them to the refuelling co-ordinates where the Boeing would be cruising patiently as an eagle awaits its fledglings away from the nest.

But these were bats.

Beautiful.

Colonel Charles A. Stone whistled quietly into his helmet. The Major, his wingman, listened, recognizing the tune.

'Dixie'.

The armoured column drove east, at best speed, through the barrier stretched across the dusty road, past the vehicle lying on its roof, away from the complex where they were to have witnessed the firing of the Supergun. The senior officers in the armoured command vehicle were unaware of the reason for their rapid departure, the unexpected and rapid hegira. But it was clear that the Great One was displeased, his anger boiling about him.

He seemed not to be enjoying the whisky from the finely cut crystal glass, especially when a deep trembling from beneath the vehicle caused the liquid to slop onto his fingers. They had looked anxiously about, all of them, wondering what could have caused the vibration, the rumbling in the ground, felt even through the solidness of the vehicle. There was puzzlement at the sound of the thunder, rolling, reverberating in the distance, where they had been, just moments before. None would venture to say what he thought had caused this phenomenon.

Perhaps after all, the Gun had been fired.

But surely, had this been so, the Great One would not have been sitting with such anger about him.

No one dared ask what had happened two short minutes earlier.

The missiles cut through the steel plating of the revolving

door, aimed unerringly at the electronic fire-control system, the nerve centre of the Supergun complex. One after another they drilled through the armour, whistling down the burning throat of the opened defensive system. The underground complex, the Supergun, its electronic control room, firing devices and ammunition exploded in a white-hot ball of greedy flame, consuming everything with its fiery touch. After the flame came the smoke, thick, black, choking and poisonous . . . Seven minutes, six point two one seconds later, four Tomahawk cruise missiles followed them in. Chuck A. Stone had taken no chances. He had called AWACS on the emergency push, who in turn talked to Base. The Commander had spoken on a satellite patch to the Pentagon, who ordered the launch from a warship in the Gulf.

Needed to be sure, he told Earl after.

Just in case we fucked up.

We *ever* fuck up, Colonel?

They were elated, all three.

Norris had made it out of the bowl, running faster than at any time in his life, flying rock and dust and sand, pieces of metal, wood and plastic, spattering into the desert around him, lending strength to his exhausted legs. Then had come the fireball, the air-consuming heat, scorching his back, singeing the hair on the nape of his neck. Briefly he had smelt his clothes burning. Alex and Nobby had watched the avalanche of boulders tumble down into the bowl, a short cliff collapse into rubble making the falling OP insignificant in comparison. And the acrid fumes that had caught in their throats, choking them. There could be no mistaking the cause of the explosions deep in the ground under the desert. Miles on they felt the reverberation through their feet as they ran, light-headed, away from the bowl that had hidden the Gun, the ridge with the OP that had brooded over it and the machine-gun that had protected it. Finally, it was over, finished, and they had done it. They ran into the sun, a euphoric, happy trio. Now, to the RV, the waiting helicopter and the escort to get them out. Fighting their way if need be. Their part of the operation was over. Let somebody else worry about the repercussions.

Major Simon Endercote, Parachute Regiment, serving with D Squadron of 22 Special Air Service Regiment, checked his gear for the tenth time. He sat, pressed against the piles of equipment stashed in the loading bay of the Chinook helicopter as it clattered out of a northern sky into Iraqi air space. He was calmer as the time for action approached, now that the rush to arrive in southern Turkey with the rest of his brick was over. There had been so little time. The charge up to London, the briefing, the civil flight to Cyprus, then the RAF VC10 to southern Turkey, behind him now.

There had been no time for rehearsals, unusual, contrary to procedures. Just the rush, the panic, to get his brick into Iraq to pull out a specialist insertion team deployed on a mission so secret none of them had been told what it was.

Endercote could hardly believe his luck. He had been with the SAS no time at all and by chance was already out on a mission. Right place, right time. The 'A' Team already deployed. He smiled grimly. This was what it was all about, he told himself. This was *soldiering*. Better than being with P Company. He had missed the Falklands campaign because he'd been serving with 1 Para up in Scotland. A home-defence battalion. Dad's fucking army. The Second and Third battalions had got the glory down south, in the fighting. One of the bastards, he never found out who, had sent him a white feather. Well, now it was *his* turn.

He wasn't sure why, but he checked his stuff all over again.

Just to be sure.

Tired, they marched all through the night, lying up whenever they heard the sound of a patrol searching for them still. Five miles, no more. They would arrive before dawn, then wait for the helicopter to come and lift them out. Richard let his mind wander, anticipating the arrival of the helicopter, smiling grimly when he remembered how he had duplicated the communications system, the information sent to his company in Cheltenham as well as to Kronk and his spooks. He pictured Kronk's face when he had received the letter from his solicitors, warning him of the consequences if their client had not returned by a certain date. He smiled at his own audacity. Alex and Nobby saw the expression and grinned too, without knowing the reason. Only that it was over. All bar the shouting.

They trudged on, exhausted now that the exhilaration had deserted them, evaporating like early-morning mist in the sun. Norris led, occasionally checking map and compass by the light of a shaded pencil torch as he calculated the distance, assessing when they would arrive and how long they might have to wait. They knew, each of them, that there would be no let-up from the searching patrols, that the hunt for them would continue unabated, more so, now that they had done their work. They travelled tactically, moving in bounds across the desert to the RV. Nobby Clarke still carried the rifle, the rifle with the three bullets in it, and, when told he should dump it, muttering that it might still be needed.

At last, they came to the cliff, a low escarpment that marked where they should be. They sat, backs to the rock, looking out into the flatness of the desert. A good place. No obstacles to get in the way. A perfect LZ for a helicopter.

Now, just sit, sleep and wait for it to arrive.

*

'We're almost there.'

Major Endercote looked up at the Load Master as he stood swaying in the Chinook helicopter. They were flying low, hugging the contours, the pilot fighting against the thermals that threatened to bounce the aircraft down into the desert, then up again, to a height higher than he wanted to be, above the radar shadow which he had diligently been avoiding since entering Iraqi air space.

'How long?' Endercote's lips were dry. Again, he fought the desire to tug the water bottle out of the holder at his belt and take a long swig from it. None of the others needed to drink. He supposed it was just him, nervous on his first mission. Stage fright.

'Two minutes.' The Load Master dropped his wrist, the sleeve covering his watch. 'We'll be on the ground for the minimum time, so you'll need to get those chaps aboard as quickly as possible. If the baddies have any anti-helicopter air defence about, ZUS 23–24, or worse, Roland, the pilot won't want to be hanging about. Any contact with them? The team on the ground?'

Endercote shook his head.

'No. Nothing. They've no ground-to-air radio. All we got was the RV, and an approximate time. This whole thing has been a rush from start to finish. God knows if they're even there.' Endercote bit back his worry, hiding it from the Load Master, the soldiers, dozing, or staring at their feet. How the hell was he supposed to know if they were there or not? And if they weren't?

'If they aren't there, at the RV? You'll put us down, and come in again when we call?'

The Load Master nodded, grinned and stuck up his thumb.

'They'll be there, Major.'

Endercote wondered if he felt as confident as he sounded.

He checked his equipment again.

He had lost count of the number of times he had done it.

The shaking at his shoulder woke him. For a moment he was lost, not knowing where he was. He was shivering, uncomfortable, stiff, his feet hurting. Moving, he shrugged away from the persistent, irritating movement, tugging at his shoulder, then at his sleeve. He tried to turn over, feeling the rough material of the rucksack rubbing against his face, hurting the soreness of his lips. He was thirsty. His body ached. He craved sleep, rest, food and drink. Most of all he wanted to drink. Something long and cool. Not the tepid, brackish water he had been drinking since . . .

Awake.

Where was he?

Cold, hurting, Norris did not want to move.

Someone was shaking his shoulder, the voice, urgent, pressed into his ear, a hand clamped over his mouth to prevent his talking, making a noise. Then, unmistakable, the high-pitched whine of an armoured personnel-carrier, driving fast, the noise dying as the BTR slowed, then stopped.

Another sound, louder, the deep punching of a helicopter.

They had come for them.

Now, their backs to the cliff, with an Iraqi APC between them and safety.

'Fuck it.' Nobby Clarke, not one to mince his words. 'How the 'ell did the Iraqis know where to find the RV?'

'Where is it? The chopper? I can hear it but—'

'There!' Norris, shaking his head, trying to come fully awake, pointed, half right. They lay grouped in close to the cliff, hidden by a pile of loose rocks. 'Look right. Two o'clock. Coming in low. The dust swirl.'

'Got it.' Alex stared at the diorama of the lightening sky, the yellows and reds and oranges, ugly in the birth of a new day, angry, as if those on the ground had done something to rile the gods, who now scowled their petulant displeasure. Charon, flexing his muscles, ready to row them into Hades. A hell of a time to go poetic.

'And there. Look.' Nobby Clarke pointed.

They saw it, Alex and Richard together, the dirty yellow-pink camouflage of the APC 200 metres from them, half left, the opposite side to the helicopter's approach path. Norris felt the despair, as the doors opened and men disgorged from the rear, already fanning out, perhaps bewildered as the sound of the rotors increased, louder the nearer the chopper got to them. There was confusion, a lack of direction, no orders to co-ordinate their actions.

Exhausted, Norris tried to think, but nothing came, no clear plan to get to the helicopter with a section of Iraqi infantry covering the ground between their position and the landing zone. As yet he did not know where the LZ would be. Not much closer in, the cliffs were a hazard. And a line of rocks jutting out from the right prevented the helicopter coming in from that side. If it landed, it would have to be at the end of this rock formation, where it was marked with a vertical pillar of big, square boulders.

Like Hound Tor, on Dartmoor.

Norris wondered he could make the comparison.

He looked again at the APC, the soldiers standing at the rear who were still not moving. One pointed suddenly, across, and up, at the helicopter hovering, moving slowly in towards the cliff. He made up his mind, not letting himself stop to think.

Instinct.

'Come on. Move!'

Without waiting to see their reaction, Norris cast off the rucksack and started running, out to his right, following the line of the cliffs in a direction that would take him away from the APC, towards the pillar of rock jutting out into the desert. That was where the chopper would make its LZ. He knew it. He wondered if the pilot had seen the armoured vehicle.

Gunshots, distant, sounding remote.

Norris looked up to see the puffs of smoke coming from the Iraqi infantry, some kneeling, others lying in the sand, a few firing as they stood. There was no sound of the heavy machine-gun mounted on the vehicle. That would come later, when someone remembered it. For the moment it had been forgotten.

Confusion.

They were seen, running, some of the soldiers now shooting at them instead of the helicopter. Norris glanced back, seeing Alex close in behind him, limping but running well, still wearing the rucksack. He reached out, gripping his arm, tugging him along, helping. Nobby, like Norris, had dumped his rucksack back in the rocks. Who the hell needed it now? Elation, then, as men leaped from the helicopter, which was still hovering ten feet above the ground. Disciplined, they spread to take up positions and return fire. They were closer now, able to make out the uniforms, the shape of the steel helmets, the black plastic rifles, the M16 Armalite, and the longer barrel of the General Purpose Machine-Gun, the GPMG, affectionately known to soldiers as the 'Gimpey'.

But there were more enemy.

Now the lighter clatter of the Russian-made helicopters as they skimmed low over the desert, hovering to offload the infantry they carried, men firing as they landed. Norris and Nobby and Alex, weaving to make themselves harder to hit, ducked the gunfire pinging into the rocks around them, thumping into the rocky gravel and ricocheting away into the far distance of the desert. They had reached the rock pillar with open ground between it and the helicopter, hovering, making dust, gunfire barking angrily from its dark interior. They were going to make it. Fifty metres, no more, then into the protective belly of the chopper, and away. Alex was limping badly, wincing as he stumbled on. The ramp, ever closer.

It was Nobby who saw them, a group of Iraqi soldiers

suddenly appearing from their right on the chopper's blind side, unseen by their rescuers. Maybe ten or twelve, yelling and shooting, the firing wide, nothing coming close. It was to frighten them and lend wings to their heels. But they could not reach the helicopter without being cut off. There was no space, no room to manoeuvre.

'Go!' gasped Nobby Clarke, already down on one knee, the AK up in his shoulder. 'I'll cover you 's best I can.'

'Nobby—'

'Go!' Screamed at them. 'Fuck off, before it's too late.'

The gun banged, close to Norris's ear, and he saw the first of the Iraqis spin as he was hit, the rifle flung from his hands. Dead, he fell in the path of the others, delaying them, making them skirt around him, unable to bring their rifles up. Norris could feel the down draught from the rotors, the stinging from the sand and dust particles thrown up into his face. Alex drew level, stumbling in his effort to keep up, his face screwed in pain. They heard the AK fire again, saw a soldier, five yards to the right of him, tumble into the dust. Slowing, Norris tried to see what had happened to Nobby Clarke. The gun barked again.

Three gone.

None left.

The AK was empty.

Richard Norris turned to look for the Corporal he had saved, so long ago on a *jebel* in the Radfan. Through the dust and the gunsmoke he saw him, legs braced, stood at the foot of the rock pillar, the rifle held by the barrel in big hands, a baseball hitter, waiting for the pitcher. A group of Iraqi soldiers edged cautiously in on him, a semicircle, closer so that they could take him alive. Nobby raised the rifle above his head bellowing from the madness in him. Norris watched, helpless as Nobby began to club at the soldiers around him.

*

Simon Endercote leapt from the belly of the Chinook, without waiting to see if he had been followed by the soldiers inside. Hunkered, he snapped the rifle up into the aim, firing at the group of Iraqis over by the APC, seeing them clearly through the aperture sight, jerking, spinning as the 5.56 mm. high-velocity bullets tumbled into them. He yelled, seeing them fall, for the moment not hearing the commands, short, sharp, coming from his NCOs as they directed fire at the APC across the desert.

He took in the scene all at once, squinting through the dust thrown up by the twin blades of the hovering Chinook, a suspicious hawk, waiting to settle. There was fire, incoming small arms, from the group over by the APC, not yet accurate, but he heard the gasp from a soldier to his left who had rolled over as a bullet had ripped into his thigh. Endercote, mesmerized, watched him roll again, coming up into a firing position, immediately shooting, not bothering to examine the wound in his leg.

He caught movement from the corner of his eye, two men, sprinting towards the Chinook, no weapons or equipment, with hessian tied to them as camouflage bouncing as they ran like tawdry scarecrows towards him. Familiar. Something in the way they were running, one of them limping. Behind them, at the base of a rock pile, another. Even at this distance, Endercote could see the big frame of the man as he swung a weapon, clubbing at the mass of men who forced in on him. He was done for, Endercote knew. They would have him in no time. One of the others stopped running, turning to witness the fate of the third, hesitating, then turning and charging back towards the rocks. The Major brought his rifle up into his shoulder, snapped off three rounds, watching the Iraqi with the bayonet pitch forwards before he could stick the man clubbing at him with the rifle. The bigger of the two, close in under the helicopter, gasped, throwing a hand up to his side, dropping to his knees, head shaking, then on to all fours, like a dog that had been whipped, the fight all but gone from it.

Familiar.

Something familiar in the way the man knelt, shaking his head. Even in the heat of the battle, Simon Endercote was disturbed, puzzled at what he had seen. A bullet cracked over his head, concentrating his mind. He forgot the big man on the floor, shooting once more into the soldiers crowded around the man fighting for his life at the base of the rock.

'Alive.' The big man, kneeling, spat blood. 'The bastards want us alive. Get to him—'

Familiar.

Blood dripping from his mouth into the sand between his hands. Like . . . like . . .

The heavy machine-gun was firing now, as someone in the Iraqi section used his initiative. Endercote, about to yell for the anti-tank team, heard the roar as the Milan fired, the missile whooshing across the gap separating them. It hit the Iraqi APC on the rear door, where the armour was at its thinnest, punching its way through to the inside, striking with a loud clang.

The explosion rocked across the desert, hurting the eardrums, drowning out the snapping gunfire, the thwacking of the rotors. The APC, one minute a dirty yellow-pink, the next a ball of fire as the missile tore through into the fuel tanks. Men around it, scattering, some on fire, others picked up and tossed away like straws in the wind. The big machine-gun had stopped, the helicopter for the moment out of danger. The Major, looking everywhere, saw the Load Master standing by the ramp at the rear of the aircraft, fist in the air, pulling it rapidly up and down, the signal, universal, understood.

Shift your arse. Let's get the fuck out of here.

Endercote looked again at the man by the rock pillar, incredibly, still on his feet, swinging the gun, felling them as they closed in on him. He was about to yell, to tell a half-section to break off and go to his aid, when he saw three of his brick running out into the open towards the pillar; two more knelt, covering them, weapons on full automatic now. One stopped briefly to change an empty magazine, done so fast Endercote hardly saw his hands move. The gun, up, firing again, the empty mag shoved into the smock.

What the hell am I doing here? These guys don't even need me.

The big man, on the ground, had rolled over on to his back, groaning, holding his side, his face distorted in pain.

'Medic!' Endercote screamed through the noise of the gunfire, intense now, as all of his brick fired on automatic, directing bursts at the enemy, cutting into them. Dimly he heard the sound of another helicopter, not one of theirs, coming in from the east, noting the change in pitch as it hovered to offload the enemy section it carried. Over his shoulder, dust clouds.

APCs. Three, maybe four.

Shit.

Let's get the hell out of here.

Norris ran, his exhaustion forgotten.

Nobby was still up, fighting, his back to the rock. Bodies of the Iraqi soldiers were piled at his feet, perhaps six or seven. Still they moved in, prodding, feinting with their bayonets, trying to get inside the gun in the wild man's hands, humming as it scythed through the air in a wide loop, occasionally striking a body or head. More of them dropped to join those at Nobby Clarke's feet. He was growling, deep in his throat, his eyes bright with the madness of the fighting.

They want him, us, alive. Richard knew. That was why Nobby had not been shot down like a rabid dog. The bastards want us alive. Another of them crumpled, adding to the pile of those dead or dying. The rifle rose and fell, blood-covered, then sweeping in its destructive arc. Nobby cried out as a bayonet thrust got through his guard, cutting through the flesh at the side of his ribs. Nobby clubbed him down, into the pile.

Dimly in the blank hole of his mind, through the pain and the fatigue and the fear, it came to him as he dashed across the desert.

Heaps upon heaps.
With the jawbone of an ass,
I have smitten a thousand men.

Then, one of them shot him.

At point blank range, Nobby Clarke was shot through the thigh.

He swung the rifle once more, yelling, the agony in the sound carried across the air. He went down. Norris saw the one who had done the shooting, braced, legs apart, the rifle, bayonet fixed to it, raised above his head. Norris screamed, watching, useless, as the bayonet drove down, through the exposed shoulders, sweat covered from the fighting and the killing, driven so hard that the soldier's helmet pitched forward over his eyes. The point burst through the chest. Then the boot, thumped into the small of the back, the moan from Nobby Clarke as the bayonet was ripped from him, twisted as it was taken, raised, ready for the killing stroke.

'Bastards!' Screamed at them.

Gunshots, automatic, close by him, three soldiers, SAS, firing into the mass of men around Nobby Clarke. They jerked, twitching as they were hit, falling, adding to the pile. He ran into the mêlée, the soldiers shooting, covering him as he heaved the bodies stacked grotesquely on top of Nobby, clearing them so that he could pull him free.

Heaps upon heaps . . .

Norris tore at the bodies, pulling them away from Nobby Clarke who lay in the dirt. At last, there, face down, not moving, the puncture between the shoulder blades bleeding darkly through the strips of cloth that had hidden him. Until now. He saw, heard nothing of the fire-fight raging about him, men yelling, screaming, dying as they stood. But, in the heat of it, he felt the SAS, fighting men, around him in a protective pocket as he reached down for Nobby. He tugged at the great weight of him, ducking to get the fireman's lift, straining to get him up, across his shoulders to carry him away from this place of killing. This, that had been Nobby's place.

... was called Ramath-lehi ...

'Here. Let me help.' A voice beside him, a figure vaguely recognized under the helmet, the dark cream spread over his face. The voice. Recognizable. The figure, tall, lean with an arrogance Norris found familiar. From somewhere, sometime.

'No. Just cover me. To the helicopter,' Norris gasped, lurching with the weight of the man across his shoulders. 'There's another of us ... he was with me. Just short of the Chinook.'

'OK. He's OK. Hit, but a medic's with him. Come on. Get the hell out of here. They'll be swarming all over us before we can blink.' Norris was too tired to recall the voice, his legs heavy as he stumbled across the desert towards the helicopter hovering so close, the SAS men withdrawing tactically, firing, moving, ever closer. His legs were buckling, Nobby's weight bearing him down. He stumbled, ran on, crumpling, dropping on to one knee. Groaning, he saw the ramp, the dark protective belly, yards from him, beckoning him to its safety.

At last he reached the ramp, men helping, one with a red cross on his arm-band, lifting Nobby Clarke from his aching shoulders, letting Norris stagger into the dark security of the helicopter. The ramp was already hissing upwards on the hydraulics. He felt it lift off, heard the change in pitch of the rotors as the vertical motion became horizontal, and the big twin-propellered machine moved ungracefully away.

It was quieter now, the vibration, the unfamiliar smells.

On all fours, his head against a pile of equipment, he tried to take in his surroundings. Fatigue washed over him. Norris fought against the tiredness that threatened to overwhelm him, prevent him thinking clearly. His brain refused to function.

Nobby.

He needed to find Nobby Clarke.

He pushed himself up, swaying as he stood, eyes blood-shot as he searched the dark interior. The medic was crouched over him, the tall figure of the team leader part obscured in the dark shadows. Norris lurched over to the group, fearful of what he might find there, then saw Alex, a hand clutched to his side, blood oozing between his fingers, the pain in his expression palpable. But he was there too, with Nobby, worried, afraid for the men who had done so much for him.

They had cut the filthy shirt open, exposing the chest, putty-white, compared to the dark skin of his forearms, the face, covered in camouflage cream hiding the stubble sprouting on cheeks and jaw. His eyes were open, barely, a spark of life, faltering then coming strong through the pain. The wound in the front of his chest was ugly, a dark puncture, weeping profusely, pale serous fluid. He coughed, Nobby did, the pink blood spurting from between lips swollen and blistered from days in the unfor-giving sun. The medic looked up briefly, not speaking, his look saying everything.

Richard knelt beside Nobby, reaching out a hand so that the big man could grip it. He felt the strength, fast escaping as he lay spread on a field-stretcher, the medic working, now on the leg where the thigh bone protruded through the blood-stained combat trousers. He knew despair, fighting to keep it from his expression as he leaned over him.

'OK, Nobby. We're going to make it. There'll be a plane to fly you to the Military Hospital in Cyprus. You'll soon be surrounded by pretty nurses, all wanting to give you a bed bath. Hold on, old friend. Not long now.' Norris thought he saw a grin in the eyes, behind the pain, but could not be sure.

'Hang on in there, Nobby.' Alex, standing huge above him, looked down at the wounded man, seeing him fighting his pain, struggling to stay alive. His own wounds were forgotten. 'Don't go quit on me now. Us, fucking officers.' He forced a grin. 'Full of piss and wind. We need you, Nobby Clarke, when the going gets tough—' Alex stopped, alarmed as Nobby's eyes closed, screwed up in pain, eating at him, hurting, his face waxy, blue-lipped as the shock set in.

Richard held the hand, saw the eyes open, briefly.

'Mr Richard.' Coughing, bleeding, pink from his lungs where the bayonet had gone into him. 'You're a bloody bandit. You ... you—' More blood, seeped from his mouth, running from the corner down on to his neck, small pink bubbles as he spoke. 'I ... I wouldn't have missed this one. Not for anything. Just ... just—' Norris felt the grip, suddenly firm, hurting his fingers.

'Millie. The cottage ... important to her.'

Norris nodded, understanding.

The tall figure of the team leader stepped forward, out of the shadows. He had been watching, listening. He spoke, letting Nobby know.

'Number Fifteen?'

Nobby looked. Realization, recognition.

'Sir?'

'Pass.'

'Sir.'

The man reached down, touching Nobby's shoulder briefly.

He turned and swayed down the belly of the helicopter to see to his brick.

Richard Norris looked at the man on the stretcher, saw

death creeping across Nobby Clarke's eyes, insidious, like engine oil spreading over the smooth surface of a stainless-steel plate. He squeezed the fingers, gentle with his own. He looked up to see the wretchedness in Alex Howard.

'The pipe, Mr Richard ... in the pocket.'

Norris found it, blood-covered, the bowl smashed. He slipped it into Nobby Clarke's mouth, only to see it tremble weakly and fall from the bruised lips and drop on to the field-dressing covering his chest. Looking up at the medic, he saw the imperceptible movement of his head. Shaking. Alexander Howard dropped to his haunches, a hand, comforting, placed on Norris's shoulder. He looked at his friend.

He wasn't sure, but he thought he was crying.

Joseph Fallon sat in front of the low table, a telephone connected to a tape-recorder close to his elbow. He dialled the number he had remembered from the old farmhouse, up country, not far from Cheltenham, which he had picked out in the beam of the flashlight. He tapped his fingers, impatient, waiting for it to be answered. On the second ring, the answering machine switched in, repeating the outgoing message. Richard Norris ... Norcom ... please leave your message after the tone ...

He held the first of the tone-diallers up to the mouthpiece, paused and pressed the transmit button. Nothing. He threw it, the one with the blue button, into a bag at his feet. He repeated the operation, this time with the yellow dialler. Again, there was nothing, just the faint crackle on the line. It was the fifth, the one with the black identifying button, before he was rewarded with the sound of an answering pip. Grimly, he smiled, pleased. He waited for the distant tape to rewind and, when he heard the tone, started the recorder on the table.

He listened to the messages on Richard Norris's answerphone. There were twelve in all, mainly men, the occasional female, probably a secretary arranging business meetings, confirming orders or rearranging schedules. Business talk that kept the economy healthy, created wealth, kept people in work. They were of no interest to Joseph Fallon.

There were two calls, both from a woman. In the first she was brief, businesslike, leaving a telephone number and a message for him to call her as soon as he got back. She had sounded like a jilted lover after a tiff, wanting to make up. In the second, she was breathless, excited, saying that she had heard the news from Old Kronkie. Her voice had been suggestive, full of mischief when she said she would be at the farmhouse to welcome him home. There was a date. And a time.

She would cook him a meal. Did he remember the meal at the flat? She had giggled.

Oh, and by the way, conspiratorial, she had got what he wanted, in more ways than one.

Umm . . .

Bye, she had said.

Her name had been Annabelle.

CHAPTER TWELVE

The wheels crunched on the gravel as he turned through the white farmhouse gate into the courtyard. At last, he was home. A wild chorus of birdsong greeted him as he got out of the car. The door clunked shut. Turning his back to the car, he leaned against it, breathing deeply, savouring the moment, letting the exhaustion fall from his body as water from an oiled swimmer as he surfaces from the ocean. Never had he felt so tired, so drained of energy, like a battery that had been used too long in trying to start a damp engine. The spark was gone from him. His body was wasted, the suit they had given him hanging listlessly about his frame, a spinnaker on a sail boat, becalmed. He walked towards the house, a scarecrow, dirty, unshaven, in need of a shower.

The key was there, amongst the dusty cobwebs on a beam in the porch.

In case Johnathan had unexpectedly come home . . .

He dropped the cheap overnight bag he had been given on to the mat just inside the door.

The old house greeted him as a long-lost friend, its cool, silent friendliness enveloping him as he opened the heavy oak door and let himself into the hall. He turned immediately to the big clock, picking open the face and winding the steel key, then swinging the pendulum to start it. The slow, heavy tick punctuated the silence as the heavy brass pendulum swept majestically across its arc, reflecting sunlight that streamed through the open door. He glanced at his watch and set the hands. He snapped it shut.

Reassured by the solidness surrounding him, he closed the door behind him. In the dim, cool interior, he let himself adjust to the familiar smells, the sounds that now surrounded him in the house that she had loved, that had once been theirs, the three of them, but could no longer be shared with them.

Bending to retrieve the bag, he saw the letter.

It was half hidden amongst the junk mail on the hall carpet.

Stooped, his hand gripping the bag, he stared, not comprehending, his mind still numb, unable to cope. He cocked his head, trying to read the address without having to pick it up. The writing was feminine. Big, bold lettering in light blue ink, the envelope, pale green. A first-class stamp. Curiosity got the better of him. He picked it up. It was addressed only to him. Mr R. Norris. No Mrs Norris.

Postmarked Belfast.

He looked at the date on his watch, then again at the letter. It had been lying in the empty house for two weeks, amongst the bills and circulars. Despite his fatigue, excitement and curiosity and a nagging fear gnawed at him. Tearing at the flap with a broken thumbnail, he read quickly, his eyes darting across the words written in the unfamiliar hand.

One page only.

He read it twice, then let his head fall back against the wall. For several seconds he did not move, his mind confused, then, shaking his head, he glanced once more at his watch, the face so badly scratched he could hardly read it. He stared at the date. Cursing, he ran down the hall to the telephone, yanking it from its cradle and dialling quickly.

Pray God that he wasn't too late.

A car, easily heard, entered the drive as he stood looking out of the french windows across the lawn, at the distant hills where the sun was balanced, about to slip down the sky into night. Soon it would be dark. The mellow chimes of the doorbell sounded a long way off, and he was irritated that this moment of peace was about to be taken from him. He turned back into the sitting room, placing the crystal glass carefully on the coffee table as he passed, wondering, then knowing, who it was.

Halfway along the hall, the sound of a key in the lock.

The door swung open as she walked into the hall. She was as beautiful as he had remembered her. Before the desert, the killing, the fear. She paused, sensing his presence, looking up to see him, shocked at the sight, the leanness, the fatigue that hung from him, the deep sorrow in his features.

Her smile was radiant as she ran to him with short, quick steps, throwing her arms about him and nuzzling her mouth into his neck, letting him feel the closeness of her, wanting him to want her.

He did not kiss her.

She stiffened momentarily at the rebuff.

'You were back, before I could get here,' she said, recovering quickly. 'The Cheltenham train was late and, as usual, not a damned taxi to be had for love nor money.' She laughed, the sound musical, delicate in the dim light of the hall. Stepping back, she looked into his face. 'My God, you look so beat. Did you get my message, on your answering machine? I left it a couple of days ago, as soon as Old Kronkie let it be known that you were coming home, that you were safe. Oh, Richard Norris, I am so happy.' She stood back another pace, looking at him, seemingly concerned at his lack of reaction to her. Perhaps it was the tiredness and what he had been through.

'It was bad, out there.' He spoke for the first time, his voice resigned. 'I can't tell you how bad. One of us, Nobby Clarke, was—' He didn't finish. She looked away, turning to drop the key on the hall table.

'I thought about you all the time. I was so worried. Kronk and Oliver kept it really close, not letting on what was happening. I dared not show too much interest. I'm not supposed to know what's going on.' She turned back to stare at him, her voice bubbling, like champagne frothing over from a flute. 'He was really pissed off, one day. I heard the two of them arguing over a solicitor's letter. I've no idea what it was all about.'

Norris smiled grimly. The letter was probably what had got them out. He wondered if the helicopter would have been there without it. He doubted it. He led her into the sitting room, conscious of her closeness, listening as she told him that she had been determined to be here to welcome him home. Looking at her, desire filled him, as it had when they had been in London, when he had given her the key, telling her to come down to the farmhouse when it was all over, when they would be able to spend some time together.

Could Felicity ever forgive him?

That had been before.

Before the desert.

'*Aysh 'amalt.*'

It had taken so long before it had come to him.

'*What have I done?*'

He shivered, then walked to the drinks cabinet.

'I'll make us a drink.'

It was all he could think of to say.

The dark-coloured car was parked, hidden along a track at the edge of the wood. He stopped before turning back into the lane, to see if it was visible. Just a faint glimmer coming from the windscreen. Walking back, he squeezed between the car and the bushes and scrub growing in close, feeling the drag against his trousers as he edged sideways, skirting round the vehicle until he could open the boot. There was an old blanket smelling of dogs, which he used to drape over the glass of the windscreen. Now, it was invisible. Leaving the car, he walked along the lane in the direction of the house.

The Kalashnikov, solid in his gloved fingers.

He followed the hedge, annoyed when his shoes squelched in the cowpat, making him slip, bringing the stink to his nostrils. How he hated the place, the brambles and the cow shit and the wet grass seeping through his shoes. But, then, this would be the last visit. Of that he was certain. At the gap in the fence, now familiar to him, he waited, looking at the house. This time, a light, shining through the curtains at the french windows, another from the upstairs landing. The excitement built in him, quickening his pulse, his breathing faster as he realized that the time was close.

A pale shadow passed behind the curtains, followed by another. The woman. She was there as he had known she would be. The lisping voice on the tape had told him. He had liked her voice, and had wondered what she looked like as he had listened through the earphone as he had lain on the narrow bed. It was an exciting voice, lisping slightly. Sex in it.

He wondered if she fucked, with Norris.

The shadow passed again in front of the pale curtains. Raising the rifle, he squinted through the sights at the shadow 50 metres away. He checked the setting of the change lever. No mistakes. The AK would cut the bastard in two from 50 metres, set like it was, on full auto.

Right, cousin Patrick.

Here we go then.

This bastard won't be taking one of ours again.

He made her a Martini, with Tanqueray gin and one olive, the glass ice cold from the freezer. He poured himself another Scotch, letting the liquid splash over the ice-cubes. Turning to face her, he studied her as he drank, his body aching with tiredness. Yet she was elated, full of life, smiling at him with those incredible blue eyes. They disconcerted him, almost diverted his attention from what he needed to say to her. Briefly, there was doubt, making him wait, delaying the moment when he would have to confront her.

He sipped his drink, watching her, wondering if he had got it right, conscious of how he felt about the woman, when she was so close to him in the same room, smiling at him, innocently beautiful. He thought about what had happened to them out in the desert, Alex, almost dying in the van, the confrontation with the soldier in the gully, when he, Norris, had nearly been killed, would have had it not been for Nobby Clarke. And Nobby, his chest stuck full of holes, lying in the helicopter . . .

Death in his eyes.

'I knew you would pull it off. It's wonderful to have you back. I'm so happy.' She laughed delightedly, showing the tiny misalignment of her front teeth that gave her the lisp, the sexiness in her voice when she spoke to him. 'And I've a surprise.' She bent to her bag, picking it up from the arm of a chair, then rummaging through it as she had the first time he had met her. He remembered what she had said, then, knowing now that she had meant it. Her hand came out of the bag, clutching a Cellophane packet. It was closed with a lead seal, a label attached to it. Her smile was radiant.

'Look.' She held it aloft, triumphant.

'Aysh haadthaak.'

'The tape. I've got the—' She stopped, realizing.

Her hand had gone to her mouth, a classic gesture, breath sucked in, knowing what she had done, that she had responded to the Arabic. The oldest trick in the world. He looked at her, knowing then, for sure.

'Why?' was all he could say.

She sagged, collapsing.

Then, she told him, hesitant, unsure, frightened.

It came, slowly at first, then spilling from her, as if eager to expunge the guilt.

'My name, my real name, is Nabela. Nabela Sa'ad. I'm half Iraqi.' She looked at him, defiant, angry. 'My father was a young lieutenant in the Iraqi Army, during the first Kuwait crisis in 1961. His jeep inadvertently strayed over the border during a sandstorm. Finally, when it cleared, he was lost, out in the open, although he must have known he was too far south, and in Kuwait.' She looked squarely at him, challenging. 'One of your precious British soldiers fired a burst at him. When my father's driver got back, he said that they had been showing a white flag which the British ignored. My mother learned he had been killed with a Vickers machine-gun, from what the driver had told her.' She gulped at her drink, looking at him, seeking understanding. 'Damn it, Richard, they weren't even married. The wedding was to be as soon as he came home on his next leave from the front. And she was already pregnant with me.'

She sat, balanced on the arm of a chair, looking at him, tears welling in the corners of her eyes, disconcerting him, making him fidget, uncomfortable, wanting this finished, to be alone.

'That didn't give you the right to do what you did, betraying us like that, especially after . . . Damn, I thought in the beginning we meant something to each other—' He didn't finish, instead shaking his head and staring into his drink.

'Richard, please, listen. Try to understand. If you only knew . . . My mother was always a romantic. She'd seen and heard all the social gossip about King Hussein, taking an English girl as his bride, his princess, and thought, in her silly, starry-eyed way, that this was what she wanted too. She'd met him as an officer cadet when he was at Sandhurst and had dated him, then lived with him in his London flat. Oh, but she loved him, Lieutenant Ismail Ibn Sa'ad.' The woman was crying openly now, sniffing, her nose running. 'You have no idea, what we went through. She, an unmarried mother, an Arab's bastard in her, swelling her belly.' She stood, pacing the room, back and forth in front of him. He stared at her, trying to understand, anguish tearing at him.

'That still didn't give you the right to do what you did. Christ, if *you* knew what *we've* been through. And all on account of your damned treachery. How did you tell them? By phone, I suppose. Damn, and you had it all, all the information. Dates, times, places. I knew something wasn't right when we were out there. God, it's easy to see now how come they were always one jump ahead.' She flopped back on to the arm of the chair and looked at him, her empty glass. He watched her, angry, wanting her, still.

'We went through hell, my mother and I. You don't know the half of it. You and your damned public-school education, living in the security of England while we—' She got up suddenly and went to the cabinet where she filled her glass with neat gin. Gulping at it, she went on: 'I was born in Bahrain. That's how I've a British passport. To start, we lived in a filthy little apartment, just off the Arab quarter. She had no skills, my mother, couldn't type or anything. They employed her as a cleaner in the British HQ, paying her what they termed Locally Enlisted Personnel wages. We couldn't live on what she earned. She couldn't look after me, so . . . Oh Richard, please try and understand.'

She half rose to walk towards him, but stopped when she saw the antagonism cloaking him, a shield she could not penetrate.

'There was only one way to make more money, and she took it. I was old enough to know that the nightly visits from the drunken sailors, soldiers, were not my uncles, as she termed them. I . . . with just the one room, I . . . I . . . could hear it, hear those disgusting creatures, fucking my mother's brains out on the narrow cot in the corner, bent over a chair, or on the floor.' She looked wretched, haggard, her beauty deserting her, her mouth, for the moment, ugly as she fought to keep her self-control and tell him what she and her mother had suffered. There was more.

'It took everything, her beauty and her reason. She looked what she was, an old scrubber.' Nabela Sa'ad had stopped crying. Norris saw the anger, the hatred, carried in her all those years. He listened, uncomfortable still, looking nowhere, an immiscible cocktail of anger and desire filling him.

'I was growing up, developing. I had inherited my mother's dark good looks, her eyes. She had started bringing Arabs home. They . . . Oh God. Damn you, Richard Norris, damn you for making me tell you this.' Her head fell forward, the black hair spilling into her lap. She looked up, tugging it from her eyes with nervous fingers. 'My mother begged me, pleaded with me, saying that it was the only way, that she was too old and ugly, and that the uncles wouldn't come to visit any more. So I had to, oh God . . . please, Richard. Don't, please don't make me tell you this.'

Norris was silent, his mind incapable of coping. He was tired, too tired to listen. His thoughts were of the fight in the desert, the killing and the fear. The loss. He drank, missing his mouth, the whisky running down his chin. He hardly listened as she told him how, finally, her mother had just given up and died, how she, Nabela, had been taken to a home, finally looked after by a woman whose husband was in the Diplomatic Service, working in the Embassy. After living with them for four years, they had adopted her, arranged the registration of her birth and obtained a birth certificate showing her to be their child. It had no mention of her Iraqi father. Her new father had held a high enough position to arrange it. Once back in England, Nabela had grown up with them, nursing her hatred. Finally, when she had been old enough to look after herself, she had left them to make a life of her own. He knew, now, why her Iraqi parenthood had never been discovered during her subsequent Positive Vetting. He stared at her as she went on.

'All through those dreadful years, when we were alone, just we two, my mother taught me to hate the British for what they had done, for killing him. Daily, in her bitterness, she drummed it into me as I grew up, through those awful times, impressing me that one day we would have our revenge. Can you understand, Richard Norris?' Annabelle, Nabela, looked at him, willing.

The tears were big, salty, as they ran down her cheeks, perhaps as they had done when he had tasted them the first time when she had lain beside him. She finished, looking at him lamely, her lip quivering, defiance in her expression as she faced him across the room. He ground his teeth, turned and walked to the window, suddenly finding the heat of the summer night oppressive, clutching at him. He dragged the curtains across, then reached for the handle of the door, intent on opening the french windows, craving clean air, as it had been in the desert. He faced her across the room.

'No,' he said finally. 'I don't fucking well understand. You took me in, deceived me, let me take two others, friends, on the mission, knowing we would be killed, that we had no chance of coming out of it alive. OK, so you went through a bad time. Yet you were prepared to let that ... that ...' – Norris chewed his teeth – 'fire a nuclear shell at Israel. You were prepared to see the terrible destruction, the death that it would have caused. To see us all killed trying to prevent it. There's no excuse for that. And after we had ... How could you see me leave, knowing what I had let myself be conned into? What are you? A Black Widow?'

'No. Wait.'

Pausing, he stared at her.

'I ... I'm sorry. You'll never understand. I can see that, now. I ... I can't really blame you, I suppose. How could I expect you to feel anything for me now?' She looked down at the tape clutched in her fingers. 'Here. Take it. At least you'll be free of them, now.' She was crying still, as she flicked it across the room to him. He made no attempt to catch, instead letting it hit his body and fall to the floor at his feet. Angry at her, he turned back to the windows, twisted the handle of the door and slid them across, opening them to the night and letting in the air.

Sipping his drink, he stood, staring out, not hearing her behind him.

He took a deep breath, grieved that it should end like this.

He heard the whisper in the earphone. Loud, yet heard by him alone.

'Bronze Three. Confirm target.'

He did not speak. Instead he blew twice into the boom mike, set close to his mouth. The procedure was not to talk when targeting from a hide. Noise travels, especially at night. So, instead, he blew quietly into his mike. It would be heard in the stuffy confines of Silver Control, where the Commander would be hunched over the map and the radio, wishing it was not his decision to make, hoping he would not have to give the order that would result in the taking of a man's life.

The man with the Parker Hale M85 sniper rifle didn't care about politics. He held the weapon steady on its bipod, peering through the SIMRAD KN 250 night-vision device fitted to the Schmidt and Bender 6X42 telescopic sight, the protective rubber eye-piece pressed close to his eye. The cross-hairs were centred on the figure half concealed in the hedgerow 200 metres away. He exhaled gently through pursed lips, expelling the air from his lungs. His finger curled around the trigger, first pad in contact with the curve, the indentations on the metal pressing his skin. He squeezed gently, taking up the first pressure of the trigger.

He waited, looking through the sight.

The target had the rifle up into the aim.

A light burst out on to the lawn as the curtains of the house were suddenly, swiftly, pulled. He did not look at the window. The light would destroy his night vision, blind him temporarily. Instead, he peered through the sight at the man in the hedgerow, neither wavering nor losing his concentration.

He began to worry.

If the order to shoot did not come soon, he would have to make a decision, based on his own assessment of the situation, his own judgement. Or, he could call into Control.

But that was contrary to procedures.

He waited.

Relaxed.

He had made up his mind.

It was a good gun, the AK74, a smaller calibre than its cousin the AKM and the more familiar AK47, yet, oddly, no lighter. He knew that there were over 35 million of them in circulation, mostly in countries that had been backed by the old Communist regime, before the Wall had come down and the USSR had disintegrated into a group of small states, arguing over who owned what, and who controlled whom.

The boys in the organization liked it, its killing power, the way that it could be put on to full automatic and fired without the tendency to climb up the target, scattering the rounds. It was the clever design of the muzzle brake that did this, and although the recoil was less than would be found on guns of a much smaller calibre, the disadvantage was in the noise it made and the lateral direction of the muzzle blast. No fun at all stood next to a man firing on full automatic.

Take your eyebrows off in no time.

But the best of it was the flatness of the bullet's trajectory when it left the barrel. At over 2500 feet per second it stopped a man. Dead. And the magazine held forty, instead of thirty, rounds. More killing to be had from it. And there was no need to alter the sight setting, below 400 metres. No wonder the Third World loved it.

He held the gun into his shoulder, concentrating, remembering the times in the tunnel range, the noise deafening, the wax balls doing nothing to prevent the pain in their ears. There were no ear-plugs now. He would hear the squealing. He did not want to miss that. The listening was important to him.

The shadow was still, behind the pale curtains, clearly defined like a target on the range. The arms were raised, the curtains dragged open, almost as if he had asked him to do it. He could see into the room now, the man Norris, standing, looking out towards him. Automatically, he moved behind the tree before realizing it was impossible for him to be seen.

The woman was behind him, over by the far wall, the door to her left. Norris, a glass in his fist, the other hand on his hip, looked tired, even from the tree line. Knackered, spent, like he'd been pushed to the edge and come back. Fallon raised the gun, aligning the distant figure on the tip of the foresight, then pressed the barrel gently against the trunk of the tree, steadying it, keeping the shake out of it. No way could he miss. Not from there. He held his breath, squeezing the pistol grip. Not too tight, not making the gun tremble.

Now . . .

The woman, behind Norris.

Christ, undressing, pulling the sweater over her head, letting her hair tumble, spilling down to her waist. No bra, and just look at those tits. Beautiful, round like grapefruit, grapefruit with strawberries stuck on with superglue. Nipples stood up in the cool breeze blowing in through the french windows, exciting him. Shit, now the skirt, being pushed down to her ankles, stepping out of it, tiny little see-through panties, no bigger than Blind Pew's eye-patch.

Would you look at that now?

Breath held, he watched as her hands went into the panties, palms on her thighs as she pushed them down. Norris wasn't even looking at her. But Fallon could not shift his eyes from the hair, thick between her legs. She moved. He watched. It was too much for him, realizing now that his penis was standing out hard from him, uncomfortable. Shit. She was going to fuck.

Norris still looked out of the window. She must have called, because Norris, the target, turned to face her. He hoped they would do it. Fuck. After, he'd blow the bastard's balls off, the same as he'd done to Patrick.

Come on, fuck the bitch.

He waited, rifle in the aim.

It was shaking, just a little.

'Richard. Richard Norris.'

Her voice was delicate, promising, disturbing him with its softness. Turning slowly, he saw her, and despite what he knew, felt the effervescent heat bubbling through him. He marvelled at the beauty of her, naked before him. She raised her hands, cupping her breasts, running her finger-tips in small circles on her nipples, knowing the movement would excite him. Her lips parted, her tongue licking them, making them wet, shiny, so that he wanted to kiss them. She walked across the room to him, standing with his back to the window, until she was close enough for him to feel the warmth of her, smell the musky, woman smell of her. Hands on his shoulders, she stood on tiptoe, reaching up to his mouth, kissing him with the wetness of her own, her tongue pushed into him.

He tried not to respond, knowing what she had done to them. To succumb, now, would be perfidious. She took his hand, placing it between her thighs, letting him feel her, and know how much she wanted him. She leaned back, her arms about his neck, hips thrust against him as she looked up at him. Her pelvis moved, gently touching him, grinding, harder. The anger had stayed with him, winning the battle of his desire for her. He was ashamed of how he had almost succumbed, relieved now that he had not. His mouth was cruel, hard, showing her what was in him. He pushed her away.

'Put your knickers back on. You look ridiculous.'

She stepped back from him, incredulous, the tears starting.

'But, Richard, I . . . I love you. Ever since . . . I tried to stop it, what was happening out there. But it had gone too far. They wouldn't listen to me. Oh, Richard, Richard Norris, say it doesn't matter now, that you will forgive me. I . . . oh God, I—'

Turning his back to her, he saw the tape, the tape that told of the killing of Patrick Donnelly, the tape that had brought this about. It lay, evil, on the carpet.

He bent, quickly, to pick it up.

Talk to me, Control, I have a target, confirmed.

But when the voice came, deep in the earpiece, it was calling Bronze One and Bronze Two.

Not him, Bronze Three.

He listened for the blowing noise in his earpiece, confirming that, like him, One and Two were on target. Nothing. A quiet buzz, deep in his head, magnified as the tension in him increased.

Talk to me, Control. My target is armed, in a firing position.

Bronze Three was sweating, just a little, the black beret too tight around his forehead. His pulse rate was higher than it had been a few minutes before. The figure, his target, dark in the pale yellow-green of the night-sight, was still balanced on the cross-hairs.

Control, talk to me.
He is about to fire. I know he is about to fire.
Control ...

The flashes from the automatic weapon were pinpricks of light, flaring in the night-scope. Seconds later, the staccato burst, crackling, shattering the silence of the night. His target had moved, fractionally, was now partially obscured by a tree. It was no longer confirmed, no longer a guaranteed hit.

'Control, Bronze Three. Target lost. He has fired. Target no longer confirmed.' He wanted to shout.

'Bronze Three. Roger. Wait.' The voice calm, not feeling the tension, like him.

Bronze Three waited, looking through the sight.

Fallon saw him, sharply silhouetted, balanced on the blade. The light from behind gave depth to the target, outlining it clearly, fused on the sight. He controlled his breathing, as he had been shown during the days practising in the tunnel range, the wetness of the south Armagh countryside outside, over his head, the others, waiting their turn to zero the weapons. The image of the target was blurred, a dark mass on the clear-cut line of the foresight. He held steady, pressed against the tree, as he had done when he had practised here before.

No way could he miss. Not from 50 metres. Not with the Kalashnikov on full auto.

Firing.

The gun juddered gently into his shoulder. Suddenly, he wondered where Norris had gone, why he was no longer there, framed in the sights, jerking as the bullets cut into him. There was just the woman, naked, with the big tits and strawberry nipples, flung backwards into the armchair against the middle of the wall, the marks where the bullets had hit her, bruising the paleness of her flesh, ugly, bleeding, easily seen, even across the distance separating them. The blood splashed from her, dark-coloured, running down the walls.

Norris was nowhere, vanished. Suddenly, the room was dark, the elongated patch of pale yellow light no longer stretched across the lawn. Blind, he could see nothing. The realization began to sink in.

He had missed.

From 50 metres, he had missed.

His target, gone.

He tried to steady himself, to control the panic that was starting in him.

His knees creaked as he bent for the tape, seeing it clearly on the carpet as he reached for it. Then the dreadful noise, the blasting whiplash of the bullets as they crackled over his head, the sickening sputtering as they slapped into the softness that had been Annabelle Sad. He looked up, saw her flung against the wall, crumpling into the chair, no sound from her, except the noise of the bullets as they struck. He had heard each of them individually as they smacked home, not the harsh crack they would have made hitting the plywood targets, when he was safe in the butts out on the 300-metre range. Instead, a dead noise, the sound a cricket bat might make if a lamb carcass hanging from a butcher's hook were hit with it.

He lay on the floor, not moving, seeing her thrown into the chair where her handbag had been earlier, before he had told her to put her knickers back on. She did not look ridiculous now, crumpled, where the force of the burst had flung her. Now, she looked grotesque, twitching still, pathetic in her dying, the blood pumping from her, oozing into the chair and running on to the carpet.

He rolled away from the window as soon as the shooting started, not knowing why he did so, only that it had been instinctive, and that, a long time ago, someone had taught him to react that way when someone shot at him.

He knew he had to make it dark, to prevent the shooter seeing him, giving him a second chance to finish what had been started. He was spread flat, in front of the couch, where he had rolled when the gun had stuttered. The woman, bleeding from everywhere, legs spread as she lay in an untidy, ugly pile in the chair. In closer, the heavy books, stacked on the ledge under the coffee table where he could reach the nearest, and heave it at the lights hanging from the ceiling, missing, but getting it with a second.

He heard the tinkling, the pop of the bulbs.

Then, the friendly darkness, rushing into the room.

The target was out in the open, running, not in a zigzag, but straight, trying to get as far away from the shooting as he could. The man in black, with the bulletproof vest, wearing a beret that was a touch too tight for him, watched the target.

Shots had been fired.

It was his decision.

His alone.

Like dreaming, he thought. This isn't happening. I am about to kill a man. Clear in his mind was what he had to do, to finish it clean, quick. Shoot to kill. No fucking about. Two hundred metres. Target, huge in the sight, going right to left. No wind to speak of. Aim off one and a half body widths . . . Breath held.

Come on, Silver. The warning.

A voice, amplified, distorted, shattered the night.

'Jesus.' Gasped from him.

He ran, away from the Norris home, away from the voice.

Again, impersonal, telling him he was surrounded, that he should throw down his weapon and surrender. Stopping, he spun in a circle, holding the rifle in tight to his hip. He fired off the rest of the magazine in the direction of the sound, somewhere over his left shoulder, yelling in exhilaration from the madness that was in him.

He didn't hear the voice again.

It came, loud and harsh in the stillness of the night.

The marksman recognized Flaxby's voice, picturing him in the unbearable heat of the van designated Silver Control. The target had stopped running, was spinning, confused, looking for the voice. The marksman had been told by those who had done this before that the silly bastards always looked for the voice. More flashes from the gun, this time fired from the hip, John Wayne style. Some of the bullets came close, slapping through the leaves of the tree just to the left of him.

He recentred the cross-hairs.

Doubt, briefly.

He pressed through the second pressure of the trigger of the sniper rifle, felt the recoil in his shoulder, deadened by the gun-pad.

The dull crump of the report.

He saw, through the ghost-green of the night-sight, the target spin anti-clockwise, stagger, then collapse into the wet grass.

It was done.

The killing, his first.

The Serious Crime Squad had come and gone, the fingerprint men, the photographers, the ballistics experts and the hard-eyed detectives with their spiral-bound notebooks and regulation-issue ballpoint pens. They had carried her away, in a black plastic body bag, letting him watch as they had run the zip along its length, stopping so that they could put the last of her hair in where it had spilled out on to the shiny surface. They had been impersonal, uninterested in what they had been doing, like meat-packers at Smithfields. They had questioned him, these hard-eyed detectives, suspicious, as if, in some way, he had been responsible for the killing at the farm-house. A telephone call, to the senior detective, had stopped the questioning. Norris was pretty sure who had made the call, picturing the good eye filled with concern. They left him alone then, going about their business as if it were routine.

He could not bear the thought of sleeping in the house after they had gone. Instead he drove into Cheltenham, found a hotel and walked tiredly into it. Lucky. A vacancy. In the room, he fell exhausted on to the bed, fully clothed, where he dozed, dreaming of climbing in a dark crack, with the sharp flash of bullets puncturing the darkness every time he stopped to rest.

Tomorrow, he would go to Ambleside and see Millie Clarke, tell her about Nobby, and give her the cheque from the government, the one Nobby had earned, so that she could buy the house and keep the bailiff away. Nobby had been specific about that. He tried not to think about the sorrow that would be in her eyes when he told her.

Then, he would go to Leeds.

He wondered what would be in store for him there, where the letter on the green paper had told him to go.

He was too tired to worry about it.

Perhaps in the morning it would be better.

At last, he slept.

A woman, short, plump, a wisp of hair hanging into her eyes, knelt on the grass as she weeded a flowerbed. She did not look up as he got out of the taxi and stood looking up the path. Concentrating on what had to be done, she stabbed, twisting assiduously with the trowel. Engrossed, she worked alone in her sorrow. He pushed open the gate, noiseless on oiled hinges, and walked quietly along the narrow path. Intensely sad, sadder than at any moment in his life, he hated himself for being here in this private world of her grief.

He must have made some small sound, for she stopped working and looked up at him, letting him see the sadness in the puffiness around her eyes, deep set in the redness from her crying. She stood, wiping her hands on her apron after she had pulled off the gardening gloves, as if worried that the sweat on her fingers would offend him, this man who had been her husband's officer, who had saved her Nobby in the desert of the Radfan.

Not in the desert of western Iraq.

'Hello, Mr Norris.' He listened to the Devonshire accent, music in the sadness. 'You put on a bit of weight since you was a lieutenant. And my, you look so tired. Come in and I'll make us a nice cup of tea. I've some scones put by. They'll be nice with a cup of tea, with some blackcurrant jam, home made. No cream though, not Devon cream, so they won't quite be right.' She walked in the direction of the cottage, to the back door leading into the kitchen, cool under the thick slate walls.

'Go through to the sitting room, just down and to the left. And mind your head, on the beam. Nobby was always hitting his head there. I put a piece of foam rubber up. Didn't hurt him so much. But 'e still kept banging it, his head.' She turned to the stove. 'I'll not be long. I always have a kettle on the go on the Aga. Never knew when Nobby would ... would—' She stopped, turning, so that he would not see her tears. He walked to her, putting his hands on her shoulders, turning her to face him. Holding his arms around her plump shoulders, he tried to comfort her, making small noises which he felt might help. Tears flowed unchecked, wetting his jacket where her face was pressed on to his lapel.

'Millie. I'm so sorry, so dreadfully sorry. I don't know what to say. About Nobby and me ... we've been through

284

a great deal together. He was always looking out for me, keeping me out of trouble. I just wish—'

"'E thought a lot of you, Mr Norris. Used to say that Mr N., 'e's a bloody bandit, 'e is. Born a hundred years too late. 'E was always saying it, my Nobby was. Thought the world of you, even before what happened in Aden. Always talking about you, them climbing trips you used to take him and the others on. Seems only like yesterday.' Gathering herself, she had turned away from him, lifting the big aluminium kettle up from the stove with both hands, pouring the steaming water into a big brown teapot with a chip out of the spout. She stirred the brew with a spoon, tapping the side of the pot so that it would mash, then placed the pot on a tray, covering it with a stained tea-cosy, keeping it warm, so that it would be right for Mr Norris, whom her Nobby had loved, had . . .

She turned and led him into the sitting room. In the cool friendly room, with pictures of thatched Devon cottages on the walls, she set the tray down and sat in a small nursing chair set to one side of the fireplace, pointing to a big armchair the other side.

He sat, knowing it was Nobby's chair.

'Now, Mr Norris.' She was pouring the dark liquid into a mug. 'Tell me about it. Tell me about my Nobby, and what happened to him out there in the desert—'

The woman was attractive, although some may have thought her clothes were too ostentatious, the sort one might expect a tart to wear. She sat in a comfortable armchair in the lounge of a country hotel on the outskirts of Leeds, her long legs crossed elegantly. Occasionally she sipped from the tall glass set on the table in front of her. The casual glances at her wristwatch became more frequent as the evening wore on, and a tiny frown creased her forehead.

The flight from Aldergrove had passed without mishap.

Now, she was full of expectancy, eager for the forthcoming meeting. She picked absently at the combs in her hair piled up on her head, then let grey, intelligent eyes drop once more to her watch.

He wasn't going to show.

She had expected too much. Perhaps he had moved, no longer living at the address shown in the file. She glanced around the room, missing nothing, then leaned forward to reach for her drink. After she had finished it, she would leave and go about her business. She could catch the morning flight back to Belfast.

There was a polite tap on her shoulder and, turning, she saw the hotel receptionist, a slip of paper in her hand.

'The gentleman you were expecting? He has just arrived. He is waiting in reception.'

Over the woman's shoulder she saw a man standing with his back to her. The lightweight suit did not fit him well, hanging on him as if it had been placed untidily on to a coat hanger. His hands were thrust deep into his pockets and his shoulders were hunched, as if to ease the fatigue in them. Even with his back turned, she could recognize the tiredness, the despair, and see that the man had suffered greatly in recent weeks.

Such exhaustion was commonplace to her, surrounded by it as she was, every day of her life. It was never ending. She hoped that what she was able to tell this man would at least alleviate some of the stress under which he must surely be living. What they had done to him was despicable, and a burning anger had welled up in her breast when she had been given access to the file.

It had been a classified file.

She reflected on its contents as she studied the man, trying to place him as a live being, bringing the tightly typed pages of script to life, giving them meaning.

So this was the father.

She had known the killer of his son.

But they had distorted the truth, and he had been usurped as a result. They had blackmailed him, threatening him with exposure, using the tape as evidence against him. Without knowing the truth, he had been forced to do as they had bid.

The receptionist spoke to him and he turned to glance in her direction. He walked towards her. She noticed that, despite the tiredness, he was light on his feet, walking with the slow languid gait of a big cat coming away from the hunt. The kill. His eyes were like hers, grey, but with more blue in them, set into a face in which none of the features was regular. Nothing matched. It was an untidy face, she decided, like an unfinished bust in clay, waiting patiently for the artist to regain interest and complete the work. The lips were cracked, the face burned by the wind and the sun. He pushed his hair off his forehead, a habit, because it fell immediately on to the line of his eyebrows again and he did nothing to remove it.

He stood looking down at her as if liking what he saw, a slow, indolent smile making his whole face change. She took the offered hand without rising from her chair, feeling the hardness of the skin against the softness of her own. His grip was firm, dry, genuinely warm. It was some seconds before she could bring herself to withdraw her fingers. At last she spoke.

'Mr Norris?'

He nodded.

'My name is Jennifer McCauley. I'm a policewoman with the Royal Ulster Constabulary. You obviously received my letter?' She felt the sudden tenseness in him.

Richard Norris reluctantly released the soft hand that had gripped his own with surprising vitality and strength. He studied the woman sitting cross-legged in the armchair, the alert grey eyes that examined him so intently. She looked, he thought, like a *fille de joie*, but damned attractive nevertheless. Fuckable. Incredibly fuckable. A soft accent, one he'd not heard since ... He shut his mind quickly, like a blade dropping, a guillotine cutting off the memory. He liked the musical lilt that emanated from the sexily pouting mouth. The sort of mouth that was slapped or kissed, he supposed, depending on the mood.

He didn't answer immediately, merely nodding to acknowledge his name. When at last he spoke, his tone was pitched low, so that his voice would not carry into the room.

'Miss McCauley. In your letter, you mentioned you could enlighten me with regard to a killing in Belfast.' He measured his words carefully, gauging her reaction, seeing the hesitancy before she replied. She stood, unfolding from the chair, stretching, catlike, almost as tall as he.

'Call me Jenny. All my friends do.' She took a deep breath. 'I know about the Donnelly killing.' She looked at him directly. 'All of it.'

His heart leapt.

Another of them.

A tiny spark burned briefly in his eyes, a sudden breeze blowing across the grey ash of a dying fire. Alarmed, she saw the sudden cruel twist that played on his mouth, his lips tugged out of shape by an unseen barb. But it was momentary, dissipated as if a cloud had sped across the sun on a blustery day. His features softened as his face creased into a lopsided smile, his lips hurting.

'In that case, Jenny McCauley, perhaps we could discuss it quietly over dinner?'

He wondered what she would tell him about the slaying of Patrick Donnelly, the IRA man he had killed to avenge the death of his son, Johnathan. He was too tired to care.

With an old-fashioned gesture, he raised his forearm for her to place her hand on it. Smiling into his eyes, she made a mock curtsy, then placed her hand on the proffered arm, suddenly comfortable with him. He guided her towards the restaurant.

Her fingers were warm on his biceps as she slipped her hand under his arm, then walked long legged beside him across the room.

She squeezed gently so that he was reassured.

He was tired now, spent.

He could not face the drive south, so instead caught a train, trying hard to sleep as it bore him away, away from the sadness he had seen. But sleep was elusive, evading him, his thoughts too preoccupied with what had gone before, his mind tormented yet relieved, the relief, like a slain deer lifted from a hunter's shoulders.

It was over.

Dear God, at last, it was over.

Now, to pick up the pieces of his life, to live once more without fear. Sighing, he sipped the Scotch as the train rushed across the points, the rhythm at last inducing sleep. The guard woke him at King's Cross. He was the last from the train and the cleaning crew had come aboard, carefully skirting around him stretched in the seat.

He crossed London to Paddington, arriving in time for the early evening train to the West Country. Twenty minutes later he arrived at his destination, Reading, the Royal Berkshire Hospital, to see how Alex was recovering. He hoped to see him well, and had been worried since leaving him in Cyprus for preliminary surgery, while he, Norris, had come back to London to debrief Kronk and Oliver.

Norris smiled.

Silly bugger, Alex, playing at John Henry under the Iraqi OP. He shuddered. If Alex hadn't been there, perhaps he wouldn't have made it out. Norris made up his mind then, never to discuss the adventure. For him, there had been too much sadness. Too much fear.

Too much sacrificed.

Surrounded by his entourage, the surgeon studied the case

notes, occasionally looking over half-glasses at the man stretched on the bed.

He would mend.

There would just be the ugly scar on his side to mar an otherwise perfect torso. The surgeon was too professional to let his curiosity get the better of him, to ask how this athletic fellow had come by such a deep flesh wound which, to his practised eye, looked as if it had been caused by a bullet. There was also the ugly discoloured puncture in the left buttock, from a none-too-clean blade of some sort, perhaps a flick-knife.

Yes, a few more days, and he could be on his way.

He pursed his lips.

'You'll make it, Mr Howard.' The surgeon flicked the notes back on to the clipboard, gently checking his pulse and temperature for perhaps the last time. 'You were lucky there was someone to give you a tetanus jab when you picked up the wound in your buttock. Fell on a piece of rusty iron, when you were working in the Middle East, did you say?'

'I didn't say,' – Alex was cautious – 'unless I've been talking in my sleep. Possible, I suppose, with what you've been shooting into me. Doc, when can I leave, be discharged?'

'A couple of days, maybe tomorrow, if you behave.' The surgeon was beginning to understand why the patient was so popular, particularly with the female staff. A handsome brute. And there had been the rumours ... Yes, it was time he left, this one.

The surgeon waited for the protest.

'But Doc, I'm fit, better now than I have been since I was admitted. A bit stiff, otherwise fine. And anyway, Sister says I'm as sprite as a ten-year-old. Don't you, ma'am?' Alex had learned to respect her. She sniffed, walking away without answering. 'Seriously, Doc, I'm fine. Fitter than a lot of those others I've seen hobbling out of here.'

'Illusionary, Mr Howard, pure illusion. Millions of flies eat horse shit. That doesn't mean it has to taste good. Let's hear no more of early discharge. You'll go on my say-so. Anyway, you have a visitor.'

The surgeon turned, leaving Alex to see who had come to visit him. A smile creased his features as Richard Norris entered the ward, an off-licence carrier in his hand, partially hidden under his jacket. The smile faltered as he noticed the state of his friend, the fatigue cloaked about him. But there was something else. Relief. Alex could not be sure. Norris reached the bed, thrusting out a hand, letting Alex take it in his own.

'Richard, you look beat. How was it up north?'

'Done. Finished. Millie Clarke was . . . well, as you would expect. I had to do something like it once before, when one of my soldiers was drowned in a canoeing accident on the Weser. Years ago, when I was a second looie.' Norris looked rueful, then at Alex directly. 'Something else. God, Alex—'

He told him about Annabelle Sad, seeing the disbelief. Then, about Jennifer McCauley.

'Richard, I just don't know what to say. I'll be damned. After Belfast, when I never heard from you, I just assumed . . . I can't believe it.'

Norris sat heavily in the chair beside the bed. He dropped his head into his hands, rubbing his eyes deep in the sockets with his knuckles. He looked up. Suddenly, he grinned. The old Norris.

'Alex, it's time you quit the insurance business. It's a waste of your talents. My company, Norcom, is expanding. There was a fax on my machine when I got back to the farmhouse. The Procurement Executive of the MoD want to run some evaluation trials on Seeker. Apparently, Walter Oliver has been pulling some strings on my behalf. He said he thought he owed me.'

The tiredness fell from him, as always when he was enthusiastic, discussing his company. He stood, thrusting his hands into his pockets, tossing the small change around, moving his fists about. 'Before this, I was working on a ground satellite system in conjunction with a US company. I had already arranged preliminary discussions with them. I need a marketing manager. He needs to be resourceful, determined, rather smooth, a touch urbane. A big, ugly bastard. You qualify for the last two.' Norris pointed with his two index fingers, the thumbs up, Colt Peacemakers with the hammers back.

'You want the job?'

Alex copied the movement, drawing the palm of his left hand back over the thumb of his right, fanning the hammer.

'What time do we leave?'

The two of them grinned.

She had banked the cheque that Richard Norris had given her, a secret smile when the manager had seen the amount, rubbing his hands as she placed it on the glass-topped desk. There was much to do, solicitors to see, the people at the building society and the travel agent to make the arrangements. Now, in the comfort of a first-class compartment of the British Rail train as it clattered over the rails on its way to London, she let her mind wander into dreamland. It was going to be all right, she told herself for the hundredth time. Everything would work out right in the end.

Not knowing her way around the capital, she took a taxi across London from King's Cross and caught another, slower, dirtier train to Woolwich, then took another taxi to the Queen Elizabeth Military Hospital. They told her where to go at reception, the floor and the ward. She rode up in the lift, feeling good in the new outfit she had bought in Carlisle, pleased she could now get into a size 14. The shoes were pretty too, even though they pinched her toes a bit.

She checked the floor number as she came out of the lift. A green arrow showed her the way to the ward. Turning, she walked along the shiny linoleum, counting off the doors as she went, the clean, disinfectant smell all around. At the first of the private wards, she paused, for a moment fearful, losing her new-found confidence. Gathering herself, she stood on tiptoe and peered through the glass and looked into the room. She smiled, then.

Quietly, she opened the door and slipped inside.

He was snoring as he slept, as he always did.

There were bandages, clean and white, and bulky around his chest. His left leg was held in traction, raised up off the bed. He was going to be all right, they had told her. His lung would recover, and with plenty of physiotherapy, his leg would mend too. Soon, he would be as sprite as before, charging around with those others, climbing men, those in the mountain-rescue team, drinking ale in her front room when they had been thrown out of the last of the Coniston pubs.

Quiet on the chair at the side of the bed, she wanted to hold the big hand in her own, to feel the strength of it, even in sleep. But the tubes inserted into his arms frightened her, worrying her, in case she should disturb them.

She was crying again, happy tears this time.

Millie Clarke sat, patient, waiting for her man to wake up.